ANTONIO

ANTONIO

A Story *of* Saint Anthony *of* Padua

By Madeline Pecora Nugent, *cfp*

Pauline

BOOKS & MEDIA

Boston

Library of Congress Control Number: 2021951760
CIP data is available.

ISBN-10: 0-8198-0878-4
ISBN-13: 978-0-8198-0878-3

Originally published as *Anthony: Words of Fire, Life of Light* (Second Edition) by Madeline Pecora Nugent, copyright © 2005, 1995, Pauline Books & Media.

Cover design by Ryan McQuade

Excerpts are taken from *Sermons for the Easter Cycle* by George Marcil, OFM (© Franciscan Institute, Saint Bonaventure University, 3261 West State Road, St. Bonaventure, NY, 14778). Reprinted by Pauline Books & Media. Used with permission.

Excerpts are taken from the *Messenger of Saint Anthony* (© Edizioni Messaggero Padova, Via Orto Botanico 11, 35123, Padova, Italy.) Reprinted by Pauline Books & Media. Used with permission.

Excerpts are taken from *Religious Dissent in the Middle Ages* by Jeffrey Burton Russell (© John Wiley & Sons, Inc., 111 River Street, Hoboken, NJ, 07030). Reprinted by Pauline Books & Media. Used with permission.

Other Scripture quotations herein are from the *The Catholic Edition of the Revised Standard Version of the Bible,* © 1965, 1966, Division of Christian Education of the National Council of the Churches of Christ in the United States of America.

Published by Pauline Books & Media, 50 Saint Pauls Avenue, Boston, MA 02130-3491

Printed in the U.S.A.

www.pauline.org

Pauline Books & Media is the publishing house of the Daughters of St. Paul, an international congregation of women religious serving the Church with the communications media.

1 2 3 4 5 6 7 8 9   26 25 24 23 22

To all holy priests of all time who, like Antonio,
preached Christ's message, namely,
"Repent and believe the good news."

Contents

Part Five

His Grace Will Come Down to Us

Acknowledgments

Thanks to the following for helping to make this book possible:

The editors at Pauline Books & Media patiently and thoroughly worked on this manuscript.

Father Leonard Tighe, Father Jack Hoak, and Father Claude Jarmak read the original manuscript and made invaluable comments. In addition to his written comments, Father Tighe also met with me in person for a lengthy and profitable discussion of my manuscript.

I also thank my husband, Jim, and our children, James, Amelia, and Frances (now Sister Veronica of Jesus, CN), for their important teenage critiques of the original manuscript.

Paul Spaeth obtained for me a pre-publication copy of the translated *Sermons of Saint Anthony of Padua* and Brother Edward Coughlin granted permission to quote from this text.

Father Sebastian Cunningham assisted in contacting Father Livio Poloniato, editor of the book *Seek First His Kingdom*. The *Edizioni Messaggero Padova* editorial staff and rights manager (Padua, Italy) granted permission to quote from this text of Saint Anthony's sermon notes, from *Praise to You Lord: Prayers of St. Anthony*, from *The Life of St. Anthony "Assidua,"* and from the *Messenger of Saint Anthony* magazine.

Father Claude Jarmak translated many of the sermon notes in *Seek First His Kingdom*, mailed me additional translated sermons not included in the book, and allowed me to quote from them. Father Jarmak also researched for me in non-English texts. He located information that I could not otherwise have found and translated information for me. He shared copies of his notes regarding the burial of Francis, the translation of his body, Francis' tomb in the basilica, and the chapter meeting of 1230, as well as copies of two bulls issued by Gregory IX. He also mailed me photocopies of articles on the causes of Saint Anthony's death and on the 1981 study of his corpse. In addition to all of this, he kindly allowed me to borrow his well-used copy of the translated *Lectio Assidua*.

Paul Spilsbury graciously shared with me his own personal translations of four early biographies of Saint Anthony and granted permission to quote from them. The texts are: *The Life of Saint Antony of Padua* by Jean Rigauld, OFM; *The Second "Life" of St Antony*, by Brother Julian of Speyer, together with extracts from *The Office of St Antony*, composed by the same brother; extracts relating to Saint Anthony from the *Dialogus Sanctorum Fratrum Minorum*; and *The Life of St Antony of Padua* by John Peckham, commonly called *The Benignitas*.

Paul Spilsbury and the publisher Edizoni Messaggero Padova also granted permission to quote from Paul's four-volume translation of Anthony's sermon notes *Sermons for Sundays and Festivals*.

Dom Julian Stead, OSB, translated from the Italian a text on the possible causes of Saint Anthony's illness and death.

Dr. Alex A. McBurney, Dr. John T. McCaffrey, and Dr. Charles McCoy studied Anthony's symptoms and physical appearance and diagnosed what could possibly have been the cause of his illness and death.

Marilyn London, forensic anthropologist for the state of Rhode Island, studied photos of and articles on Anthony's remains and offered medical judgments about his health.

Sister Mary Francis Hone shared valuable information on the lives of the Poor Ladies of the time and verified some information on Sister Elena Enselmini and Brother Philip. She also made available an English translation of the first biography of Saint Anthony.

Father Michael Cusato, Jean François Godet-Calogeras, and Father Claude Jarmak offered insights into events involving Brother Elia.

Franciscan scholar Jean François Godet-Calogeras answered many questions and clarified several points, including how to write names in Italian and whether Anthony made more than one trip to the pope.

Franciscan Pilgrimage director Bret Thoman, OFS, was extremely helpful regarding the Umbrian language and place and character names in this book.

Therapists Thomas Carr and Sister Katherine Donnelly were extremely helpful in understanding the possible psychology of Mestre João. Mr. Carr edited the chapter concerning this abusive prior.

Professional artist Joseph Matose read the manuscript and created a drawing of Saint Anthony which accurately captures his personality and which was used in the first edition of this book. Mr. Matose also fervently prayed for the completion of the original manuscript.

Joan and Butch Hitchcock of Signal Graphics spent much time in reproducing out-of-print texts to use in this research.

Dr. Michael DeMaio translated the beginning sentences of *Quo elongati*.

The library staff at Salve Regina University in the reference and library loan departments, particularly Joan Bartram, Nancy Flanagan, and Klaus Baernthaler, researched and obtained through their interlibrary loan most of the texts used in writing this book.

Reference librarian Theresa Shaffer and others in the reference department at St. Bonaventure's Library researched Sister Elena Enselmini, Brother Luke Belludi, Brother Philip, the *Second Life of St. Anthony*, and the papal bull *Quo elongati*, and also photocopied and mailed materials to me.

Thanks to Elizabeth Lemire, Sue Swank, Erica Faunce, Erica Noll, Sandy Seyfert, Tish Sak, and Kay-Marie Bougher, who worked tirelessly from October into January in the CFP Holy Angels online gift shop so that I could take that time to update this manuscript prior to its third printing.

My deepest thanks goes to all those who prayed for me and for this text, particularly my mother, Amelia Pecora, and my ecumenical prayer group, for their fervent and continual prayers for the original edition. Subsequently, thanks to the numerous friends, the Poor Sisters of Saint Clare and other religious, and my Franciscan brothers and sisters in Christ who supported this effort with their prayers from the very beginning and continue to do so now. I also especially thank Leonardo Defilippis and Father John Randall, whose prayers enabled me to complete the chapter on Brother Elia, Saint Anthony himself, and the Trinity, whom I invoked daily. Anything good in this book is the result of powers far more perceptive than my own.

Introductory Materials

"Tony, Tony, come around,
Something's lost and can't be found."

Saint Anthony is the only Doctor of the Church who is invoked when someone loses a pencil. Why? Because Saint Anthony cares. And he is effective.

Anthony was born eight hundred years ago, but his message is as fresh as if he were living now.

Today our Catholic Church is challenged from within and without. Some who call themselves Catholic openly challenge Church teaching on the sanctity of human life, God's divinity, or humankind's redemption by Christ. Some reject the Church's interpretation of certain Bible passages. Anthony faced the same challenges. Society seems to value capable, intelligent, and healthy people more than the incapacitated, mentally deficient, and incurably ill. This was also the society in which Anthony lived and preached.

Anthony was loyal to his Church and fiercely in love with God. His knowledge of and insight into Scripture was phenomenal. Called in his own day "the Hammer of Heretics" and "the Ark of the Testament," he battled heresies that questioned the value of all life, the authority of the Church, and the very nature of God. He was eloquent and effective in preaching the truth to a society that was generally ignorant of it. Moreover, he not only proclaimed the Gospel, he also totally lived it so that his very life was a witness to the profound truth of his words.

Anthony tenderly ministered to people whom others considered unimportant. Although he lived at a time when some Catholic clergy were dissolute and avaricious, he maintained his own purity and holiness by constant prayer and vigilance. He spoke out forcefully against sin and offered Christ's infinite mercy and forgiveness to those who repented. Thus, he was one of the most forceful and yet most gentle of saints.

Anthony believed that a preacher's goal must be to bring listeners to repentance and penance, and he designed every one of his sermons with this in mind. Repentance means a total and genuine desire to turn away from sin, not just major sins but all sin. Penance means conversion of the individual's entire spirit, a conversion from sin to goodness, from the world to Christ. Penance necessarily involves contrition, confession, and satisfaction for sin, but not in a superficial sense. Anthony advocated sincere sorrow, thorough confession, and complete and cheerful restitution. Neither repentance nor penance come about by saying a certain number of prayers given by the priest in the sacrament of Reconciliation. They come about by an absolute renunciation of a sinful life (and every person's life is sinful to some degree) and by entirely embracing and submitting to a completely new life centered in God and God's perfect will for each person.

Saint Anthony has a powerful message for our time. We need to return to and embrace his values, to experience the breadth and depth of his faith, and to know and love his Christ. We need to totally relinquish our own will as Saint Anthony did so that we may wholly do God's will for us. Only then will we truly "repent and believe the Good News."

Early Sources

Saint Anthony is a wonderful saint but most frustrating to write about. We know more about his faith from his sermon notes than we can glean from his biographies. He was asked by his superiors to write these notes as homily outlines for other preachers. Only in modern times have his sermon notes been translated from Latin into English.

Father Livio Poloniato's book, *Seek First His Kingdom*, has excerpts of many of Anthony's sermon notes and is an excellent introduction to his spirituality and faith.

Father Claude Jarmak translated many of Anthony's beautiful prayers in the book *Praise to You, Lord: Prayers of St. Anthony*.

The Franciscan Institute has translated Anthony's Easter Cycle of sermon notes (*Sermons for the Easter Cycle*), which includes his complete sermon notes for Easter and the six Sundays following.

Paul Spilsbury translated all of Anthony's sermon notes in a four-volume set, *Sermons for Sundays and Festivals*.

Although we have these marvelous works, no stenographer took down word for word what Anthony actually preached. Very few of his spoken words are recorded. When speaking and preaching, he must have often expressed the same ideas that he wrote in his sermon notes, but just what did he say?

In this book, Anthony speaks, for the most part, words he either said on a particular occasion or wrote in his sermon notes. If he had read his sermon notes word for word as his homilies, his listeners would have been lost in a quick barrage of references, history, and allegory. But the notes were not meant to be preached verbatim. They were intended to give his fellow friars source material from which to build their own sermons. So he himself must have developed his themes, expanding on one point before moving to the next. His sermons and counsel in this book, using his own written words as much as possible, attempt to follow that pattern. The notes at the end of each chapter tell which sermon notes provided the basis for his counsel, prayer, or preaching.

Saint Anthony is called "the miracle worker." Yet most scholars accept only a few miracles during his lifetime as genuine, and different traditions accord these to different locations. Many other miracles took place following his death. Were some of these transposed, in the oral tradition, as taking place during his lifetime? The chapter notes detail the current scholarship.

Biographers during Anthony's time recorded few personal details about their hero. Later writers fleshed out his history, but how accurately? Again, the chapter notes tell of some of the discrepancies in his story.

This book looks at Anthony through the eyes of those who knew him, thus giving the reader a sense of what it may have been like to know the saint. Most of the characters in the book actually existed. Any fictional characters and imagined details are indicated in the chapter notes. In all cases, descriptions of historical places and events are as accurate as possible. The book remains true to Anthony's teaching style and vocal expression. The background and miracles attributed to him are in the histories. Scholars can refer to the references at the end of this book for a more in-depth study of what we know and believe about Saint Anthony.

This book is about Saint Anthony and those whose lives he touched. In that sense, it is a book about us. In many characters, readers will find some characteristics of their own. By identifying with those who knew the saint, we meet the saint. By God's grace, may Saint Anthony help us to come to genuine repentance and heartfelt penance that enable us to more deeply know, love, and serve the Lord to Whom Anthony so totally and freely gave his life.

Notes on Chronology

Certain dates in the life of Saint Anthony, like the dates of the first Franciscan martyrs, his entry into the Franciscan Order, the death of Saint Francis, and the issuing of *Quo Elongati*, are recorded in history. The exact dates for many other events in his life are uncertain. Regarding the events recorded in the life of Saint Francis, this book generally follows the chronology in the French edition of *Early Documents* with emendations suggested by Jean-François Godet-Calogeras, professor emeritus of theology and Franciscan studies at Saint Bonaventure University (Saint Bonaventure, New York) and general editor of *Franciscan Studies*.

Antonio: A Story of Saint Anthony of Padua helps the reader to see Anthony through the eyes of his contemporaries without replicating events covered in *Francesco: A Story of Saint Francis of Assisi* and *Chiara: A Story of Saint Clare of Assisi*. This book can be read on its own. However, reading all three books will give a more complete picture of how each of these saints, all contemporaries of one another, helped determine the direction of the early Franciscan movement.

Francesco portrays the friendship between Francis and Elia, Francis' conversion, the early brotherhood, and its expansion and magnetism. It also relates how laypeople, like this book's Count Tiso da Camposampiero, lived the penitential *Rule of Life*, written for them by Cardinal Ugolino at Francis' request.

Chiara details the sisters' life in the convents of the Poor Ladies, such as that of Sister Elena Enselmini, whose spiritual director was Anthony. Several of Anthony's sermon notes expand themes for instructing enclosed religious women. *Chiara* also continues the life of Brother Elia after Anthony's death.

In addition to this general outline, specific incidents covered more completely in the other books are:

1220: Cardinal Ugolino, at Francis' request, becomes Cardinal Protector of the Order: *Francesco*, chapter 98.

1221: Additional information on the Pentecost Chapter: *Francesco*, chapter 106.

1221–23: The progression of Francis' Rule for the Lesser Brothers: *Francesco*, chapters 105, 113.

1224: Unrest over Elia's governance of the Lesser Brothers: *Francesco*, chapter 117.

1224: Francis receives the stigmata: *Francesco*, chapter 119.

1226: Francis' progressive illness and death: *Francesco*, chapters 123 through 127.

Anthony's Appearance and Health

A 1981 study of Saint Anthony's skeletal remains and the historical record of his appearance and health history yield some important information. He was robust and just under five feet, six inches tall, slightly taller than a medium-sized person of his time. He had a long, narrow face with large, deep-set, penetrating eyes (presumably black or dark brown since he was Portuguese), dark hair, and an aquiline nose. His legs and feet were very sturdy, and his hands were long with thin fingers. His beautiful, regular teeth showed very little wear for a man of his age. This means that he ate little, probably mostly vegetables.

In 2014, these findings were verified by a group of forensic experts. In a team effort that included the University of Padua's Anthropology Museum, the Antoniani Studies Center, and a 3-D tech group, these experts reconstructed the face of Saint Anthony from a digital copy of his skull. The reconstruction revealed a long-faced young man with deep-set eyes, a prominent, straight nose, small, narrow lips, round cheeks, and a peaceful expression.

Examination of Anthony's skeleton revealed knees that showed signs of long hours spent in kneeling. The left knee had evidence of bursitis and osteitis and an infection under the kneecap. This could have been caused by a fall or, more likely, by excessive kneeling on that particular knee. His three lower ribs on the left side were also distended abnormally. This could have been caused by any number of factors: carrying heavy loads on that side (his books and manuscripts, perhaps?), or kneeling, or the swelling of an internal organ (perhaps a lobe of the liver), or pressure of some sort on his corpse.

Anthony is variously described as being a bit stocky as a youth, then growing thin upon entering religious life (presumably from excessive fasting), and then, later in life, as corpulent. His skin is described as being brown, ruddy, bronzed. When he died, it immediately whitened and became like an infant's.

Anthony suffered a severe fever in Morocco; no one knows what this was. However, he was ill off and on during the remainder of his life and many scholars of the saint believe that the fever was responsible for this chronic illness. We do know that, later in life, he suffered from dropsy (edema), which is water retention in the body tissues. This was most likely the cause of his corpulency.

By studying paintings of Anthony by contemporaries, his description in the histories (see, for example, Purcell 91), and his bodily remains, one may make some very tenuous conclusions about the illness that caused this man to die before the age of forty. Innumerable causes of dropsy exist, including a poor and unsubstantial diet. Some diseases that cause dropsy are kidney disease, heart disease, some cancers, and hepatitis.

No one can say with certainty what caused Saint Anthony's final illness and death. At least one author attributes the cause to asthma and diabetes. This book describes Anthony's physical appearance without diagnosing its cause. The description closely resembles that of a person afflicted with chronic active hepatitis, which he may have contracted from unsanitary conditions or contaminated fish on his journey to Morocco.

Anthony's Intellect

Anthony was a brilliant man. Calling him "the Ark of the Testament," a pope declared that, if the Bible were lost, Anthony could rewrite it from memory

(*Assidua* 13, Rig 12, Ben 3, *Dialogus* 2). Scholars know that he had the Bible memorized because he occasionally misquotes a reference in his sermon notes. He used this knowledge not only to enliven the faith of his Christian audiences but also to refute heresy, which was rampant at that time. So effective were his arguments that he was remembered as the "Hammer of Heretics" (Ben 4).

His studies as an Augustinian grounded him not only in Scripture but also in natural sciences as they were known at the time. Apparently he memorized a medieval bestiary that shared biological information (as then known) along with scriptural allegory about the beasts discussed. He frequently used and expanded such references in his sermon notes. No doubt he also preached on these topics, thus enthralling his audiences with the spiritual relevance of both exotic and mundane creatures.

Anthony's Preaching

When Anthony entered the *religio*, the Rule stated, "Let no brother preach contrary to the rite and practice of the Church or without the permission of his minister. Let the minister be careful of granting it without discernment to anyone" (FA:ED I 75). All the brothers, however, had permission to share a simple exhortation encouraging the people to repentance (FA:ED I 78). While exhortation involved a call to repentance, preaching expanded that call by developing themes using Scripture and Church doctrine. Permission to preach was granted to priests and canons who had an educational background in spiritual matters and whose preaching could hold an audience's attention and move them to spiritual reform. Fra Elia, minister general of the Lesser Brothers, granted Anthony permission to preach.

Helpful Cultural Information

Biblical Quotations: At the time of Saint Anthony, there were no standard verse divisions in the Bible, and standardized chapter divisions were just being introduced. In this book, biblical quotes are from the *Revised Standard Version, Catholic Edition*, except when they are part of a quotation from the writings of Saint Anthony or another early source. The citations are given in the notes found at the end of each chapter.

Canonical Hours: Time was divided into three-hour segments. The friars, like all penitents, clergy, and religious at the time, prayed, at specific "hours," certain set prayers called "offices." The modern name for the "hour" is given in parentheses:

> Matins (Office of Readings): First prayer of the morning, usually combined with Lauds
>
> Lauds (Morning Prayer): Prayer at dawn
>
> Prime (This office is no longer prayed): 6 a.m.
>
> Terce (Midmorning Prayer): 9 a.m.
>
> Sext (Midday Prayer): Noon
>
> None (Midafternoon Prayer): 3 p.m.
>
> Vespers (Evening Prayer): between 3 and 6 p.m.
>
> Compline (Night Prayer): 9 p.m. or when darkness was falling

Capitalization: All pronouns referring to God, Christ, and the Holy Spirit are capitalized except those which Anthony or his copyists did not capitalize in his quoted writings.

Cathars: The term "Catholic," used in reference to the followers of the Bishop of Rome, came into use only around 1600. The Christian faith, which we now call the Roman Catholic faith, was the one accepted by papal authority. Sects, who called themselves Christian but didn't accept papal authority, were considered heretical. The Cathars (Albigensians) were a prominent heretical sect that was making many converts in northern Italy and southern France. Anthony was sent to preach the true faith in these areas.

The Cathars believed that sexual procreation was from Satan and that the good God was spirit but the evil god made the material world. They did not eat any food that came from sexual intercourse. Fish was considered to be a clean animal, as well as all amphibians (toads, frogs), because they were believed to reproduce by spontaneous generation.

Chapter Notes: Chapter notes at the end of each chapter provide important and interesting background information. They indicate some of the major references used in that chapter, including the source of Saint Anthony's words, and distinguish material in the historical record from what is supposition.

In these notes, the references generally refer to the earliest mention of the incident in the historical record. Later histories may also mention, and often expand, the incident or information.

Characters: Names of the characters are as they would have been in their native tongue. People are named in relation to their ancestors. In Umbrian, Francesco di Pietro di Bernardone means "Francis, son of Peter who is the son of Bernard." The word "di" may be written as "de" or "dei" and in this usage means "child of" or "from." Other than Francis, Clare, Anthony, and the popes, history records little, if anything, about the physical appearance of most of the people in this book.

Social Class: Medieval people were honored according to their social class, e.g., emperor, king, queen, lord, lady, baron, count. In the Church, clergy were also ranked: pope, cardinal, bishop, priest, deacon, cleric. The term "prelate" referred to any religious authority. The poor had no titles.

Social Mores: Power rested with the nobles, high religious leaders, and military. The merchants and middle classes were attempting to rise in power. The lower classes were powerless and generally disregarded. Below them were the beggars and then, at the lowest social level, the lepers, robbers, and other outcasts.

Stages of Becoming a Religious Order: Francis began his conversion as a voluntary penitent. His first brothers were also lay penitents. Clare followed this example as well as that of other penitents whom she knew. However, penitents generally lived in their own homes, not in community. As Francis gained followers who lived a common life with him, their group began to resemble a "religio."

"Religio" was the canonical term applied to a group of Christians who lived together a faithful life with certain common practices. The Church monitored a religio closely. Should it become sufficiently organized, a religio could become an approved "ordine" (religious order). The Church required a religio to submit a written rule of life, which the Church had to approve before designating a religio as an ordine. When Anthony joined the brothers who were following Francis, the group was a religio. It became an ordine when the pope approved Francis' Rule in 1223.

In the early times when the friars became organized into provinces, each province (*provincia*) was divided into custodies (*custodia*). At the head of the province was a provincial minister, and at the head of each custody was a custos. The superior of each convent was called a guardian.

Time: In Anthony's time, the new year began on March 25, the feast of the Annunciation. However, because that system confuses modern readers, the years in this book reflect current usage.

Titles: Titles for the major sections of this book are from Saint Anthony's sermon notes on "The Litanies" (SSF IV, pp. 231–46).

Titles for Francis and His Brothers: At some point, Francis was ordained a deacon, but he never became a priest. Out of respect, the brothers sometimes called Francis "Father" because he was a spiritual father to them. Generally, the brothers humbly called one another "Fra," which is a short from of *frater* or *fratello* (brother), even though some of these men were ordained priests. In this book, all of the brothers, no matter their nationality, are called "Fra" among themselves.

The title of respect for a Franciscan Order priest, used by those not in the brotherhood, was Padre in Italy and Père in France. Diocesan and Benedictine clergy were titled Dom, which is a short form of *Domino* (Lord).

In papal documents from 1219–28, the brotherhood was called the "Lesser Brothers" (FA:ED I 558–64). With the issuance of *Quo elongati* in 1230, the designation changed to the "Order of Minors" (FA:ED 570).

Tonsure: Hair was an object of beauty in the Middle Ages. Tonsure, which involved cutting the hair in unattractive ways, was a sign that a person had abandoned a sinful life and was consecrated to God. A male religious kept his hair short and had a bald patch shaved in the center of his scalp. He went bareheaded except in inclement weather, when he might wear a cap or a hood. A female religious had her hair cut up to her ears, kept her hair short, and covered her "baldness" with a veil.

Translation of Foreign Words Used

Buono: Good

Cathar, Cathars (plural): A heretical sect that believed the material world was evil

Comune: City-states that developed throughout northern and central Italy in the twelfth century

Consolamentum: A Cathar rite of spiritual baptism by which one was made a perfecti

Custos, custodes (plural): Governing friar of a custody

Del, della: "Of" ("I Piazza del San Rufino" means "the Piazza of the Cathedral of San Rufino")

Dom: Title of respect for secular and diocesan priests

Fra: Colloquial name for a religious brother, shortened from Fratello

Grazie: Thank you

Madame: My lady

Madonna, Madonne (plural): Informal Old Umbrian term for My Lady (My Ladies), used for noble girls and women

Mamma: Mommy, Mum

Mercato: Marketplace

Merci: Thank you

Messer, Messers (plural): Old Umbrian title of respect for a man: Mister, Sir, Lord

Mestre: Master

Monte: Mountain

Nonna, Nonno: Grandmom, Grandpop

Ordine: Religious Order

Oui: Yes

Pace e bene: The greeting Francis gave his brothers to use: "Peace and all good"

Padre: Priest

Papà: Daddy

Père: Father (priest)

Perfecti: Highest rank among the Cathars, the "perfected one." Comparable to a priest.

Piazza: A wide, open space where several streets come together

Podestà: The elected head of the comune, who had a council to advise him

Porziuncula: Little portion of land

Religio: Intermediate step in becoming a religious order (ordine)

San/Santa/Sant'/São: Saint

Seigneur: Lord (as in the title of a nobleman)

Sì: Yes

Suor: Colloquial name for a religious sister

Sometimes history did not record the name of a real character. At other times a character was created to illustrate a certain point. In both instances, characters were assigned names or names were created for them that indicate one of their qualities. In this book, the created and assigned names and their meanings are:

Agathe: French name for "kindhearted woman" (peasant woman who hosted Anthony in her house)

Amélie: French for "hardworking" (maid sent to bring vegetables to the friars)

Aroldo: Italian for "army ruler" (superior of Monte Paolo)

Cerf: French for "deer, hart, stag" (Lord of Châteauneuf-la-Forêt)

Drago: Italian for "dragon" (robber band leader)

Fabio: Italian name for "boy who grows beans" (robber converted by Anthony's preaching)

Gifferd: French male name for "plump-faced" (martyred notary)

Martin: French Saint Martin of Tours (novice who stole Anthony's psalter)

Minette: French name meaning "faithful defender" (fictitious prostitute as an example of the many prostitutes converted by Anthony)

Scettico: Italian for "skeptic" (cardinal who felt Anthony's canonization was rushed)

Varden: Old French name meaning "from the green hills" (fictitious heretic as an example of the interactions between Anthony and heretics)

Penance—Then and Now

Penance means conversion as well as the sacrificial methods that foster it, such as fasting from food, giving alms, confessing sins, praying, living chastely, having minimal possessions, and doing good works.

Modern minds associate the season of Lent with penance. Lent is a time to see where one has strayed from following God, then do what is necessary to draw closer to Him. However, we are called to conversion and good works not only during Lent, but always. Penance turns us away from self-indulgence and turns us toward God.

For many people in Anthony's time, penance was more than a seasonal practice. Since they saw hell as a very real possibility for those who sinned seriously, it was appealing as a means of gaining heaven through expiating serious sins. By defeating sinful human desires, penance also kept a person from seriously sinning again.

In medieval times, those who confessed grave sins were enrolled in the Order of Penitents, a recognized order in the Church, until completing the satisfaction given for the forgiveness of these sins. Penitents who had sinned mortally might be told, for example, to take a pilgrimage (or pilgrimages) to holy places, to build a hospital or a church, or to abstain from conjugal relations for a time.

Before Anthony was born, a great penitential movement began to sweep Europe. No one knows exactly how it began, but many people began to see the need for a deeper relationship with God and realized that living a penitential life was a means to that end. Because they had not sinned mortally, they were not required to enter the Order of Penitents. Nevertheless, many laypeople voluntarily began to live penitential lives because they wished to distance themselves from worldly concerns. Voluntary penitents embraced prayer, fasting, abstinence from food, simplicity of life, and doing good works as disciplines to help them surrender their own wills to God. Saint Francis of Assisi began his conversion as one of these voluntary penitents.

The Lay Franciscan Charism Today

An Internet search will reveal numerous Franciscan male and female religious orders. Some of these evolved from Francis' original foundation, while others are trying to live his original expression today. Lay expressions of the Franciscan charism include not only the largest group, the Secular Franciscan Order (OFS), but also many smaller ones. Those seeking a lifestyle resembling that of Francis' first lay followers, among them Count Tiso da Camposampiero, may wish to consult the Confraternity of Penitents, whose members "live the Rule of 1221 as closely as possible to its original intent." For more information, see www.penitents.org or write to Confraternity of Penitents, 1702 Lumbard Street, Fort Wayne, IN, 46803, USA.

May the Lord direct you as you seek to know Him better and serve Him more faithfully!

Abbreviations for Primary Sources Referenced in the Chapter Notes

Early Documents Regarding Saint Anthony

Assidua: *The Life of Saint Anthony* by a contemporary Franciscan (1232)

2LJS: *The Second "Life" of St. Antony* by Brother Julian of Speyer (1233–34)

Dialogus: *Dialogus Sanctorum Fratrum Minorum* (1246)

Ben: *Benignitas*

Rig: *Rigaldina*

Writings of Saint Anthony

Praise: *Praise to You Lord: Prayers of Saint Anthony*

SE: *Anthony of Padua: Sermons for the Easter Cycle*

SK: *Seek First His Kingdom*

SSF: *Sermons for Sundays and Festivals*

Early Documents Regarding Saint Francis

FA:ED: *Early Documents I (The Saint), II (The Prophet), III (The Founder)*

Later Biographies

Fortini: Helen Moak's 1981 English Translation *Francis of Assisi* of Arnaldo Fortini's *Nova Vita di San Francesco*

Purcell: *Saint Anthony and His Times* by Mary Purcell

Adm: *The Admonitions* (undated) (FA:ED I 128–37)

2LF: *Later Admonition and Exhortation to the Brothers and Sisters of Penance (Second Version of the Letter to the Faithful)* (1220?) (FA:ED I 45–51)

IC: *The Life of Saint Francis* by Friar Thomas of Celano (1228) (FA:ED I 180–308)

AP: *The Anonymous of Perugia* composed by Friar John of Perugia (FA:ED II 34–58)

L3C: *The Legend of the Three Companions* composed by three of Saint Francis' early followers, Friars Leo, Angelo, and Rufino (FA:ED II 66–110)

AC: *The Assisi Compilation* seemingly compiled by Friars Leo, Angelo, Rufino, and possibly others (FA:ED II 118–230)

2C: *The Remembrance of the Desire of a Soul* by Friar Thomas of Celano (FA:ED II 239–393)

Other Biographies and Books

1.5C: *The Rediscovered Life of Saint Francis of Assisi* by Friar Thomas of Celano

13CC: *Thirteenth Century Chronicles*

1MP: *Mirror of Perfection* (Lemmens Edition)

3C: *Treatise on the Miracles of Saint Francis* (FA:ED II 399–468)

LMj: The *Major Legend* by Saint Bonaventure (FA:ED II 525–649)

Fioretti: *The Little Flowers of Saint Francis* (abbreviated *Fioretti*, its name in Italian)

24Gen: *Chronicle of the Twenty-Four Generals of the Order of Friars Minor*

Fortini: Arnaldo Fortini, Assisi mayor and historian, delved into Assisi archives and shared his research in *Nova Vita di San Francesco*. References in this book refer to Helen Moak's 1981 English translation unless otherwise stated.

PROLOGUE

The Eyes of His Mercy

Scettico,
Cardinal of the Holy Roman Church

Bedchamber, Rome, Italy (Spring 1232)

The old cardinal lay in bed, tossing and turning in the total blackness of his cold, damp sleeping quarters. This room always felt dank. Often he'd considered it a privilege to suffer the chill for the love of Christ, but tonight the nip in the night air of Rome was troublesome.

Or maybe it wasn't the frost in the room. Maybe it was the chill in the consistory court. He didn't like to make enemies, and here he was, making plenty. Sure, he was skeptical. So skeptical that he overheard some of the other cardinals calling him Cardinal Scettico. If that were to be his new nickname, so be it. He liked it, actually. A cardinal of the Roman Church shouldn't be gullible.

The whole city of Padua and its surrounding towns hated him. Whom did he number among his adversaries? The common people. The Order of Minors, known as the Lesser Brothers until just a few years ago. The Poor Enclosed Ladies. The priors of several monasteries. The university students and faculty. The podestà who governed Padua and his council and knights. The bishop of Padua and the bishop of Palestrina. Ottone, the son of the Marquis di Monteferrato. The cardinal of San Nicola. He had made enemies of all of them. All because he was cautious. They wanted Antonio of the Order of Minors canonized now. Scettico wanted to wait.

Over these past days, he hadn't been the only one, but he'd been the most pugnacious of those who insisted that canonizing Antonio was a bit premature. The man hadn't even reached forty when he died, a young age to achieve the ranks of sanctity, and he hadn't been dead even a year. Certainly, the Church's declaration of sainthood should stand the test of time, not be in response to some popular movement to canonize a hero. Why, less than a month after Antonio's death, bishops and clergy, government officials and nobility, commoners and knights had sent a delegation to the papal court. They had come with a long list of extraordinary miracles taking place at his tomb and begging Lord Pope to begin the canonization process. Then the letters began to come, and more envoys, month after month in a continuous stream, all begging the same favor. Canonize Antonio.

Scettico turned on his pillow, burying the prickly gray stubs of his whiskers into the silk coverlet. If only he could stop reliving the afternoon. The images kept tumbling through his brain like a glass, bouncing, bouncing when it should have shattered. Fifty-three miracles attributed to Antonio's intercession, and approved, all but one of them taking place after his death. That afternoon in the consistory, Fra Giordano, prior of San Benedetto, had read the list orally in his deep, monotone voice.

A hunchbacked woman straightened at Antonio's tomb.

A man severely crippled in a fall from a church tower able to walk away from the tomb without his crutches.

A blind brother from the Order of Friars Minor restored to sight after venerating Antonio's relics.

A man deaf for twenty years hearing laughter again after praying to the dead friar.

A young man, unable to speak his entire life and painfully bedridden for fourteen years, carried to Antonio's tomb, walking away freed from pain and paralysis and singing loud praises to God.

And that image of the glass. That one image that Scettico couldn't erase from his mind. After Antonio's death, a heretic knight from Salvaterra had come to Padua. At lunch, his family and friends were praising Antonio's miracles. Angry, the knight emptied his drinking glass in one huge gulp and challenged, "If he whom you call a saint will keep this glass from breaking, I will believe all that you say about him." Scettico kept seeing the knight flinging the glass against the stone floor. The glass bounced, bounced again, and finally slid to rest. Unbroken. Believing, the knight carried the glass to the friars, where he confessed. Now that knight was proclaiming the wonders of Christ and beseeching Lord Pope for Antonio's canonization.

The miracles were authentic. Jean of Abbeville of France, Archbishop of Besançon and Bishop-Cardinal of Santa Sabina, and his learned committee had investigated every single miracle carefully. They had discarded many. But these fifty-three they accepted. Oh, they were authentic, all right. But make Antonio a saint? Now?

The haste troubled Scettico. Antonio had barely died at the convent of the Poor Enclosed Ladies in Arcella when the nuns and the friars who lived in Padua began to argue over which convent should house the remains. What an embarrassing mess that was, with townspeople taking up arms and choosing sides. Peace returned only when the bishop of Padua and the clergy plus the minister provincial of the friars declared that the brothers would get the body because Antonio himself had requested burial at the friars' Church of Santa Maria. Backing up the decision were the podestà of Padua and his city council.

So Antonio was buried at Santa Maria, where the processions to his tomb were outlandish. The numbers visiting choked Padua, and the murmuring of prayers at his grave sounded persistently like the hum of crickets in the swamps at night.

Worst of all were the outrageous candles lugged by pilgrims to the tomb. Each new devotee seemed determined to outdo the others. Many candles were so huge that they had to be lopped off to fit in the church. Others were so heavy that two oxen pulling a cart could barely drag them. Many tapers were ornately decorated with churches or flowers or battle scenes of wax. So much flame surrounded the tomb, both inside and outside the church, that night was as bright as day. It was another miracle that neither the small wooden church nor the town of Padua caught fire. This was faith that bordered on superstition; this was hysteria that pushed for canonization.

Scettico's pinched nose had smelled heresy in the air for three quarters of a century. His dark eyes, once gentle as a deer mouse's, had grown wary as a rat's for having seen the brutal slaughter of an infidel and the equally vicious butchering of a Christian missionary.

He had watched Pierre Vaudès appear, dressed like John the Baptist and preaching repentance and poverty. His followers claimed to imitate Christ and the apostles, but after twenty years, the Church denounced Vaudès' teachings. He had blasphemed the Church, its customs, and its clergy. He claimed that his group alone was the Church of Christ, obedient to God alone, and refused to submit to papal authority and excommunication.

Scettico had seen, too, the growing strength of the Cathars, a more dangerous heretical sect. They rejected the very foundation of the faith by claiming that Christ had never taken human flesh, for flesh was created not by God, but by Satan.

Scettico had seen supposedly holy priests fall into sin and generous monks grow greedy. He knew that time is a great test of sanctity and wondered why so many wanted to rush this particular follower of Francesco into heaven. Was it because this Antonio had been the noble son of a Portuguese knight? Had the public been snared by the romance of a young dandy giving up his riches to embrace the poverty of Christ? And had the romance given weight to the miracles and perhaps even caused them through some public mass hysteria and adulation?

Scettico had come to see his mission as defeating the canonization. Yesterday he had pressed his points in the consistory. The pope had listened intently. He seemed to agree that perhaps he was acting too hastily in canonizing Antonio now. Tomorrow the consistory would meet again. This time ambassadors from Padua would be present. Scettico would press on. If God knew that he was right, the canonization would wait a few years until the world was certain about this Antonio's holiness.

Scettico pressed his palms against his temple. All he wanted was a little rest. If only he could relax. He tried to lie still. Eventually he drifted into a fitful sleep troubled by glasses bouncing through candle flames and knights kneeling at tombs.

Then the quality of his dreams changed. The vision clarified and became a scene. The pope, dressed in pontifical vestments, stood before the altar in a church that had to be new since every stone, every slab glimmered without a scratch, without dust, without the stain of candle smoke. Around Pope Gregorio IX, cardinals were clustered, Scettico among them. The stately prelates in red stood prayerfully as the pope proceeded to consecrate the altar, then looked about in confusion. He could find no relics of the saints to seal within the altar.

In the center of the church stood a casket in which lay a body covered with a white veil.

"Take relics from that," Lord Pope said, pointing down the aisle toward the corpse.

The cardinals exchanged glances, their noses wrinkling slightly at the idea. No one moved.

"Lord Pope, there are no relics. Only a body," one cardinal said.

"Take courage and go quickly," the pope said. "Take off the cloth and see what is inside. The body will provide new relics."

Finally, one cardinal pursed his lips and nodded slightly. He bowed to the pope and stepped forward, walking down the aisle with a purposeful gait.

The others followed. The first cardinal lifted the veil and touched the long, thin fingers that lay folded in prayer on the bosom of a patched gray habit. A fragrance so sweet that Scettico could smell it in his dream wafted from the corpse. The scent was of myrrh, incense, and aloes.

"Sant'Antonio," one of the cardinals said with reverent softness. The word swept through the group. "Sant'Antonio! Sant'Antonio!" The cardinals began to pluck at the body, at the wool habit, at the black hair cut in a tonsure, each greedy to snatch a relic to hide away for his personal reverence.

Scettico woke in a cold sweat. Too shaken to move, he lay staring into the darkness.

"Messer Cardinal, it's dawn. Are you praying your morning Office today?"

Scettico roused himself at the cleric's voice. Ugh! Candlelight brightened the bedchamber. The clerics who were his aides hadn't overslept. They'd lit the candles as usual.

Scettico pushed back his coverlet and waved the cleric aside. "Go ahead. I'll be right there."

Scettico secured his breeches and under-tunic, then wrapped himself in his mantle and hurried through the torchlit halls to the house chapel where the three clerics and some others were waiting. As soon as Scettico stood in his place before the altar, the assigned cleric began the Office.

Scettico tried to focus on the words in his worn breviary, on the chants and the prayers. Instead, he kept remembering that corpse in the coffin. As he struggled to pray, calmness seeped into his soul like broth into newly baked bread. He looked up from his breviary to a cross of the crucified Christ suspended above the altar.

You want this, don't You?

Scettico didn't need an audible answer. He knew.

He was fully dressed and on his way to the consistory when he met the ambassadors of Padua on their way there as well. Before they could speak, he held up his hand and noticed with wonder how vividly his veins stood out in the sunlight. "I'm an old man, beyond my usefulness," he said. "I fully opposed Antonio's canonization and had resolved to do all I could today to stop it." He watched a shadow of pain cross the face of the plumpest, most highly adorned fellow. He knew that he, like a magician, had the power to change that look with a word. "Today God gave me a dream and I am of a totally different opinion now. I know well that Antonio is a saint and is worthy to be canonized. I will do all in my power to hasten his canonization." He beckoned the ambassadors to follow him, almost feeling on his back the glow on the plump one's face.

Scettico was as good as his word. Not only did he speak eagerly of Antonio's greatness, but he also spent the greater part of the day sidling up to opposing cardinals and persuading them to yield to the judgment of those who favored Antonio's cause.

The cardinals agreed. The pope consented. The Church decreed.

On May 30, 1232, the Solemnity of Pentecost, the canonization took place in the cathedral of Spoleto, where Scettico sat with the other cardinals.

As Pope Gregorio IX read the decree of canonization, Scettico allowed himself to grin in public. To him, the words sounded as forceful as if they came from Christ Himself.

"Surely God . . . frequently is pleased to honor . . . his faithful servants . . . by rendering their memory glorious with signs and prodigies, by means of which heretical depravity is confused and masked and the Catholic religion is more and more confirmed. Of this number was Blessed Anthony . . . of the Order of the Friars Minor. In order that a man be recognized as a saint two things are necessary; namely, the virtue of his life and the truth of the miracles. We have been assured of the virtues and of the miracles of Blessed Anthony, whose holiness We have also experienced . . . when he dwelt for a short time with Us. We have decided . . . to enroll him in the number of the saints . . . and We request that you should excite the devotion of the faithful to the veneration of him and, every year, on the thirteenth of June, that you should celebrate his feast."

Scettico sighed and closed his damp eyes momentarily. Antonio belonged to the world but lived in heaven. Scettico had done what God had wished. It mattered little if he died that very moment, for now his mission was complete.

NOTES

Upon Antonio's death, the convent at Arcella and the Monastery of Santa Maria at Padua contested for his remains. The bishop of Padua declared that the remains should be interred at Santa Maria (*Assidua* 26–38, 2LJS 7–8, Rig 17).

Thousands of pilgrims flocked to his tomb. Following custom, many brought votive candles—some so huge that sixteen men had to carry one candle into the church. One candle that had to be lopped off to fit into the church was donated by university students (*Assidua* 41, 2LJS 9, Rig 17).

Miracles due to Antonio's intercession were reported in abundance. His cause for canonization was introduced and the pope appointed a learned committee to study the matter. The committee approved fifty-three miracles (2LJS 10–11), including the ones mentioned in this prologue: cure of a hunchbacked woman (*Assidua* 50–51); cure of a man who fell from a church tower (*Assidua* 60); cure of a blind friar (*Assidua* 63); cure of a man deaf for twenty years (*Assidua* 65); unbroken glass (*Assidua* 70–71).

One unnamed cardinal opposed the canonization but changed his mind following the dream described. His words to the Paduan ambassadors are on record (*Assidua* 42–48, 2LJS 9–10, Rig 17–18).

Antonio was canonized on Pentecost Sunday, May 30, 1232, by Pope Gregorio IX. Some of the pope's actual words are recorded in the prologue.

On the day of Antonio's canonization, the bells in Lisbon began to ring of their own accord, and the people danced with joy (Ben 13).

Antonio's tongue and larynx, which remain incorrupt to this day, can be seen in his basilica at Padua. The aromas of incense, myrrh, and aloes, exuding from his corpse, were again noticed when his remains were studied in 1981.

Lack of reliable information about Antonio begins with the year of his birth. Traditionally, this has been given as the feast of the Assumption, August 15, 1195. This would make him nearly thirty-six when he died. However, recent scientific dating of his remains indicate that he was thirty-nine years and nine months old at the time of his death, which would put his birth in 1191. Because the day and year of his birth are contested, this book is purposely vague about his age.

PART ONE

Go to Christ Your Friend in This Night

1

Mestre João

Santa Cruz Monastery, Coimbra, Portugal (1220)

Mestre João was sitting in his cell at Santa Cruz Monastery in Coimbra, Portugal. Before him on a small table lay an open text of Saint Augustine's work, *On True Religion*. Next to it lay the Scriptures, open to Matthew's Gospel. Mestre João was preparing his lesson for the following day when he heard a tap at his door.

"Come in," he said as he pushed his body to standing position and shook out his arthritic knees.

As João started toward the door, his hand outstretched in greeting, he saw that the one who had knocked was a slightly built young priest. João broke into a grin. Even his weak eyes could tell who the young man was.

"Fernando, my star student!" João clasped Fernando's forearm and shook it heartily. Fernando returned the gesture.

"Which philosopher have you come to discuss today? Aristotle? Or the writings of the saints? Bernard, perhaps? Jerome? Gregory? I'm working on Saint Augustine for tomorrow's lecture. Perhaps you could enlighten me."

Dressed in the white linen rochet and cord worn by the Canons Regular who followed the Rule of Saint Augustine, Fernando smiled. "I think not, Mestre. You're the teacher."

"Here. Sit down." João tugged him toward the extra chair that stood beside his desk, waiting for inquiring students just like Fernando. As João eased his bulky body into his own chair, he winced at the pain in his knees. "Don't mind me, Fernando. I'm getting old."

Fernando settled into the chair, his long hands clasped in his lap. "We're all getting old, Mestre."

João propped his elbow on the small table. He planted his chin on his upraised fist and made himself comfortable. He always enjoyed Fernando's visits. Their discussions often went far into the evening. "So, you didn't come to talk about age. What is it today?"

"Mestre, I have asked the Lesser Brothers to accept me into their religio."

What? Had João heard that correctly? His fist fell to the table and he sat bolt upright.

"The Lesser Brothers? Mendicants? They aren't even an ordine. Since when have you been thinking of this, Fernando?"

"For a long time, Mestre."

"A long time? You, Fernando, who are the son of a noble knight? Those men live more poorly than Christ Himself. What do they have? A patched tunic. A frayed cord for the waist. Not even sandals. God alone knows the condition of their breeches. They're beggars. They plead for alms like beggars, sleep like beggars, smell like beggars."

Fernando was staring at João with that intensely deep look of his. "I know, Mestre. Here we have a powerful priory, lands, a subsidy from the king. The Lesser Brothers have nothing but God. That's what I want."

João rubbed his bald head in confusion. "But Fernando. It's poor enough here at Santa Cruz. Prior João has kept us all in misery with his mishandling of the monastery finances." Their prior's sins of usury had gained him money paid back with unlawful interest, yet he had used none of that ill-gotten money for the monastery. João had complained to Lord Pope, but Prior João's excommunication had done nothing to remedy the matter. "You are already in poverty. We all are."

"I'm speaking of poverty of spirit, Mestre. This is what I need."

Poverty of spirit? What did that mean? Suddenly João knew what the real reason for Fernando's decision must be. Prior João. Had he accosted Fernando?

Mestre João fought to keep the fury out of his voice. "Fernando, has Prior João been making advances toward you?"

Fernando shook his head. "Not anymore."

João closed his eyes and groaned. "Not anymore. What did he do to you?"

Fernando's voice was steady but pained. "Nothing, Mestre. His looks at me seemed strange at times. Sometimes he touched my wrist in a way that was too tender, not of God's love but of man's passion. I pulled away. He never tried anything more with me. He hasn't bothered me for years."

João threw back his head in relief. "Thank God, Fernando!"

For he had touched many, male and female, Christian and non-Christian alike. Despite being sent into the desert to do two years of solitary penance for several years of these crimes, the elderly prior hadn't repented. Mestre João had no solid proof, but he knew. A few canons at Santa Cruz too frequently "consulted" Prior João for "spiritual guidance." The prior made continual excursions into the city on "business" as well. From there, gossip about him seeped into Santa Cruz.

"Fernando, you don't have to leave. I've written to Lord Pope again, asking him to investigate Prior João. You'll see. He'll be dismissed."

"Mestre, I'm not leaving because of Prior João."

"But you said yourself, in one of your sermons—I remember it so well, I wish I had said it—you said, 'Sham sanctity is a thief that goes about in the dark of night.' I was sure you meant Prior João and those like him. And then I remember, too, in another sermon—how did you put it?—'The false religious are errant stars who, in the dark of this world, lead others to shipwreck.' You're right, Fernando."

Fernando leaned toward João, his palms extended slightly upward, his long, expressive fingers fanned, as if to hand João a message. "Prior João and the others are not beyond hope. Aren't you praying for them daily as I am? God's grace and the Church are calling them to repentance. If any one of them responds, the devil will forsake his soul and he will be lifted up by God. As the twenty-seventh Psalm says, 'My father,' the devil, 'and my mother,' carnal concupiscence, 'have forsaken me; but the Lord has raised me up.' There's hope for those men. I'm not leaving because of them."

"Then why, Fernando?"

Fernando closed his dark eyes and brought his clasped hands toward his bowed chin. When he lifted his head, his gaze at João seemed to plead his words. "Please try to understand. It's no longer enough for me to fast and pray, to celebrate the Mass, to preach. I'm happy doing these things, happy, too, with receiving guests in the refectory and scrubbing the kitchen and circling the garden in prayer. But they're not enough. Even my night watches aren't enough, although I begged Prior João to be allowed to continue them. I haven't given up all, Mestre. I have held on to my life. I want to give God my life so that I may merit eternal joy."

"Have you prayed about this, Fernando?"

Fernando's voice trembled. "I have been praying and praying. He wants me to give Him my life."

João groaned. Of course Fernando had been praying. Ever since he arrived at Santa Cruz eight years ago, he had been praying. When João's arthritis kept him awake at night, he often paced through the monastery to walk the pains out of his feet. Countless nights he had caught Fernando deep in prayer in the chapel. Sometimes Fernando would be kneeling before the altar, his eyes fixed somewhere above it, as if looking at Someone no one else saw. Other times he would be before the alcove of the Blessed Mother, his left knee on the floor, his body bent over his right leg, his hands on his right knee. More than once João caught him totally prostrate, facedown on the stone floor. Ever since King Afonso had placed the silver reliquaries of the five martyred friars in the chapel at Santa Cruz, Fernando had prayed there, too, his head pressed against one reliquary or the other.

"Fernando," João would say, "go to bed." Always the slight shoulders would droop just a bit with disappointment and the deep-set eyes would look sorrowful. But the silent nod of obedience always came.

What did all these prayers mean? Could God have truly spoken to the person sitting across from him? João leaned toward Fernando. "God has told you to join the Lesser Brothers?"

Fernando's gaze was unwavering. "Not in so many words. I heard no voice, if that's what you mean. But I must do it."

"Why?"

"Because I want to give God my life. This is what He wants me to do."

"Can't you give it to Him here?"

"That's what I thought, Mestre. But I no longer think that."

João leaned back in his chair. "Fernando, you know there is a rule. No one may leave the monastery without the permission of all the canons who live here. Not everyone will give you permission." João placed his arm on the table and leaned into it. "You're a priest, one of the youngest we've ever ordained. We had to have an exemption from Church law to ordain you, but it was done because you are full of promise."

As he spoke, João saw the color rise in Fernando's dark face at the compliment. He knew that compliments made Fernando uneasy, but sometimes the truth had to be told.

"We are sixty canons here, Fernando, and you, despite your youth, are the brightest man among all of us. Admit it, Fernando. You love books. I've heard you in your room, studying, reading aloud Scripture, philosophy, the natural sciences, the writings of the saints. You drive them into your brain with your recitations until they become a part of you. You know history, science, nature, all the controversies of our faith. Your memory is phenomenal. Have you ever read one thing that you've forgotten? I think not. You'll throw all this away to beg for scraps with men who cannot even write their names? Fernando, that religio's founder, Francesco, won't allow the friars to own even a breviary. Your knowledge will be wasted."

Fernando's eyes were downcast at the tirade, their gaze resting on his hands clasped again in his lap.

"You're a preacher. You love to preach. No one else can speak like you. Your words bring repentance and conversion to those deepest in sin. I've never heard of one decent preacher in the Lesser Brothers. Join them and you'll throw away your gift."

João paused. What else could he say?

Fernando's voice came steady, but his gaze remained on his hands. "Mestre, don't credit me for what others understand through my words. Unless there is inwardly He Who truly preaches, my tongue labors in vain. My preaching is good for preparing the way. But it is the inner anointing through the inspiration of grace, along with the outer anointing of the sermon, that teaches about salvation. When the anointing of grace is missing, my words are powerless."

"They are never powerless, Fernando."

"That can be a great source of pride. And pride keeps a person from Christ."

"Do you want to give up preaching? To protect yourself from pride? Is that it?"

"I don't know if that's it." Fernando lifted his left hand toward Mestre João as if begging him to understand. "The Lesser Brothers have given God everything. *Everything*. I must do that. I must give God everything. Even my preaching, if that's what He wants. Everything. Mestre, I haven't given God my life."

Suddenly João remembered. Fernando had been praying at the tombs of the five Lesser Brothers who were martyred in Morocco. He chose his words carefully. "If you become a Lesser Brother, you will be a martyr. That's what you think. That's what you desire."

João expected his statement to make the young man fidget. He was wrong. "Oh, if only God would count me worthy to share the martyr's crown! What joy, Mestre! I have asked the brothers to accept me on the condition that they send me to Morocco."

João slapped the table in exasperation. "They agreed to this?"

Fernando shrugged and nodded.

João pushed back his chair with such force that it toppled beneath him. "Well, why not agree?" he shouted at Fernando. "That religio has no form, no rule, no novitiate! It has nothing but Francesco! You know yourself, Fernando, that had Francesco not returned from the East when he did, his ragtag band of serfs and free men would have splintered into disaster. You have fallen under the spell of the crazy son of a merchant!"

Fernando looked up at João with that penetrating gaze. "I'm not joining because of Francesco. I'm joining because of Christ."

João paced around the table. "Why do you keep saying 'am joining'? You will never get permission to leave here."

"The brothers are returning tomorrow to invest me."

"Tomorrow!" João's fist slammed onto the table so suddenly that *On True Religion* jumped and tumbled to the floor. As Fernando bent to pick it up, emotion swelled inside of João's gut and threatened to overcome him.

His voice came shaky but subdued, his back to the priest so that Fernando could not see the trembling of his mouth. "Leave me, Fernando. And pray. Pray hard. Discern. Does God want you to die? Or do you?"

"I will pray, Mestre."

João heard the rustle of cloth, the shuffle of sandals, the soft closing of the door to his cell. Turning to the table, he sank to his knees and buried his head in the volume Fernando had just placed on the wood.

Fernando, Fernando! You could be all I never was, all I wished I could be. You'll go to Morocco and be killed? For what?

João's breath came in great gulps as Fernando's life sped like a gale through his mind. He was as powerless to stop the recall as a sapling is to impede a tempest.

Prior Gonzalo of Lisbon had shared with João the tale of Fernando's early life. His father, Martino, who was a wealthy Lisbon noble, made certain that Fernando was well-educated so that he could skillfully manage the family's estate and lands. Fifteen-year-old Fernando must have assumed that Martino, who attended daily Mass, would never object to his son becoming a priest, but the young man had been wrong. Nevertheless, his persistence eventually wore down Martino's opposition.

Once he gained his father's permission, Fernando sought out Prior Gonzalo of São Vicente Abbey, which lay just outside the walls of Lisbon. He asked to be admitted, telling Gonzalo that he was worried about his salvation if he remained on his current path. Worldly goods and honors attracted him. Temptations to fleshly lust were strengthening. He felt dangerously close to falling into serious sin. He wanted to live his life for God but felt too weak spiritually to do it on his own. Gonzalo understood. He had admitted Fernando as a novice.

"He was plump, pampered, and pale when he arrived," Gonzalo had laughed, "but within three months, he had shaped up." Of course! The monks not only prayed in their torchlit chapels but also toiled on their monastery grounds, pulling weeds, hoeing vegetables, and trimming fruit trees, not to mention harvesting the growth of their labors. When, after a year or more's time Fernando requested a transfer to Santa Cruz, his arms had grown muscular, his complexion ruddy, and his temptations diminished.

When he arrived at Santa Cruz, here in Coimbra, João questioned him about the reasons for his transfer. Fernando had replied, "Too many friends and family members visited me there. They were drawing me back into the world."

Smart man, João had thought. Not many people would make a two days' journey just to visit.

In João's classes, Fernando excelled. He was insightful, quick, genteel, graceful, a young man whose nobility was evident at a glance. When assigned to the kitchen, he was an efficient cook and housekeeper, equally at home with pots and brushes as with books. At work in the garden, he tilled, planted, and harvested with as much diligence as he put into his studies. In his free time, he lived in the library, absorbed in books, or in the chapel, sunk in prayer. When he preached at Mass, the congregation sat awestruck.

Since Fernando mastered languages easily and his manners were impeccable, Prior João had made him guestmaster. In the guesthouse, Fernando both distributed alms and received visitors from all nationalities and walks of life. These included priests, paupers, bishops, lepers, nobles, beggars, Queen Urraca of Portugal, and the Lesser Brothers.

The Lesser Brothers lived at the monastery at Olivares, given to them by Queen Urraca herself. Fernando had become friends with many of the mendicant brothers. When one of the martyrs, Fra Questor, died, Fernando confided a vision to Mestre João. "While celebrating Mass, I saw Fra Questor's soul winging its way through purgatory, ascending like a dove into glory."

João should have attached more importance to Fernando's fascination with these men, especially with the five who had come begging alms on their way to Morocco. Fernando had ceaselessly talked about their desire to bring Christ's message to those who had never heard it. At recreation, Fernando, in his usual theatrical way, had told his fellow followers of Saint Augustine about his encounter with these followers of Francesco. "Fra Berard said he was going to die for God's glory. Fra Pietro agreed. Fra Otho joked about being food for ravens. Fra Adjutus spoke little but laughed with him. Fra Accursius said that nothing better existed than to die for God Who died for us."

The five Lesser Brothers had gone to Morocco as chaplains to the sultan's soldiers under Dom Pedro, brother of Portugal's King Afonso. Dom Pedro was the well-paid head of the sultan's armies.

Dom João Roberto had gone into exile with Dom Pedro. But when Dom Pedro sent the martyrs' remains to Santa Cruz, he sent João Roberto along with them. From João Roberto, the monks at Coimbra had heard the stirring details of the martyrs' deaths.

In Morocco, João Roberto said, when the brothers had spoken about Christ, the sultan thought them mad and ordered them either to return to Europe or to be silent. They refused. So the sultan punished them with twenty days of imprisonment, starvation, and torture.

Upon their release, they returned with joy to exhorting the people, thus infuriating the sultan, who ordered Dom Pedro to put them aboard a ship and send them home. Having earlier tried to persuade the brothers to moderate their zeal, Dom Pedro now twice attempted to deport them to Spain. But the stubborn men would listen to no reason and, eluding their guards, found their way back to the sultan.

When Berard mounted the sultan's chariot to speak, the sultan's temper snapped. "Enough!" he had cried. He ordered them to be tortured and killed and, thus, the blood of the five brothers had been spilled in Morocco.

Moved to tears, Dom Pedro had used his political influence to claim the bodies and encase them in two silver caskets. The remains made their way throughout Spain and then into Portugal, finally reaching the capital city of Coimbra. Not knowing whether to bury them in the monastery at Olivares as befitted their humility or in the cathedral as befitted their martyrdom, Afonso's wife, Queen Urraca, who had gone on foot to meet the procession, declared that the mule bearing the reliquaries be released to go where it pleased. To everyone's surprise, it plodded to Santa Cruz, where it knelt before the altar until the holy burdens were removed from its back.

Mestre João had seen this mule's behavior and had thought it odd and yet glorious. God had wanted the martyrs to be enshrined here at Santa Cruz. But why? Now he felt angry with God. Had God brought the martyrs here so that He, through their presence, could claim Fernando?

For no one could deny that the presence of the martyrs' bodies had wrought a change in that young priest from Lisbon. His voice cracking with emotion, Fernando had preached at the Mass of the martyrs. Then, many times afterward, João had caught him praying at their reliquaries, his head resting against the gleaming metal, his cheeks often streaked with tears.

Had Fernando been praying to die?

Tomorrow he would leave. God wanted this? *Why, God? Why Fernando?*

João knew that he must pray. He was still kneeling at the table, his head buried in the book. Now he pushed to his feet, pains once again shooting through his knees. He would go to the chapel and pour out his heart to God.

Fernando, however, had beat him there. Before the alcove of the Blessed Mother, Fernando bent almost prostrate to the stone floor.

João slipped into a pew toward the chapel's rear. *Why, God? Why Fernando? Are You calling him, Lord? In every life, You give a call. Many calls. To do Your will is to submit, to obey. Are You calling him to the Lesser Brothers, Lord? To die? He has such potential. Lord, can You want this? Are You calling him, Lord? Lord, I beg You, if this is from Fernando and not from You, foil his plans.*

Then from deep inside João, like a furtive mouse, poked a thought. *If You are calling, Lord, this monastery will allow Fernando to leave.*

The next day, the entire monastery gathered in the meeting room, each in his accustomed place on the benches arranged along the walls. Fernando, standing in the room's center, presented his question. Whispers swept along the walls. Although Mestre João's poor vision blurred the men's faces, he'd grown accustomed to nuances of speech. He had anticipated a gasp of shock. He didn't hear one. That could mean only one thing. Fernando had spoken to each monk earlier, one by one.

Or perhaps God had.

The monks began to cast their votes. One by one they agreed with Fernando. Reluctantly. Sorrowfully. Against their better judgment. But they agreed. With each vote, João's spirit fell. They were voting to send Fernando to his death. He could see the budding lily of Fernando's promise being crushed by a massive, fatal paw.

Now it was João's turn to vote. He stood uncomfortably. "Fernando, why would God want your life? But if He truly wants it, then you must give it. You've made it clear that you've prayed, that this desire for martyrdom is not only from your own will but also from God Himself. What we, in our poor understanding, deem folly, God often sees as wisdom. If it is God's will that you go to Morocco, then you must go." João's voice began to quaver as he limped toward the young man with the anxious face. "Fernando, I won't oppose you." João extended his arms to Fernando and embraced his trembling body. João's voice was thick. "Go, then, and become a saint."

"Oh, Mestre," Fernando whispered, his voice quivering, "when you hear of that, then you will praise God."

Late in the day, two Lesser Brothers, one of them Fra Giovanni Parenti, the provincial minister, came bearing a coarse gray habit. In the guest receiving room, in the presence of Mestre João and all the canons of the monastery, Fernando removed his white rochet and cord and kissed them. He handed them to Mestre João and slipped into the rough-looking, floor-length tunic. Around his waist he tied a frayed length of rope. Then he walked around the room and embraced each canon before stepping out of his sandals and leaving barefoot.

NOTES

Antonio was baptized Fernando. His family, education, religious history, and reasons for transfer to Santa Cruz follow the historical record (*Assidua* 3–4, Rig 1–4, *Dialogus* 1, 2LJS 1). Purcell details the martyrdom of the five friars and the transferal of their remains to Santa Cruz (pp. 67–73).

São Vicente's was a daughter monastery to Santa Cruz, thus easing Antonio's transfer. At Santa Cruz, he was guestmaster, receiving visitors from all walks of life and distributing alms. His dealings with the Lesser Brothers, including Fra Questor and the five martyrs, are accurate, as are his obtaining the permission of all the monks to leave the monastery and the dialogue "Go, then, and become a saint" (*Assidua* 4–7, Rig 2–3, 2LJD 1–2, *Dialogus* 1, Ben 1).

Some scholars believe that Antonio was ordained a priest after he joined the Lesser Brothers, placing this ordination at Forli in 1222. Others believe that he had been ordained while an Augustinian, since history claims that he offered a Mass for Fra Questor and, in 1221, was assigned to Monte Paolo to offer Mass for the brothers. Other ordinations show that Portugal was in the habit of making exceptions to the Church rule that men could not be ordained prior to the age of thirty. As a priest, Antonio almost certainly preached.

Antonio's teacher, Mestre João, accused Prior João of the charges listed in this chapter. In 1222, Pope Onorio III ordered three of Lisbon's priors to conduct an inquest into these charges, since Prior João had ignored several excommunications. Prior João was relieved of his post and died in 1226, the same year that Francesco of Assisi entered eternal glory. Purcell details the sad story of Prior João (pp. 55–60, 67, 79–80).

Antonio's words are from SerE 63, 148, 173 (sham sanctity, false religious, and hopeful words on repentance of the corrupt clergy); SerE 186 (preaching and God's anointing); and Psalm 27:10 ("My father and my mother . . .").

2

Maria

Santa Maria Maior Cathedral, Lisbon, Portugal (1220)

The small, stocky lady, dressed in the pale, beaded gown of a noble-woman, walked slowly down the aisle of Santa Maria Maior Cathedral. Some said it was the most magnificent church in all Portugal. Before the main altar, a monk intoned a hymn, his thin whisper magnified in the vastness of the sanctuary. Maria was aware that those kneeling in prayer, more poorly dressed than she, were watching her curiously, but she had learned to ignore their stares decades earlier when she was a child. Conscious of the rustle of her gown in the holy stillness, she made her way to the alcove of the Blessed Mother, to the left of the main altar. There she knelt on the hard marble kneeler, her back straight as she had been taught from her youth to carry it, but her head bowed. She did not pray aloud; she never did. Yet, in her heart, she spoke clearly and, she hoped, poignantly.

Blessed Mary, my Mother, Mother of my Fernando, look into your tender soul and have mercy on me. Where is my son, Blessed Mother?

"Take me to Coimbra," she had begged Martino that night months ago as they lay in bed. "All Lisbon is talking about the miracles of healing at the tombs of the five martyred friars."

Martino had rolled toward her and lightly kissed her cheek. "The five martyred friars are buried in the church of Santa Cruz. Isn't that where Fernando is?" His voice had a touch of pain that it always had whenever Maria mentioned their oldest son.

"You know I would like to see Fernando, too."

"If he had stayed home," Martino said with a hint of bitterness, "and had taken over the estate as I wished him to, you wouldn't have to go to Coimbra to see him."

Maria flinched at this reminder of her husband's broken dreams. Kissing Martino's cheek lightly, she pleaded, "Martino, the time for resentment is passed. Fernando left us years ago. He's happy as a monk. He would have been miserable here."

Martino groaned. "I know. He moves souls. He could have moved men."

"He's doing God's work, Martino."

Martino stroked Maria's hair. "I know, my sweet joy. I miss him as much as you do. We'll leave once the sowing is done." He had planted a kiss on her lips and continued to love her, a regular occurrence that seemed remarkable to her now that her black hair was flecked with gray and her once firm breasts were sagging. Martino still called her the name he had used on their wedding night. His "Venus."

The journey to Coimbra had seemed to take forever as it always did. She worried whether the nurse would properly care for the children she left behind. Would the nurse see that Pedro ate well? Would she be tolerant of young Maria's moodiness? Would she insist that Feliciana practice her stitchery?

Martino never worried. "The children are big enough," he always told her before these journeys. "They can care for themselves."

Nevertheless, she worried. The Blessed Mother understood. The Blessed Mother must have worried about her own grown Son. Hadn't He left their dwelling, challenged the religious authorities, and traipsed all over the countryside with no place to call home? Surely, He concerned her. Once, with His relatives, she went to call Him. Jesus ignored her, saying, "Who is my mother, and who are my brethren? Whoever does the will of my Father in heaven is my brother, and sister, and mother." Grown children could be a worry. The Holy Virgin understood.

When she had arrived at Santa Cruz, Maria had encountered the unexpected. Fernando was gone. "He's joined the Lesser Brothers," the guestmaster told her. He directed her and Martino to the nearby Brothers' abbey of the Olives.

Maria, Martino, and their entourage of horses, mules, baggage, servants, knights, and nobles wound their way through gnarled olive groves where the delicate lace of the olive leaves brushed Maria's face. With a smile, she knew what only a mother would know. Fernando would often stroll under the olives, seeking the leafy softness as another man might seek his lady's caresses.

Then she had seen the abbey and her smile died as swiftly as a crushed gnat. The abbey was a hut. Worse. A shack. Fernando here? Against the abbey leaned hovels of wattle. As her horse strode past, she glimpsed two figures inside one of these rude dwellings. One friar lay on a bed of straw, his head on a stone, his bare and dirt-blackened feet splayed out beneath a ragged, tan woolen tunic that was splashed nearly to the knees with caked mud. Another friar was bending over him, swabbing the prostrate one's neck with a gray, dripping cloth.

Fernando here? Even as she silently screamed *no*, the doctoring friar turned toward her and stood.

He's no more than a boy, she thought with a start as she noticed the scraggly beard just beginning to sprout. *Where's your mother? Why did she let you come here?*

He saw the questions on her face but misread them. "He has a fever," he said, nodding at the ill friar.

"We're looking for a priest named Fernando," Martino said.

"Fernando?" The young man was obviously puzzled.

Maria found her voice. "Our son. A friar with black hair, dark skin. About medium height. Well-bred," she added. "He joined you from Santa Cruz."

The youth smiled. "You mean Fra Antonio. He does resemble you," he added with a bow. "But he's no longer here. He and Fra Felipe and Fra Leo left several days ago for Morocco."

She felt her face go ashen.

"This had been his cell, here in the olive grove," the youth said, "but shortly after he left, Fra José grew ill. Our guardian ordered him to come here. Fra Antonio's cell was newer than Fra José's. More watertight," he grinned.

"He's not here, Maria," Martino had said. He grabbed her horse's reins in his own strong hands and turned the beast back the way they'd come.

"Godspeed!" the youth called as he stooped into the hut.

Oh, Blessed Mother, Maria prayed now in the cathedral, *how my own silk sheets and down comforters mock me! Fernando on straw? Oh, Blessed Mother, have pity! And he's not even at Olivares. He's sailed for Morocco!*

Morocco. Morocco. There in the olive orchard, Maria had wanted to shriek like a peasant woman who hears that her son has been run over with a plow. If only she could faint like a coward at the sight of blood. Or beat the earth with her fists like a knight knocked to the dust in a tournament. But the wife of a court noble does no such thing, so she sat straight in her saddle. The beast under her pulled against the taut rein as the cortège headed back to Lisbon.

"Morocco." Maria whispered the word in the cathedral. The word sounded like the first note of a dirge. She boldly raised her eyes to the icon. The Blessed Virgin's gentle face was tilted to the right. Her dark eyes seemed to look pityingly into Maria's own.

Blessed Mother, Maria pleaded, *those in Morocco don't believe in your Son. Nor do they wish to hear of Him. Those who speak of Christ there die for their valor. The five holy martyrs were killed there. Is that what Fernando wants? To die for your Son? Let it not be, my Mother.*

Maria's gaze wandered to the Holy Infant Who stood in the crook of His Mother's left arm, His chubby hand stroking the Virgin's cheek.

Wasn't it enough that your own Son died? Death was your Son's mission. It's not my son's.

Blessed Mother, you know how I prayed to you for this child. How I gave him to you from the first moment that I knew he was growing beneath my heart. You accepted my gift. You saw that he was born on the feast of your Assumption. He's not yet thirty, Mother. Even your Son survived to thirty-three. Can my son not have at least as many years or a few more?

Maria was weeping in silence as a faint memory returned, suddenly strong: the sweet, sweet smell of slippery newborn wetness. How tenderly, eagerly her infant had tugged at her breast, his dark eyes fixed on her face as his mouth pulled!

Could she leave those memories in the sands of the desert? Those and other recollections. The young Fernando noticed what everyone else overlooked.

Sunlight snagged on the steep terraces and stone walls of his neighborhood. The anguished cries of seabirds that flew between the River Tagus and the Lisbon shore. The peculiar moaning of sea and wind on stormy nights. What would he notice in Morocco but the glint of steel honed to kill, the shouts of men out for blood?

Oh, Mother of mine, he's worth more than his blood. Maria remembered him, a chubby little boy in a tunic too long for his short, plump legs. The sleeves hugged his arms. The low neck was embroidered with golden curls and loops, her design, her art. She combed his hair and sent him to school. So near their house, yet so far for a child of seven.

"Your Blessed Mother will be with you when I'm not," she had told him.

"She's as sweet as you, isn't she, Mamā?" he asked.

"Sweeter," Maria said, kissing his head and sending him off.

At the bishops' school attached to this cathedral, he did very well in his studies. Fernando didn't brag about his abilities, but his uncle, Canon Fernando, who taught at the school, frequently told Maria and Martino how brilliant his little namesake was. How quickly Fernando grasped writing on a small wax tablet with a stylus! With what confidence he memorized Old Testament genealogies and lists of vices and virtues richly engraved on framed sheepskin hides! His teachers praised his memory, his behavior, his cheerfulness. As he grew older, the praise increased. All subjects seemed easy to him. Arithmetic. Geometry. Botany. Medicine. History. Philosophy. Music. Rhetoric. Natural science. He would come home from school eager to tell Maria about the precious gems or exotic beasts or diseases of the body which he had studied that day.

Surely, his teachers said, Fernando would make a fine knight, an asset to the king's court. But Martino said no. Fernando was too small, too weak to be a knight. Why waste his brilliance on combat when he was more suited to intellectual pursuits? Fernando would write the accounts for his father, manage the castle, inherit the estate. He had the intelligence and grace to rise in society. He would be a noble in every sense of the word.

Martino's plans thrilled Maria. She had not wanted to see her son wield a sword. Better for him to be at home, safe, than risking his life in combat. Better to be respected for wisdom than for prowess.

You know how Fernando loves you, Mother of God. Ever since I sang "O Glorious Lady" to him, over and over when he was an infant, it has been his favorite song. Every Mass he ever served as an altar boy he dedicated to you. When we would walk the streets and pass a church, he would ask to go inside and pay you a visit. Even the cathedral school that educated him bears your name.

Why has he gone to Morocco, Blessed Mother? Is the devil drawing him there to be rid of him?

Maria had thought that Fernando was done with demons. Years ago, when he was praying before the Blessed Mother's shrine here, he had encountered a devil, a hideous creature that had appeared at the altar. Frightened but not frightened off, Fernando remembered the Son of God. The boy traced a cross on the marble step on which he knelt, whispering as he did so the precious name of Jesus. The creature vanished. Fernando raced home to Maria to tell her, to pull her back to the church and to show her the spot of the apparition.

Oh, Blessed Mary, I thought I had lost him when he told us that he wished to join the Canons Regular of Saint Augustine. The convent of São Vicente was nearby, but it might as well have been in Germany, for he was giving up all his life to enter there. He wasn't yet twenty.

Maria had dreams. She had envisioned Fernando's wedding, his wife, his children on her lap. She had seen him riding across his estate seeing that the serfs who worked his land had food and goods. She pictured him endowing cathedrals and schools with his funds.

A priest had no place in Maria's daydream or in Martino's. They told their son that he was throwing away his life. He told his parents that he was saving his soul. They showed him what he would be losing. He told them all that he would gain. In the end, Maria and Martino relented. Fernando accepted the white robe and black, hooded cloak of the ordine.

Maria and Martino saw him often. So did his friends. He was hardly a man when he asked to leave São Vicente's monastery and Lisbon. Martino promised that his family would visit him wherever he went.

Oh, Blessed Queen of Heaven, beg your Son not to take mine. The monks at Coimbra praise Fernando's preaching. He has a gift, they say. Let him use it, Blessed Mother.

Sweet Mother, have mercy on the tears of this mother, your daughter. Fernando, I know, is praying to you, too. He is begging to die for his faith. Merciful Mother, I am older and wiser than he is. I know his gifts even if he wishes to disregard them. Won't he do God more good alive than dead? Don't listen to his prayers, dear Lady. Answer mine. Spare my son.

NOTES

Antonio's first biography states that he was born of young, noble parents in Lisbon (*Assidua* 3). A later biography states that "He was of noble birth, his father being Martin, a knight of Afonso [or: Martin (son of Afonso, a knight)]" (Ben 1). Afonso was the king of Portugal.

In Antonio's day, several classes of nobility lived in Portugal. The lowest class was the villein-knights who were able to own a horse and arms of their own. These knights frequently settled in such border towns as Lisbon where they could acquire small (for the time) territories and protect the castles and towns of the realm. If Antonio's father were a member of this class, as seems likely, he would have been a member of the lower nobility (Purcell 24–25).

Thus, it seems likely that Antonio's father, Martino, was a knight and that his mother, Maria Teresa, was a noblewoman, although their class is disputed. Antonio had two sisters, Maria and Feliciana, and a brother, Pedro. Maria became a member of the community of nuns of Saint Augustine, which was attached to São Vicente Monastery, the very monastery that Fernando entered. Pedro became a wealthy man who bequeathed some houses he owned to the cathedral canons. Feliciana married. Some writers claim that Antonio raised to life her dead son.

As a child, Antonio, then called Fernando, was educated well. He apparently had a prodigious memory. Fernando had a great devotion to the Blessed Mother, which he learned from his own mother. He assisted at daily Mass and would go into any church that he passed to pray. Once, while at prayer, a demon appeared to him, and he repulsed the creature by tracing the sign of the cross on the marble step (Purcell 26).

When Fernando entered the Franciscans, he took the name Antonio after Saint Anthony of the Desert, for whom the monastery was named. He hoped this new name would make finding him more difficult for his family and friends (*Assidua* 8, Rig 4).

The monastery at Olivares consisted of rude huts thrust against the walls of the abbey. The friars slept on straw with stones for pillows. They worked the land and begged alms. Within two weeks to six months of his joining, Antonio, Felipe, and Leo were sent to Morocco.

Antonio's traditional birthdate is August 15, the feast of the Assumption of Mary.

The Scripture is from Matthew 12:48, 50 ("Who is my mother . . .").

3

Emílio

Ship Bound for Portugal, Mediterranean Sea (Early Spring 1221)

Emílio raised his gnarled fist to the sky and shook it at the swirling black clouds. From the moment he had arisen, an hour before dawn, until now, the wind had crested from a moan to a roar. The ship was pitching in the tempestuous Mediterranean Sea. Much as he wanted to shave the gray stubble poking out on his weathered face, he'd not risk the razor today. On the rolling ship, he'd likely slice himself deeply and add another scar to cheeks that had sustained too many wounds in tavern brawls.

Emílio hated storms because his unshaved beard always itched during them. For all the pain and discomfort he'd experienced at sea, he didn't know why the facial irritation bothered him so much, but he accepted it just as he accepted the knee cramps that seemed almost constant now that he was getting too old for life at sea. He must be past forty, he thought, but how could he return to the land after spending nearly his whole life on the waves?

Of course, if he gave up sailing, he could sit indoors during storms and maybe even enjoy a warm fire. Right now, that sounded tremendously alluring. Any moment, he expected to be pelted with rain and perhaps hail. "Cursed be all ye demons in hell," he muttered as he strode across the narrow, shifting deck of the ship.

He paused at the hold in the ship's belly from which wafted up the sweet odor of lemons and limes from Morocco, piled in bins for sale in Lisbon.

"Hey, ya brothers down there? Ya'wake?"

"We are," a sturdy voice called out of the darkness.

"And a good morning t'ya, though ya'd not know it from the sky," Emílio yelled above the wind. He shoved his head down into the narrow opening. "I'll help ya git the good padre on deck, Fra Felipe."

The young brother's face appeared in the gray circle of light at the foot of the ladder. Then Padre Antonio's ashen face moved into the glow. He was young, too. Emílio could tell that, but the flush on his sunken cheeks aged him.

"Ya look peaked ta-day, Padre!" Emílio shouted. "Ya better get up here and take some air before she starts ta rain."

Tall Felipe supported the shorter padre from below as he climbed the ladder. Emílio's muscular arms grabbed the padre's thin ones and pulled him out into the light.

"Don't know why the captain took ya on," Emílio said to Antonio, who stood unsteadily on the pitching ship. "He knew ya was sick. How ya going ta work yer way ta Lisbon?"

He looked at the young brother who was now standing on deck, too, staring at the angry sky. "Now, Fra Felipe, ya kin work fer yer passage all right. I seen ya yesterday, hoisting them sails like an old sea dog when ya ain't hardly even old enough ta be a man yet. Swabbing the deck like ya was born with a rag in yer fist."

Emílio gave his arm to Antonio to steady him. "I know. Ya try, Padre. Ya do a passable job. Don't know how ya keep yer legs under ya. I seen ya a couple times, leanin' into the railing, sick with fever. Ya don't eat, not much anyway. How ya gonna git strong if ya don't eat hearty?"

He sat Antonio on the deck between a pile of rope and a creaking mast. "Course, maybe ya don't wanna muscle up. Maybe ya wanna die. Hey, I heard the stories. The whole ship knows the two of ya and yer friend Leo sailed ta Ceuta ta die. Course, only Leo got his wish."

Emílio avoided looking into the padre's eyes as he fished around under his grayish shirt for the bread he'd stashed there.

"All right. Ya didn't go there ta die. Ya went ta preach about yer Savior. But the sultan wants nothin' ta do with yer Savior. He made vulture bait of five other of ya guys who came here. And yer friend Leo, too. Ya knew what would happen when ya came. Aren't those first five brothers buried in yer city? I don't think King Afonso cared much about them, the king bein' out of the pope's graces and all that. But Dom Pedro welcomed their bones like they was angels, I hear. Stuffed their dust into silver boxes. Silver! Is that what ya two want? Silver don't do no good unless yer alive ta spend it."

Emílio found the loaf and, squatting on the deck before the two brothers, tore at it with his greasy hands.

"Look. Ya wanted ta die. Ya might get yer chance. Naw, the captain wouldn't touch ya. He claims he's a follower of yer God. So yer God don't mind if the cap'n's got a woman in every port, sometimes two? A God like that I might believe in. Might, ya hear. Don't go preaching ta me again. I ain't ready ta hear it."

He tossed a hunk of bread up to Felipe, who was standing as sturdily as a column beside him.

"Naw, ya needn't worry about the cap'n. It's yer God ya need ta worry about. Ya, Padre, ya told me that He got the sea and the sky in His hand like I got me this bread. He does what He wants with them, ya said."

Emílio put a hunk of bread into Antonio's hand.

"He's doin' a rotten job right now, Padre. Us out of port just barely a day and this wind comes up outta the west. Wind? This ain't no wind. This is a gale. A maelstrom. We're barely through the strait, so close ta land yet. So intense. Seems unearthly. Ya been praying ta go back ta Portugal, back ta yer community, ya told me. Ya better pray harder. This ship ain't going nowhere near Portugal in this storm."

He looked at the two brothers, who were still holding their bread. "Why don't ya eat? When the rain starts, the rest o' the bread will rot."

"First, we pray," said Antonio, bowing his head.

Emílio didn't listen to the words. He heard instead the first splatters of rain thrown across the ship like pellets of ice.

Three days later, Emílio found a length of soaked rope behind one of the water barrels and went looking for the brothers. He found the two of them kneeling in the hold, wedged one behind the other in the narrow walkway between two bins of fruit, their heads bowed in prayer. The boat was pitching from side to side and the ankle-deep water in the hold washed from one side to the other, flowing up against the men, around them and down with each toss of the vessel. The lemons and limes were shifting first to one side, then to the other, straining against the wooden slats that kept the fruit in check.

Water sloshed in Emílio's boots as he waded over to the brothers. He didn't care if he interrupted their prayer. "Listen, ya guys. Where's yer God? Three days in this tempest. Not even the cap'n knows where we are. Ya better pray. We're goin' down if this keeps up."

Then he felt a tinge of remorse. He was used to storms, though he had been in few as violent as this. These men were only on their second sea voyage.

"Yer holdin' up in this, ain't ya?" he asked more tenderly. "Ya all right, Padre?" Emílio grabbed the shoulder of the brother closest to the ladder.

"Hey! Wake up!"

Antonio lifted his head and looked at Emílio. Emílio felt as if the priest could see his innards and, even worse, his sins. He thrust the rope at Antonio, knowing that he would look at the tether rather than at the sailor.

"Cap'n told me ta give ya this. He's afraid these bins is gonna bust open. An' if they do, ya won't be able to stay down here. Ya'll have ta be on deck. If that happens, Padre, ya lash yourself ta the mast. Fra Felipe, he's sturdy enough ta hang on. But you? Ship's heavin' too much, pitchin' worse. Yer red with fever. Cap'n's afraid ya'll wash overboard. Bad luck for us all then. Tie yerself ta the mast, ya hear?"

Antonio nodded. Just then, a shriek came out of the west, an ungodly scream of wind, and the ship rolled almost completely over. The lemons and limes heaved against the wooden slats and a horrible crack burst through the hold. The fruit to the left of the three men came pouring out upon them in an avalanche and bumped across the hold. Suddenly, the water was a soup of green and yellow fruit. The three men pushed toward the ladder. As Emílio lost his footing, two pairs of wet, wool-covered arms reached out for him and heaved him erect.

"Thank ya, brothers," he managed to sputter as he spat out the water he had gulped.

As the men reached the deck, Emílio grabbed the padre and pulled him toward the central mast. The ship pitched again and threw Antonio against the upright wooden log. Emílio snatched the rope from his hands and swiftly began to lash him fast.

"Now don't ya preach ta me," he said as Antonio began to speak. "Ya didn't git to preach to the Saracens, so don't preach ta me." Then he felt a wince of pity at the man's lost dreams and changed his mind. "Well, go ahead, preach. Ya didn't see an infidel in Morocco, did ya, but I'm pretty close ta one in belief anyhow. I heard ya was sick with fever when ya landed in Ceuta 'bout the start of the year. Ya'd have got yer wish ta die there if it weren't fer yer friend. Him runnin' around, gittin' ya eats, bathin' yer fiery body, that's what kept ya alive."

"And his prayers," Antonio said. "He prayed, too."

"And his prayers, too, if ya say so. I seen these fevers. Seen lots a sailors die from 'em. Sickness hits the weak ones. Why'd ya think ya was strong enough ta stand the desert? But then, maybe ya didn't care if ya snuffed out like a candle."

Emílio cinched the knot. Twice.

"Have you ever loved anyone enough to die for them?" Antonio asked.

"What kind of stupid question is that? I live fer me self. If I die, it'll be fer me."

The ship lurched again and a swell of water washed up over the prow, burying the deck.

"Yer fast now, Padre. You'll not roll. I'll be back with a tarp fer ya if the sea don't git me first. Cap'n wants ya to have it. Course, I don't know what good it'll do. Ya already look like a drowned rat."

"A drowned rat must look more handsome than I do." Those black eyes were twinkling. "Or than you do. Or Fra Felipe."

Emílio chuckled. "We're drownin' 'n yer jokin'. Yer all right, Padre. Say yer prayers. Prayers is all we got left."

The next dawn, just as the blackness of night was reluctantly yielding to the thick grayness of day, a sickening scrape ripped through the wind and the boat shuddered like a horse in its death agony. Emílio had felt this once before on a vessel bound for France. The ship had run aground. They were going down. He had half a mind to jump and save himself, but he couldn't leave the brothers.

Pulling his knife from his belt, he worked his way up the tipped deck to where Felipe was frantically trying to untie the padre's ropes.

"Ya need a knife, boy," he said, pushing the young man aside. "Padre, I'd not leave ya here. I'll have ya loose quick now." One of Emílio's gnarled hands grabbed the swollen cord, thick as a sausage, while the other worked the knife. The blue veins on his wrists protruded and throbbed like worms.

"We two will stay with ya, won't we, Fra Felipe? Ship's goin' down. We struck something. Damn night. Sorry. Didn't mean to offend yer sensibilities. Cap'n couldn't see a thing. Couldn't avoid the reef if he had. Sails no damn good in this wind."

The rope split. "Yer loose, Padre." Emílio pulled the cord away from the woolen habit. It had stuck fast to the waist. "When we go down, grab yerself a plank, ya hear? You'll wash in an' maybe yer God'll keep ya from grinding ta pulp on the reef."

The ship was tilting more dangerously now but no longer pitching so violently. The wind seemed quieter, as if the storm were breaking up.

"Uh, Padre, if ya don't mind. Could ya, like—uh, bless me? I been baptized. My ma saw ta that. Ain't done nothing with my faith since then. But bless me now. I don't want ta die without a blessin'."

The ship shuddered and sighed. A rush of water flowed up over the dipping prow. "Quick," Emílio commanded. "She's shiftin'. What do I say?"

"In the name of the Father, and of the Son, and of the Holy Spirit."

Emílio repeated hurriedly. "In the name of the Father . . ."

Not long after, the ship sank slowly into the sea.

Emílio washed in with the tide. So did the lemons, the limes, the captain, the crew, and the brothers. Emílio and Felipe found Antonio lying facedown in the sand at the edge of the tide. They dragged him out of the water's reach to an outcropping of granite, where Emílio left them while he went in search of civilization. After walking inland for a short time, he found a village where people who spoke a strange dialect clustered about him. He finally understood that he was in Sicily. As best he could, he told them about the wreck and about the two brothers and that one of them was ill. Was there any place around here they could stay?

The crowd of men, women, and children all nodded and spoke in a jumble. He was able to comprehend that some distance up the beach in the town of Messina was a community of Lesser Brothers. A lanky, black-haired farmer with a cart volunteered to take the brothers there.

The two brothers were still sitting in the shelter of the rock when Emílio and the farmer arrived.

"Naw, I ain't goin' with ya," Emílio said as he hoisted Antonio into the straw. "Cap'n wants me ta stay here with the ship and the rest of the crew. Seems like we somehow all made it out here alive. Must be yer prayers, Padre. We're gonna see if we kin salvage anythin' before we outfit again fer Portugal."

Then he had a thought. It had been nagging at him ever since the storm started, really. But he had been able to crush the idea pretty well until the ship broke up. Then he'd made that promise.

"Look, Padre, before ya go, would ya hear me confession? I mean, I kinda promised God I'd go when I was out there fightin' the sea. Promised I'd go if I lived, that is. Don't like ta break promises, I don't. I mean, any man who's blown this far off course and survives the deep should keep his promises, don't ya think? Do ya mind, Padre? Ya folks with the cart kin wait 'til I'm done, can't ya?"

The farmer and Felipe nodded and considerately walked off along the beach, leaving Antonio sitting in the straw and Emílio leaning awkwardly on the cart.

"Climb up," Antonio said with a smile.

Emílio had sat in lots of places, places he knew a priest would never go. None of those bars or brothels had embarrassed him like being in this cart did. But he climbed in obediently and attempted to kneel.

"Sitting is fine," Antonio said.

So Emílio sat. "How da I begin, Padre? I got I don't know how many years ta talk about."

Antonio smiled. "You start like this: 'In the name of the Father . . .'"

Emílio thought he'd have trouble remembering years of sins, but they kept tumbling out like dried beans from a clay crock. Didn't seem to matter that he didn't tell them in order. The padre listened and nodded and kept asking if he had any more to confess. Emílio had no idea how long it was before he couldn't think of another thing. Then Antonio put a firm hand on Emílio's head and said something in a strange but clearly spoken language.

"Now for this absolution to be effective, there is something you must do."

Do?

"You must avoid all these sins you confessed."

Sure. He knew that. He'd try. Didn't know how he could do it. But he'd try.

"And every day you must pray for someone else who needs to confess, and offer to God one difficulty of your day for that person."

"Every day?"

"For the rest of your life. Every day."

"Why?"

"So that person, too, can go to heaven."

"But I don't even know that person."

"You will when you both get to heaven."

"Is that where I'm goin'?"

"If you don't sin any more, heaven is where you'll be going."

Heaven. Sounded wonderful.

Emílio searched his mind for a person. "Who should I pray fer?"

"How's this? Pray, 'Lord, I'm praying for someone You know who needs to confess. And I offer You this one trouble today for that person.' And then think of some difficulty to offer as a prayer for him or her."

"Like this stubbly beard here?" He rubbed his fuzzy cheeks. "I hate it."

Antonio laughed. "Like your beard. Or this." He touched Emílio's arm where the ripped sleeve revealed a gash where the blood had caked. He hadn't even noticed that. "Or that." Antonio pointed to Emílio's bare feet. He'd lost his boots in the sea.

He was starting to understand. He felt light, pure, as if he could skip across the sky like the white clouds in the wake of the storm.

Goodness. The brothers better get moving! He beckoned to the farmer and Felipe. Within moments the brothers were settled in the straw and the farmer was taking up the reins.

"Padre, ya take care," Emílio said. And he meant it. "Yer fever's still warm. Git better now. I don't know much about prayin', but I'll put in a word fer ya. Thanks fer hearin' my confession. I'll be prayin' for that somebody, Padre! God knows I got enough troubles ta use in them prayers. God bless ya!" he called out to the bumping cart. "This ain't Portugal, but ya'll be okay here. Pray fer me."

He hadn't had to ask. The padre's hand was already tracing the sign of the cross in Emílio's direction as the cart rounded a dune and disappeared from sight.

NOTES

Antonio and Fra Felipe of Castile sailed for Morocco probably around December 1220. Some sources say that a Fra Leo of Lisbon was martyred in Morocco at this time. Purcell (p. 79) believes that Leo was Antonio's traveling companion rather than Felipe, but it is very possible that the three friars, Leo, Antonio, and Felipe, all traveled to Morocco on the same boat.

Either on board or immediately after disembarking, Antonio fell ill with a violent fever so extreme that he was bedridden for months at the port of Ceuta. Had someone not tended him, he likely would have died. It is improbable that Leo could have been tending Antonio and also sharing Christ's message with the Muslims. If Leo were martyred, how did Antonio survive on his own? Another brother must have tended him, and that would have been Felipe.

Antonio's extreme illness was so persistent that he either decided to return to Portugal or was recalled there. Felipe went with him.

In this chapter, the return voyage to Portugal is seen through the eyes of a fictitious crew member, Emílio. Shortly after setting sail from Ceuta, Antonio's ship was caught in a storm so violent that it blew the vessel 1,500 miles off course, across the Mediterranean to Sicily. It ran aground near Messina, where the Lesser Brothers had a convent. Antonio and Felipe were taken there (*Assidua* 8–9, Rig 4, 2LJS 2, *Dialogus* 1).

4

Fra Felipe

Porziuncula, Assisi, Italy (1221)

Tall, eighteen-year-old Felipe leaped across the grassy meadow and arched into the air. His palm solidly met a small ball and whacked it upward over the heads of his French teammates and across a crude net strung between two saplings. The ball sped downward on the other side of the net, where a sturdy young brother raced toward the hurtling object, slammed it with his palm, and sent it back across the net.

The ball plunged to the right of the net in Antonio's direction. Antonio took a running jump and slapped the ball just as it dipped toward the ground. His strike was solid but short. The ball flew over the net and dived earthward so close to the net that no one on the opposing team could reach it before it bounced through the grass.

A cheer shot from the opposite side of the net, loudest of all from Felipe. It rang across the meadow and through the glades where other brothers were sitting, watching the game or chatting.

The winning teammates bounded together and began to pound each other's backs in hearty appreciation. Then, as one group, they hurried over to the losers and patted their backs, too.

"Good game."

"Luck."

"We prayed harder."

"Like fun."

"You got more Romans on the winning side and this is Roman territory. We French aren't used to the soil here."

"You Frenchmen taught us this game. You ought to know how to play it."

Gradually the banter ended. Felipe helped the French brother who had painstakingly knotted the net untie it from the saplings and roll it up.

"Merci," the brother smiled as he tucked the net under his arm and plopped the ball into his hood. He said something about Toulouse, but Felipe couldn't quite understand all of it. He assumed that this French brother may have been assigned to that French city.

Felipe nodded to him and then looked around for Antonio. He wanted to find him before Compline.

Over there. Sitting on a grassy knoll, his face flushed from exertion.

Felipe bounded over and sat beside him as Antonio lay back and stared up at the sky, where the sun that had burned so fiercely in the afternoon smiled less intensely now that evening approached.

"Do you ever miss home?" Felipe asked, lying down beside the priest.

"Sometimes."

"I've been thinking often about Spain. About the girls in flamenco dresses at festival time in Castile. Is that wrong?"

"I would say that's normal."

"I bet you never think about women."

Antonio chuckled. "Brothers are not to bet. And if you did bet on that, you'd lose."

Felipe sighed. The warm sun on his forehead felt like a soft maiden's palm. "Did any woman ever tempt you, brother?"

"Once."

"What did you do?"

"I sent her back to serve her mistress."

"So she was a servant girl. I used to like a girl once, too. She tended pigs. Sometimes I still think about her. Do you ever think about that servant girl?"

"Occasionally."

"What do you do when you have these thoughts?" Felipe watched the clouds.

"I do what Fra Francesco told us to do. I use the discipline. Or run. Or plunge into an icy stream."

Felipe sighed. "I've done that, too. It does work." He was silent for a while, then asked, "Do you ever miss your family?"

"Sometimes."

"What do you do about that?"

"I've written to them."

Felipe had never thought of that. His parents couldn't read, but the lord of their estate could. Felipe couldn't write, but some of the brothers could. He'd ask one to write for him. Once he knew where he would be assigned, he would ask permission of his new guardian to beg a parchment and a quill.

Oh, how could he make his parents understand what joy he felt at following Christ and at telling others about Him? He imagined himself in his home, sharing with his parents the words Francesco wanted all the brothers to use to exhort the people to repentance. Felipe had learned these words from the convent guardian.

"When you approach a town," Francesco had instructed, "and see the church spire, kneel and pray." First the Our Father and then Pope Innocenzo's prayer composed in honor of the Crusaders' victory at Toledo. "We adore you, Lord Jesus Christ, in all your churches throughout the whole world, and we bless you, because by your holy cross you have redeemed the world." After praying, the brothers were to approach a gate of the city or town and then loudly and joyfully call the residents to do penance.

"Fear and honor, praise and bless," the brothers were to call out, "give thanks and adore the Lord God, Almighty in Trinity and in Unity, Father, Son, and Holy Spirit, the Creator of all." Then the brothers would proclaim: "Do penance, performing worthy fruits of penance because we shall soon die. Give and it will be given to you. Forgive and you shall be forgiven. If you do not forgive people their sins, the Lord will not forgive you yours. Confess all your sins. Blessed are those who die in penance, for they shall be in the kingdom of heaven. Woe to those who do not die in penance, for they shall be children of the devil whose works they do and they shall go into everlasting fire. Beware of and abstain from every evil and persevere in good till the end."

The homily was fixed and straightforward, easy to remember. Felipe had seen it convert a peasant here and there when he had recited it with fervor. Fra Antonio had exhorted the people, too, in similar words spoken with deep conviction. But when Antonio spoke, Felipe always felt a sense of uneasy longing, as if Antonio had within him so much more to speak and was holding back.

A wheezing grunt startled him. Antonio. The priest's eyes were closed, his mouth slightly open. Antonio was asleep.

Felipe smiled. Of course Antonio was worn out. He'd been ill when they arrived in Messina, and the two months of restored vigor before they left for this chapter meeting would have dissipated by the time they finally arrived. First that short boat ride across the strait to Calabria and then a trek of several weeks to reach Assisi. The arduous journey tired even Felipe.

As the small band of Lesser Brothers had approached Assisi, however, Felipe's fatigue yielded to excitement. Could they have arrived at a fair? Dusty brothers like themselves clogged the roads. Knights and ladies rode by on horses decked with colorful ribbons and small, furled banners. The townsfolk of Assisi had festooned their homes with leafy garlands and banners, but although many wanted to be hospitable and offer the brothers lodging, so many thousands had come that the houses didn't have enough room. So the brothers went into the meadows and woods and constructed wattle huts in which to stay and reed mats on which to sleep.

For a week, Felipe and Antonio and brothers from everywhere had slept and prayed and feasted out in the open on huge tables laden with delicacies served to them by the lords and ladies who had brought them. The chapter gathering was supposed to last only a week, but now it was Tuesday and the brothers were still here. Francesco said they had to stay until they consumed all the food. Felipe had never experienced anything like it.

Goodness, just remembering the exuberance of the past week was draining. All that eating, fellowship, prayers, preaching, meetings, plus the tension of wondering where he'd be assigned for the next year—his "obedience," as the brothers called it. Felipe was to receive his the next morning. And the next morning, he did.

Gathered in a cluster of gray-clad brothers, Felipe heard his name called and his obedience given. Città di Castello. He didn't know the language of those brothers, but it seemed similar to his own. *I think I can learn quickly,* he reasoned.

Where was Antonio going? Felipe had missed his name being called. As the group of brothers wandered off straggler by straggler as names and assignments were called, he could see Antonio sitting on the grass. Felipe bounded over to him.

"I'm going to Città di Castello tomorrow. They say it isn't far from here. Where are you assigned?"

"I'm not assigned."

Not assigned? "Didn't you ask the provincials to take you? I saw you asking when I did."

"No one accepted me."

No one accepted Antonio? Why? Then he thought of how the rather average-sized, frail priest, still thin from his bout with fever, must have appeared to the provincials. Not capable of the rigors of the religio. They no doubt thought he'd be a burden.

"Didn't you tell them you were a priest?"

"No one asked."

"What did you tell them?"

"I asked them to instruct me in spiritual discipline and I offered to clean the kitchen for them and do household work or beg."

Antonio's humility frustrated Felipe. "You can't stay here with nowhere to go."

"Fra Felipe, I went to Morocco because I was certain that God wanted me there. I still feel that He did. Yet He resisted me all winter by striking me with that fever. Thus, God foiled my desire to die for Him, the desire that I was certain was His will."

Felipe groaned. Antonio had spoken to him several times about the confusion that he felt over his desire for martyrdom. If God had truly called Antonio to Morocco, then why hadn't the Lord allowed him to preach there? If God gave Antonio a burning desire to die for Christ, then why hadn't that desire been fulfilled?

Antonio gazed at Felipe with eyes that seemed pained. "I don't understand, Felipe. Did I misread what I thought the Holy Spirit wanted me to do? Was the desire to die for Christ from me and not from God? Please try to understand, brother. I didn't think that I wanted my own will then, but maybe I did. I know now that I only want God's will. I will wait here until God puts me where He wants me."

Antonio was praying for God to bring him wherever God wanted him to be. Felipe started praying, too. *Lord, You need to help him.*

Just as quickly, the thought came. Go FIND A PROVINCIAL.

Me?

"Wait here," Felipe told Antonio. And he was off.

Where?

Over there. A group of brothers, some young, some older. Felipe hurried toward them. "Pace e bene, brothers. Can any of you point me to a provincial?"

The brothers all turned toward an older brother in their midst.

"I'm a provincial. Fra Graziano," the square-jawed, big-eared friar said. "My province is the Romagna. And you, brother?"

"Fra Felipe. From Castile. But this isn't about me. I'm assigned, but I have a friend who isn't. Fra Antonio. From Coimbra. He's a priest."

"I know of no Fra Antonio from Coimbra."

"He's been a member of the religio less than a year. He had been ordained at Santa Cruz monastery in Coimbra, under the Rule of Saint Augustine."

Graziano ran his hands over his thick black beard. "I may have use for him."

When Felipe found Antonio, he was kneeling at prayer in the Porziuncula, the little church that Francesco had repaired in the early days of his conversion. Felipe also knelt in the back and prayed until the hour sounded for Prime. He met Antonio coming out of the chapel.

"I've found a provincial who may take you! Will you ask him?"

"If you wish," Antonio said.

As the friars gathered for prayer, Felipe looked for Graziano and found him in the crowd. "There he is," Felipe said, "the big man with the black beard. Go and ask him to take you."

Antonio smiled. "You're still taking good care of me, brother."

"Go ask."

Nodding, Antonio approached Graziano. "I'm Fra Antonio," Felipe heard him say. "I'm not assigned. Will you accept me in your province and assign me to a hermitage where I may learn spiritual discipline?"

Graziano glanced at Felipe, then at Antonio. "So you are a priest?"

"Sì," Antonio said.

"If Fra Elia approves, you're welcome in my province. I have there a small hermitage, Monte Paolo, in the Apennines, about half a morning's walk from Forli. You will learn spiritual discipline there. The six brothers there have been going to Forli or Cesna for Mass and the sacraments. They've repeatedly asked me for a priest, but I've had none to send them. Are you willing to go there and celebrate Mass for the brothers?"

"I'm willing to do whatever you tell me, brother."

"Buono. I shall ask Fra Elia at once. I'm sure that he'll approve."

Following Prime, Felipe looked about for the group bound that morning for Città di Castello. He spied them amid other clusters of brothers, but before he joined them, he had to bid farewell to Antonio, who was standing with the Monte Paolo group. The two men embraced, promised to pray for one another, and wished each other God's peace. Maybe they would meet at another chapter meeting. Felipe hoped it would be so.

NOTES

The nature, goals, festivities, and prayers of this chapter meeting, which began on Pentecost, May 23, are accurate (13CC 30–32).

Francesco's instruction to pray the Our Father and the "We adore you" prayer are in the early histories (FA:ED I 388), as is the simple sermon the brothers were to give (FA:ED I 78).

"The game of the palm," or *jeu de paume*, originated in France in the 1100s or 1200s and eventually evolved into tennis. No record exists of friars playing this game, but it is entirely possible that they did, since Francesco encouraged joy among his followers.

Antonio's earliest biography states that he was "tempted beyond normal" by "passions of the flesh," but, "mastering the weak human condition, he tightened the reins over the impulses of carnal concupiscence" (*Assidua* 4). Felipe and Antonio's discussion about sexual temptation is a postulation about what these temptations may have been. Whether Felipe had a similar temptation is pure speculation.

The assignment of Fra Felipe and the progression by which Antonio was sent to Monte Paolo follow the historical record, although some historians have Antonio being assigned to Monte Paolo when he, not Felipe, spoke to Fra Graziano.

5

Fra Aroldo

Monte Paolo Monastery, Between Arezzo and Forli, Italy (1222)

A roldo, the big-boned guardian of Monte Paolo, was wedged into a tiny wooden chair at his desk in his narrow cell. He was reading for the third time Fra Antonio's commentary on the Psalms. If he hadn't been so engrossed by the words before him, he would have realized how cramped his thick muscles had become.

As a squire, Aroldo had learned to read. As a knight, he had enjoyed stretching out in his large chair by the fireplace to study by candlelight his single, precious text of Scripture. Since becoming a brother and traveling here to these mountains between Arezzo and Forli, he had nothing to read at all. This poor, out-of-the-way hermitage owned not a single manuscript. Then Fra Antonio had arrived and requested writing materials. Aroldo had given him permission to beg for them provided that the young priest submit his work to Aroldo's scrutiny. He would have preferred to read the commentary outdoors where he could prop his bulky back against a huge oak, but the mountain breezes were tricky. Aroldo feared that a gust would catch one of the carefully penned pages and snatch it forever from him.

So he remained in his cell. He stretched against the wooden chair and realized with a start that his neck and ribcage felt stiff.

"Fra Aroldo? You called for me?"

The quiet voice at his door startled him.

Aroldo pushed back his chair too abruptly, catching it swiftly as it nearly toppled to the floor. He arched his back and stretched his arms wide. They nearly touched the two walls of his cell.

The friar at the door hadn't moved. "Come in, Fra Antonio!" Aroldo bellowed. "I've been reading your work."

Antonio walked softly into the cell and stood before Aroldo. "They're only my thoughts, brother. Is there anything wrong with them?"

Wrong with them? "Brother, this is the first material I've been able to read since joining the religio."

"My words are better than nothing. Sì?"

"Better than much that I've read. You have tremendous insight. I'd never applied Psalm 127 to myself: 'Your children around your table like new olive plants.' I had thought that verse was for families. Right here you've written," Aroldo said, picking up the page and reading, "'Your children, dear Jesus, are Christians whom You have given birth to in the labor pains of Your Passion.' And here," Aroldo said, flipping a page, "you wrote, 'These children are indeed Your children since You have redeemed them with Your own Blood, O Lord. Would that they really be Yours and not their own, that is, given up to their own flesh.'" He put the page back onto the table and smiled at Antonio. "I don't think that I'll ever again see an olive shoot without thinking of myself as a child of God."

"Did you call me here to discuss my work?"

Glancing down at Antonio's pages, Aroldo stretched again. "You don't mind a walk along the mountain, do you?"

Antonio laughed. "Do I mind going to God's garden?"

"So that's what you call these glades," Aroldo said as he led the way out into the sunlight and in the direction of Antonio's cell. He said no more until the two men had moved beyond the small cluster of cells and the cultivated garden plots where a brother, bent over his hoeing, paused to nod at them. When the two arrived in the thick of the forest where the sound of the hoe could no longer be heard, Aroldo spoke again.

"Are you happy here, Antonio?"

Antonio threw up his arms as if to embrace the wood and turned about slowly, his hands and face upraised to the branches above him. "Are the sparrows happy here?" he said, pointing to a few who winged above from branch to branch. He paused, then knelt and scratched apart the pine needles at his feet. When he stood, an earthworm crusted with dirt squirmed in his palm. "Are these happy here?" He bent to drop the worm back onto the soil, then sprinkled dirt and dry needles over it again. "All creatures are happy in the Creator's garden, including me."

"The cell that you have been using? It suits you?"

Again the smile. "Fra Artigiano was very kind to let me use it. He removed the tools he stored there so I could replace them with myself, this hunk of obstinate metal and unbendable wood."

"And is the metal becoming malleable and the wood pliable?"

"I would hope so."

"May I see your cell?"

Antonio led Aroldo to a nearby narrow cave. Someone, perhaps another brother, had hewn—with great difficulty, no doubt—the cramped cavern from a huge rock thrusting out of the mountainside. Near the opening stood a rough-looking table and rustic stool. "You made those?" Aroldo asked.

"Fra Artigiano let me use his tools."

Aroldo laughed. "Fra Artigiano, is it? That is your name for him? A good name, too."

In the rear of the cell lay a mound of straw with a stone for a pillow. Against the wall, at the head of the pillow, leaned a scourge of tufted marsh plants. Stream rushes. Pliant. Sturdy. When used to lash one's flesh as a discipline or as a deterrent to temptation, they stung like slender whips.

Aroldo saw all these things in a glance and knew what they meant. His smile disappeared. He turned and looked directly at the priest. "The brothers tell me that you take no bread or water with you to this cell and sometimes, when the bell rings for the evening meal, you are so weak that they must support you as you walk."

Antonio returned the gaze. "I've never missed a meal."

"Nor a prayer either. You're faithful and prompt." Aroldo looked again at the rushes. They were green, yet shredding, a sure sign of frequent use. "I want you to relax the discipline. And I want you to eat more, if not in this cell, then at table." Aroldo squeezed Antonio's right arm through the sleeve of his habit.

"You're bones, Fra Antonio. You came to us barely recovered from illness."

"You were good to take me. I'm better now."

"Barely recovered from illness," Aroldo repeated as he lightly shook the thin arm. "You're no good to us dead, brother. A dead priest can't celebrate Mass. Less discipline. More food."

Antonio's shoulders, always so regally carried, fell just a bit. "Sì, brother."

"Doesn't Scripture say 'to obey is better than sacrifice'?"

"Sì. 'Having purified your souls by your obedience,'" Antonio confirmed Aroldo's Scripture verse with another. "Less discipline. More food."

Aroldo released his arm and turned away from the cell. He began walking again into the forest. "The kitchen has been spotless, brother. Every pot and pan is scrubbed and in place. You do well with this job you requested."

"Grazie."

"You feel better about eating now that you're a servant?"

Antonio grinned.

"You weren't born a kitchen drudge," Aroldo said, turning back toward the hermitage.

"What makes you say so?"

"The carriage of your back. Your steady gaze. Your confident and clear manner of speech. These are part of you. From infancy, serfs learn to act as serfs, nobles as nobles. You bow, brother, and avert your eyes as a serf might do, but you do these consciously. These mannerisms aren't part of you, just as they aren't part of me."

"I'm sorry that they're not."

"Never be sorry for what God has created in you."

The two walked in silence, listening to the birds twittering and the breeze soughing through the pines. Soon the hoe sounded in the woods. "I'm glad Fra Graziano sent you to us to celebrate Mass," Aroldo confessed.

"So am I."

"And I'm grateful that you allowed me to read your commentary. It's opened my eyes as nothing I have ever read before, except perhaps Saint Augustine."

Aroldo glanced sidelong at the priest to see how he would receive this compliment. A bit of color rose to Antonio's cheeks. "I'm no Saint Augustine."

"If only Fra Francesco could see this. Perhaps he would change his mind about allowing the friars to be educated. You've explained our Lord's teaching well."

"It's easy to do. The Gospel is the kiss of God."

Aroldo nodded. The kiss of God. What a beautiful phrase!

The sound of the hoe was just beyond the next thicket when Aroldo stepped over a huge toppled tree trunk and sat down. Antonio sat next to him.

"In Ember Week there will be an ordination at Forli. Some of our brothers and some of the Preaching Brothers will receive Holy Orders. I'm requested to attend and would like you to be my traveling companion."

"I would like that."

Aroldo clasped Antonio's two long hands in his own huge paws and shook them heartily.

"Then we have a pact. To Forli."

"To Forli."

NOTES

Historians disagree on the exact location of Monte Paolo. Some place it near Forli, others near Arezzo, others near Bologna. Purcell (p. 93) has placed it four miles from Forli. This text reflects that opinion.

At Monte Paolo, Antonio asked for a small cave hewn out of rock, which had been used by a brother to store tools. Here he prayed, fasted, used the discipline, and worked on a commentary on the Psalms. He always left his cell for meals and prayers even though, at times, he was so weak that he had to be assisted in walking. He also celebrated daily Mass for the brothers and asked to clean the kitchen. When an ordination of Franciscans and Preaching Brothers (Dominicans) was to be held at Forli, he accompanied the unnamed superior (assigned the name Fra Aroldo in this chapter) as a traveling companion (*Assidua* 9–10, 2LJS 2–3, *Dialogus* 2, Rig 5–6).

Antonio's words are from SK 32–36 (comments on Psalm 127) and Purcell 223 (the Gospels as the kiss of God). The Scripture is from Psalm 128:3 (then numbered as Psalm 127: "Your children around your table . . ."), 1 Samuel 15:22 ("to obey is better . . ."), and 1 Peter 1:22 ("having purified your souls . . .").

6

Fra Graziano

Convent of the Lesser Brothers, Forlì, Italy (March 19, 1222)

Graziano always enjoyed an ordination because the ceremony meant more priests to bring the sacraments to the people.

Yes, the convent must seem shabby to Bishop Alberto, who had ordained the new priests from both the Lesser Brothers and the Preaching Brothers, but the tasty meal that they were now enjoying would, Graziano hoped, compensate for the poverty of the surroundings. The portions were small, as they should be during Lent, but the Lesser Brothers had prepared the food well.

Graziano was just now relishing pan-cooked spring greens seasoned with olive oil and garlic. As a yeoman, he had observed with what delicacy the noble lord he had once served ate his meals. In attending to him, Graziano had picked up some of the refined eating habits of the nobility. He hadn't forgotten them by becoming a follower of Francesco. Right now, he was sharing his table with Bishop Alberto. He didn't want his table manners to appear coarse to the prelate.

As the men chatted and filled their stomachs with roasted nuts, Graziano swallowed his last delicious mouthful and pushed away from the table. The meal was ending and the men were growing louder. Now seemed the best time for the dinner speech. One of the brothers who belonged to the ordine founded by the forceful Domingo de Guzmán must have been assigned to prepare the message.

Their mission was preaching. Graziano would find out who was to speak and quiet the men.

He located the provincial of the Preaching Brothers, a stern-looking gentleman with a pointed white beard.

"Brother, who has been appointed to preach at this time?" Graziano asked. "I'll introduce him now."

The black-robed friar opened his hands wide. "No one asked us to provide a speaker. We assumed that, since the ordination was at a convent of the Lesser Brothers, you were providing the preacher."

Graziano scowled and then immediately tried to smile. He knew his tactic was fruitless. He had never been able to make his face move into contortions that his emotions warred against.

"We're not prepared," Graziano said in desperation. "Would you care to speak?"

"I'm only good at preaching when I'm prepared," the priest said, his beard bobbing up and down with his words. "Why not ask some of my friars? Perhaps one will agree."

With a glimmer of hope, Graziano moved along the table, sending the question before him. Would one of the followers of Domingo be willing to preach? They all had the same excuse. No one was prepared.

As Graziano moved back toward his own brothers, Bishop Alberto waved him over. Graziano came reluctantly. "Is something wrong?" the prelate asked. "By comparison to your face, a prune would look handsome."

Graziano stifled a grin. "Messer Bishop, don't bother yourself about my problem."

"Come. Tell me what it is. We can't have your sourpuss ruining this delicious meal."

"Messer Bishop, no one is prepared to speak."

"Aren't you provincial? Choose someone."

"We're all brothers here. Except a few."

"Preach yourself. You're a priest."

Graziano moaned. "I'm not prepared."

Bishop Alberto propped his chin upon his fist. "Don't you have anyone who will preach out of obedience?"

Graziano glanced around the room. His gaze fell on Antonio seated at the rear table, speaking softly to Fra Aroldo from Monte Paolo. This was the thin, sickly-looking young priest whom Graziano had sent to Monte Paolo last year. Since then, the brother's face had plumped a bit. *Monte Paolo has restored his health,* Graziano thought. Then he remembered something else about that brother.

"Back there is a priest who once told me that he would do whatever I said," Graziano told Bishop Alberto.

"Call him up here," the bishop ordered.

As Antonio knelt before the bishop, Graziano looked with dismay at the priest's rough, chapped hands, clasped before his chest. Obviously, Fra Aroldo had made him a kitchen drudge.

I have brought a man who washes pots and sweeps floors to the bishop as a speaker, Graziano thought miserably.

"Can you preach?" the bishop asked Antonio.

"Sì, Messer Bishop."

"Then I order you, under obedience, to give a toast."

"But Messer Bishop . . ."

"Under obedience."

"Sì, Messer Bishop."

"You are to take as your text, 'Christ became obedient unto death, even to death on a cross.'"

"Sì, Messer Bishop."

"And speak whatever the Holy Spirit may give you. I bless you now in the name of the Father, and of the Son, and of the Holy Spirit." The bishop made the sign of the cross over Antonio, who blessed himself with the words. Then Bishop Alberto lightly touched the top of Antonio's head. When he removed his hand, Antonio looked up at the prelate, who said, "You may begin."

Graziano prayed rapidly as the average-looking friar made his way to the front of the table, all eyes on him. *Holy Spirit, give him the words.*

Antonio stood still, his head bowed but his back straight, as a murmur sifted through the room and died. The men shifted in their seats and then the sounds of creaking faded. Antonio lifted his head and looked slightly upward, as if to Someone he alone could see.

"'Christ became obedient unto death,'" he spoke. His voice seemed to quiver before gaining strength. "'Even unto death on a cross.'" His gaze spanned the men before him. "In the name of the Father and of the Son and of the Holy Spirit."

The friars crossed themselves.

Antonio's voice came again, louder. "Christ." A pause. "Became." Pause. "Obedient." Pause. "These words find their first expression early in Scripture in the Holy Gospel according to Luke. After Mary and Joseph found Jesus in the Temple, 'He went down with them and came to Nazareth and was obedient to them.' He came to Nazareth, that garden of humility, and 'He was obedient to them.'"

Antonio paused and gazed from one attentive face to the next. Suddenly he called out, "Let all boasting cease, let all impudence disappear in the face of these words: 'He was obedient to them.' Who was He, Who was obedient? He Who has created everything from nothing."

Antonio raised his eyes and stretched out his arms to heaven as he spoke. "He 'Who,' as Isaiah says, 'has cupped in His hand the waters of the sea and marked off the heavens with a span; Who has held in a measure the dust of the earth, weighed the mountains in scales and the hills in a balance.'

"Who, as Job says, 'shakes the earth out of its place, and the pillars beneath it tremble; Who commands the sun, and it rises not, Who seals up the stars; Who alone stretches out the heavens and treads upon the crests of the sea; Who made the Bear and the Orion, the Pleiades and the Constellations of the south; Who does great things past finding out, marvelous things beyond reckoning.'"

Antonio lowered his arms and gazed again at the friars. "He Who does all these things 'was obedient to them.' Whom did He obey? A carpenter." He held out his left hand. "And a poor, humble virgin." He extended his right hand. "He Who is the Beginning and the End, the Ruler of angels, made Himself obedient to human creatures. The Creator of the heavens obeys a carpenter, the God of eternal glory listens to a poor virgin. Has anyone ever witnessed anything comparable to this? Has any ear heard anything like this?"

Antonio drew his hands to his chest, placing them over his heart. "And we would hear even more profound wonders, for He, the Christ, the Creator, became obedient, not only to Mary and Joseph who nurtured His life but to death, death on a cross."

And so he spoke. Graziano lost all track of time. He had heard countless sermons. Many priests had Antonio's conviction. Some had his grace. But no one he had ever heard possessed such depth of knowledge or breadth of spirituality. Antonio was opening up the Scriptures, shining on the word "obedience" a radiance that could only come from God Himself.

"And thus the Son, obedient to His Father's bidding, ran to meet death, death on a cross." Antonio stretched his arms at his sides. "Therefore, 'He stood with His hands outstretched' on the cross 'between the living and the dead.' He was stretched between two thieves, one of whom was saved and the other condemned; He stood between those who were being kept in prison in the netherworld and those who were living in the miseries of this world's exile. All of these the Son delivered from the blaze of diabolic persecution when He offered Himself to the Father in the sweet fragrance of sacrifice."

Graziano felt himself to be a witness to something wonderful, something unfolding and rising like the wings of the Spirit filling the room.

"In His arms outstretched on the cross, Christ gathers us." Antonio's arms reached to encircle, as it were, the brothers and to lift them to his chest. "He lifts us to the bosom of His mercy as a mother takes her child. He nourishes us with His Blood as if it were milk. And He has carried us in His arms extended on the cross. Therefore, rejoice because Christ has died for you."

Antonio's voice rose as he called out, "To the ends of the earth, O preachers, proclaim this word of joy. Proclaim it not only to the just who are in the Church's midst, but to the outer bounds of the Church, outside the precepts of the Lord within which we must live. Let the world hear the word of joy so that all people might obtain the full joy which has no bounds. For Christ became obedient unto death for us, thereby bringing us to eternal life. Let us become obedient unto Him and proclaim to all that He, our obedient and merciful Savior, is to be praised. He is the beginning and the end, wonderful, ineffable for all ages. Amen."

On the very edge of Graziano's consciousness, he watched Antonio return to his bench and sit. No one else stirred. After a lengthy silence, a murmur broke across the room. Graziano could feel excitement stirring his soul.

The bishop was smiling at him. "An excellent choice, Padre. He must be a great asset to your province."

Graziano grinned. He pushed out of his bench and ordered his legs to walk, not sprint, to where Antonio was surrounded by a cluster of chattering brothers. He drew aside the guardian of Monte Paolo, who was sitting quietly, staring at Antonio and the brothers around him.

"You've kept him to yourself for nine months," Graziano said eagerly. "Now he belongs to our entire province. He must go throughout the Romagna to preach."

"Brother, he never preached for us. We thought him incapable and never asked."

"I'll send a message to Fra Elia this very night," Graziano continued. "As minister general, he would want to grant him permission to preach such words as he has spoken to us. Rimini is rife with heretics. I'll ask Fra Elia to allow him to make his way there, preaching as he goes."

NOTES

March 19 or September 24 are both possibilities for when the ordination at Forli took place. By some oversight, no one had been asked to preach, so Antonio was ordered to do so by Fra Graziano and Bishop Alberto. The text he was given is the one stated in this chapter, and he was to speak as the Holy Spirit directed him. No words of his sermon were recorded. However, whatever he said must have been more than the simple exhortation to repentance that all the brothers could offer (FA:ED I 78). Only an educated brother would have been able to develop a theme using Scripture, theology, and studies of the day as Antonio must have done. Fra Elia, the minister general, soon granted Antonio formal permission to preach as a regular part of his ministry.

Antonio's sermon on "Christ became obedient" is from SK (156–60) and SerE (107–08, 194–96, 204). The Scripture referenced is Philippians 2:8 ("Christ became obedient . . ."), Luke 2:51 ("He went down with them . . ."), Isaiah 40:12 ("Who has cupped . . ."), Job 9:6–10 ("Who shakes the earth . . ."), and Numbers 16:48 ("He stood with his hands . . .").

Part Two

In Such Need of Bread

7

Benedetto

Shore of the Marecchia River, Rimini, Italy (1222)

Benedetto was squatting along the shore of the Marecchia River. His toes dug into the cool, wet sand. His skinny hands swiftly plucked fish from the netted mass directly in front of him. In the near distance where the Marecchia met the Adriatic Sea, the dull roar and crash of the tide broke on the beach. To avoid being blinded by flinging sand, Benedetto had turned his back to the brisk sea breeze that now whipped his thick black hair around his face.

Even though the eastern sky was just beginning to turn pink, Benedetto could see clearly enough to sort the saleable from the useless fish and drop them into the proper baskets. He had been fishing for fifteen years and probably could have sorted the fish by touch.

Right now, he wasn't even thinking of fish. Perhaps the last time he had been truly conscious of the fish was when he was an almost-grown man, several years after he'd begun working the nets with his father. Then, he began to think of girls. His thoughts had been deliciously new and strange and, as he grew older, forbidden. But he had tried to censor those lewd ideas, for God would disapprove.

When he was barely a man, his thoughts had turned to Gionata, who was barely a woman. She was the one his father had chosen for him, the daughter of a fishing acquaintance from Pesaro. Benedetto had seen others more beautiful than Gionata, for her nose was a bit too big for her slender face, but he noted in her an inner loveliness. She loved the good God and the Church as he did, an unusual attribute in this area.

Today, as he sorted the fish, he was thinking of Gionata, big with their third child. Would she be calling the midwife even now? Would he return home to a third son? His first two boys, as custom dictated, had been named after his and Gionata's fathers. A third son would bear Benedetto's name. Benedetto's heart swelled at the thought.

But when the child did come, he would be unable to share his joy with the men who fished the sea with him. Benedetto glumly thought of Giuseppe and Rodrigo, whose boat flanked him on the right, and Isidoro, who was sorting his fish to the left. All three were Cathars, believers in that sect that was destroying the Church not only in the Empire but also all over the world.

Giuseppe and Rodrigo constantly harangued Benedetto about their heretical faith. Cathar meant "the pure." They promoted a "pure" religion. The Cathars were especially strong in a French city called Albi, so these heretics were called Albigensians there. They went by other names in far distant lands like Germany and a place at the end of the sea called England.

Giuseppe and Rodrigo so much as said that Benedetto and Gionata were sinners because they were begetting children. "Don't you know that sexual appetite comes from the devil?" they asked him more than once. "Sexual union is sinful." They were sure about that because, they pointed out, "The good God is pure spirit and the Creator of everything spiritual and good. The evil god created the visible world and every living thing in it, including human bodies. Satan uses human bodies to imprison apostate spiritual beings who once rebelled against the good God. These souls have to do penance and free themselves of all flesh if they are ever to enter heaven."

Thus was their religion. Then came their accusation. "You and your wife are in league with Satan because you're creating children in whom spiritual beings are held hostage." If Benedetto believed these men, he would find no joy whatsoever in his children.

Benedetto pushed the black hair out of his face and glanced at the boat next to him. The men were sorting the fish. Quickly. *If only they'd sort out their lives,* he thought. *Forgive me, Lord. That was uncharitable.* He made a speedy sign of the cross as a spiritual apology.

He knew Giuseppe and Rodrigo lived impure lives. Unlike the *perfecti* in their sect, whom the rogues called the "Good Men" or, even more blasphemously, "Good Christians," the two scoundrels had not yet received the *consolamentum*, the Cathar secret rite of baptism. Thus the men were free to live loose and licentious lives, for the sacrament, they claimed, would purge them of all sin. Once they took the *consolamentum*, which they planned to do on their deathbeds, they were assured entrance into heaven. Should they die too swiftly, their souls would be reborn in the bodies of other humans until they would do sufficient penance and become *perfecti*. The souls of Benedetto and Gionata, who believed in the Roman Church, were condemned to endless cycles of rebirth and death until they, too, embraced the Catharist truth.

Benedetto had no patience or love for Giuseppe and Rodrigo. They were Cathars so that they could sin without the guilt they would have to face were they members of the Roman Church. At night, the men's raw, drunken laughter would echo through the Rimini streets as they made their way to the town brothel. Their beastly existence held no lure for Benedetto.

Isidoro was different. Benedetto glanced at him sorting his catch methodically, almost reverently. In the red-bearded teen's presence, Benedetto felt sinful and confused. Isidoro didn't talk about his faith, but all the fishers in Rimini knew how he lived. He embraced his faith as fully as if he were a Good Man himself. He killed no birds or four-footed animals, for he said that was sinful. He ate no meat, not even the fish he caught for a living. He drank no wine, courted no woman. Three times a week, while the other men were pulling out sausages and cheese for lunch, Isidoro was fasting on bread and water. Having received the first part of the *consolamentum*, Isidoro was now worthy to pray the "Our Father" several times daily. Benedetto noticed that he frequently paused his work and stood unmoving for a few moments, his head bowed. Once a month, he attended a service presided over by the Good Men.

Isidoro's holy life mocked Benedetto, who sometimes felt too exhausted to attend Sunday Mass, even though he always went, and who often resented fast days and the hunger pains that accompanied them. Would God take him to heaven despite his faults? The idea of receiving the *consolamentum* and being assured of eternal reward was appealing. Increasingly, he began to wonder if he were holding on to his Roman faith only because he had been raised in it.

Benedetto had to admit that Isidoro's condemnation of Dom Alonzo was justified. The parish priest ate his fill of sweets purchased with, so the rumor went, money donated for the poor. His house was anything but simple. Benedetto often saw him weaving his way home from the tavern, where drink and loose women were both equally accessible.

In contrast, the perfecti, as Isidoro often pointed out, put their faith in the good God and lived the poverty, purity, and charity they preached. They owned nothing, lived on alms, fasted, and prayed frequently. They refused sexual relations of any kind and were quick to offer solace, help, and encouragement to the needy.

"How can you believe priests like Alonzo?" Isidoro would challenge. "Would God make Himself into lowly bread, and at the bidding of a sinful priest? It would be holier to pray in a barnyard than in that priest's church."

Isidoro made Benedetto think. Sometimes he felt as stupid as the fish that lay limp at his feet. He tossed a plump fish into one basket to save and sell, and a tangle of seaweed into another to discard. Which basket was he in: God's or Satan's? How about Isidoro and the Good Men? Whose basket claimed them?

"Hey, Benedetto! Here comes your new priest!" shouted a deep, raspy voice from the next craft.

The call of squat, muscular Giuseppe punctuated the soothing lap of the river's waves against the smooth hull of Benedetto's boat. Benedetto strained his eyes to stare down the beach. Far away, just emerging from the spot where night and dawn merge, was the silhouette of a man who walked with the straight carriage and purposeful gait of a noble, but who was clothed in coarse beggar's wool. Fra Antonio.

"I hear that priest is even holier than you and Isidoro," Rodrigo called.

"Then maybe he's Christ returned," Giuseppe roared. Benedetto's ears burned at the blasphemy.

Antonio had arrived in town two weeks ago and had been preaching throughout the city as the Cathars did. Audiences would gather to listen. Benedetto himself had listened several times. Antonio was not from the

Romagna—Benedetto could tell that—yet he spoke the language well. Even more than that, he spoke of God as forcefully as the Catharist preachers. Benedetto had never before heard any priest speak like that.

On Sunday, Benedetto, Gionata, and the children had gone to Mass, at which Antonio presided with Dom Alonzo assisting. There Benedetto participated at Mass as never before. Although he did not fully understand the Latin that Antonio used, he knew that the words differed in pronunciation, and perhaps in meaning, from those Dom Alonzo spoke.

Antonio preached. Benedetto had never heard anyone preach at Mass. He had learned his faith from his parents, from the paintings on the walls of the church, and from the Apostles' Creed and the Our Father, which Dom Alonzo had everyone recite. But until Antonio had spoken, Benedetto had not really thought about the love of Christ.

At Mass, Fra Antonio had said that Jesus' disciples were fishermen. As Benedetto continued to sort the fish, he wondered if Jesus could call someone as sinful as himself to follow the Lord. Now his gaze was following Antonio as the priest made his way down the beach. Antonio was pausing at each boat, taking time to speak to each man. Benedetto suddenly reddened over his uncultured manner, his clothes and body reeking of fish, his hands covered with slime. He wanted to run and hide, but his fingers kept up their mechanical task of sorting the fish.

Now Antonio was standing beside Isidoro's boat. The two men were speaking so softly that Benedetto couldn't hear. Then Antonio nodded and moved down the beach toward Benedetto.

"I'm Fra Antonio," he said with a smile and a slight bow toward Benedetto.

Benedetto didn't know what to do with his hands. They seemed unable to leave the fish.

"I know, Padre. I've heard you speak."

"Then you know how proud you should be of your occupation. Jesus chose men who fished to tell the world about Him. He made one of them the head of the Church."

Benedetto blushed.

"What's your name?"

"Benedetto."

Antonio smiled. "'Blessed' is the meaning of Benedetto. A good name for you, too. God has blessed you with a sturdy back and a good wife and family. Soon to be increased."

Benedetto grinned. "How did you know?"

Antonio laughed gently. "My eyes work as well as yours, Benedetto. I saw you and your wife standing in church on Sunday. In so small a crowd, how could I miss you?"

"This is a poor town for preaching," Benedetto said bitterly. "They are all Cathars here." He glanced sidelong at Giuseppe and Rodrigo. "The true faith is almost gone."

Antonio shrugged. "Gone? You know, Benedetto, a fish symbolizes faith."

Benedetto squinted in confusion. "Faith?"

"Faith. Like a fish that is born, nourished, and lives in the deep waters of the sea, faith cannot be seen with the human eye. Like a fish, faith in God is born in the dark recesses of one's heart. It is sanctified by the invisible grace of the Holy Spirit by the waters of Baptism. Have you been baptized, Benedetto?"

"Sì, Padre," Benedetto said with pride.

"Buono. Then you have faith. But you must allow the invisible help of Divine Providence to nourish that faith lest it grow weak. For true faith, like a fish pounded by the sea's waves, is not destroyed by life's adversities. Ask God for this faith. Say, 'Give me the grace to live and die in the faith of the holy apostles and of your holy Church.'"

Benedetto pursed his lips. Did Padre Antonio know that he'd been questioning his faith? "There are many in this town who don't care about the holy Church. Their reasons are sometimes convincing."

Antonio looked toward Isidoro. "I know."

"They're hopeless, Padre."

"Hopeless? So it is as hopeless for the Cathars to return to true faith as it is for these fish before you to return to the sea?"

"The Cathars are snared," Benedetto shrugged, "just like these fish."

Antonio reached down at Benedetto's feet and picked up a squirming fish. "May I have this one?"

"Of course."

The priest held the fish firmly, walked down to the waves, and waded into the river. Benedetto saw the water creeping up along his robe to his waist. Then he dropped his hands into the water and, when he lifted them up again, the fish was gone.

"Swim, fish!" Antonio called out. "Swim to the sea, your source and sustainer of life!" Then he turned back toward the shore and his voice swept over Benedetto like a breaker on the beach. "We're all snared. But God gives up on no human being. Christ can set you free to seek the Source and Sustainer of your life. But first you must know that you are caught and helpless. Then you must trust the nail-pierced hands of the One Who can release you. In the world, all freedom is slavery. With God, all slavery is freedom. Do you wish to be snared by the world? Or do you wish to be free in Christ?" Benedetto had a sense that the priest's ringing voice wasn't meant for his ears alone. "Today I'll be preaching here at the hour of Sext. Will you come?"

Benedetto would be here at Sext, mending his nets and rubbing down his boat. So would the other men. Antonio would have a captive audience.

At Sext, the sun was high overhead, but the wind blowing off the water moderated the heat of its rays. Benedetto was scraping the hull of his boat. He had sold his fish. He had visited Gionata, who assured him that today she would not give birth. He had told her about Padre Antonio coming to the beach to speak. Gionata had wanted to come, too. Benedetto scanned the small crowd that was gathering along the shore. Men. Women. Children of the town. He knew most of them. A smattering of people, about equally divided between followers of the Roman Church and Cathars.

"Papà!"

Benedetto broke into a grin as two pudgy arms twisted about his neck from behind. He stood up and swung around in a circle with four-year-old Alfredo clinging to him for dear life. Two more tiny arms grabbed his left leg. Benedetto swooped up Attilio and swung him into the air. Benedetto plopped Attilio into his boat and then peeled Alfredo from his neck and placed him beside his brother.

He looked down the beach. Gionata was trudging toward him, a basket weighing on her arm. Benedetto knew what it held. Bread and cheese, dried fish and wine. They wouldn't be hungry while Padre Antonio spoke. And soon he arrived, climbing onto a rock that jutted above the beach not far from Benedetto's boat. Like the shells that dotted the coast, a small crowd spread out along the shore.

"'Your children around your table, like new olive plants.'" Padre Antonio's voice resonated like a trumpet. He repeated the text, which he said was from the Psalms. Then he proceeded to explain it. Time passed. Benedetto and his family ate their lunch. The priest kept preaching. The crowd, including the Cathars, remained attentive. Benedetto began knotting a net while Alfredo and Attilio clambered into Gionata's lap and fell asleep.

"We can speak of three different kinds of tables," Antonio called out, his voice resounding easily above the slapping of the waves. "Each of the three tables offers its own proper nourishment. The first table is that of doctrine, of the teachings of the Church that Christ founded upon Himself. The second table is that of penance, the payment back to God for our wrongdoing against Him and against one another. The third table is that of the Eucharist, where the faithful partake of the Body of our Lord and Christ at Mass."

Benedetto became aware of a murmur, a rustling, a shuffling. The shifting sound of people ill at ease. He looked up from his nets. Isidoro's slow easing to a standing position in the hull of his boat caught Benedetto's eye.

"The first table is that of doctrine," Antonio continued. "'You have prepared a table for Me, against those who afflict Me,' the Psalmist said in Psalm 22. This refers to Christ. Those who afflict Christ are heretics who choose what they will believe of the teachings of the Church. They are much like pampered children who choose their sweets from the plate held before them. God wishes us to have all good, not only part. Christ is truth and truth does not change; truth does not divide."

From behind Benedetto, Giuseppe rasped, "Hey, Rodrigo, we've heard enough, eh? This work can wait until tomorrow. Let's go home and have a nap."

Twin dull thuds of feet hitting sand told Benedetto that the men were leaving. The two companions were part of a momentum that was slithering through the crowd. Certainly the focus on doctrine, Eucharist, and penance, all three of which the Cathars denied, was causing the breakup. Benedetto saw the people begin to move apart as bread slowly drifts into crumbs when thrown into water. Isidoro himself seemed transfixed between Antonio's stare and Benedetto's, as if he wanted to hurry off yet wished to stay.

"So I've said things you don't wish to hear," Antonio's voice rang out above the dispersing crowd. The brother lifted his eyes heavenward and paused for the briefest moment. Then he leaped off the rock and strode toward the river.

"Listen to the word of the Lord, you fish of the river and the sea," he called out, facing the waves, "since the unfaithful heretics chose to regard it with contempt."

Benedetto stared at the priest. The sun and the disappointment at how his words were received must have made him feverish.

"My brother fish!" he called to the sea, "you are bound to give great thanks to your Creator, according to your capabilities, since He has given you a noble element in which you live according to what suits your nature—namely, the sweet," Antonio stretched his arms toward the sea, "and salty waters. There you can find many places in which to shelter, in order to avoid the discomfort of stormy waters. He has given you an element that is transparent and clear, many ways that you can follow while swimming, and also abundant food."

The friar was attacking the very foundation of Catharist belief. He was saying that the good God, the only God, and not Satan, had created the physical world. This world embraced the sea and the fish in it; God's Holy Spirit resided in these lowly creatures of flesh.

Suddenly, Benedetto heard a surging that he recognized. His gaze flew automatically beyond the friar to the river. There a swarm of fish surfaced, their shiny heads emerging, their mouths open as if to feed. Up and down the river, as far as he could see, fish were surfacing. The smaller fish were closer to the shore and bigger, brawnier fish farther out in deeper water. They were all the way out to the mouth of the Marecchia where it merged with the Adriatic.

"In the beginning of the world, you were blessed by God and were given the command to multiply. During the flood, you alone were preserved without harm among all the other animals that were outside the ark. You have been adorned with fins and have the strength to go wherever it pleases you."

Benedetto heard another sound, this one from the shore. Here and there among the dispersing people were excited mumblings, tugging at departing friends, pointing to the water. Some scattered folk turned on their heels and ran in the direction of Rimini.

"You received the command to preserve Jonah, the Lord's prophet, and after three days to place him back on dry ground. It was you who provided the Lord Jesus Christ with the coin in order to pay the tax, since he was poor and did not have any money. After the resurrection you provided food for the eternal King. So for all of these many graces you are bound to praise and bless the Lord, since you have received unique and good gifts among all the other animals."

Benedetto didn't know where to look. To the beach, on which the fickle crowd was beginning to surge toward the priest. To the water, which was shimmering with rows of slender fish. To Isidoro, who had turned in his boat and was staring at the river. Or to Antonio, whose gaze swept the gentle waves from east to west as if he were exhorting reasonable creatures to the praise of God.

"Blessed be the eternal God, to Whom the fish in the waters render more honor than heretics, and to Whose words the irrational creatures give heed more than men who are unfaithful."

Then Antonio turned ever so slowly back toward the gaping crowd. From the direction of Rimini, people came running.

"Even the beasts of the earth recognize the table of the Lord's doctrine. They believe Christ's teachings in their entirety, for they recognize the holiness of the One Who created them and Who taught us. But only those made in God's image have been invited to God's second and third tables, those of penance and the Eucharist. For beasts, unable to sin, have no need of repentance. And beasts, unable to be saved, have no need of the Bread of Life."

Suddenly, Benedetto felt his boat shift. His worried glance caught Gionata. Her falling to her knees had caused the craft's drift. Beside her, Alfredo and Attilio stared over the water. The dancing ribbon of fish was so close to shore, dangerously close, where gulls could have easily snatched them.

The gulls. Where were the gulls? With so many fish this close to the surface, the white predators should have been swooping into the river in massive winged clouds, their raucous shrieks knifing the air. Where were the gulls?

"'The rest of your table shall be full of rich food,' God says in the Book of Job. The rich food of God's forgiveness comes when we cry out our sins to our Father and beg His mercy. And who among us has not sinned? Have we sinned with money, with lust, with pride, with possessions? Have we neglected our Father or our families? Have we turned from Christ, true God and true Man, to follow the heresies of mere men? Have we, like Pharisees, thought ourselves better than the rest of humanity? No sin can come into God's presence. 'All have sinned and fallen short of the glory of God.' Oh, what rich food we consume when we admit our sins and beg God's mercy. Then God feeds us with the grace of forgiveness until our souls are full."

As Antonio continued to speak, people here and there began to kneel. Benedetto sank into the sand, his head in his hands. How quick he had been to see the sins of others while remaining blind to the darkness of pride and a judgmental spirit in his own soul! Didn't Catharist doctrines tantalize him? Yet Antonio had shown that God was in control on this very beach in the fish He had created. If fish knew and bowed to the Lord, why not Benedetto?

"We receive God's forgiveness. Then we are worthy to receive in abundance at the table of the Eucharist where 'you cannot be partakers of the table of the Lord and of the table of devils.' For God and demons are enemies and those who do not serve the One surely serve the other. At which table do you wish to be seated? The food served at the first table, the table of doctrine, is the word of life. The feast at the second table of penance is the food of groanings and tears. The meal at the third is the Body and Blood of Christ. Must you choose your table? No! God calls you to all three."

Benedetto stayed on his knees, his soul weeping softly as Antonio continued to speak. He dared not look up at the holy priest, for he felt that, if he did, the whole town would see the tears glistening on his cheeks.

"So come like children 'around the table,' seeing all that God has to offer, taking all that God wishes to give you. Come. Believe firmly. Approach reverently. Admit the unworthiness of such great grace given to you. Eat of the tables of God with humility. Oh, Christ, may we nourish ourselves at Your threefold table so joyfully, humbly, and trustingly that we may merit to be nourished at Your eternal table in heaven. Amen."

As Antonio's words faded, soft sounds of sobbing people and splashing fish mingled.

"My good people and my dear fish, thank you for listening with your hearts. Now return to your homes in peace."

The waters surged and gurgled. By the time Benedetto wiped his eyes and could see through their glaze, the river surface was covered with rapidly widening eddies where thousands of fish had dipped below the waves.

On the beach, another surge rippled through the crowd. Open weeping. Scattered cries of "God have mercy." Benedetto could no longer see Antonio, so dense was the crowd thronging him.

Benedetto turned to Gionata, who, still kneeling, was staring at the mob. "Gionata," he choked, "I must go to confession. Today."

Gionata nodded. "I, too, Benedetto."

They waited. As the sun was dipping behind Rimini, they finally reached Padre Antonio and confessed to him beside the Marecchia River. They would have had longer to wait, but Isidoro, who was in front of them, saw that Alfredo and Attilio were getting drowsy. He gave Benedetto and Gionata his place in line.

NOTES

Benedetto, his family, his fishing companions, and Dom Alonzo are fictitious characters based on personalities of the time.

The doctrines of the Cathars as discussed are accurate. The perfecti, who had completed the consolamentum, were called the "Good Men" who preached in northern Italy and France. Believers who had not taken this sacrament fell into two categories. Some lived chaste lives. Others planned to sin until they neared death, when they hoped to receive the consolamentum and be purged of their sins. The Cathar influence spread because their holy Good Men were living in stark contrast to some clergy in the Roman Church.

Catholics and heretics existed side by side in most of the areas in which Antonio preached. He was commissioned to preach not only to enliven the faith of Catholics but also to refute and convert heretics.

Rimini is one of the principal towns of the Romagna, to which Antonio had been sent (*Assidua* 12–13, Rig 12, Ben 4, 2LJS 4). Most historians claim that the miracle in this chapter happened at Rimini, although one (Rig 13) favors Padua.

Antonio's words are from: "God's Love for His Children," in the magazine *Messenger of Saint Anthony* (comparing a fish to faith); FA:ED III 33, 510–21, 632–36,

24Gen Section 1 pp.164–65 (his sermon to the fish and the crowd's reaction); SK 32–36 (sermon that caused the crowd to disperse; however, no record exists of the sermon that he preached that caused this dispersal).

The Scripture is from Psalm 128:3 (then numbered as Psalm 127: "Your children around your table . . ."), Psalm 23:5 (then numbered as Psalm 22: "You have prepared a table . . ."), Job 36:16 ("The rest of your table . . ."), Romans 3:23 ("All have sinned . . ."), and 1 Corinthians 10:21 ("You cannot be partakers . . .").

8

Bononillo

Saddle Shop, Rimini, Italy (Holy Week 1222)

Bononillo's bulbous nose loved the smell of leather. In his saddle shop, he was stooped over a saddle, tacking the softest leather to the bows. Even to his weathered hands, which had worked on saddles all his life, properly tanned leather still felt softer than the skin of an infant. Bononillo liked to work with materials that he could see and touch. Wood that he could carve. Leather that he could coax into shape. And sometimes, for a duke or a lord, rich paints that he could delicately dab onto the pommel and cantle and create a work of beauty.

A shadow fell across the saddle and Bononillo looked up. Antonio stood in the doorway.

"Ah, my friend, what a beautiful job you do during this holiest of weeks," Antonio said. "God has given you an eye and a hand to do this work well."

Bononillo's sharp black eyes looked up at the priest. "My hands are as strong—even stronger—than they were when I was hardly a man and opened this shop."

"Then I bet you thought you were in your prime. You thought you knew all there was to know about making saddles. And about life in general as well."

"How did you know that?"

"Because all youth are the same."

Bononillo nodded his nearly bald head. "You're young yourself. When you get old like me, you'll realize how little you know now."

"True. There's always so much more to know about God. This is a very great week to learn."

Bononillo pressed into the leather with his cloth, rubbing briskly. He had picked up the young priest's second hint about Holy Week. "You're hoping that I will confess this week and go to Eucharist on Easter, aren't you?"

"Is that such a bad hope?"

"I can't remember the last time I've been to confession and Eucharist."

"It isn't yet the hour of Terce. I have all day to listen."

Bononillo lifted the saddle to the morning sun. The buffed leather shone in the rays. "It's not sin that keeps me from confession, Padre. You know that it's the Eucharist. We've had this conversation several times since you came to Rimini. Your arguments are no more convincing than those of Dom Alonzo where the Eucharist is concerned. Dom Alonzo is a lax priest. Why would the holy Christ agree to rest in Dom Alonzo's hands, even in the form of bread and wine?"

Antonio groaned. "Dom Alonzo holds the office of priest. He has been ordained to consecrate bread and wine into the Body and Blood of Christ. His sins do not affect this function."

Bononillo shuffled through a pile of fresh rags that lay in a tub at his feet. "God allows scandal if He permits men like Dom Alonzo to consecrate His Body and then distribute it to others."

"May I come in?"

Bononillo shrugged.

Antonio sat on a wooden stool beside the saddler. "That ring on your finger, Bononillo. It's made of gold, isn't it?"

"Are you hoping I will donate it to the Church?"

Antonio burst out laughing. "If you want to, Bononillo. I'll sell it and give the money to the poor. But no, I wasn't thinking of that. I was thinking of a story in the Passion of Saint Sebastian. The story tells of a king who had a gold ring adorned with a precious stone, much like yours, which he liked very much. One day the precious ring fell into a sewer. The king was heartbroken. What would you do if you were the king, Bononillo?"

Bononillo was buffing the saddle. "Get someone to get it out."

"And suppose no one would."

Bononillo rubbed the pommel. "I'm not stupid, Padre. I'd go in myself and get it."

"And so the king did in this story. You will notice, Bononillo, that the sewer didn't deter the king from seeking the ring. Why not?"

"Because the ring was valuable."

"Correct. And if your ring fell into just such a sewer, wouldn't you retrieve it? Wouldn't you wash it clean and treasure it?"

Bononillo turned the saddle over and gave the underside a hearty buff. "I told you, I'm not stupid."

"So you aren't, Bononillo. The ring is of the same value and luster whether or not it lies in refuse or encircles your finger, correct? In the same way, the office of a priest doesn't change even if the priest is defiled by sin. It's a permanent office, just as gold is a permanent metal. Defilement changes neither gold nor the priestly ability to consecrate the Eucharist."

Bononillo turned the saddle upright again. "Are you defending Dom Alonzo's lifestyle?"

Antonio rose so abruptly that the stool toppled. The friar stood it in place as he spoke. "You've heard me speak, Bononillo. You've heard me say more than once that those who abuse the inheritance of Christ by their immoral lives shall be cut off from the kingdom of God. They are like idols in the Church, fit only for hell. I don't defend immoral clergy. I defend the Eucharist."

Bononillo angrily threw the rag into the dust. "The Eucharist. The Eucharist. Suppose you are right about Dom Alonzo and his priestly office. But the Eucharist?" Bononillo thrust the saddle toward the priest. "You can see this. Feel it. Smell it. It's leather. You claim that the Eucharist is the Body and Blood of Christ. Yet I can see it, feel it, smell it. It's bread. Wine. I had eaten it myself for years before I realized what foolishness it is to believe. Then I could receive the Eucharist no longer or I would be pretending to believe what's so obviously false."

Antonio took a deep breath. "Bononillo, I've told you before. Christ said, 'Take, eat; this is my body,' and 'this is my blood.' Don't you believe your Lord?"

Bononillo groaned. He picked up the rag and shook out the dust. "I want to believe, Padre, but I can't. I've spoken to my sons about this and to my grandsons who are now having sons. None of them can explain it to me. Dom Alonzo can't explain it. The Cathars say there is no sacrament. I don't believe much of what else they say, but they are right about the Eucharist. I know you're a holy man, but you're mistaken. I see bread. I see wine. I eat bread. I drink wine. I know what flesh is, Padre. The Eucharist isn't flesh."

Antonio clasped his hands behind his back and slowly paced the short length of Bononillo's shop. Bononillo went back to polishing his saddle.

"Even the beasts recognize the Creator."

"I know. I heard you speak at the river. I saw the fish. I believe in God. I believe everything you say. But the Eucharist? It's unbelievable."

"The form of the bread, of the wine, remains the same. The substance changes. The substance is Christ."

"God asks us to believe that? That's absurd."

"You're as thick-headed as a horse, Bononillo."

"A horse is smarter than you, Padre. A horse knows bread from flesh."

Antonio stopped pacing. He stood facing the doorway, his back to Bononillo, his head bowed, his hands clasped behind his back. Bononillo watched him curiously. Abruptly, Antonio raised his head and tilted it backward as if he were gazing transfixed at something in the sky. He maintained this posture for so long that Bononillo stopped watching him and returned to buffing the saddle.

Suddenly Antonio called out, "If your horse recognized Christ in the Eucharist, then would you believe?"

Bononillo snickered. "My horse?"

"Would you believe?"

"Sì! I would rejoin the Church and take my entire family with me."

Antonio turned toward Bononillo. "Starve your horse for three days. Then, on Holy Thursday, after Mass at Prime, bring her to the village square along with some oats and hay. I'll bring the Eucharist. We'll see what the horse will do."

Bononillo shrugged. "She'll eat the hay and oats."

"If she does, then the fault is mine, not God's. Just remember that. My sin, not God's lack of presence in the Sacrament."

"You really do believe, don't you?" Bononillo felt a tinge of pity for the young, idealistic fool. "All Rimini will be there to watch. If your test doesn't work, you'll lose the town. The church will be empty for your Easter sermon."

The priest smiled thinly. "If the test does work, God shall resurrect your soul and perhaps a household of souls. I'll let God take charge of the outcome."

Bononillo nodded. "To God, then."

Bononillo spent the next three days feeling sorry for poor Enrica, who had no way of knowing why her food supply, including even the straw on which she bedded, had disappeared. He spent extra time grooming her while pushing her away from trying to nibble his tunic or cap. By the third day, the horse was shaky. Nevertheless, her big watery eyes looked trustingly at the master who had always cared so lovingly for her. She shuddered a bit as Bononillo flung two packs, one of oats, the other of hay, across her back. He had chosen his best saddlebags to display to the crowd.

"Soon you will eat, my good worker." He patted Enrica and led her out into the street, which was flooded with light from the rising sun.

"Here comes Bononillo!" shouted a child to some playmates. "Come on!"

Bononillo felt as if he were leading a parade. All of Rimini had heard about the challenge. Neighbors drifted out of their homes and shops and clustered about him as he made his way to the village square. Everyone liked a good prank and this was one the visiting priest was about to play on himself.

Besides, this was Holy Thursday, the day on which Christ first changed bread and wine into His Body and Blood. If the first miracle were true, perhaps the people would see a second such occurrence today. The potential of such an occurrence seemed slim, yet what if it did happen? Who would want to miss seeing it? Bononillo felt the tiniest thrill of fright shiver along his body. What if he was about to witness a miracle?

The square was crowded with people when Bononillo arrived. He and Enrica stood awkwardly among the city folk who made a tiny circle of space around them both. How wise he had been to choose his best saddlebags!

The restless crowd began to murmur. "Where's the priest?"

"I saw him in church."

"He's been in church the past three days, praying."

"Oh, that's why we haven't heard him preach."

"Where is he now?"

"Someone, run to the church and tell him that Bononillo is here and his horse is hungry."

A young boy sprinted away from the crowd in the direction of the town chapel. Twenty minutes later, he bounded back to the crowd. "He was saying Mass. But look, he's coming." The boy pointed down the street from which he had just run.

Sure enough, coming around the corner were Dom Alonzo and one of his young assistants, bearing candles, and a third man, swinging a censer. Behind them walked Antonio, a small, cross-topped silver tower held high above his head. Bononillo had not seen one of those since he had left the Church, but he remembered what they held. The Eucharist. Following the procession were people, mostly women, who probably had been at Mass. The procession walked silently and slowly. As the tower approached, many in the crowd fell to their knees and made the sign of the cross. As Antonio moved into the cluster of people, he nodded to Bononillo.

"Put down the hay and oats."

Bononillo pulled the bags off Enrica's back and tore them open. He tumbled the hay before the mare and then spilled the grain on top of the pile. As he did so, Antonio walked next to the pile of food. His gaze was fixed on the little tower held high over his head.

Enrica turned toward the priest. First one knee and then the other buckled under the horse until the beast was kneeling before the Eucharist. The animal's head bowed.

Bononillo felt as if he were no longer in his body. He seemed to be watching a drama or a dream. A massive feeling of relief swept his soul. The Eucharist was true. How it was true, Bononillo didn't know. Antonio's words about substance and form still made no sense. But he could see Enrica. Enrica recognized Christ. Bononillo crumpled to his knees, his arm around Enrica's neck, his eyes looking at the elevated tower, his soul seeing Jesus. He was again free to believe.

"Come," said Antonio, "it is time for the hungry to be fed. Enrica, you may rise now and eat."

The horse sprang to her feet, shaking off Bononillo as she did so. Her mouth dipped into the hay and oats and a loud *crunch* broke the quiet. Spontaneous laughter rang through the crowd.

Antonio was grinning. "For hungry beasts, oats and hay. For believers in Christ, the Bread of Life. Enrica has been without food for three days and see how famished she is. Bononillo, you have been without the Food of Life for years. Are you famished, too?"

Bononillo's voice was too thick to answer. He merely nodded.

Antonio held the Eucharistic tower toward the crowd and moved it in an arc around them. Many of those still standing fell to their knees and hurriedly crossed themselves. "And you, how hungry are you?" he addressed the people. "How long has it been since you have feasted on the Body and Blood of Christ? 'Unless you eat the flesh of the Son of man and drink his blood, you have no life in you.' 'For my flesh is food indeed, and my blood is drink indeed.' Come and confess your sins. Then your souls will be pure to receive the risen Christ on Easter."

That morning, Bononillo and a long line of other penitents went to confession. On Easter, they received the Eucharist from Antonio's hand.

NOTES

The miracle of Bononillo's beast of burden and his subsequent conversion are related in the historical record (*Assidua* 13, 2LJS 4, *Dialogus* 2, Ben 4–5, Rig 13). No mention of his occupation exists.

Depending on the account, the animal is called a mule, horse, or mare. Bononillo's name is spelled Bonvillo, Bonillus, and Bonello. Various locations are given, among them Toulouse, Bourges, and Rimini. One historian says it was repeated three times, once at each location.

At this period of history, the Eucharist was kept in a small gold or silver dove or tower which could be removed from the church.

Antonio's words to Bononillo regarding the ring in the sewer are from his sermon "Washing the Feet," in *Messenger of Saint Anthony*. The Scripture referenced is from Matthew 26:26, 28 ("Take, eat . . .") and John 6:53 ("Unless you eat the flesh . . .").

9

Dom Vito

Rectory, Bologna, Italy (Early 1224)

As he approached the hearth in the poorly built hovel that served as his rectory, elderly, stooped Dom Vito stepped over Cidro, the skinniest beggar in Bologna. Cidro lay on the floor, snoring and curled up before the dying embers. His big, sooty feet were so close to the fireplace that if there had been any flames, his heels would have been singed.

With his bony fingers, Vito drew the huge black kettle toward himself. Stepping over Cidro again, he carried the kettle outdoors to the well.

Through the thin rags that wrapped his feet, old Vito's toes curled at the cold of a delicate, fresh layer of snow. With hands already tingling from the dawn's chill, Vito let down the water bucket. He heard a feeble crackling as the wood smashed through the fragile ice that had formed on the water overnight. Then he drew up the water, poured it into the kettle, and lugged the kettle indoors.

On the small, rickety table on which he ate, he found the wrinkled carrots, sprouting onions, and softening garlic that he'd brought up late last night from the root cellar. Yesterday a matron had brought him a gigantic cheese. He had shared it with the six men and women who were sleeping in his room just now and then saved some for today in the little larder near his bed. When Vito took out the cheese, he noticed that it was smaller than when he had put it in.

The gray-haired priest glanced around the room at the rag-covered bodies on the floor and at the curled-up form on his bed, that of crippled Maria with her infant asleep in her arms. Who had sneaked a night nibble? Crooked-nosed Donte, the leper? The big-eyed orphan girl, Tazia? Or old Cidro? No matter. Vito crumbled the remaining cheese into the kettle, then sliced the vegetables and added them as well. He brought the kettle to the hearth and added wood to the embers. As a tiny flame leaped up, Vito tugged at Cidro's feet, dragging them out of danger.

From the mantle above the hearth, Vito took a thick, well-worn book, its pages neatly penned in small script. Kneeling next to Cidro, he opened the breviary and began to silently recite his morning prayers. By the time he finished them, the beggars were awake. They walked with him to the little church where he would prepare to offer Sunday Mass and they would take their familiar spots around the steps to beg alms. Once Mass began, they would creep in to huddle at the rear of the church. After Mass, they would scurry outdoors again to beg of the worshipers as they left. After begging, they would slip into the streets of Bologna and, if the night was warm, sleep there. But if it was cold, as it had been last night, they would be back at Vito's door. He would give them soup to eat and a place to sleep, for in them he saw Christ.

Vito had been in the church but a moment when the visiting friar arrived. Fra Antonio taught theology to the Lesser Brothers at their little convent in the city. He was, Vito had heard, a mighty preacher. He and Antonio would celebrate Mass together, with Antonio preaching the sermon.

Soon, after greeting and vesting, after processions and incense, after prayers and readings, Antonio stood in the pulpit while Vito sat to the side of the altar and gazed at his motley congregation. On the floor in the back of the church, the beggars clustered. In front of them on wooden benches perched the well-dressed lords and ladies of Bologna. Some of the wealthy listeners were responsible in part for the wretched plight of those who huddled behind them. Every Sunday, Vito looked down at this congregation while his soul seethed. How could the usurers sit there in comfort while the poor whom they swindled stared at their backs?

Each week, it seemed, Vito spoke out against the crimes of the rich and the plight of the poor. Today Antonio was speaking of it himself.

"The Psalmist says, 'This vast ocean,' which is the world, 'stretches its arms wide. In it, innumerable reptiles swarm. Here live creatures small and great, swimming in the waters as ships sail by.'" Antonio paused to sweep the church with his gaze. "The sea is the world, full of bitterness, yet vast in riches, wide and teeming with delights. Its arms are open wide to gather in the greedy." Antonio threw open his arms to their fullest breadth.

"Saint Matthew says it well. 'Wide is the way leading to destruction.' Who goes this way? Certainly not Christ's poor who enter by the narrow gate. The way to destruction is a wide sea through which the usurers swim on their way to hell. These greedy people swarm throughout the entire sea, having the whole world in their grasp."

How could those most insidiously guilty listen with ears of stone? Vito wondered. How could they listen week after week and not be moved? The poor of Bologna were in misery because of usury. Swindlers loaned the needy money at thirty, fifty, even eighty percent interest. How could the poverty-stricken, wasting away in wretchedness, possibly pay it back? Sometimes, in desperation, the borrowers hired assassins to slay the men to whom they were financially bound. Meanwhile, the usurers grew fat and drunk on choice wines that might as well have been distilled from the sweat and blood of the destitute.

"Look at the usurers. Look at the hands that dare to come to church and offer alms. Such hands are dripping with the blood of the poor. Oh, there are innumerable reptiles in the great sea of this earth. One kind, most plentiful," Antonio said, lowering his voice to a hissing sort of whisper, "hide themselves from sight as best they can, crawling and groveling in the shadows. These furtive yet loathsome creatures are those who practice usury in secret. This very day, they sit among us with their ill-gotten coins lining their pockets. Then there are those more visible small creatures of the ocean. These are the swindlers who practice usury openly," Antonio's voice rose, "but who charge moderate rates of interest. How generous they seem, how merciful! Let your mercy be that of Christ, Who gave to all freely, expecting nothing in return!"

He paused and then his voice trumpeted through the church. "Finally there are those powerful and vicious animals of the ocean from whom all other life flees in terror. These usurers are evil, lost, professional souls who ply their trade unashamedly in the full light of day."

Ah, there in the congregation sat confident Messer Zaccaria and his youthful-looking wife, Madonna Odilia. Comfortably warm in his gray fox cape, raven-haired Zaccaria was one of those powerful and vicious animals of the sea about which Antonio preached. Vito had many times spoken to him about the evil in his life. His words had left as much an impression on Zaccaria as an inchworm leaves on the bark of an oak.

"These miserable persons care nothing for the realities of life. They never think of how they entered this world in utter nakedness, nor do they think that they will leave it wrapped in a few rags. How have they come to possess so many things?" Antonio paused. "Through theft and cheating."

Antonio held his left palm toward the congregation. "Can you see what I hold here? Probably not, for it is so small that, to you, it appears to be only an insignificant husk. And so it actually is the husk of a dung beetle." Antonio plucked a tiny black knob from his palm and held it between two fingers so all could see.

"Who has not seen a dung beetle? This creature, when alive, is cloaked in an iridescent shell. What finery of black, purple, blue, green, bronze, or gold he wears! Why, he gleams in the sun like a precious metal. How beautiful and impressive he seems! And what does this vivid creature do? He gathers much dung and with great labor makes a round ball; but in the end a passing ass steps on both beetle and ball," Antonio brought his fist down upon the dried-up beetle, "and in a moment destroys it and all it labored so long over."

He's as superb as they say, Vito thought. *I'm glad I invited him to preach.*

"In the same way, the miser or usurer gathers long the dung of money, and labors long; but when he least expects it, the devil chokes him. And so he gives his soul to the demons, his flesh to worms, and his money to his family."

Antonio curled his fingers around the dead beetle and dropped it on the pulpit. He looked from one face to the next of his listeners. "Alas! It is not enough for the wretches to extinguish or drive out the inspiration of divine grace in themselves; but they must also persecute and expel it from those about them—children, wives, and so on!" He paused, then spoke again, forcefully. "For instance: Suppose the son of a usurer is struck with fear of the judgment, or of the pains of hell, and resolves to live an honest life and bewail the misery of this life. If his father gets to hear of it, he persecutes this grace in him with all his power, and so for his daughter, his wife, his whole family."

Vito scanned his congregation. Here and there he saw faces averted from the preacher and foreheads blushing. Antonio's words were hitting home.

"See what evil deeds these murderers perform! They kill in themselves and in their families the strife of penance and the remembrance of the Lord's Passion, which was given as a blessing by God the Father to the whole world."

Antonio turned away from the people as if to walk from the pulpit. Then abruptly he turned back. "But does God abandon those who gather the dung of riches or who swim about the vast sea of the world in so much foolish confidence and unconcern? Not at all. So that they might do penance, the ships, that is, the preachers of the Church, pass by." Antonio turned and nodded at Vito, who amiably nodded back. "They need only approach the ships to be lifted out of the water of temporal greed and into God's kingdom."

Antonio raised his arms and face upward. "'Lift up your eyes on high,' says the prophet Jeremiah." He lowered his arms and his gaze. "Sea creatures do not lift their eyes on high. Their eyes are so placed that they must look to the side or below. But Jeremiah says, 'Lift your eyes on high.' Who looks on high? The person who acknowledges the malice of his deeds and confesses them openly, sincerely and without reservation."

Vito could see Antonio peering into the congregation, catching first one face and then another in his gaze. "Therefore, lift your eyes on high. Do not cast them down or sideways. Do not be ashamed. Do not fear. If you lift your eyes on high and acknowledge your sins, you will 'surely live and not die.' Abandon yourself completely to the judgment of the priest. Make your words those of Saul, who became the Apostle Paul: 'Lord, what will you have me do?'"

Vito sighed. If only the priest's words could penetrate the oaken hearts that listened! If only tears of repentance would flow! As Antonio continued to exhort his listeners to repentance and confession, Vito lifted his heart in prayer. *Lord, let Fra Antonio's words penetrate the heart of this congregation. Let them have an effect, Lord, so that the dignity of the poor may be restored.*

"Let us give thanks, then, to Jesus Christ, the Son of God, Who cast out the devil and Who can save us from the deep and carnal waters of this earthly life. Let us devoutly and humbly beg Him to give His grace to each of us, to enable us to acknowledge our sins, to confess them, and to faithfully obey the counsel of our confessor. May the Lord Jesus Christ, to Whom be honor, majesty, power,

praise, and glory throughout all ages, grant this to all of us. And let every creature who swims in the sea of this world answer, 'Amen!'"

As Antonio descended from the pulpit, Vito pleaded, *Lord, let his words
bring fruit.* That was his offering for the remainder of the Mass and for the time
afterward when he and Antonio took their seats on stools in the rear of the
church to hear the confessions of those waiting in line. In Antonio's line, Vito
noticed, stood Messer Zaccaria and Madonna Odilia.

As Vito listened to the sins of skinny Cidro, a great bubble of envy swelled
inside the old priest's soul. For years he had urged Zaccaria to confession. For
years he had preached the very message that Antonio had preached today.
Zaccaria had never once confessed. Today he was.

Vito had prayed for this moment. Prayed fervently. Had even prayed today.
He had thought Zaccaria would come to him to confess. Instead, he had gone to
Antonio.

Antonio was young, good-looking, straight and noble in carriage, with eyes
so large and deep-set that they seemed to probe a person's soul. He was articu-
late and intelligent, his voice strong with youth and conviction. In contrast,
stoop-shouldered Vito was nearing the end of his long life, his face dotted with
warts and brown age spots. Vito's voice was high and shrill and his small eyes
red-rimmed and watery. He often fumbled for words, for his education had
been minimal.

Antonio and Vito had preached the same message, but the preacher and the
delivery were different. Today Zaccaria was confessing to the young, vibrant
priest. And Vito knew beyond a doubt that what he had suspected for several
months was true. He had grown too old to be effective.

Vito absolved Cidro, who had confessed to stealing the cheese. Then Vito
listened to Maria's sins. All his beggars, he noticed, were in his line. Precious
people. They trusted him. Antonio's line was a colorful thread of fur capes,
jaunty caps, and high boots. Why was Vito even the pastor of this church if only
the poor came to him? A younger priest should take over. A younger priest
could get the response that this young priest got today. Vito knew God and
loved Him, but he was too old to influence the young. Vito could exhort. But a
young priest, full of the fire of faith, could convert.

Confessions continued until the final beggar was absolved. Antonio still had two more richly dressed penitents. Vito would wait. He wanted to thank Antonio for preaching today. He wanted to congratulate him on his success with Zaccaria.

Vito closed his eyes briefly and leaned back into the corner of the wall. He had slept on the floor last night beside Donte, having given his bed to Maria and the baby who had fussed with fever throughout the night. The fussing had disturbed Vito's sleep.

Now Vito dozed. As he napped, he saw Antonio approach him. "Why are you jealous of me? There's no need," the young brother said. "Come and speak to me."

Vito woke with a start. Antonio was nowhere near him. He was in the far corner of the church, dismissing his final penitent. As the plump matron started toward the door, Vito knew what he must do. He had long ago learned to distinguish a mere dream from a God-given vision. This was a vision. God wanted him to speak to Antonio. He wouldn't protest to God. Pushing erect, he approached Antonio, his arm outstretched in friendship.

"Fra Antonio, your words are powerful," Vito said. He grasped Antonio's forearm and embraced him. "My church is poor. Yet you came to speak in it. Grazie. You have converted people I couldn't reach."

Antonio shook his head. "Dom, I speak words. The Lord grants conversion."

"Your words brought it about. I'm envious."

"I've observed you with your poor. I, too, am envious."

"No, brother. I really am envious. I've tried to reach Messer Zaccaria for years, to no avail. Today, for the first time, he confessed to you."

"Messer Zaccaria? The usurer in the fox cape?"

Vito nodded.

"He told me that many times you had spoken to him about his crimes." Antonio glanced toward the door of the church. "Dom Vito, come with me."

Vito followed Antonio to the door, where Antonio stepped outdoors into a lightly falling snow. As his bare feet left toe tracks in the whiteness, Antonio stooped beside a patch of ground to the right of the church door. "On my way into church, I noticed the garlic here popping up through the snow. Did you plant it?"

Vito looked at the little green shoots pricking like tiny blades through the snow. "Sì. I always plant garlic. In the fall."

"Like all good farmers and gardeners do." Antonio stroked one of the tiny plants. "You don't expect to eat the garlic today, do you?"

"I wouldn't even be able to get them out of the frozen ground," Vito said. "And they're not grown."

Antonio looked up at Vito. "But they'll continue to grow in the early rains of spring and the late rains of summer until harvest. Sì?"

The friar stood. Vito observed the young face, the snow alighting on dark lashes and black hair. "You're a good farmer, Dom Vito. Saint James writes in his letter, 'The farmer waits for the precious fruit of the earth, being patient over it until it receives the early and late rain.' The farmer is the preacher. A preacher such as yourself sows the seeds of preaching and implants the desire for eternal life in your listeners. In the meantime, there is need for patience. Sometimes a soul is in winter, as it were, when no growth occurs and grace seems ineffective. But life in the soul is still present, just as it is present in your garlic."

Vito gazed at the tiny green shoots and nodded.

"Then comes the 'early rain,' which is premature grace through the hearing of God's message. It is premature for it comes too soon for harvest. This is the grace that your words have given Messer Zaccaria and several others who confessed today."

"But you're the one who brought about their confession."

"I was merely the 'late rain,' coming at a later time. Through my words, God's Spirit brought conversion today." Antonio reached out and laid a firm hand on Vito's shoulder.

"You'll bring late rain, too, if you're patient. When you bear your trials with patience and joy, you will receive the 'early rain' of grace yourself and you will be able to dispense it to others. You will receive the 'late rain' of glory in the future when those whom you have been tending and watering with your words convert and when you yourself enter eternal life. You have planted and watered the seed for years, Dom Vito. I have appeared only at harvest time."

Vito disagreed. "But I've been unable to harvest anything. The young merchants and usurers won't listen to me. I'm getting too old. A younger man like yourself would be much more effective."

"Youth means nothing," Antonio smiled through the drifting snow. "Faith means all. I say to you what Paul said to the Galatians, 'Let us not grow weary in well-doing, for in due season we shall reap, if we do not lose heart.' Do not lose heart, Dom Vito. You will reap."

Vito shook his head. "Brother, I want to believe you're right." Antonio, Vito saw, was growing white with snow. He glanced at Antonio's bare feet. "Would you like to come into my house? I have a fire on the hearth and soup in the kettle."

"I would like that."

Vito's house was just five steps away. The two priests shook the snow from their tunics as they entered. Vito pulled two scratched wooden bowls from a shelf and ladled the bubbling soup into each. As he and Antonio sat at the table, a knock sounded at the door.

"Come in," Vito called.

The door pushed open and snow-covered Maria crept in on her knees, her useless, twisted legs dragging behind her. The woman's whining baby, wrapped in a tattered length of wool, was clutched to her chest.

"Maria," Vito said. "I'm glad you came. Come have some soup with us."

The woman smiled, the wide spaces between her teeth showing.

"Take my chair, Madonna," Antonio said, rising. He reached out his hands toward her infant. "May I hold your sweet child?"

"He's got a fever, Padre," Maria said, handing him the baby.

"So I see," Antonio said as he pulled back the dirty blanket and stroked the infant's forehead. Antonio made the sign of the cross over the infant and then over Maria, who signed herself and then pulled herself into the chair.

As she sat, Vito placed a bowl of soup before her and noticed that her stubby, twisted feet were raw and bleeding. He fished beside the hearth for some rags and dipped one into a pail of water that he kept filled next to the hearth. Squatting beside her, Vito began to swab her bloody toes.

"Maria, where are the shoes I gave you yesterday? Madonna Serena gave me only that one pair."

Maria blushed. "Donte said the lepers hadn't any. I told him to give them mine."

Vito sighed. Beggars. Some of them were more generous than the wealthy could even imagine being.

Vito dried Maria's feet and returned to the hearth for some additional rags. As Maria lifted the bowl of soup to her lips, Vito wrapped her feet snugly in the tattered cloths.

"Maria," Antonio said, "you have given away your shoes. You are as merciful as the Virgin Mother of Christ whose name you bear." Hugging the whimpering child to his chest and rocking back and forth, Antonio smiled at the exhausted mother. "You are blessed to bear the sweetest name of any woman on earth."

Maria put her soup bowl down and grinned at the priest. When a smile flooded her dirty face and huge mouth, she looked, Vito thought, almost pretty. Antonio smiled back. "Jesus loved His mother more than all women, Maria, since He had received from her His human body. She found more grace and mercy in Christ than any other woman. Oh, what a blessed name is Maria!"

"My mother named me, Padre. After the Virgin. That was what she always told me."

"So your mother was faithful as was our Lady's mother. Do you know that your name, Maria, means 'star of the sea'?"

Maria shook her head. "I didn't know it meant anything."

Antonio spoke as he rocked, his words louder than the fussy cries of the infant. "The name is most appropriate for our Mother in heaven. Mariners watch the North Star for safe passage while sailing. It is a fixed star in the heavens and, by watching it, they are able to find their bearings in any sea. Mary is like this star. She is a star that indicates a clear path to all those tossed about on the turbulent waters of life. Mary is a name beloved by angels and feared by devils. I imagine, Maria, that you often find life difficult." Antonio was rocking the infant more slowly now. The whimpering had stopped.

"Sì, Padre. But Dom Vito helps. He's a good priest."

Antonio glanced at Vito. His eyes seemed to twinkle. "So I can see. And Dom Vito often finds life difficult, too. That I can also see."

Vito bashfully turned his eyes away from the friar's.

"I'd like to teach you both a prayer to our Lady, a prayer that will guide you through difficult times."

"I'd like that," Maria said.

Antonio held the child in his arms, pressed close to his chest. The infant was quiet, possibly asleep. Bowing his head, Antonio began to pray in a soft, gentle voice. "We pray to you, our Lady, our hope. We are tossed about by the storm of life's seas. May you, Star of the Sea, enlighten and guide us to our safe harbor. Assist us with your protective presence when we are about to depart from this life so that we may merit to leave this prison fearlessly and reach happily the kingdom of endless joy. We hope to receive these favors from Jesus Christ, Whom you bore in your blessed womb and nursed at your most holy breast. To Him be all honor and glory, forever and ever. Amen."

"Brother, would you repeat the prayer again so that we may learn it?" Vito asked.

So Antonio, gazing at the sleeping child, repeated it. At the end of the third repetition, with Maria and Vito praying the words with Antonio, the baby began to wriggle and whine, his little mouth rubbing back and forth against Antonio's tunic. Antonio laughed and held the child toward Maria. "I cannot give him what he wants now. You take him and nurse him."

Maria bubbled with joy. "If he wants to nurse, he'll get well." As she enfolded the infant in her arms, she grinned. "He's no longer hot. The fever has broken."

"Thank God!" Vito exclaimed. Then he added, "Maria, perhaps if you lie down and nurse him, he'll fall asleep." He pointed to his bed, which he always invited beggars to use when they visited. It was the only luxury Vito had, but when the needy slept at Vito's, he slept on the floor.

Clutching the baby who was rooting eagerly at her chest, Maria crawled to Vito's bed and climbed in, lying down with her face to the wall.

Antonio smiled as he sat at the table. "I envy you, Dom Vito. Your name means life, and you have given life to so many people. How many of the poor in Bologna love and need you? You not only speak to them of Christ. You show them Him in who you are. Without an exemplary life, Dom Vito, no one can assemble the people, since a preacher's words have no effect if his life is held in contempt."

"Sì, people like Maria listen," Vito said. "But those who confessed to you today do hold me in contempt, brother. They don't heed me at all. Some speak against my taking in people like Maria."

"That happens to everyone. I constantly find people who spare neither the saint nor the sinner from their detraction. These people perversely claim that good is bad and that bad is good. They call darkness light and light, darkness. They turn what is bitter to sweetness and what is sweet to bitterness."

"Some pastors in this city do that very thing." He hated to admit it, but it was true. "I see their fine churches and the alms they gather. If I spoke as they do, I wouldn't anger men like Messer Zaccaria. Then perhaps people like him would give me money to care for the people who come to me for help."

Antonio, who had been sipping the soup, lowered his bowl. "Dom Vito, Christ says, 'I am the Truth.' Whoever preaches the truth preaches Christ. Whoever conceals it in his preaching denies Christ. Truth leads to hatred, and so, not to incur anyone's hatred, they cover their mouths with a veil of silence. If they preached the truth as it really is, as truth requires and as Holy Scripture clearly commands, then (if I am not mistaken) they would incur the hatred of carnal people. Correct?"

"All the time."

"Do not fear these people, Dom Vito. Because they go by human standards, they fear human scandal, whereas truth should not be abandoned because of scandal. O you blind preachers! You fear the scandal of blind men, and so incur blindness of soul! Like fine, fat cows, some wealthy men give the dung of temporalities to the preacher, so as to escape his criticism. But I beg you to be an authentic preacher who thinks nothing of silver and gold. So Peter says to prelates and preachers, 'Feed the flock of God which is among you, taking care of it, not by constraint, but willingly, according to God; not for filthy lucre's sake, but voluntarily; neither as lording it over the clergy, but being made a pattern to the flock.' And he adds, 'If any man speaks, let him speak as the words of God.' Whoever 'speaks the words of God' is afraid of teaching anything beyond God's will, beyond the authority of Holy Scripture, or not useful to his brethren; and he fears to be silent about the things he should teach."

"I've tried to do this, but it seems to bring about no change in anyone."

Antonio drained the soup from his bowl and then turned it upside down. "What is this little tunnel?" he asked, pointing to a thin, serpentine groove in the wood.

"The gnawing of a woodworm. It was in the wood when I carved the bowl. I'm sorry I have no better bowls to offer."

"The bowl is fine." Antonio pointed to the tunnel. "You say a woodworm made this. A worm bores and gnaws away at wood. So must a preacher bore and gnaw away at hearts hardened by sin which bear no fruit. Nothing is harder than a worm when it bores into wood. Yet nothing is softer to the touch than a worm. So must a preacher be tender, treating repentant and humbled souls with compassion and mercy. Thus, when you preach the word of God, preach with determination and firmness to move the hearts of your hearers. But if those listeners hurl insults and affronts at you, remain soft, forgiving, and friendly."

Vito's gaze was fixed on the tiny, twisting tunnel. A worm is both hard and soft, rigid and flexible. He would never have thought of himself that way.

"Mercilessly kill all sins in yourself so that you may show mercy first toward yourself and then toward others. Thus, you will fulfill the precept of Jesus, 'to be merciful as your Father is merciful.' When you are merciful to yourself, Dom Vito, then you will feel confident to show mercy to those who confessed today. You are the one who must nurture their faith."

Antonio placed the bowl on the table and touched Vito's hand. "Late last year, Pope Onorio wrote to our universities and religious houses commanding them to send preachers to France to combat the heresies there. The minister general of the brotherhood is sending me to France; I'll be leaving soon. In Bologna, the newly born in Christ will come to you, not to me."

A knock sounded at the door. "Come in," Vito called.

Zaccaria stood in the doorway, his fox cape flecked with snow. The usurer shook the snow from his cape, then stepped inside the house and knelt before Vito.

"Dom Vito, I've come to make restitution and to ask forgiveness," he said, his head bowed. "You've spoken to me for years and I didn't listen. I ask God to forgive me, for cheating the Church and the poor."

Vito swallowed the amazement in his voice. Placing his hand on Zaccaria's shoulder, he said, "I forgive you, and may God forgive you, Messer."

Zaccaria looked up at Vito, his eyes glistening with tears. "Grazie." Then he turned toward the door and called, "Bring in the coins."

A stocky youth in a black fur cape walked into the room, carrying with him a fat leather pouch. Rising from his knees, Zaccaria took the pouch and dumped its contents onto the table. Coins of all denominations bounced against the wood until a great heap lay there.

"There will be more," Zaccaria said. Vito was speechless as Zaccaria took Vito's hand in his right hand and Antonio's in his left. His grip was firm as he said, "Grazie, both of you. You've given me life."

Then, dropping his grip on the hands, he unfastened his cape and stepped over to the bed. Gently he draped the fur over Maria and her sleeping infant. Then he silently walked to the door and out into the storm. The groom followed, closing the door behind them.

Antonio touched Vito's wrist. "That is your first newborn, Dom Vito. Nurse him well with the milk of God's holy word so that he may grow up strong in Christ."

NOTES

Although all of this chapter's characters, except Antonio, are fictitious representations of real personalities, the usury in Bologna is accurately represented. It was excessive in many cities in Europe, and Antonio preached against it frequently. Zaccaria's reaction to the sermon is a typical reaction of usurers as recorded by biographers in Antonio's story.

Dom Vito's vision of Antonio is based on similar visions in the historical record. People reported that Antonio or others appeared to them in dreams, urging them to confess. Following Antonio's death, people claimed that he appeared to them and named the friar to whom they were to confess.

Woodworms are common pests in Italy.

Historians are unsure of exactly when Antonio went to France. Apparently, he was there by the fall of 1224. Almost certainly he was sent there in response to the pope's request for able preachers to be sent to France to respond to heresy. The pope sent this request to universities and religious houses sometime in the fall or early winter of 1223. By the time Antonio received his orders to report to France, winter had likely arrived in Bologna. This chapter reflects that possibility.

Antonio's sermon against usury is from Purcell 149–50 (see also SSF I 44–45) and "To See, To Speak, To Hear" in *Messenger of Saint Anthony*. His illustration involving the dung beetle is taken from SSF IV 22. His words to Vito are from SSF I 399–401, as well as from the following sermons as translated in *Messenger of Saint Anthony*: "Knowledge, Virtue, and Faith"; "The Preacher Warrior Against Sin"; and "You Will Find an Infant." His praise of the Virgin Mary, the explanation of her name, and his prayer to her are from SK 71–84.

Scripture cited in this chapter is from Psalm 104:25–26 ("This vast ocean . . ."), Matthew 7:13 ("Wide is the way . . ."), Jeremiah 3:2 ("Lift up your eyes . . ."), Ezekiel 33:15 ("You will surely live . . ."), Acts 22:10 ("Lord, what will you . . ."), James 5:7–8 ("The farmer waits . . ."), Galatians 6:9 ("Let us not grow weary . . ."), Isaiah 5:20 (that good is bad and bad is good), John 14:6 ("I am the truth"), 1 Peter 5:2–3 ("Feed and tend . . ."), 1 Peter 4:11 ("If any man speak . . ."), and Luke 6:36 ("be merciful . . .").

10

Fra Giusto

School of Theology, Bologna, Italy (June 1224)

Fra Giusto liked the novelty of having an evening class at Bologna's School of Theology. He was seated with his fellow theology students, grateful for the shade of a huge oak that towered over all of them and over their teacher Fra Antonio.

"Let me tell you briefly what Pope Innocenzo wrote about the name of Jesus," Antonio was saying. Giusto couldn't see the learned man's face because everyone had pulled their hoods over their tonsured heads to discourage the swarms of gnats and flies that, like the students, had sought the evening shade.

"The name of Jesus is made up of two syllables." Antonio paused. "And five letters." Pause. "Three vowels and two consonants."*

Giusto was grateful for the pauses. They allowed the information time to penetrate the mind.

"The two syllables in the name Jesus are symbolic of the two natures in Jesus, the divine and the human. The divine nature comes from the Heavenly Father, the human nature from His earthly mother."

---

* The name Jesus is spelled *Iesus* in Latin. Antonio uses this spelling in his explanation of the Holy Name. The two consonants are s and s; the three vowels are I, e, and u.

Antonio was scanning the crowd. When he turned toward Giusto, the young man was gazing into the priest's intense, deep-set eyes. "Note that a vowel is a sound that can be pronounced by itself, while a consonant needs another sound with it as it cannot be pronounced alone."

Giusto nodded. He understood. Antonio's gaze shifted to another student. "The three vowels in Jesus' name signify the divinity which, although One in itself, exists in Three Persons. In First John, we read, 'There are Three who give testimony in heaven: the Father, the Word, and the Holy Spirit. And these Three are One.'"

Antonio paused again. Then he continued, pausing between phrases.

"The two consonants—both s's—in the name of Jesus signify humanity." Pause.

"Although humanity is made up of two substances—that is, body and soul—nevertheless, like the consonants, neither body nor soul can stand alone." Pause. "Each must be joined with other substances to form the unity of a person."

Giusto wondered if anyone else was suddenly thinking of himself as a unique individual with a unique body and a unique soul. He had never considered that.

"Just as a rational soul and body form one person, so God and man form one Christ. Christ is both God and man. He can subsist by Himself in as far as He is God—part of the Trinity—but He cannot subsist by Himself in as far as He is human—that is, body and soul." Pause.

Giusto hadn't ever thought about that either. He lingered on the idea that Christ needed a body to be who He was.

"The Acts of the Apostles tells us, 'There is no other name given to us whereby we must be saved.' May we be saved by God through the name of Jesus Christ our Lord, Who is blessed above all things throughout all the ages. Amen."

And so ended the lecture. The students rose, stretched, and made their way to the chapel for Compline. When that ended, the light was dying. Giusto and the others made their ways to their tiny huts, where they would sleep.

But Fra Giusto couldn't sleep. Not tonight. Not last night either. When had he last enjoyed a good night's sleep? He lay on his straw mat staring wide-eyed into the darkness as if, by looking hard enough, he would see his turbulent thoughts take on demonic form. The calm night mocked his anguish. The soft snoring of peaceful brothers came from nearby huts. Crickets chirped. Night frogs croaked their love songs to each other.

The same thoughts had come so many nights before. During the day, when Giusto begged alms or bent his muscular arms to hoe the friars' vegetable patch or listened to lectures or studied, he could push the thoughts deep inside. At night, when his body and mind were too tired to fight them any longer, the questions would emerge to terrify him.

What if the Bible were wrong? Such a blasphemous thought shouldn't even enter a brother's mind. Yet he had asked an even more heretical question. Did God exist? And, if He did, why was He so cruel?

Why do you fast, pray, discipline yourself when it is to no avail? his mind would ask. *Can't you see that the Bible is the product of men's minds? Look at those around you. Fra Giovanni goes about with lowered eyes and appears so pious. Yet how many times have you seen him dropping candle wax on the heads of those below him in choir? And Fra Bertrado. How can he follow Fra Francesco when he must daily have five boiled eggs for breakfast?*

Even yourself. The others look at you and say, "Giusto is a model of virtue." They say this because you, a baron, left all your inheritance to follow Christ, thinking to gain a greater reward in eternity. They say this because they don't know how often you cheated your serfs of their just produce from your meadows or how disdainfully you treated your grooms and squires. They know nothing about Madonna Elena, whom you courted while her husband fought the Crusades. They had never seen how you squandered money on fine silk stockings and fur capes when it should have been given to the poor. How proud you were, Giusto! Your pride will damn you to hell. If the other brothers knew the real you, they'd expel you like a dog. How wisely Jesus spoke of you—outwardly white like a marble tomb, inwardly full of uncleanness and corruption. Wasn't it this way with those who lived in years past? Those who wrote the Scripture chose pious words, but their deeds were far different. Didn't David compose the Psalms yet sin with Bathsheba? Didn't Moses write God's commandments yet kill an Egyptian? Even the books of God were written by such men who looked holy but committed evil deeds. Certainly if God existed, we would see no such wickedness. God wouldn't allow these questions to torment you, nor would He allow evil to exist in the world. The very presence of doubts and disasters proves that God is merely an idea created by men to pacify others.

Pulling his thin woolen blanket with him, Giusto rolled over on his belly and thrust his face into his hands. *Stop!* his mind shrieked. *The torment must stop!* His mind would crack if these questions continued.

"God," he whispered, "if You do exist, tell me Who You are and show me what You can do. I cannot bear these trials much longer."

GO SEE FRA ANTONIO. The thought was gentle yet firm.

Fra Antonio is asleep, Giusto argued.

GO SEE FRA ANTONIO.

How could he go to see Fra Antonio? Giusto had no personal relationship with his theology teacher, whose reputation had preceded him. Fra Antonio was intimidating!

Antonio had preached in Vercelli and Milan. Heretics who heard him returned to the Church. The faithful who heard him flocked to confession.

Antonio had received instruction from Abbot Thomas de Gaule, a saintly mystic and author. Some teachers here at the school claimed that Abbot Thomas was the world's greatest living doctor of theology. However, Thomas had reportedly claimed that he had no need to teach Antonio anything because divine grace aided him. Antonio had expounded so thoroughly on the different orders of angels that his fellow students at Vercelli and even Abbot Thomas had felt as if they were in the presence of the heavenly hosts.

Antonio had been chosen by Francesco to accompany him to the papal court to discuss their new Rule of Life. Lord Pope had approved that Rule, thus changing the status of the brotherhood from a religio to an ordine. Surely Antonio played some role in obtaining that approval. Antonio had received Fra Francesco's permission to teach the brothers theology. Francesco had granted this permission to no one else. Antonio was joyfully hailed as "my bishop" by Francesco. What greater compliment could be paid?

Antonio. Giusto felt unworthy to breathe the same air that sustained a man like that. And now he was to wake him in the middle of the night? All he needed was to add that impudence to his sins.

GO SEE FRA ANTONIO.

No! What good would that do? God was a righteous judge. Didn't Scripture say that the righteous would scarcely be saved? Jesus, Who claimed to be the very Truth, said, "He who is able to receive this, let him receive it." Didn't that mean that not every person could receive the faith or do good? Surely Giusto was one of those who would never be saved. And God, should God exist, saw these torments and tears and cared not at all. How foolish it was to persist in useless prayers! The prophet Ezekiel said, "The soul that sins shall die."

Giusto had sinned exceedingly and still sinned by his doubts. Even Scripture stated that "all have sinned and fall short of the glory of God." God, if He existed, was just and must punish wickedness. If God were a mere phantasm of the imagination, Giusto had no hope. If God were real, he still had no hope. Why did he think that joining these followers of Francesco would be his salvation? He had no salvation.

Go see Fra Antonio.

How could Antonio understand Giusto's torment? The man was totally devoted to God, totally devoid of unclean desires.

Go to Fra Antonio. Only in the name of Jesus can you be saved. Go to the priest.

It was dark. How could he go in the dark?

He opened his eyes. It was light. Moonlight flooded his cell through the cracks.

Giusto pushed back his blanket. In the glimmer, he could see his breeches and coarse tunic. Dressing quickly, he stepped out into the ghostly glow of moonlit fog.

Antonio's hut, five away from Giusto's, looked as if it were dissolving into the mist. Outside the priest's cell, Giusto stood motionless. Now what? How dare he wake his teacher? Should he call out? Tap lightly? Go in and wake him?

Inside the still hut, coarse cloth rustled. Soft footsteps. Antonio stood in the doorway.

"I thought I heard someone. Fra Giusto, what troubles you?"

Giusto's knees crumbled beneath him. He was kneeling in front of the priest, sobbing uncontrollably.

He felt two firm hands on his shoulders.

"If we speak here, we'll disturb the sleeping brothers. Come."

Antonio helped Giusto to his feet and guided him away from the cells toward the winding road that led to the town fields. The night was perfectly still, the moon a fuzzy, bright orb in a vaporous shroud of sky. As the men's bare feet scratched the dust, crickets in the tall weeds on either side of the road momentarily ceased chirping. The mist opened before the men and closed behind them.

For a long while, Giusto poured out his sins, fears, and questions. The priest listened without speaking. Finally, when Giusto had no more to say, they walked on in silence. At last, Antonio turned off the road and pushed through a ribbon of high, dew-soaked grass until he stood at the edge of a newly plowed field. Giusto obediently followed.

"Fra Giusto," the priest began, "this field represents the body of Christ. God says in the Book of Genesis, 'Let the earth bring forth vegetation.' This cannot happen unless the soil is first broken."

Antonio stooped to the earth and scooped up a handful of rich, moist soil. Still stooping, he gazed up at Giusto. "The earth is Christ, crushed for our sins, pierced by a lance and nails. Just as the earth, plowed and broken in springtime, produces abundant harvest, so the bruised and broken body of Christ gained for us the harvest of heaven."

Antonio rose and pressed the soil into Giusto's hand. It felt delightfully cool, almost alive. "This field, brother, is also you. When a person is contrite for his sins as you are, he is like a piece of soil that has been reduced to dust. Crushed by sorrow for his offenses, the sinner can turn his mind to God and make of it a delightful garden. What other possible pleasure or joy can satisfy a man when he stands before God, from Whom and in Whom everything that exists is true? You have stood before God, Fra Giusto, and have admitted that you are nothing in yourself.

"When have you done this? In the desert of your questioning." Antonio rubbed his hands on the moist grass to cleanse them. "Brother, there are three stages in our spiritual life. God describes them through the mouth of the prophet Hosea. 'I will nourish her; I will lead her into the desert and speak to her heart.' With God's grace, a beginner in the spiritual life is 'nourished,' becoming stronger and stronger in the practice of virtue. This you have done by overcoming your carnal desires.

"Now you are passing through the second stage of spiritual development. In this stage, God 'leads the soul into the desert.'"

Antonio led the way back to the road and began walking again, going deeper into the pasture lands. Giusto thought momentarily of the robbers on the roads at night, then dismissed the thought. Robbers wouldn't harm them. They knew the followers of Francesco had nothing to give but their tunics and breeches.

"Where did God speak to John the Baptist? In the desert, 'parched, lifeless, and without water, where I have gazed on you,' as Psalm 62 states. John came as 'a voice crying in the desert.' A voice is a preacher and the desert is a symbol of the cross on which Christ died, abandoned, naked, and crowned with thorns. From the desert of the cross, Christ cried, 'Father, into Your hands I commend My spirit.' Thus we must do this as well, when we are in the desert of our own questioning."

"It's so difficult, brother, to give my soul to God when I question His very goodness and existence."

"Ah, very difficult. Most exceedingly difficult. For Satan's influence is always present in the desert."

Giusto clutched the soil in his fist. "Are you saying that my thoughts have come from Satan?"

"This may well be, brother. Yet God has permitted these thoughts, hasn't He? They have clouded your mind just as this mist clouds the night. And you wonder why God has permitted your torment. Because one stage of the spiritual life is the desert. In the desert, when one submits to God, one can also find peace and quiet, away from the tumult of internal unrest. Here God 'speaks to her heart' the way a loving mother speaks to her child. Can you hear God speaking to you in the desert of your thoughts?"

"I believe God told me to come to you."

"Perhaps to help you see that what you are experiencing is neither unusual nor evil, for it will bring you to the third stage of spiritual development. In this third stage, the soul experiences the complete joy of God's presence within it. What a superabundance of love, joy, and zeal a soul experiences when it possesses God! Certainly, Fra Giusto, you are looking for that joy."

"Who isn't looking for it?"

"But you think that you must have faith without reason. No, brother. To have faith is to exercise the most reason. Saint Peter in his first letter writes, 'As newborn babies, desire the rational milk without guile.' Something is rational when it is done according to reason. Reason is a faculty of the soul which recognizes truth. It also means the contemplation of truth or the truth itself. Jesus said, 'He who knows the truth listens to My voice.' He said this because He is the Truth, as He said, 'I am the Way and the Truth and the Life.' We are to be 'rational' toward God, always seeking the truth. Truth does not come except to those who seek it. One way of seeking is through questions."

"But I have questioned the very existence of God and His goodness."

Antonio stopped and moved his arm in an arc. "What do you see, Fra Giusto?"

"Just a bit of the road and some grass beside it, an edge of meadow beyond. Nothing else. It's too dark and misty."

"And do you question if all that you see is all that is?"

"Of course not. I know that meadows extend to the left and right as far as the eyes can see and beyond them the Apennine Mountains."

"How do you know?"

"I've seen them before."

"And is that everything that exists? Or is there more to the world than you can see at any one moment?"

"Bologna lies behind us, and beyond that all of the Romagna. Then, to the north, France, and to the south, the sea, and beyond that, the ocean and other nations."

"Have you seen them?"

"I've never left the Romagna."

"Yet you believe. Why?"

"Others have seen and written of these places or brought back tales of them."

"And you believe them. Then look at the Bible, brother. It was written by those who saw, those who witnessed. Look at Jesus. He is the writing of the Father. Saint John calls him the 'Word of God.' Read that 'Word' for your answers, Fra Giusto, and 'do not be faithless, but believing.' I will pray for you."

Antonio swung around on the road and headed back through the fog to Bologna. The men walked slowly and in silence. Giusto knew that the priest was already praying for him, and he sensed a strength and calm coming from those prayers. To know Antonio was to know a man who understood and loved and lived the "Word." To be in his presence was to meet the Truth. The Truth was the Son, rising now in Giusto's soul to warm away the fog of doubt. Giusto was glad that he had gone to see the priest.

NOTES

The facts concerning Antonio's teaching and various duties, including the papal audience, follow the historical record. The brothers asked Francesco to allow Antonio to teach them theology (24Gen Section 1, p. 177).

Sometime after November 29, 1223, when Pope Onorio III approved the Rule for the brothers, Francesco sent a brief note to Antonio, stating, "I am pleased that you teach sacred theology to the brothers provided that, as is contained in the Rule, you 'do not extinguish the Spirit of prayer and devotion' during study of this kind" (FA:ED I 107). Antonio began to teach after receiving this permission.

Antonio taught the brothers theology at Bologna (Ben 3), Montpellier, Toulouse, and Padua, and in other locations in Italy and France. Some historians claim that he held the office of lector of theology at universities in some of these cities, but this seems inaccurate since most of the universities had not established this position prior to Antonio's death. Likely, he instructed the friars at their own convents, not at the universities. Some sources say that he inaugurated a school of theology in 1223 for the friars of Bologna that eventually developed into the school of theology for the university of that city. Quite likely, Antonio wrote some of his sermons as notes for teaching these classes.

Biographers of the saint record several instances in which he counseled religious of his order and other orders, advising them against temptations and confirming them in their faith. Fra Giusto is a fictitious character whose temptations are patterned after those of a Bavarian monk, Othloh, who took his final vows in 1032. Othloh's autobiography, some of which is quoted in *Life in the Middle Ages*, contains a vivid picture of his temptations and questions and the torment that they caused him.

Antonio's words are from SK 24–27 (teaching on the name of Jesus) and SK 9–18, 85–88, 161–65 (his comments to Giusto).

Scripture verses are from Matthew 23:27 ("Outwardly white . . ."); 1 Peter 4:18 ("The righteous are scarcely saved . . ."); Matthew 19:12 ("He who is able to receive it . . ."); Ezekiel 18:20 ("The soul that sins . . ."); Romans 3:23 ("All have sinned and fall short . . ."); Acts 4:12 ("There is no other name . . ."); Genesis 1:11 ("Let the earth bring forth . . ."); Hosea 2:14 ("I will lead her . . ."); Psalm 63:1 ("Parched, lifeless . . ."); Isaiah 40:3 ("A voice crying . . ."); Luke 23:46 ("Father, into Your hands . . ."); 1 Peter 1:23 ("As newborn babies . . ."); John 18:37 ("He who knows the truth . . ."); John 14:6 ("I am the Way . . ."); John 1:1 (the Word of God); and John 20:27 ("Do not be faithless . . .").

PART THREE

A Serpent Creeps by Hidden Ways

11

Fra Monaldo

Chapter Meeting, Arles, France (September 1224)

F ra Monaldo sat on a wooden bench in the very back of the room. His arthritis was bothering him as it always did, but he refused to lean against the wall. No one must know that he was in pain.

Monaldo had chosen this seat as the one best fitting his station. Here no one would notice the tiny old man whom his fellow friars lovingly called Fra Mouse. With his patched gray tunic hanging loosely over his stooped shoulders and his brown eyes bright in his thin face, Monaldo did resemble the furtive little creatures that he and the other brothers sometimes surprised around this monastery.

Arles was suffering under a mid-September heatwave. Had there not been a light rain today, the friars would have assembled outdoors under the grape arbors that surrounded the monastery. It would have been pleasant there, with the breeze rippling through the wide grape leaves, the thick purple clusters almost ripe enough to pick.

As it was, Monaldo's guardian thoughtfully rearranged this room at the convent so that the benches for those who would address the chapter were directly in front of the open door. Here his guests would catch any breeze that might filter through the arbors to relieve the stifling humidity. Other benches

were arranged to face the two in the front. Monaldo, being at the rear of the
room, caught very little fresh air. He didn't mind. With age had come a perpetual chill in his bones. Today, while many other brothers periodically wiped the
sweat from their foreheads with the sleeves of their tunics, Monaldo, except for
his arthritis, felt quite comfortable.

How fortunate he was to be present at this chapter meeting! Only the
ordine's younger, more vigorous provincials and delegates had been invited.
Had he and his convent mates not lived here at Arles where the chapter meeting
was being held, they never would have been asked to attend. As it was, their
guardian allowed them to sit in on the meeting. However, they were not to
speak unnecessarily to the important delegates. They were to sit only after everyone else was seated. They were to assist any visitors.

The brothers agreed. A few of the dignitaries had asked some brothers for
drinks of water. No one had asked Monaldo for anything. The brothers had
obediently allowed the visitors to sit first, then took the best seats left. Monaldo
sat down last. Let the younger men claim the seats that afforded a better view of
the proceedings. They were more able than he to absorb the fire of Francesco
and healthy enough to bring it to the world.

Monaldo had seen Fra Francesco a few times at chapter meetings of the
entire ordine. Joy and holiness radiated from the scrawny, short man who had
once been a merchant's son courting dreams of knighthood. Not many ordines
began with a poet and a dreamer like Francesco, whose love for God radiated in
his words and actions. Monaldo had never spoken to Francesco personally, nor
even approached him. He felt that between Francesco and him lay a chasm of
difference: the one man with a foot already in heaven and the other no holier
than the dust beneath his feet.

Francesco was not at today's regional chapter meeting. As the number of
Lesser Brothers grew, so did the number of such regional gatherings, and
Francesco, whose stamina was waning, could no longer attend them all. In fact,
he was ill in Assisi at this very moment and, the brothers knew, burdened with
worries over the ordine. How fervently they offered daily prayers for him and
for themselves!

Not everyone agreed with the reforms begun by the current minister general, Fra Elia. Some brothers feared that Francesco's simple Rule of poverty,

chastity, and obedience would be destroyed, and with it, the very soul of the ordine. Yet Francesco had submitted himself to Fra Elia in strict obedience. Monaldo could only imagine the struggle and pain Francesco felt as Elia worked to bring structure and direction to the brotherhood. Francesco, who to Monaldo seemed as free as a lark, could only have seen Elia's efforts as trying to cage a flock of sparrows.

Where did Fra Giovanni Bonelli of Florence, their provincial who had called this chapter meeting, stand regarding the Rule? No one was certain. He hadn't discussed it, although the chapter had already covered many issues on which the brothers held differing opinions—disciplining lax brothers, owning convents, teaching theology, battling heresy, ministering to lepers and the poor.

Before the men grew too burdened with dry and discouraging problems, Fra Giovanni called a brief recess. Monaldo remained in his seat, content to rest. Despite the drizzle, many other brothers ventured outdoors to walk briefly under the arbors. When they reassembled, the room smelled of wet woolen tunics and sweat.

"Before we begin our discussion again, we need to return our thoughts to Christ," Fra Giovanni said. "He must be the Beginning, the End, and the Means by which we do all. I have asked Fra Antonio to address you on the inscription on Christ's cross, 'Jesus of Nazareth, the King of the Jews,' and on His sufferings for our sake."

Antonio was one of those young, vigorous men whom Monaldo admired. When Monaldo had been Antonio's age, he was working in obscurity as a serf on a baron's estate. And so he continued until he was past fifty, when he heard some followers of Francesco speak. Then he left the nothing he had to embrace the Everything the friars offered. With them he begged, prayed, and tended the poor in obscurity. Obscurity was all he knew, all he wanted, all he merited.

In contrast to Monaldo, the young man who knelt before Fra Giovanni to receive a blessing was becoming a legend. Some said that he was closer to Francesco in his beliefs than any other brother. Some wanted him to be minister general of the ordine. Many brothers, including Monaldo, had never heard him preach, but they had heard that the fire of God burned in him as he spoke throughout the area.

In his rain-splattered tunic, Antonio stood to face the gathering. His tonsured hair and his eyelashes glistened with mist as he bowed his head and lifted
his hands in prayer.

As Antonio began speaking, Monaldo swelled with warmth and devotion
to the Son of God. He lost track of time and forgot his pains as Antonio progressed with his sermon.

Now Antonio's gaze was steady on a spot just above the heads of his listeners, as if he were seeing the One he described.

"Let us raise our eyes and fix them on Jesus crucified, the author of salvation. Let us contemplate our Lord pierced with nails and suspended from the
cross." He paused before continuing. "How can you not believe when your life
is hanging before you from the cross?"

Antonio looked at the faces lifted toward him, his own face beaded with
sweat. "What is more important than a man's life? The life of the body is the
soul and the life of the soul is Christ. Here, then, your very life hangs from the
cross. How can you not feel any pain? How can you refuse to identify yourself
with His suffering? If Christ is your life, as He truly is, how can you keep from
following Him, ready with Peter and Thomas to be thrown into jail and to die at
His side?"

The priest's gaze focused on Monaldo. "Christ hangs from the cross before
you to invite you to share in His suffering. He never stops calling to us, 'Come,
all of you who pass by the way, look and see whether there is any suffering like
My suffering.'"

Antonio bowed his head and raised his hands skyward. "How easily do they
fall away, they who were redeemed at the cost of so much pain!"

Again, his head lifted as if he were gazing at Christ Himself. "His Passion
was more than sufficient to redeem all humanity and still many head toward
perdition. What could cause greater grief when no one recognizes or worries
about this tragedy?"

Antonio's voice trembled. "It is truly frightful that the God Who once
regretted having created us will one day feel sorry for having redeemed us."

He turned to face the doorway, his hands sweeping toward the grape arbors
that were dripping with rain. His voice rose above the patter on the roof and
filled the room. "If after working all year long in his vineyard a farmer is

disappointed because he cannot find ripe grapes, how much more bitter will be God's disappointment at our fruitlessness. God lamented in the Book of the prophet Isaiah, 'What more was there to do for my vineyard that I had not done? Why, when I looked for the crop of grapes, did it bring forth wild grapes?'"

Antonio turned back to the friars. "God is deeply disappointed when instead of justice in conversion and penance, He finds iniquity. He expects righteousness and honesty to be practiced toward one's neighbor, but instead He hears the cries of the oppressed."

He clenched his fists, then opened them and looked at them as if they held the grapes about which he spoke. "This is the bitter fruit that the vineyard yields after the Passion of its Divine Landlord." His fingers curled around the imaginary grapes. "It deserves to be ripped out at its roots and thrown into the fire."

The priest's hands swept outward and then upward. Again, he raised his eyes. "Your Life hangs before you on the cross so that you might see yourself as in a mirror. You can thus see how serious were your wounds and that they can be healed by no other medicine than by the Blood of the Son of God. And, if you pause to reflect deeply, you can also come to understand how sublime is your dignity. How lofty is the greatness of your human person for which it was necessary to pay so incalculable a price. The 'mirror' of the cross shows you what you are in the present; it teaches you to what depths you must lower your pride, how you must mortify the desires of your flesh, how you ought to pray to the Father for those who persecute you and place your spirit in His hands."

Monaldo noticed the slightest flicker of movement in the doorway behind Antonio. A figure entered the room. Monaldo broke into a grin. Fra Francesco!

Even as he smiled, he squinted. Francesco was not wet with rain. Monaldo saw the little man fling his arms open wide in the form of a cross and then rise until his head and shoulders were above those of Antonio. Antonio continued to preach as if totally unaware of Francesco's presence.

"But you do not believe in Christ, in your Life, Who assures you, 'Just as Moses raised the serpent in the desert, in the same way the Son of Man must be raised up, so that whoever believes in Him may not be lost but have eternal life.' To see and to believe is the same thing because, in this case, you see only as much as you believe."

Francesco brought his arms before him and, with his right hand, blessed the brothers over Antonio's head. Then he smiled and traced a cross directly above the shaved scalp of Antonio, who was preaching beneath him.

Antonio was gazing intently at the brothers, his voice a plea, "Believe firmly in Jesus crucified, the Life of your life, so that you may be able to live with Him, Who is Life itself, forever and ever. Amen."

Antonio bowed his head and walked back to the bench on which he had been sitting. Behind him, through the doorway, Monaldo saw the wet arbors. Francesco was gone.

In the hushed, prayerful silence, Monaldo struggled with a holy torment. TELL THE VISION, the Spirit was saying to his heart.

How could he, a nobody, have been granted such a divine favor?

I am not worthy to have seen it, Monaldo argued. *Let the others who have seen it speak.*

I DETERMINE WHO IS WORTHY. NO ONE HAS SEEN MY BELOVED FRANCESCO BUT YOU. TELL THE VISION.

No one moved. All were deep in prayer and meditation.

TELL THE VISION.

Finally Fra Giovanni rose. "Thank you, Fra Antonio. Has anyone anything to share regarding what our brother preached?"

TELL THE VISION.

No one spoke. Each seemed to be waiting for the other.

TELL.

Monaldo stood. His legs felt weak. "Fra Antonio, while you were speaking, Fra Francesco came in the doorway and blessed us and you." He sat down.

"Did you see this, brother?" Fra Giovanni asked.

"Sì," Monaldo said in a squeaky voice.

Some brothers turned to look at Monaldo. Others knelt in thanksgiving. Antonio dropped to his knees, his head bowed to the floor.

Fra Giovanni spoke, a tremor in his voice. "I had been praying for the spirit of Francesco to strengthen and guide this meeting. Praise the Lord for having granted my prayer."

NOTES

Monaldo's vision of Francesco, his blessing Antonio while he preached on the Passion, and the inscription on the cross are in the historical record (FA:ED I 225, 390; FA:ED III 92–93, Rig 12, Ben 5, 2LJS 5). Most locations name Arles; one names Provence (2LJS 5) as the convent where this took place. The generally accepted time of this meeting is around September 14, 1224, the feast of the Exaltation of the Cross, although 1225 or 1226 has been suggested. Biographical information about Francesco and the response of the friars toward him are in the histories.

History records no description of Monaldo, the weather, the business under discussion, the fruits grown at the convent, or the words that Antonio preached.

Antonio's words are from SK 146–50. Scripture verses are from Lamentations 1:12 ("Come, all of you . . ."); Isaiah 5:4 ("What more was there . . ."); and John 3:14–15 ("Just as Moses . . .").

12

Fra Martin

Road from Montpellier to Arles, Montpellier, France (Spring 1225)

The theft had been almost too easy. Fra Martin had lagged behind while the other brothers assembled for choir; then he slipped into Antonio's cell. Here he quickly found what he was seeking: Antonio's personally hand-penned *Commentary on the Psalms* lying on a small table near the priest's sleeping mat. Martin had left the convent immediately, giving the impression that he was hurrying to join his brothers at prayer. Instead, he had skirted the church and then, on long, thin legs, raced through the streets of Montpellier. He ran until he reached the road that followed this tributary of the Rhône River, a road that led to Arles. In Arles, he would sell the *Commentary*, purchase some useful clothing, and give the tunic he now wore to a beggar.

He realized how odd he must appear to travelers who walked the road with him. The Lesser Brothers always traveled in pairs, and he was alone. Yet no one stopped to ask, "Where's your companion?"

He had been too young to enter the ordine, he told himself, and too wicked. He was, after all, the son of beggars, a beggar himself. He had slept with the beggar women of Béziers and paid them with coins or food he had stolen. Perhaps he had even fathered a child. Then he had seen the holy beggars of Fra Francesco and longed to be like them. They possessed a God-given peace and joy that he longed for. How could he have been so foolish to think that he, a sinner, could become a man of Christ?

The brothers welcomed him lovingly. The ordine had been good to him. He had food to eat—not much, it was true, but then he didn't need much. He was used to eating little. He had a place to sleep—only a mat of straw, but he needed no more. His needs were met and he had begun to learn of the God for Whom he hungered.

When he had come to Montpellier to learn from Fra Antonio, everything had improved. Antonio's teaching had deepened his faith and knowledge. How little he knew, but he was learning. How poorly he believed, but he was trying. And, in Montpellier, the convent was comfortable and the food plentiful. That was because Montpellier, unlike many other cities in the province, had never gone over to the Cathars. Remaining faithful to the Church, Montpellier was quick to house and sustain any true sons of Christ.

And so Martin the thin-armed beggar had become Martin the thin-armed novice. But now he knew that donning a tunic couldn't change a sinner into a saint. True, he had worked at his faith. True, he hadn't stolen or been with any woman since he'd joined the brothers. But as the months went on, he grew weary of repairing chapels and praying and fasting. Out in the streets as a beggar, he had been destitute and maligned, but he was free to do as he pleased. In the convent, he seemed always surrounded by other brothers, hemmed in by doctrine, constrained by holiness. Sometimes he felt as though he were suffocating. Finally, he came to realize that he could never be a brother. Sin was too entrenched in his soul and the desire for freedom too keen.

Right now, it felt good to be walking down this road, a stolen book hidden in the folds of his tunic, his eyes gazing longingly at each woman who shyly passed him. He knew that he shouldn't feel this pride, this lust, but the desires were there, surely as much a part of him as his fingernails. They proved to him again that he wasn't meant to be a holy man. Fra Antonio might be, but not Martin.

Then the thought struck him. Fra Antonio had received orders to preach against the heretics at Toulouse. Within days he would be leaving and would want to take his book with him. Most likely he'd be back in his cell by now, searching for the volume. Suppose he appeared to Martin. The novice shivered with fear and shook his head. No, such a thing wouldn't happen. Still, what had just happened on Easter? Didn't Fra Antonio seem to be in two places at one time on that day?

Martin and several other brothers had been chanting their prayers in the convent choir while the faithful townsfolk were with Antonio as he celebrated Mass in the cathedral. When the moment for chanting the Office arrived, the brothers waited expectantly for the one designated to begin. It was Antonio's turn. Surely he had found a replacement. The men's heads were bowed in respectful silence when suddenly they heard Antonio's gentle song. From the corner of his eye, Martin could see Antonio standing in his usual place, singing the Alleluia. Mass must have ended extremely early for the priest to return to choir. Once Antonio finished singing, the brothers had resumed their prayers in unison. When they finally disbanded to return to their cells, they heard the clamor of worshipers leaving the cathedral. The Mass Antonio celebrated was just over.

Just a few days ago, while Antonio was teaching the friars theology, one of the brothers who had served Mass with the priest spoke up, "Brother, you say that we must have silence in which to pray. Is that why, on Easter, during your sermon you so abruptly drew your hood over your face and sank back in the pulpit, being silent for so long? When you drew the hood back and resumed your sermon, you said nothing about it. Were you expecting that we, during the time of silence, would reflect on the glory of the risen Lord?"

Antonio had smiled. "That would have been a worthy reflection."

The incident on Easter seemed spookier each time Martin thought about it.

By now, the sun was high overhead and Martin's legs were growing weary. Directly ahead was a bridge across the Rhône River. How cool and comfortable appeared the shade underneath it! There, before continuing his journey, he could rest a bit. That is, he could rest if the frogs that lived along the banks would cease their incessant croaking.

As Martin picked his way down the slope to the shade under the bridge, he thought of Fra Antonio. If Fra Antonio were here, he would have begun noon prayers after asking the frogs to maintain silence. At the Montpellier convent, Antonio had blessed the water of a pond and asked the noisy frogs in it to be quiet. Ever after, they no longer croaked. One friar claimed that he had taken a few frogs from the Montpellier pond and brought them to another pond, where they began to call out. So he took a few from the opposite pond and brought them to Montpellier, where they maintained perpetual silence. The frogs were quiet in the Montpellier pond but noisy anywhere else. Strange. A lot about Fra Antonio was strange.

Martin was not about to silence the frogs or pray. He was totally exhausted. The previous week of restless nights had drained him. He had never before planned a theft with so much agitation. If he lay down here on this bed of thick grass, he would most likely fall asleep no matter how loudly the frogs croaked.

He could not have been sleeping long when the silence awakened him. Why were the frogs still? He knew. Someone was here. Or something. He leaped to his feet. Perhaps a bandit. Then, to his right, obscured by the arch of the bridge, a dark bulk moved. In a moment of confusion, he thought it was Antonio. Then he saw bristly black fur and a thick black snout. Martin scrambled up the bank and made for the bridge. The huge monster was on the bridge.

Take the book back to the priest, a voice seemed to command as the unidentifiable beast lunged toward Martin. *Take it back or I shall kill you and throw your body into the river.*

Martin had never seen a demon, but he knew such creatures existed. Only a demon could speak. The black monster must be the devil himself. Martin spun on his heels and bolted back the way he had come, not sparing one second to see if the beast were lurching after him.

The sun was dropping in the darkening sky by the time he returned to the convent. How would he get the book to the priest? He would simply leave it on the chapel step and someone would discover it and return it to its owner. He didn't plan to stay at the convent himself. Tales of discipline in other convents had reached this one. He was certain that Antonio would act as other priests did. Wasn't this man nicknamed the Hammer of Heretics? Hadn't he silenced opposition in the provinces of Aquitania, Narbonne, and Languedoc? A man as forceful as he would punish the crime of theft. Antonio would strip Martin naked and beat him nearly unconscious while the other brothers watched.

As he laid the book on the chapel step, the voice came again. *Take the book to the priest. To the priest.*

Martin drew back. What was that shadow just around the corner of the chapel?

He grabbed the book and, forcing himself to walk to preserve the rule of the ordine, entered the convent, and tapped at the door of Antonio's cell.

"Come in."

Martin knew he had better look contrite. Opening the door, he fell on his knees, his head bowed.

"So. You've returned my book," a kind voice said. "God has answered one of my prayers." The priest put his hand on the youth's trembling shoulder. "Why are you so frightened? I'm not going to hurt you."

"Brother, I am a wretched sinner." He hoped he sounded sorry. Very sorry. "Forgive me."

To Martin's shock, the priest sank to his knees before him, his bowed head touching the ground, his voice almost a sob. "Lord, I realize that, if you were to remove your compassion from me, I, too, would become a victim of my own wretchedness." Then Antonio raised his head and placed his hands on the youth's shoulders. Martin flinched at the unexpected touch, but the grip was gentle instead of severe. With his face lifted heavenward and his eyes closed, Antonio whispered, "O Lord, our protector, look upon the face of Your Anointed. O Lord, do not look upon our sins, but look at the face of Christ, Your Anointed, covered with spittle, swollen with bruises, and covered with tears on our behalf. Have mercy on us, O Lord, because of the face of Christ. Be merciful to us who have been the cause of His suffering."

Then Antonio released his gentle touch and raised his arms to God, his prayer continuing to flow as smoothly as a placid stream. The mildness astonished Martin as the weight of his own pretended contrition crushed him. He was a sinner. He deserved to be beaten within a breath of his life. Martin pulled the too-wide tunic over his thin shoulders. The garment slid down, crumpling about his knees, its sleeves clinging loosely to his wrists. The young man knelt, bare-backed and still, his eyes downcast and closed, while Antonio continued to pray.

A beating would feel good. A beating would thrash the guilt and deceit away.

Martin heard the priest shift before him. He was rising, he knew. He heard soft footsteps circle him to the right. Without thinking, Martin tightened his back muscles, then flinched at the first touch on his shoulders. It was his tunic being gently lifted back into place.

"The wounds of Christ on the cross speak to the Father of forgiveness, not vengeance, my little one." The priest tucked the garment into place. "I had prayed to have my book back. And I had prayed for you to return with it. The book has returned. Have you?"

Martin couldn't bear to look up. With bowed head, he whispered hoarsely, "Brother, I cannot. I'm not like the others. I'm wicked. If you knew . . . I feel trapped here."

The youth felt a tender touch on his hand, warm fingers enclosing it, a gentle tug upward.

"Come with me."

Martin rose and followed Antonio out of the convent. Why was he going with him? Martin only knew that he must.

In silence, the two men wound their way through the streets of Montpellier, with Antonio pausing to chat with or bless several townspeople who stopped him.

This man is the Hammer of Heretics? Martin thought. True, to crowds Antonio spoke forcefully against sin. Yet he urged mercy toward the sinner. No Crusader could use Antonio's words to justify the slaughter of heretics. His correction began and ended with love. What had he counseled the brothers? Martin struggled to recall that class. "With a fallen brother, we must show ourselves neither too tender nor too hard, neither soft as flesh nor hard as bone; in him, we must love our own human nature while hating his fault. Saint John exhorts us to fraternal charity, comparing it to and wishing us to model it on the charity that God has shown to all of us. 'By this has the charity of God appeared to us, that God has sent His only begotten Son into the world, so that by Him we may have life.'"

How had Martin forgotten those words? He shouldn't have feared this man.

When the two men arrived at the outskirts of the town, Antonio commented, "We've just preached a good sermon, Fra Martin."

What a startling comment! "We haven't said anything."

"Our peaceful manner and modest looks are a sermon to those who have seen us. It can often be more influential to be than to say. Now, look." Antonio pointed to the peaks of the Cevennes Mountains thrust across each other far in the distance. "When did Jesus go up to a mountain, taking with Him Peter, James, and John?"

Martin reached into his memory for that lesson that Antonio, the teacher, had given. Finally, the answer came. "At the Transfiguration, brother."

Nodding, Antonio struck off the main road and led the way along one of the many winding paths that shepherds used to drive their flocks up to higher pastures.

"The three apostles, Peter, James, and John, were special friends of Christ. These three men represent three properties of a soul. Without these properties, a soul cannot ascend 'the high mountain of light.' It cannot establish a relationship with God. Do you want a relationship with God, my brother?"

"I do. But for me, it's not possible. I don't fit in here."

"Let us see if you fit in or not. Peter, James, and John were coarse fishermen. They didn't 'fit in' to an ordine either. Yet they followed Christ, didn't they?"

Martin agreed.

"Nor were they without sin. What can you tell me about that?"

Again Martin searched his memory for the knowledge that he had gleaned in class.

"Peter cut off a servant's ear. He denied knowing Christ. James and John— they argued about who would be greatest in heaven. And . . . and they wanted to call down punishment on a town that wouldn't accept them. Is that right, brother?"

Antonio grinned and playfully slapped the youth's shoulder. "You have a good memory. Now let's look at the names of these three men. Each name has a meaning. Peter means 'an admission.' James means 'a conquest' and John 'the grace of God.' Do you believe in Jesus and hope for salvation, my brother?"

"Oui. But is salvation possible for me? I'm so wicked."

"There you go calling yourself wicked again," Antonio said. "We're all wicked. Didn't Christ come to save sinners?" Antonio pointed to the mountains, which seemed no nearer the closer they approached. "Only sinners may approach God on His high mountain of prayer. If sinners could not come to God, no one would go. Suppose we asked all the saints ever born on earth, with the exception of the always sinless holy Mother of Christ, whether they were without sin? What do you think they would answer if not to repeat with John the Apostle, 'If we say we have no sin, we deceive ourselves and the truth is not in us.'"

Antonio smiled at Martin. "So do not be afraid to approach God. When you do, take with you Peter as Jesus did when He went up to the mountain. Take Peter and admit your sins, as did Peter. What sins? All of them. The pride in your heart. Your lust of the flesh. Your greed for material possessions. These are sins of which we all are guilty."

Martin hung his head. No one was guiltier of these sins than he.

Antonio continued to walk across the vast meadow toward the peaks. "Take James with you also. James is a conquest. Overcome and conquer these sins. Destroy the pride in your heart. Mortify the carnal desires of your flesh. Curb the vanity of a deceitful world."

"How can I do that? I've just stolen your book. On the road, I've just looked lustfully at women."

"You can curb your sins if you take yet one more person with you when you ascend to God's transfiguring presence. Take also John, the grace of God who 'stands knocking at your door.'" Still walking, Antonio turned to Martin. "God is ever ready to enter your heart, brother. And He will enter it. You need only to open the door of your spirit. God has revealed to you the evil that you have done and that you still struggle with inside. That revelation is the gift of grace. Now, in God and God's grace, preserve the good which you have begun. What good, you say? You have returned my book. And you have returned yourself."

"But I can't stay."

"Do you wish to be happy?"

"With all my heart."

"I've not yet taught about the Book of Tobit in Scripture. Perhaps I should take that up soon with you students. Fra Martin, take to heart the words that Tobit spoke to his son on his deathbed. 'Remember the Lord our God all your days!' All your days, son of Tobit. Remember the Lord all your days and then you will be happy."

"Is it possible to be truly happy?"

Antonio smiled. "It's possible. Look around you."

The men halted. They were standing in the center of a field cropped low by countless sheep and goats. Far off to their right, a herd of white, black, and speckled ewes and lambs bleated intermittently. Two shepherds were seated beneath a tree at the edge of the clearing.

"This is a beautiful scene. Surely God dwells here. When God dwells in the soul, the soul becomes even more beautiful than all of this. For who can be more blessed or more happy than one in whom God has set up His dwelling place? What else can you need or what else can possibly make you richer? You have everything when you have within you the One Who made all things, the only One Who can satisfy the longings of your spirit, without Whom whatever exists is as nothing."

Antonio took Martin's hands in his own and raised their arms skyward. Martin, following Antonio's example, lifted his face to the heavens growing dusky with evening. Antonio's voice rang out with joy, "O Possession Which contains all things within Yourself, truly blessed is the person who has You, truly happy whoever possesses You because he then owns that Goodness which alone can make the human mind completely happy.

"But, dear God, what can I give to come to possess You? If I give away everything, do You think that I will have You in exchange? You are much higher than the highest heavens. You are deeper than the deepest abyss, longer than the longest distance, wider than the widest ocean.

"How, then, can I, a worm, a dead dog, a tiny flea, a son of man, come to possess You?"

Antonio paused and Martin felt the anguish of the priest's cry echoing in his own heart. How could he, a sinner, possess the happiness that comes from possessing God?

With his arms and face still stretched heavenward, Antonio continued to cry out, "Job rightly says, when he speaks of divine wisdom,

'It cannot be valued in the gold of Ophir,
in precious onyx or sapphire.
Gold and glass cannot equal it,
nor can it be exchanged for jewels of fine gold . . .
the price of wisdom is beyond pearls.'

O Lord God, I do not have these riches; what, then, can I give to possess You?"

The boy's hands were stretched to their uppermost limit and then slowly lowered. As Antonio lowered his hands, he also dropped his voice in prayer,

"O Lord, I already know Your answer. 'Give Me yourself,' You say, 'and I will give you Myself. Give Me your mind and you will have Me in your mind. Keep all your possessions, but only give Me your soul. I have heard enough of your words; I do not need your works; only give Me yourself, forever.'"

The men's hands were dropped before them, still joined. *Lord, let me give myself to You,* Martin prayed. *Take my poor gift, Lord, and make me happy.*

The question came softly. "Do you want to have God always in your mind?"

Martin's voice trembled. "Oh, brother, I want it. I want it so much."

"Then obey Him. We must be obedient to Christ rather than to our own whims, for we must not serve our Lord only with words. If the heart is humble, the body is obedient. Humility begets obedience. Fra Francesco knows that humility is best supported by poverty. He calls us to follow Lady Poverty, for whoever possesses poverty is rich and wealthy. Where there is real poverty, there is found abundance. Do you understand this?"

"I want to understand it."

Antonio raised his eyes heavenward. "O inestimable worth of poverty! Who does not possess you, possesses nothing, even though they may possess everything. What joy there is in you! For when we are poor and humble, we empty ourselves of all that we possess. Then we are hollow, able to contain anything poured into us. Into us, O God, pour an infusion of divine grace until we overflow with joy."

"Lord, let me have nothing so that I may have everything that is You," Martin whispered.

The joy in Francesco's followers had attracted Martin. The joy in Antonio inspired him. If only he could possess God! Then he would need nothing else, neither the freedom of the streets nor the love of women nor the assurance of gold. God alone would be sufficient.

Martin squeezed Antonio's hands. "Brother, how can I return to the ordine?"

Antonio, who was still gazing upward, lowered his glance. His dark eyes found Martin's.

"You have never left the ordine. The book is back. You are back. No more needs to be said."

Martin dropped to his knees before the priest. "Brother, forgive me." This time, his sorrow was genuine.

Placing his hand on Martin's shoulder, Antonio pronounced absolution. "For your penance, you must daily practice emptying yourself to be filled totally with God. When you have done this completely, you must speak to the people of Montpellier about the possession of God. Find those who will listen, even if there are only one or two. Tell of the Possession Who will possess you. Urge them to empty themselves to the One Who can fill them. Will you do that?"

Martin nodded. The joy in his heart was bubbling up, overflowing.

"God, empty me of myself and fill me with You," he begged.

The joy in his heart began to thaw the iciness in his spirit, melting out of him greed, lust, and desire, and spreading in its place a tiny, warm glow of the Son. A great ledge of ice still clung to his soul, but he would beg God to melt it all. When the Son totally filled him, he would spread His brilliance to others. He would illuminate Montpellier with the light of Christ.

NOTES

In the history of the saint, an unnamed novice at Montpellier stole Antonio's *Commentary on the Psalms*, with the likely intent of selling it and leaving the order. Antonio prayed for the return of the book. A hideous beast appeared to the novice, threatening to kill him and throw his body in a river if he didn't return the volume. The young man returned the book, was lovingly forgiven by Antonio, and returned to the order to become a model religious (Purcell 131–32). Today the Franciscan friary in Bologna claims to have preserved the stolen book.

History records the incident of Antonio silencing the frogs at Montpellier during prayer (Purcell 132). It also tells how Antonio and another brother walked through a town without saying a word. Following their journey, Antonio remarked that they had preached well by example.

Hagiographers also record the miracle of Antonio disappearing from Mass in the manner described in this chapter, and, at the same time, singing the Office with the brothers, then reappearing to complete his homily. Some accounts claim that this miracle happened at Easter in Montpellier (Rig 7, Ben 5). Others have it occurring on Holy Thursday in Limoges.

Antonio was known as the Hammer of Heretics (Ben 4). The whipping that Martin feared was part of the discipline in some other orders but not generally in Francesco's convents.

Antonio's words are from SK 9–13, 19–23, 71–75; and Purcell 125.

Scripture verses are from 1 John 4:9 ("By this has the charity . . ."); 1 John 1:8 ("If we say . . ."); Revelation 3:20 (image of God knocking at the door); Philippians 1:6 ("Preserve the good . . ."); Tobit 4:5 ("Remember the Lord . . ."); Job 28:16–18 ("It cannot be valued . . .").

13

Seigneur Varden

City Square, Toulouse, France (Summer 1225)

Under a high summer sun, Seigneur Varden perspired in his black robe while he preached from a wooden platform at the edge of the main square of Toulouse. His tall, slender stature and white hair accurately gave him the look of austerity and holiness. Like all perfecti, he fasted three days a week on bread and water and never ate meat, eggs, cheese, or milk. Several times daily, he recited the Lord's Prayer sixteen times in succession. He considered the world's goods and attractions to be little better than a dog's vomit.

When he had become a perfecti, he had deeded his small estate and castle over to the elders of his faith. They had retained him as landlord, but he now owned nothing but his faith. His life, he realized, had not begun until he had joined the Cathars. Prior to that time, worries about his family and his lands had consumed his attention.

Seigneur Varden's grandfather had owned a huge estate here in the Languedoc, but the custom of dividing inheritances equally among descendants had sliced his lands into smaller sections. Each of his grandfather's eight sons had to share in the property.

Seigneur Varden's father had sired nine surviving sons, so Seigneur Varden's inheritance had amounted to only seven acres near Toulouse, part of it swamp and much of it forest. For all his married life, he had struggled to keep his wife decently clothed and his children fed. But how to divide his minuscule inheritance among his own three sons? What could they do with little more than two acres of ground apiece? And what dowry could his two daughters bring to a marriage?

One June market day many years ago, when Seigneur Varden had not solved these difficulties, he had ridden into Toulouse to visit Renault the weaver. Renault was a huge man with hands as thick as turnips, yet he wove the most delicate kerchiefs. His prices were steep, but the lord wanted to purchase something lovely for his lady's feast day.

Seigneur Varden had looked at Renault's wares and then asked, "Have you anything more?"

"I have more precious goods than these," Renault had replied. "Would you like to know more about them?"

Varden was curious. "Oui."

"My goods are from God, and you may know God as well." Renault spoke softly, "Such goods will kindle in your heart the love of God."

"I attend Mass every Sunday and holy day," Varden had said.

"Is that enough?" Renault had asked. "If you would like to learn more of what I have to give, come to me today at the hour of None and I will teach you."

Thus had begun Seigneur Varden's conversion. Two years later, with Renault at his side, he received the consolamentum and became a perfecti. Later he had deeded his castle to the Cathars, enrolled his daughters as perfecti to live there in the hospice, and watched two of his sons and his wife also become believers.

Through his frequent preaching, Varden had made many converts among the people of Toulouse. He knew that his way of life meant as much as the words he spoke. Both together might convert another soul in the cluster of people who today had come from market to listen attentively. If any expressed an interest in learning more, either he or Renault, who was part of today's crowd, would teach them.

The crowd was attentive but obviously minding the sun. Here and there some folks fanned themselves with their hats or even their bare palms. Those near the market stalls hugged the shade. Varden decided to be brief.

As he spoke, he noticed a gray-robed brother slip into the crowd not three yards from Renault. The difference in size between the two men made Varden envision a black bear about to pounce on a gray mountain goat. The comical image didn't humor him. The brother hadn't come to be converted. He came to refute.

The lord felt a surge of bitterness. Ever since he had become a perfecti, the Roman Church had been warring against the Cathars in the name of religion. He remembered well the year of his consolamentum. Not two months after, Père Domingo de Guzmán had walked barefoot into Toulouse to preach against the Cathars. Domingo had called the Good Men Albigensians after the town of Albi in which many of the Cathars lived. Seigneur Varden had listened attentively to public debates between preacher and perfecti. Often these culminated in angry verbal exchanges in which each party accused the other of being the Antichrist.

Two years later, the easily disliked preacher, Pierre de Castelnau, was murdered, and Pope Innocenzo III called for the first Albigensian crusade against the Good Men. Warfare consumed the territory of the Languedoc, with many towns around Toulouse falling to the crusaders. Tales of massacres, rapes, mutilations, burnings, and dismembering on both sides filtered into the city. Battles became political with counts vying for whatever territories they could conquer, no matter what religion their inhabitants espoused.

Twice Toulouse had been viciously assaulted. Twice it had repelled the enemy. Now the Catharist sympathizer, Count Raymond VII, held nearly complete control of the area. Despite the count's promise to the pope not to protect the sect, the Catharist bishop still remained safely in the city. Any gray-robed brother who tried to stir up the followers of Rome against Seigneur Varden would instead rally the Cathars to the lord's defense.

Seigneur Varden decided to assume the offensive. He would turn the crowd against the brother.

"The clergy tell you that serving God consists in attending Mass," he projected his voice to the farthest corners of the square. "But listen to the Gospel of John: 'Jesus rose from supper and laid aside His garments and took a towel and girded Himself. After that, He poured water into a basin and began to wash the disciples' feet.'"

Varden walked back and forth as he preached, his hand and head movements emphasizing certain key points. "He said to them, 'Do you know what I have done to you? You call Me Master and Lord and you say well, for so I am. If I then, your Lord and Master, have washed your feet, you also ought to wash one another's feet. For I have given you an example, that you should do as I have done to you.' So we must humbly serve one another as Christ commanded."

He gestured toward the brother. "But do the Roman clergy do this? Listen to the Gospels of Matthew and Mark." As the lord plunged into Christ's long denunciation of the evil and hypocrisy of religious leaders, he was certain that his words would be effective. During his own conversion, Renault had quoted him these very passages. Seigneur Varden then asked the crowd the same question that Renault had asked him.

"To whom do these passages refer?" And he gave Renault's answer. "They refer to the clergy and the monks."

The crowd shifted and several turned to stare at the brother. Those standing near him, including Renault, sidled away until he was left standing alone in a small, cleared space.

"The doctors of the Roman Church are proud of their dress and carriage. They love honor and to be called Père, but we do not have such honors. They frequently visit women of the town, for reasons that you certainly can imagine, but we each have a wife and live chastely with her.

"The clergy are rich and want more, taking even the money of poor widows to support their ceremonies and buildings. But we are content with simple food and clothes and want no more. Look at the knights and the bishops who send them to battle with the Church's blessings. They fight and war and burn and kill the poor, but Christ said, 'He who takes the sword will perish by it.' We suffer from them for our righteousness, for, as you well know, they have killed several of our members and warred against our city."

A cry of support rose from the crowd as they recalled the bitterness of their city's siege and their own united, desperate struggle to beat back the crusaders.

"Their clergy do nothing, but we work with our hands. Only their clergy may teach and no one else, but among us women as well as men may teach. In fact, a disciple of seven days may instruct another."

Seigneur Varden paused as he swept his arms before him as if to encompass the entire city. "Hardly a teacher among them knows by heart three connected chapters of the New Testament, but nearly all among us can recite the text in our own tongue, for we have our own Scriptures written in the language that we speak. And because we have the true faith of Christ and teach a holy life and doctrine, the Roman Church persecutes us without cause, bringing some of us even to death."

A murmur of assent swept through the crowd. Varden noticed a swift motion near the brother. Two brawny youths pushed toward the man, but Renault leaped in front of them and, with outstretched arms as thick as clubs, blocked their path. Like all perfecti, Renault opposed violence. The youths backed off, and Varden continued to speak.

"The clergy say much but do nothing. They bind heavy burdens and place them on their followers, but we practice what we teach. They insist that traditions of men be followed more than the commandments of God, to observe their fasts, festivals, Masses, and other human institutions, but we persuade others only to keep the doctrines of Christ and of the apostles. They load penitents with the most grievous penances, which they do nothing to relieve, but we, following Christ's example, tell the sinner, 'Go and sin no more,' and remit all his sins by the imposition of hands, therefore paving his way into eternal life in heaven. On the other hand, they, by their rigorous teaching, send almost all souls to hell. Think which faith is more perfect: ours, or that of the Church of Rome?"

Varden paused. "If you wish to learn more, come and speak to me now. I, as well as other Christians, will teach you." With that, he turned and descended the platform, the wild applause of the crowd sounding in his ears.

As the applause died, a deep, firm voice shot forth, "Who among you destroys his entire garden because worms and rot have ruined five cabbages?"

A hush fell over the crowd as heads turned toward the brother. He was speaking even as he walked toward the platform.

"The Church was commended to Peter by Christ with the words, 'Feed My lambs,' not once but three times. Not once did he tell Peter to shear them or to fleece them. It is as if Jesus said, 'If you love Me because of Myself, feed My sheep, not your sheep but Mine. Seek My glory among them, not yours; My gain and not yours, since the love of God is proved by the love of one's neighbor.'"

The friar bowed to Seigneur Varden as he climbed the steps to the platform. As he reached the flat planking, he turned to Varden and called out, "He who just addressed you was right in condemning the corrupt clergy."

A whistle of amazement swept across the square. Even Seigneur Varden, who had heard many preachers, hadn't heard one condemn other members of his Church.

"Woe to that shepherd of the Church who does not feed his sheep even one time, but shears and fleeces them three or four times. To such a shepherd, God says in Genesis, 'The king of Sodom,' who is the devil, demands, 'Give me their souls. The rest you can keep for yourself.'"

The friar seemed to gaze intently at each person before him. "I ask you again. Do you destroy an entire garden because worms and rot have ruined five cabbages? Don't you instead pluck the cabbages and throw them on the dung heap, then return to cultivate and enjoy the good fruits of your garden? God agrees with the lord who just addressed you. The rotten clergy will be plucked out of God's garden that is the Church. God will give their souls to the devil, who will throw them into hell to rot."

He paused momentarily. "Come here tomorrow at this time and learn about God's garden of true faith that can become for you the garden of paradise whose fruit is eternal life."

The brother descended the steps, bowed to Varden, who still stood by them, and walked off toward the convent of the Lesser Brothers.

As the brother disappeared, Renault touched Varden's shoulder. "Your speech almost got him beaten."

"Who is he?"

"They say his name is Père Antonio."

The next day, under a hotter sun than the day before, Seigneur Varden and Renault joined a small crowd in the main square of Toulouse. When they had come within three yards of the preaching platform, they stopped. Here, a few other Catharist believers congregated.

The day was sultry. Every inch of shade was crammed with bodies. Those standing in the sun fanned themselves with scraps of cloth. Beads of sweat were glistening on nearly every forehead when the news rippled through the group, "Here he comes."

Two men dressed in patched gray tunics approached the platform from a tiny side street. The heavier one remained at the steps, while Père Antonio ascended the platform, raised his hands over the crowd for silence, and then bowed his head. After a few moments, he raised his eyes to heaven and, in a sturdy but gentle voice, began to pray.

"O Light of the world, infinite God, Father of eternity, Giver of wisdom and knowledge and ineffable Dispenser of every spiritual grace, You know all things before they are made. You Who make the darkness and the light, put forth Your hand and touch my mouth. Make it like a sharp sword to utter eloquently Your words. Make my tongue, O Lord, like a chosen arrow to declare faithfully Your wonders. Put Your Spirit, O Lord, in my heart that I may perceive. Put it in my soul that I may retain. Put it in my conscience that I may meditate. Lovingly, holily, mercifully, clemently, and gently inspire me with Your grace."

As Antonio continued his prayer, Varden surveyed the crowd. The fanning and shifting had decreased as if Antonio's prayer had been a gentle breeze to drive back the heat.

"'God said, "Let there be light," and there was light.' In the name of the Father and of the Son and of the Holy Spirit." Antonio crossed himself as he spoke, and those followers of Rome did the same.

"Let us examine the seven days of God's creation, beginning with the first, and apply them to our life as followers of Christ."

Seigneur Varden nodded. Antonio was going to directly attack Catharist beliefs. He was speaking from the Old Testament, which the Cathars knew was written by Satan. He stated that God created the material universe when Satan, not God, had done so.

"The first day represents the Incarnation of our Savior. Without our Savior, we would be faithless and lost. Without light, our world would not exist. The light is Christ, 'Who dwells in unapproachable light' and 'gives light to every person coming into the world.'"

The Cathars knew that only those of their faith had God's true enlightenment.

"When the Father said, 'Let there be light,' He was also speaking of His Son's Incarnation. Saint John expresses this more succinctly: 'The Word became flesh and made His dwelling among us.'"

Renault leaned toward Seigneur Varden. "As I expected. He claims that Christ was truly human flesh instead of spirit alone."

"When the prophet Ezekiel writes, 'the hand of the Lord came upon me,' he is referring to the Son in Whom and through Whom the Father created all things."

Varden tried to calculate how many teachings of his faith Antonio was disputing. Was this the fourth or fifth? The Father created only spiritual things. The Father created the Son.

"God said, 'Let there be light,' and the Light of the world was born of the Virgin Mary. 'The darkness which covered the abyss'—that is, the hearts of men—was dispelled."

Six. Christ's birth through Mary was an illusion. God would not have entrapped himself in human flesh to be born in a human way from a woman's womb.

"On the second day, God said, 'Let there be a vault in the middle of the waters, to divide the waters in two.' The vault is Baptism, which, like a vault, divides the deep from the shallow waters, believers from unbelievers."

Following the example of the evil John the Baptizer, the followers of the Roman Church espoused water baptism, even for infants. The Good Men, knowing that water was material, and therefore the creation of an evil god, followed Christ, who baptized with fire and the Holy Spirit.

"God set a vault between the waters to divide them. This vault is Baptism. Sinners, however, break the pact which they made with God at Baptism. The earth, laboring under the sins of greed, lust, and pride, merits the curse pronounced upon it in the Book of Revelation, 'Woe to the inhabitants of the earth.'"

As Antonio continued to expound the sins of humanity, Varden glanced about the crowd. The priest was speaking to followers of Rome now, for they were the ones consumed by these vices.

"On the third day, God said, 'Let the earth bring forth vegetation, every kind of plant that bears seed and every kind of fruit tree on earth that bears fruit with its seed in it.' The earth, plowed and broken up in springtime, produces abundant fruit at harvest. Thus, the earth represents the Passion of our Lord Whose bruised and broken Body, 'crushed for our sins,' produces the abundant fruit of the heavenly Kingdom."

Christ had not really suffered and died, for He had no real body. The Passion was but an illusion.

"On the fourth day, God said, 'Let there be two lights in the dome of the sky.' The sky is the risen Christ, resplendent like the sun in the glory of His resurrection and incorruptible in His Body like the moon. Thus, the fourth day prefigures the resurrection of our Lord."

As Christ's death was illusion, so was His resurrection and incorruptible body, for He never had and never would assume evil flesh.

"On the fifth day, God made 'birds of the air.' This text recalls the mystery of the Ascension when the Son of God flew like a bird to the right side of His Father."

Where did Antonio get these comparisons? His theology was heretical, but his knowledge of Scripture and its applications was stunning. As a preacher, Varden recognized and admired talent when he heard it. If only this man were a Cathar!

"On the sixth day, God said, 'Let us make people in Our image, after Our likeness.' God blew into the man's nostrils the breath of life, and so the man became a living being."

Satan had taken apostate spirits who had rebelled against the good God and, forming bodies of earth, had imprisoned those spirits in them. The devil, and not the good God, had made humanity.

"The image of God in humanity, deformed and obscured by sin, was restored and illumined by the Holy Spirit, Who breathed the breath of life into each person. Thus, the sixth day represents the sending of the Holy Spirit into the world at Pentecost. The Holy Spirit, given at Pentecost, impresses on our hearts the Spirit of God and so makes of each of us 'a living being.' Due to the gift of the Spirit, we can recognize the Father in the face of the Son and we can follow that Son through the light of faith."

Not everyone possessed the Holy Spirit. God granted this gift only to those who had received the consolamentum.

"'Since on the seventh day God was finished with the work He had been doing, He rested.' On the last day, the faithful will also rest from all their work and suffering and God 'shall wipe every tear from their eyes.' The seventh day is the gift of eternal life. On that day, the Church will be welcomed by Christ, her

Spouse, who will 'give her a reward of her labors and let her works praise her at the city gates.' Those gates are the final judgment, at which Christ will say, 'Come, you have My Father's blessing.' May each of us be counted worthy to enter those gates and forever 'feast in the kingdom of God.' Amen."

Cheers rose from the crowd as Antonio descended the platform. Some surged toward him. Renault and Varden remained like statues of stone in the shifting mob.

"He is forceful," Renault said.

To Varden's right, three Catharist believers were kneeling, their backs bowed. "And effective," he added. "Apparently, he has made some converts."

The two men worked their way toward the kneeling trio. They must be won back to the true faith before they succumbed to Antonio's words. The remainder of the day, Renault and Varden worked with the men until they finally accepted an invitation to a gathering in the castle that Varden had deeded to his Cathar superiors.

In the evening coolness of the castle's sitting room, the talk was of Antonio. Residents, both perfecti and believers, tore apart his speech as wild dogs rip to shreds a fallen stag. As one of the elders, Seigneur Varden took the lead in the discussion. The sun dipped lower. The trio from the square excused themselves and started home. Discussion continued among those left. Only past midnight did Varden and two other remaining perfecti finally surrender to weariness and retire for the night.

Varden, however, lay awake. Antonio troubled him. The priest was sincere in his heresy. How could he so firmly believe falsehood? Varden would listen to him preach again and would find the holes in the fabric of that man's faith.

Four days later, Seigneur Varden was again preaching. He had decided to attack head-on the core of Antonio's speech—namely, that God created the world. The sky was overcast and the day pleasant. The crowd was ample. Again, Antonio was in the gathering.

"It is perfectly clear from the Scriptures that the god and lord who is the creator of the world is different from Him to Whom the blessed commend their spirits," Varden began. "Our opponents say that according to Genesis the Lord is the creator of the visible things of this world: the heavens and the earth, the sea, men and beasts, birds and reptiles."

He glared at Antonio. Several listeners did the same.

"But I say that the creator of the visible things of this world is not the true God. And I prove this from the evil of his words and deeds and the changeable character of his words and deeds as described in the Old Testament. Where should I begin? The whole Old Testament is filled with the evil of this god.

"Abram, who was called by this god to leave his homeland, gave his wife Sarai to the Egyptian king and said that she was his sister. The king intended to commit fornication with her because of this lie. This same Abram committed adultery with a slave woman so that he would father a son."

Seigneur Varden continued to name men and women who served the Old Testament god but whose lives were sinful—Jacob, Rachel, Rahab, David. He gave examples of slaughters of many innocent people, all done in the name of this god.

"It is evident enough to the wise that the true God could not be the creator who mercilessly tempts men and women to destruction. The good God is the God of the New Testament, the God of the Spirit, the God of Jesus, the God we serve. To Him be all praise and glory and honor. Amen. Alleluia!"

The following day, while Seigneur Varden and the other residents were taking a light breakfast in the lord's castle-turned-hospice, a servant brought him a message.

"Père Antonio is here to see you, Seigneur."

So, his rival had come! Varden wished to speak to him privately. "Lower the drawbridge and bring him into the sitting room," he commanded.

With a sip of wine, he washed down his final bite of bread, then bid good day to his fellow perfecti and believers.

In this sitting room dwelled ghosts of memories. Here, before joining the Cathars, Varden had often sat to work on accounts and ledgers. Here his sons had shown him little boats they'd made of wooden planks and his daughters had sung their childish songs. After the castle had become a Catharist hospice, Varden's wife, little more than an enfleshed reed, had lain upon a bed here. She had received the consolamentum here and had every sin forgiven. Then, to ensure that she would sin no more, she had voluntarily begun the final, suicidal fast called the *endura*. After five days of bloodletting in warm baths and eating and drinking nothing, she had entered eternal life from this very room. Here, not two weeks ago, Varden had presided at the consolamentum of the city coppersmith, whom he had sent to Carcassonne to preach. Now he would confront a man whose faith he had rejected.

"You are dismissed," Varden waved to the servant as he ushered Antonio into the room.

Now alone, Varden and Antonio bowed to each other, then broke into grins. "So each of us recognizes the other's breeding," Varden said, extending his hands.

Antonio grasped Varden's hands in his own. "Your hands are as rough as mine," he said. "It seems that we have both exchanged breeding for weeding."

"I have plucked a few rotten cabbages out of my garden," Varden admitted.

Antonio laughed.

Varden nodded toward a small side table around which three wooden chairs were arranged. "Have a seat."

As the men sat, Varden asked, "Have you come to convert me?"

Antonio was still smiling. "I can't do that, Seigneur. Only God can convert."

"He seems to work effectively through you."

"Any victory is His, not mine. But I did come to speak to you about Him, if only to satisfy myself that I've done so."

"Your Church is in heresy. It abandoned the way centuries ago. We have returned to faith as it was meant to be."

"You have made yourself superior to God." Antonio's voice was gentle but firm.

Varden had submitted himself to God. "What do you mean?"

"God is the author of our life and our freedom. Without God, we would not exist. Do you agree?"

"Oui."

"Yesterday, you questioned the Old Testament's apparent evil done in the name of God. You concluded that the God of the Old Testament cannot be the God of the New. By denying the goodness and wisdom of the Old Testament

God, you deny the goodness and wisdom of Christ, Who quoted the Old Testament extensively."

"Christ commanded us, 'Love your enemies and pray for those who persecute you. If any one strikes you on the right cheek, turn to him the other also.' He said, 'Every one who is angry with his brother shall be liable to judgment,'" Varden argued. "The killings, fornications, and deceits of the Old Testament, done in the name of God, do not follow these dictates of love."

"'O the depth of the riches and wisdom and knowledge of God! How unsearchable are his judgments and how inscrutable his ways!

For who has known the mind of the Lord,
or who has been his counselor?'"

Varden knew that argument. The priest had backed him into a corner by implying that no human could understand God's mysterious ways. Before he could think of a rejoinder, Antonio asked another question.

"Do you remember what Christ said about abolishing the law?"

"Oui. 'Think not that I have come to abolish the law and the prophets; I have come not to abolish them but to fulfill them.'"

Antonio smiled. "Oui. And how did He fulfill it? Precisely by taking upon Himself all the deceits, murders, fornications, lies, and every other sin of the past, present, and future and nailing them with Himself to the cross. God broke His Own law against killing by delivering Himself up as the Son to be crucified. He did this for our total and greater good."

Varden interrupted, "Christ's death was an illusion, not a fact."

"So you say. By denying Christ's death, you deny His humanity. Thus you negate the very foundation of Christianity."

"God, Who is all good, would not have taken to Himself sinful flesh."

"The beginning of the Gospel of John, which you quote, states, 'And the Word became flesh and dwelt among us.'"

Varden knew the answer to that objection. "This illusion is pointed out by Saint Paul in his letter to the Philippians where he writes, 'Christ Jesus, who, though he was in the form of God, did not count equality with God a thing to be grasped, but emptied himself, taking the form of a servant.' The word 'form' is used."

"And yet the passage continues, '. . . taking the form of a servant, being born in the likeness of men. And being found in human form he humbled himself and became obedient unto death, even death on a cross,'" Antonio countered. "In his first letter to the Corinthians, Saint Paul writes, 'If there is no resurrection of the dead, then Christ has not been raised; if Christ has not been raised, then our preaching is in vain and your faith is in vain.' You deny the actual death of Christ and His actual, bodily resurrection. How can you deny the eyewitness accounts of the Gospels?"

"The apostles and Saint Paul were deceived by what they saw. They could not differentiate between illusion and reality."

"You were married, were you not?"

The lord nodded at this sudden change in subject.

"A wedding celebrates the union of two people, a bride and a groom. Many times weddings are arranged between two contending families to produce peace between them, the man taking a bride from his rival's family. In the human race, dissension existed between God and humanity. God wished to establish peace. All the messengers and legates sent by God could do nothing, so God the Father consented to send His Son, Who united Himself to our human nature in the womb of the Virgin Mary. Thus, the union of God and man was complete in the Son. Two disparate natures joined. In Christ, we are granted union with the Father, forgiveness of sins, and a share in eternal life."

"You must know that you will never convince me of your heresies."

Antonio stood. "God enlightens souls, Seigneur, not I."

Varden stood as well.

"Do not trouble yourself, Seigneur. I can find my way out."

"Nonsense. I will walk with you to the gatehouse." Varden smiled weakly. "Have I disappointed you by not rushing to embrace your God?"

Antonio laughed as the two men came out of the sitting room. "With God there is always hope that misguided souls will know the truth. I am only to tell of His truth." Antonio turned to Varden as the men walked into the sunlight. The priest's black eyes were bright with earnestness. "There is truth, Seigneur. Christ said, 'I am the way, and the truth, and the life.' Saint John tells us that 'in him there is no falsehood.'"

Antonio's gaze was unsettling. "Père, I admire your sincerity."

"And I admire yours. But it often happens that sincere people are sincerely wrong." Antonio bowed. "I will continue to pray for you, Seigneur."

"And I for you."

At the gatehouse, the two men grasped hands again before bidding farewell.

Weeks passed. Seigneur Varden preached. Antonio preached. Usually they were in each other's audience. Sometimes sentiment supported one, sometimes the other.

Antonio's crowd was swelling. Certain shopkeepers closed their doors on the days the priest spoke and came to hear him. If he was speaking at noon, women would begin to arrive in the morning in order to claim a spot near the platform. Always, after he preached, Antonio would be mobbed. Varden often thought of approaching him, but he had no reason to do so. He didn't believe the Roman theology. Nevertheless, he couldn't discount Antonio's holiness. He was teaching the Lesser Brothers theology at their convent. He was said to have cured paralysis and epilepsy with the sign of the cross. People claimed that he spoke in strange languages.

Where were the holes in the fabric of his faith?

One warm Saturday, under a clearing gray sky, Antonio was on the platform preaching. Seigneur Varden stood about ten yards from him in a crowd that was packed so tightly in the square that a horse and rider would have had great difficulty pushing through. With all eyes on him, Antonio said, "And so, my people, today will be the last time that I preach to you. Tomorrow after Mass at dawn, I will be leaving for Castres."

A cry went up from the crowd. Antonio raised his hands for silence.

"So I want to leave you with this final message."

Here it comes, Varden thought. *Now he will pit them against us. This crowd will want to show him how deeply they love him and his God. Trouble will begin with this speech.*

"The Apostle John tells us that, following Christ's resurrection, 'when the doors were shut where the disciples were assembled, Jesus came and stood in their midst and said to them, "Peace be with you." When He had said this, He showed them His hands and His side.' Saint Luke, who describes the same incident, says that Christ told the apostles, 'Look at My hands and feet. It is really I.

Touch Me and see, for a spirit has no flesh and bones as you see I have.' When
He had said this, He showed them His hands and His feet."

Antonio looked squarely at Varden. "It is my opinion that Christ showed
His apostles the wounds in His hands, feet, and side for four reasons. First, He
showed the wounds to prove to them that He had really risen."

Antonio looked across the crowd as he held his long, expressive hands,
palms outward, toward them. "By showing His wounds, Jesus intended to dem-
onstrate that the faith of His disciples had nothing to do with current or popular
opinion about Him. It had nothing to do with theories or interpretations of
Scripture. Faith was based instead on the direct knowledge and experience
which His followers had gained through their familiarity with Him. By showing His wounds, He wished to remove all doubt from their minds. May He
remove doubt from the minds of any of you present."

I have no doubt, Varden thought. *My faith is secure.*

"Second, He revealed His wounds to the Church and faithful souls because
within those wounds is a place of refuge." Antonio raised his left hand skyward
and brought it down gracefully to rest in the palm of his right hand. "Just as a
dove builds its nest in a safe place to protect itself against the attacks of a hawk,
so Christians find shelter from the attacks of the devil by constructing for themselves a nesting place within the wounds of Christ." He held his hands, one
nesting within the other, toward the crowd. "Nest there and find solace."

IN WOUNDS THAT ARE ILLUSORY, SOLACE IS IMPOSSIBLE. The words
that came from nowhere pricked Seigneur Varden's soul.

"Third, Christ showed His wounds to impress on our hearts the signs of His
sufferings, and fourth, to evoke in us compassion so that we would not crucify
Him again with the nails of our sins."

Antonio's voice rose with fervor as his eyes sought each person present.
"Christ shows us the wounds in His hands, feet, and side and says, 'See the
hands that made and formed you; see how they have been pierced by nails.
Behold My side, pierced by a lance, from which came forth My Church, like
Eve who came from the side of Adam. The angel, stationed at the gates of
paradise after Adam's sin, has been washed away by the blood flowing from
My side. The water flowing from My side has extinguished the flame of his
fiery sword.'"

Antonio's gaze again caught Varden's. "'Do not crucify Me again. Do not pollute the blood of the covenant by which you have been sanctified.'"

He paused and lowered his voice. "When our Lord had shown the apostles the wounds in His hands, feet, and side, He repeated, 'Peace be with you.' Only if we keep in our hearts the memory of Christ's wounds and listen to His words will we find true peace in our hearts."

Seigneur Varden had found peace with the Cathars. He had been assured of eternal life through the remission of his sins. He had provided for his children. He had friends and supporters in the faith.

"May the true Lord, Who is true God and true man, grant you the peace that comes from knowing, loving, and obeying the truth. Amen."

Today no wild cheers swept the crowd. Instead, a hush punctuated by quiet sobbing lay like a shroud on the audience. As Antonio descended from the platform, people threw themselves on their knees before him.

"Don't leave us, Père."

"Before you go, bless me, Père."

"Bless me, too, Père."

"My child, Père."

"May the Lord have mercy on me."

"Père, forgive me."

The pleas of stricken individuals around Antonio gradually grew fainter as Varden and a good portion of the crowd slowly pressed out of the square. Varden had found the holes in the fabric of Antonio's faith and they were not mere holes at all. The holes were the wounds of Christ. Had Varden believed that those wounds were real and not mere illusions, he, too, would have proclaimed the Roman faith to the world.

NOTES

Antonio was sent to the Languedoc "to preach against the heretics." So state his biographies. No details are given. Toulouse was a stronghold of the Cathars *(Ben 4)*, who were called the Albigensians by those not adhering to the Catharist doctrines. The name came from the town of Albi, a Catharist stronghold and the source of the heresy in France.

Antonio taught theology to the friars in Toulouse and engaged in open debates with the Cathars. Seigneur Varden and the other Cathars in this chapter are fictional characters who most likely had real-life counterparts in Toulouse. They accurately represent the lifestyles, ceremonies, and beliefs of the Cathars of the period.

Antonio's words are from Stoddard 53 (prayer before his sermon), SK 14–18 (his preaching on the seven days of creation), SK 54–57 (why Christ showed his wounds), SK 111–15 (his condemnation of corrupt clergy), and SK 89–93 (his comparison of the Incarnation to a marriage).

Seigneur Varden's sermon against the corrupt clergy and Renault's conversion of the lord are based on writings by former Catharist Reinerius Saccho, in Maitland's book, *Facts and Documents Illustrative of the History, Doctrine, and Rites of the Ancient Albigensians and Waldenses* (pp. 400–437). The same book's "Sentences and Culpa from the Book of Sentences" (pp. 271–87) describes the *endura* undertaken by Varden's wife. Seigneur Varden's sermon on the creator of the universe is from a Catharist book entitled *The Instruction of the Simple* as described in Jeffrey Russell's book, *Religious Dissent in the Middle Ages* (pp. 74–75).

Scripture verses are: John 13:4–5 ("Jesus rose from supper . . ."); John 13:12–15 ("Do you know what I have done . . ."); Matthew 26:52 ("He who takes the sword . . ."); Matthew 23:4 ("They bind heavy burdens . . ."); John 21:15 ("Feed my lambs . . ."); Genesis 14:21 ("The king of Sodom demands . . ."); Genesis 1 and 2 (the creation story); 1 Timothy 6:16 ("Who dwells in unapproachable light . . ."); John 1:14 ("The Word became flesh . . ."); Ezekiel 37:1 ("The hand of the Lord . . ."); Revelation 12:12 ("Woe to the inhabitants . . ."); Isaiah 53:5 ("Crushed for our sins . . ."); Revelation 21:4 ("Shall wipe every tear . . ."); Proverbs 31:31 ("her a reward . . ."); Matthew 25:34 ("Come, you have my . . ."); Luke 13:29 ("Feast in the kingdom . . ."); Matthew 5:44 ("Love your enemies . . ."); Matthew 5:39 ("If any one strikes you . . ."); Matthew 5:22 ("Every one who is angry . . ."); Romans 11:33 ("O the depth of the riches . . ."); Matthew 5:17 ("Think not that I have come . . ."); Philippians 2:5–8 ("Christ Jesus, who, though . . ."); 1 Corinthians 15:13–14 ("If there is no resurrection . . ."); John 14:6 ("I am the way . . ."); John 7:18 ("In him there is no falsehood . . ."); John 20:19–20 ("When the doors were shut . . ."); Luke 24:39–40 ("Look at my hands . . ."); Song of Solomon 2:14 (image of dove building its nest); and John 20:21 ("Peace be with you . . .").

14

The Seigneur de Châteauneuf-la-Forêt

Chateau, Limoges, France (Early Spring 1226)

The Seigneur de Châteauneuf-la-Forêt knocked on the door of a little house in Limoges. Although the house belonged to Saint Martin's Church and was under the auspices of monks who followed the Rule of Saint Benedict, the monks didn't reside here. They had their own much larger monastery. In this house lived the Lesser Brothers, as poverty-stricken as their name implied. Young and vigorous, the Seigneur de Châteauneuf-la-Forêt nevertheless preferred the presence of these simple, humble men to that of his hunting companions.

The tall, auburn-haired young baron hadn't always been spiritually minded. As a boy, he had loved games, surprises, and feasts. As he grew older, his tastes included lovely damsels. But he had always had a serious side, one that told him that things of the world could never fill the longing in his heart. As he entered maturity, he had turned more completely to the One Who could fill him. He retained a priest to celebrate daily Mass in his chateau's chapel. He gave away his silks and began to live as simply as possible. To put his enlivened faith into action, he himself gave alms to the poor, which included these joyful, faithful brothers. How unaware they were that their grateful response to his provisions was their gift to him.

After a few moments, an unfamiliar brother answered his knock. Startled at first, the baron suddenly had an insight.

"Pardon, but might you be Père Antonio?"

The short, black-bearded brother grinned, his deep-set eyes sparkling. "Oui. How did you know?"

"The brothers said that a Père Antonio, a teacher at their convent school at Toulouse, was coming to become custos here. What do you teach?"

"Scripture. The faith. How to reason. How to pray."

The young baron nodded enthusiastically. "How I would love to learn those things! Might you permit me to join your classes? I know it's an unusual request . . ." His voice trailed off.

"I don't think that's permitted," Antonio remarked.

"I thought not," the baron mumbled.

"But nothing prevents me from holding a class of one. For you, if you wish."

How he wished it! Speechless, he could merely nod.

"Do you wish to have your first class now, Seigneur?"

"Oui! But I had better give you this first."

He turned to his gray-dappled steed and untied a plump leather-wrapped bundle from his saddle. "Two days ago, I was hunting and a stag fell to our dogs and arrows. Here is a shoulder for the brothers."

"Must have been hefty. Very large antlers, I imagine."

"Very large."

Père Antonio took the heavy package. "How generous of you!" He propped the bundle against the house. "You use dogs to hunt. May I ask you if what natural history says about hunting stags is correct?"

"I may not know, but I'll tell you what I do know."

Antonio nodded. "Is this how the hunting is done? Two men go, and one of them whistles and sings. The stag follows the song, taking pleasure in it. Then the other man takes his spear and strikes the stag and kills it."

"That's the customary way."

"Do you realize that the hunting of the rich is the same?"

The comment jolted him.

"The two men are the world and the devil. The world whistles and sings in front of the rich man, who is the stag, showing him pleasures and riches and promising him them. When the stupid fool follows, taking pleasure in them, he is killed by the devil and carried off to hell's kitchen to be skinned and boiled."

"That's precisely what I don't want to have happen to me!"

"Then you wish to be like a wise stag. Such a one is accustomed to leap over thorny and pitted places. When it hears the barking of dogs, unlike the stag that fell to your skill, it makes its way downwind so that its scent is blown away. In the same way the penitent or just man, who it seems you must be, directs his course by practice of devotion so that he may run well and unweariedly toward the prize of his heavenly calling."

That unassuming wrapped shoulder was leading to some undreamed-of insights. "The thorny and pitted places. Those are places of sin, oui?"

"Oui!" Antonio agreed. "The penitent also grows accustomed to leaping over—that is, despising—the thorny places of temporal riches and the pitted places of bodily pleasure and so is no longer captive for destruction but instead released into freedom."

The baron was following these analogies. "We don't release a stag. We boil him!"

The priest chuckled. "But you, Seigneur, wish to avoid boiling! I imagine that when you sense the barking of dogs—that is, the suggestions of the devil—you make your way of action 'downwind.' That is, in all your actions, inward and outward, you take refuge in humility."

"I hope that's so."

"You know, the stag pants after the fountains of water. So the penitent sinner pants after the fountain of confession where he may drink the water of tears. By humility he will immerse himself in that fountain of confession. There, he puts away all that is superfluous and harmful and so grows spiritually young again."

The young man intuited the unasked question. "Oui, I would like to confess."

Antonio smiled. "Allow me to take this shoulder in to the cook. I will return in a moment, Seigneur Cerf."

Seigneur Cerf. The baron beamed at Antonio's new nickname for him: the French word for stag.

NOTES

Antonio became custos of Saint Martin's (Rig 1), which the Benedictine abbot allowed the Lesser Brothers to use. The postulated year is 1226.

While history doesn't physically describe the Seigneur de Châteauneuf-la-Forêt nor give his age, it records that he was devoted to the friars and to Antonio and was, therefore, likely a holy man. This chapter imagines the relationship between the baron and the saint. The gift of the stag's shoulder to the brothers and Antonio's nickname for the baron are fabricated.

This chapter is one example of how Antonio frequently used information from the natural sciences and a medieval bestiary to teach a moral lesson. It also postulates how benefactors supported the Lesser Brothers.

Antonio's words about the stag are from SSF IV 156, 283–284, 286.

15

Gifferd

Saracen Encampment, Jerusalem, Palestine (1226)

Gifferd lay in a small, sturdy hut abuzz with swarms of flies. As a youth, he'd been nicknamed Gifferd because his face was so round and plump. If those who had coined that name saw his gaunt face now, they would be shocked. Outdoors beneath the sun, the sand of the Holy Land had been hot beneath his feet when he had been taken, stripped, and scourged. Now the sand in the hut's shade felt cool to his quivering cheek, cool and wet from the blood that oozed out beneath his half-closed eyelids. How feebly those eyelids fluttered to keep the grains from the now-hollow sockets! Until an hour ago, those sockets had held his eyes. Now his eyes and fingertips were gone.

Outside the hut, voices muttered in a language he couldn't understand. Guards. Why would the head Saracen post guards at his door? Certainly Gifferd was going nowhere. The torturers had broken both his legs.

"Jesus," he choked through a throat parched with thirst. For three days he had been given nothing to eat or drink. Now what moisture he had left in his body was seeping into the sand along with his life.

The world had condensed to a pulse of pain. Despite spasms of agony, images played in his mind. At the judgment, one's whole life races swiftly before one's mind. Was this his judgment?

He saw himself as a child in Le Puy-en-Velay, France, tagging along with his parents to Mass and being enthralled by the incense and the strange language of the priest. Then as he aged, religion had grown boring and annoying.

He had become a notary by studying hard and earning higher marks than other students in his class. He began settling suits between this Christian and that one. Up close, he saw backbiting, scandal, and greed. How many men had he represented who were ready to cheat and lie to get money or land? Nearly all of these went to Mass and piously dropped small sums into the poor box.

How sick he became of religious hypocrisy! He had begun to believe that the Church and its doctrines were a farce. The Eucharist no longer made sense. He had been taught that God was loving and just. But God seemed vicious and unjust. God struck everywhere with pain, suffering, and death. Gifferd had seen his brother's children die of a strange, spotted fever. He had watched his saintly grandmother linger painfully for months, barely able to eat, until death finally claimed her. He had held his dead sister's matted head against his breast while the stillborn baby whom she had been struggling to give birth to lay cold and blue in a blanket at her side. His mother had prayed and lit candles for each of these people. What good had come of her hours spent in his family's chapel before a tapestry of Christ's birth? God was deaf, if God existed. Or else God was cruel and unjust.

He preferred to believe in no God rather than in a cruel, insensitive, and unjust one. He began to say that those who believed in God were stupid. Unlike himself, they refused to admit that the God of their belief couldn't be the God of the world.

Since God didn't exist, Gifferd could do as he pleased. He started by ceasing to pray. Then he stopped attending Mass. He began to frequent taverns and brothels and he made his work his god. He craved success more than money.

If he had to cheat and lie to win his case, he did so. And he was successful. Merchants, barons, and counts came to him with their quarrels. He nearly always won.

In early October 1225, Antonio came to Le Puy-en-Velay as guardian of the convent of the Lesser Brothers. Soon Gifferd heard some of his clients speaking about the new priest. "He speaks words of fire," they said. "Everyone is going to hear him."

Gifferd had no desire to hear him.

But meet him he did. Gifferd had been riding home after visiting one of his more prosperous clients, a baron who was squabbling with his brother over a portion of the family estate. Each claimed that their recently deceased father had promised them the choicest fields and manor house. The father had died without a will. The family had summoned Gifferd in an attempt to prevent bloodshed.

Gifferd liked to be neatly dressed, for the better dressed he was, the more his clients trusted him and the better they paid. So that day he had worn his blue-and-yellow button cap with blue stockings and yellow outer bliant skirt, slit in front and back so that he looked quite fashionable astride his black steed. He had chosen his cherry-red cloak and fastened it at his shoulder with a large, round brooch of gold. A steady breeze was blowing the cloak behind him like a banner. How impressive he must have looked to the raggedy children who were playing toss with fruit pits in the garbage-strewn streets!

He turned down one street and saw an unfamiliar gray-robed friar walking toward him. As Gifferd drew near, the friar gazed at him, then dropped to his knees and bowed with his head to the ground. Gifferd rode on.

The new friar must think I'm a king, he thought.

Within a few days, Gifferd again met the friar. This time Gifferd was reeling half-drunk from the local tavern with one of the town whores clinging to his arm. Again, the brother knelt and bowed his head to the ground.

The next day, when Gifferd's mind cleared, he thought of this second act of respect.

Perhaps he's mocking me, he thought.

Twice more the same sort of incident happened. By then, Gifferd knew who that new friar was. Père Antonio. Everyone was talking about him. They imagined him to be some sort of holy wonder-worker.

Gifferd began to feel uneasy. He watched where he walked or rode. And if he saw any gray-robed friar on the same street, he took another route.

One day he was playing dice with the town candlemaker when he idly remarked, "You're more of a challenge at this game than Jules."

"You won't have any more easy wins with him," the candlemaker said, rolling the dice. "He's gotten holy and given up the game."

"Jules? No."

"I win this round," the candlemaker said, sweeping Gifferd's coins into his pile. He gave Gifferd the dice. "Jules has been converted by Père Antonio."

"Jules told me he never wanted to hear or meet Père Antonio." Gifferd rolled the dice.

"Nor did he want to. His wife wanted to go to hear him preach and Jules refused. He was sick in bed with some sort of stomach upset and told her that she had to stay home to care for him."

"Most likely too much sour wine." Gifferd watched his opponent sweep a few more coins away.

"Most likely. His wife was upset, but she opened her window to see the friar at least. You know you can see straight down into the valley from their home, and the friar was preaching in the town square. She could see all the way down there quite well."

"How stupid! The friar would have looked no bigger than a gnat."

"Are women known to be smart?" The candlemaker rolled the dice again. "Not only did she see him, but she also heard him. And so did Jules."

"Heard him? How?"

"I don't know how. But hear him they did. And Jules gave up drinking and dicing. Now he brings wood to the convent. Père Antonio, you know, is guardian there." The candlemaker slapped his knee when he saw the dice. "You've had ill luck today. That last coin of yours is mine."

Over and over, Gifferd asked himself the same question. How could Jules convert? He and Gifferd had been in a contest of sorts to see who could lead the most dissolute life. And now Gifferd had won because Jules had converted.

The following Sunday afternoon, on a day too cold for late October, Gifferd had ridden through a forest swept with colored leaves to Jules' house on the mountain. He must see if the candlemaker's story was true.

The big woodcutter invited Gifferd in and they both sat, warming themselves in the fire's glow.

"You must go to hear Père Antonio." Jules' black eyes were earnest with pleading.

"The clergy are all hypocrites. You know what they do in the dark. You've seen it yourself."

"No. His is a life of light. Even in the dark."

"How can you be sure what he does in the dark?"

"Because I can tell by his works," Jules said. "You know Old One Eye, the crazy beggar?"

Gifferd nodded. Who didn't know the man who, oftentimes naked even in winter, begged and moaned in the town square?

"Last Sunday, during Père Antonio's sermon at Mass, Old One Eye wandered in. He began moaning and begging in that loud voice of his. Père Antonio came down from the pulpit and made his way to him. He touched Old One Eye's arm and asked him to be calm and quiet."

"As if Old One Eye would understand."

"He did understand. He said, 'I will be quiet if you give me your cord.' So Père Antonio smiled and gave it to him. And Old One Eye tied it around his waist and then sat down and listened to the rest of the sermon in perfect quiet. Go see him tomorrow, my friend. He only begs now. He no longer moans. He's no longer crazy. Through the priest, God has cured Old One Eye."

"You're crazy," Gifferd said. "You yourself agreed that God doesn't exist."

Jules grabbed Gifferd's arm. Through the warm woolen sleeve of his green tunic, Gifferd felt Jules' too-tight grip. "I used to believe that. Then I heard Père Antonio. I've seen Old One Eye cured. My friend, if God doesn't exist, whether you live a good or bad life, when you die, that is the end of you."

"I prefer a bad life. It's more interesting."

Jules' fingers tightened. "But if God does exist, you will live forever. If you love and serve God, you will rejoice for all eternity in the bliss of heaven. If you hate and reject God, you will suffer for all eternity in the flames of hell. Life on this earth is short, my friend. What are fifty or seventy years or less in comparison to eternity? If eternity does exist, would you rather spend it in bliss or in anguish?"

"If eternity does exist, there may not be a hell. Or God may send no one there."

"But if He does, where are you going, my friend?"

Gifferd had ridden home, more troubled than ever. The next day, he combed the streets looking for Old One Eye. When he found him clothed in a ragged, filthy cape and sitting beside one of the town wells, Gifferd purposely rode directly up to him. He fully expected to see the scrawny, dirty man weaving back and forth, moaning and holding out his trembling hands as he had always done.

But not today. With his head cocked upward toward Gifferd, Old One Eye spoke the first words that Gifferd had ever heard him speak. "A coin for a beggar?"

"I have none today," Gifferd said.

"Then God bless you anyway," Old One Eye said, winking his one good eye. The man was sane.

Not many days later, Gifferd was summoned to a cloth merchant's house. The man was having difficulty collecting payment from a certain noble who had ordered but never paid for several bolts of fine silk and linen. The merchant wanted his money.

Gifferd was riding through the crowded marketplace when he rounded a farmer's stall and met Antonio face to face. Again, the priest knelt and bowed.

At the suppressed giggling of two daintily dressed young ladies, Gifferd snapped. "Priest, I ought to strike you with the sword to punish your mockery. What do you mean? Why do you bow to me and make of me a public fool?"

The young ladies gasped. Gifferd could feel the stares of many curious eyes.

Antonio raised his head and peered at Gifferd. But he didn't rise. "O, brother, you don't know the honor that God has reserved for you. How I envy your happiness! I became a poor Lesser Brother because I wished to be a martyr for God's glory. I even journeyed to Morocco but became so ill that I had to be sent home before preaching one word about my Lord. It was not God's will that I shed my blood for His name. Yet God has revealed to me that one day you will achieve the dream that I had for myself."

Gifferd burst out laughing. "How ridiculous!"

"When your blessed hour arrives, I beg you to remember me."

"Priest, you are deluded." Gifferd spat in the friar's upturned face and spurred his horse on.

"May God bless you," Antonio called after him. "And when your hour comes, pray for me."

When Gifferd arrived at the cloth merchant's house, the merchant greeted him cheerfully.

"Come in," the young, bearded man hailed. "You'll get my money for me and I'll use it to host a huge baptismal party for my firstborn son. Come. Let us drink a toast to him." He led Gifferd into his ample kitchen.

Gifferd grinned. "So your child has been born. I had not heard."

"Oh, no. My wife hasn't yet given birth. It's too early." The merchant summoned a servant. "Wine for us."

"Then you and I may be toasting a daughter instead of a son."

"No. He's a son. Père Antonio said so."

Gifferd felt the blood drain from his face, and he knew that the merchant noticed it.

"My wife has been going to hear him preach. Surely you have heard him, too. Just two weeks ago, she asked him to pray for her and her child. So he began to pray at once. Then suddenly he paused and told her that we would have a son who would become a brother like himself and a martyr for Christ. We're naming him Philippe, and we will gladly give him to our Lord."

The cloth merchant's tale and Gifferd's own encounters with Old One Eye and with Antonio tormented him for days. Then there was the nagging reality of Jules' conversion. And other things, too. Oui, the brothels and taverns and dicing tables were still busy. But something seemed somehow different. One day, while ordering a new pair of shoes, he knew what it was. The squabbling in the streets had decreased. He hadn't seen a beggar taunted for weeks. And, on Sunday mornings, the streets were quite empty. Nearly everyone was in church.

Days passed. November arrived, and with it, the chill of autumn. Gifferd didn't change his lifestyle, but something inside of him had changed. Then one day, he knew why.

Antonio must be praying for him.

So he rode to the convent to see the friar and to tell him that he needed no prayers.

"He's not here. He's gone to Bourges," he was told.

Three weeks later, the cloth merchant invited Gifferd to his newborn son Philippe's baptismal feast.

The banquet was full of well-bred guests. The merchant bragged about his son and retold several times Antonio's prophecy of his martyrdom. One noble after another spoke of conversion because of Antonio's words. But their words weren't as powerful as the lusty cry of a little newborn boy. Gifferd gazed at the child in awe. He had never before seen a martyr.

Then with a start he was brought back to the present, to the little hut in Jerusalem, where the voices of the guards were growing louder. Gifferd heard a clamor. The bishop's deep voice, considerably weaker, preached still. There were voices of other Crusaders, some pleading for mercy, others preaching Christ. *They're gathering us together to kill us,* Gifferd thought. What sweet relief!

Conversion had come slowly, like the incessant dripping of water wearing an impression in stone. After Philippe's baptism, Gifferd began having difficulty sleeping. Images troubled him. Images of his childhood, his life, his faith, of Père Antonio and Old One Eye, of the converted Jules and newborn Philippe. In this turmoil, winter passed and spring arrived.

In the cool dawns of spring, Gifferd rose early because he couldn't sleep and rode out into the quiet country, where he wandered among vineyards bursting forth new buds and fields freshly plowed for seed. Always he returned to the same questions. What if God did exist? What if God were just? Where would he spend eternity?

One morning, when the birds were full-throated with mating lust, he stopped his horse beside a clear stream and prayed while the animal drank deeply. *Lord, if You do exist, let me know what to do.*

Every day for a week, he rode to that same spot and prayed the same prayer.

Then the bishop came to Le Puy-en-Velay. He preached fiery words to the people. He exhorted them to join him on a Crusade to the Holy Land to convert the Saracens to true faith in Christ.

Gifferd had always scoffed at these harangues. Surely the bishop couldn't believe that every Crusader was interested in the glory of God or converting the Saracens—some were in it for their own glory or for the spoils of war. The bishop skipped over that truth. Instead, he emphasized that those who went on crusade received an indulgence remitting all their sins. Those who died there in the cause of Christ were assured of heaven.

This was his answer—a chance to remit his sins. Deep in his soul, he knew that he wouldn't return from the Holy Land. Hadn't Père Antonio predicted it? So he sold all his property and joined the Crusade. On the way there, at daily

Mass and in prayer, his faith coalesced and deepened. He marveled at how blind he'd been when he hadn't believed.

When the band of Christian knights and believers reached Jerusalem, the bishop began to preach. To Gifferd, his words seemed too kind and soft, the moderate words of a man who had never lived evil but had only seen or read of it.

Unable to contain himself, Gifferd silenced the bishop and began to preach himself. He told the followers of Mohammed of his own life and its wretchedness and proclaimed the greatness of Christ as the true Son of God. "Those who know of Christ and reject Him reject God," he cried out.

Angry shouts rose from the infidels. Rough hands grabbed him and hauled him and the others away. They had all been tortured. And now they all would die.

Strong hands grabbed Gifferd's ankles and spun him around. As he was dragged out of the hut and across the burning sand, his body shrieked with pain. *Jesus,* he implored through the anguish. *Remember me. Forgive me. Take me home.*

Then he remembered: *Père Antonio asked me to pray for him.*

With a petition for the priest on his lips, he was thrown onto the sand. Someone shoved a block of wood under his neck.

Lord, bless the priest. Bless his mission, he prayed as he heard the motion of a sword thrust toward his neck.

NOTES

Antonio became guardian of the convent at Le Puy-en-Velay, where he not only ministered to the friars but also preached frequently in surrounding towns. He assumed this role in either 1225 or 1227. Since Francesco died in 1226, and Antonio was extremely busy in Italy thereafter, he may not have been able to return to France and assume guardianship of a convent. Hence, 1225 was the date chosen for the flashbacks in this chapter.

Antonio's reverence toward and prediction regarding the scandalous unnamed notary of Le Puy-en-Velay is true (Da Rieti 49–50). The notary converted (the records do not tell how this conversion came about) and joined the bishop's Crusade to

Jerusalem. There he forcefully spoke about Christ and subsequently was tortured for three days and then killed. The type of torture was not detailed. Historical records give no indication that the notary ever heard Antonio preach.

The incident regarding the woman and husband converting after hearing Antonio preach at a two-mile distance is recorded in some of Antonio's biographies (Ben 6). The histories also record the healing during Mass of a deranged beggar (24Gen Section 1, p. 175) and Antonio's prediction about a yet-unborn son who would become a Franciscan martyr (Da Rieti 49–50). Occupations of the adults in these stories are not given.

The infant Philippe eventually became a Lesser Brother and asked to be sent to the Holy Land. He "arrived at Axoto (Azot, today Azotus) which at that time had fallen into the hands of the Saracens, who, as soon as they occupied it, condemned to death all the Christians, numbering about two thousand." Philippe asked that he be the last to be beheaded. While he waited, he comforted the other Christians and encouraged them to remain true to Christ. When the Saracens realized how Philippe was encouraging the others, they flayed him and cut off his tongue. Nevertheless, he continued to preach by signs and example. All of the Christians maintained their faith and were martyred, with Philippe being executed last of all (Da Rieti 50–52, Purcell 137).

16

Seigneur Cerf

Châteauneuf-la-Forêt, Chateau, Limoges, France (Mid-1226)

S eigneur Cerf de Châteauneuf-la-Forêt watched with pleasure as Père
Antonio heartily ate his substantial meal. Cerf had gone to hear him
whenever he preached in Limoges or nearby. While Antonio was away
visiting other convents under his jurisdiction and preaching in those towns,
Cerf continued to bring food to the Lesser Brothers at Saint Martin's. They
always told him when Antonio would be returning to Limoges.

Sometimes they told him stories, like the time Antonio had fallen ill in
Solignac. The followers of Saint Benedict had a monastery there where Antonio
convalesced. One of the monks suffered from a temptation so severe that he
despaired of life. Intending to kill himself, he confessed to Antonio, who told
the monk to put on the tattered, worn-out tunic that the holy men had insisted
Antonio discard. When the distraught man clothed himself, his temptation
vanished.

Antonio had recovered and returned to Limoges, where Cerf had spoken
with him several times. How might he get closer to God? How might he pray
more deeply? Antonio had always counseled him wisely, but a few days ago,
Cerf had deeper concerns. He asked Antonio to dinner to discuss them. He
also promised him use of a room in which he could work on the Easter

sermons that his superiors had requested for other priests to use. Antonio had agreed to Cerf's invitation because here, far away from the crowds who pressed him in Limoges, he could spread out the Scriptures and write in solitude.

Now the intended meal was ended and the priest was rising from his seat at Seigneur Cerf's immense oaken dining table. "A superb meal as usual! Merci!" the priest exclaimed. "And there is still time for a stroll around your magnificent estate and that discussion you requested."

Indeed, the sky was ablaze with evening light. The priest and the baron walked together out of the great hall and down the chateau's wide steps into the courtyard. Each time Antonio accepted a dinner invitation to the chateau, the two men followed the same pattern of a meal followed by a stroll and counsel.

Seigneur Cerf spoke frankly. "Père, I pray and ask God to guide me as you have encouraged me to do. But I still don't have the peace that you have. How do I find this peace, Père? Is it possible?"

Antonio shifted his gaze to one of the many turrets of the castle on which a flock of gray doves perched. "'Who will give me wings like a dove that I may fly and be at rest?' David asked in the Psalms. It's your question, isn't it?"

"Oui."

Antonio pointed to the birds. "David's cry is the cry of a soul that is weary of this world and longs for the solitude and peace of life in a cloister."

"Père, I have thought about the religious life. Yet I have obligations here. Many people are in my employ. If I abandon all this and sell it, where will these people go?"

Antonio smiled at the lord. "It's possible to have a cloister in the heart."

"The heart?"

Antonio pointed to the castle walls and gestured beyond them.

"Jeremiah said, 'Leave the cities and dwell in the rock, you that dwell in the country of Moab; and be like the dove that makes her nest in the mouth of the hole in the highest place.' 'Leave the cities' refers to the sins and vices that dishonor, the tumult that prevents the soul from rising to God and often even from thinking of Him."

Vice no longer tempted Seigneur Cerf. He hadn't engaged in drinking, gambling, or licentiousness for years. But tumult? His responsibilities were many. Always tools were breaking, serfs were ill, weather was uncooperative, household helpers were arguing. Tumult. The word described his life well.

"'Moab' is the world. The world is a place of pride. All is pride in the world. There is pride of intellect, which refuses to humble itself before God; pride of the will, which refuses to submit to the will of God; pride of the senses, which rebel against reason and dominate it. Do you see yourself in any of this?"

Cerf saw himself juggling ledgers and extracting tithes from the peasants. He saw himself caught up in his own knowledge, insight, and administrative talents, efficiently running his estate. He prayed much, but he left God in the chapel. Pride.

"To leave the world, to live remote from the tumult of cities, to keep oneself unspotted from their vices is not sufficient. Therefore, the prophet adds, 'Dwell in the rock.'"

Antonio turned and pointed to the cross that rose over the chateau's small chapel. "This rock is Jesus Christ. Establish yourself in Him, Seigneur Cerf. Let Him be the constant theme of your thoughts, the object of your affections. Jacob slept on a stone in the wilderness, and while he slept he saw the heavens opened and conversed with angels, receiving a blessing from the Lord. So will it be with those who place their entire trust in Jesus Christ. They will be favored with heavenly visions. But the soul that does not repose upon this rock cannot expect to be blessed by the Lord."

Cerf ran his long fingers through his thick auburn curls. "I want to do this, Père. But how can I trust God? How can I abandon myself that completely?"

Antonio moved toward a thick staircase that led upward to the highest walls on the chateau. Cerf walked along with him. "Scripture holds the answer, Seigneur. 'Be like the dove that makes her nest in the mouth of the hole in the highest place.' Doves do not nest on the ground as hens do or in low shrubs like sparrows. You know where their nests are."

"In the turrets, Père." As the two men ascended the staircase, startled doves perched on the heights flew before them.

"Oui, in the nooks in high, rocky places. Jesus is the rock and the hole in the rock is the wound in Christ's side. That wound is the safe harbor of refuge to which Christ calls the soul in the words of the Canticle: 'Arise, my love, my beautiful one and come! . . . My dove in the clefts of the rock, in the hollow places of the wall.'"

As the men continued to climb, Antonio's hand swept across the span of the castle walls. "The Divine Spouse speaks of numberless clefts in the rock, but He also speaks of the deep hollow. There were indeed in His Body numberless wounds and one deep wound in His side. This wound leads to His Heart, and here, Seigneur Cerf, He calls you. He extends His arms to your soul. See how He opens wide His sacred side and Divine Heart so that you may come and hide therein."

Abruptly, Antonio paused and pointed ahead and to the left. There, in one of the battlements through which archers might shoot in a siege, a dove was nesting. "By retiring into the clefts of the rock, the dove is safe from birds of prey while also enjoying a quiet refuge where she may rest and coo in peace. So you will find in the Heart of Jesus a secure refuge against the wiles and attacks of Satan and a delightful retreat. But you must not rest merely at the entrance to the hole in the rock of Christ. You must penetrate its depths. In the depths you will find the Precious Blood, which has redeemed us. This Blood pleads for us and demands mercy and calls us to Its very source, to the innermost sanctuary from which It springs, the Heart of Jesus. There your soul shall find light, peace, and unimaginable consolations."

A warm love seeped over Cerf's spirit like blood from a fresh wound. How he wanted to find that Precious Blood, to find his peace in the Heart of his Redeemer!

The men continued their climb while the dove watched them warily, but without taking flight. Farther along, Antonio pointed to another cleft in which a flattened nest lay.

"What is a dove's nest made of, Seigneur?"

"Little bits of straw, Père, and grasses."

"And where does she get them?"

"Wherever she finds them. The stable. The pasture. The garden."

Antonio bent down and picked up a few straws that had fallen from the nest to the step on which the men stood.

"The dove uses these little bits of straw that the world tramples under its feet to build a secure and comfortable nest," he said as he stood. He pointed to the nest. "The virtues we must use to nest in Christ are like these cast-off, simple grasses. The world despises them and, indeed, never notices them, yet Christ Himself used them to submit to His Father."

Antonio turned to Cerf. "What are these virtues?" Taking Cerf's hand and opening his fingers, Antonio tapped the palm. "Here are the virtues we must use to nest in Christ." Antonio began to place one straw after another into the palm as he spoke. "Meekness. Humility. Poverty. Penance. Patience. Mortification." He tapped the little mound of straw in Cerf's hand. "For the soul, these are nesting materials for life in the hollow of the rock, in the Heart of Jesus."

Antonio closed Cerf's fingers around the straw. "Make your nest away from the tumult of this world. Make it deep in the Heart of Christ and build it of the virtues of Christ. Dwell there and you shall have the peace you seek. In the hollow of the Rock, you shall know God."

They spoke of other matters of less importance, and soon the sun was sinking low. Cerf led Antonio into the chateau and bid him goodnight outside the room he allowed the priest to use whenever he visited. Antonio always stayed several days, for the chateau was a good morning's ride from Limoges, where he continued as custos of the Lesser Brothers. Antonio rode out here if he could hitch a ride on a cart. And, if he couldn't, he walked.

Cerf was not yet ready to retire. He wished to pray as Antonio had just suggested. In the chateau's chapel, he knelt before a tapestry of Christ's agony in the garden. Two flickering candles illuminated the chapel, just down the hall from his own bedchamber. The cooler night air blowing softly through the open windows caressed the baron's thinly bearded face and ruffled his long chestnut tunic as he knelt.

He remained still, his head bowed, his thick auburn curls falling over his neck. At his sides, his arms hung utterly relaxed as he probed deeper into the Heart of Christ. In a short time, he was no longer conscious of the tapestry or the flickering candles or the breeze. He was deep in the cleft of Christ's Heart. As he penetrated that Holy Wound, he found himself meditating on one thing and then another. Christ's Passion. His mercy. His love. The Heart of Christ held him, with all his sinful imperfections, in the very center of Christ's love. And not Cerf alone but every human soul ever to have lived and to live still. Cerf's head bowed almost to the floor as he thought of Christ's great humility not only to become human Himself, but also to nurture every other human in His own Precious Heart. God in human flesh loved humans whom He had made in His own image for no other reason than love.

Lord, make me grateful to You for Your love, he prayed. *Lord, please make me more like You.*

So his meditation and prayer continued until he felt the images fading and his body stiff from lack of movement. With a deep sigh of longing to be one with Christ, Cerf opened his eyes and raised his head. He pushed upright and shook the tightness out of one knee and then the other. Leaning forward, he kissed the tormented face of Christ on the tapestry, bowed, and left.

The hallway leading to his bedchamber was dimly lit with a single torch in the center. Just prior to Cerf's room was Antonio's. The priest would be writing. Cerf expected to see the flicker of candlelight under Antonio's door. What he noticed was a flooding radiance. At the same moment, he heard the babble of a child in the room.

How puzzling! None of the household servants had a small child. The serfs who did wouldn't be in his castle at any time, much less at this hour. Had a mother come to see the priest? But why would she come in the thick of night? No one had asked him about admitting a woman and child to the chateau, and no one should have been admitted without his permission.

Now the child was giggling. Who had come to see the priest without Cerf's knowledge or approval?

Bending down, he peeked in the wide keyhole and caught his breath. Antonio was kneeling at the ample writing table on which lay two open books, one of which appeared thick enough to be a Bible. To one side were pushed a parchment and a reed pen. On the other side, a candle flickered.

Antonio was bathed in light, and the light was coming from a chubby-legged infant who was sitting a bit unsteadily on the thickest book.

As Cerf watched, Antonio held his hands in front of the child, his two pointer fingers extended toward the infant. The child reached up and grabbed one finger in each fat fist, then, with the priest's help, pulled himself up on tip-toe. The baby's legs danced up and down while the child laughed with delight. Then, suddenly, one toe slipped and the boy lost his balance. Swiftly, the priest scooped the baby up in his arms before the plump-cheeked, dark-haired head could strike the table. The child laughed and kicked against Antonio's habit, then reached up toward the priest's grinning mouth and fingered his lips. Antonio kissed the tiny fingers.

With one hand gripping the priest's lower teeth and the other the neckline of his tunic, the child pulled himself erect in Antonio's arms. Then the boy tugged at Antonio's ear, bringing it down to his mouth as if to whisper into it.

The priest turned his face to the door as the child suddenly thrust his arms directly toward Cerf. As the child stretched in Cerf's direction, almost tumbling out of Antonio's arms, Cerf bowed his head in awe for just the briefest second. When he looked up again, Antonio's arms were empty and the only light in the shadowy room came from the flickering candle.

Cerf dropped to his knees. He was too overtaken with deep joy even to weep. The door in front of him opened. He raised his head. "Père, what was He saying to you?"

Antonio took Cerf's right hand in his palm and raised him to his feet. "He said that your house will flourish and will enjoy great prosperity as long as it remains faithful to Mother Church. But when it goes over to heresy, it will be overwhelmed with misfortune and will become extinct."

Cerf caught his breath at the prophecy. He had expected nothing like that.

"Seigneur Cerf," Antonio said softly, "Christ has permitted you to see Himself and to receive His message. Praise Him for this vision but tell it to no one. I beg you. Tell this to no one, at least not while I live."

Cerf's voice was tight with joy and sorrow, wonder and fear. "Oui, Père. I will tell no one. Until its telling can no longer draw the curious to you, I will tell no one."

NOTES

Antonio wrote his Easter sermons at Limoges, probably around April 1226. Whether the vision described here occurred at that time is questionable. However, the lord of Châteauneuf-la-Forêt did give Antonio a room in his castle. It seems probable that the saint, who sought out caves for privacy and discipline, would not have accepted this luxury without reason. Having a place to write these sermons seems to be a sensible motive.

The vision of the Christ Child is recorded by several historians, although some modern historians question whether or not it actually happened. Biographers who agree that it did happen disagree on where the vision occurred. Some say at Châteauneuf-la-Forêt, others at Padua, and some at three other locations. The gentleman who saw the vision variously saw it through a keyhole or window. In some versions, Antonio holds the Child. In others, the Child is floating and a heavenly fragrance and singing fill the air. In most versions, Antonio asks that the spy keep the vision secret while Antonio lived. He may have asked this either the night of the vision or the following morning. Whether Antonio had one or several visitations of the Child is unknown.

Antonio's prophecy came true. In the seventeenth century, the then Seigneur de Châteauneuf-la-Forêt rejected the Catholic Church and the house fell (Purcell 155–57).

Antonio's cure of the Benedictine monk is in the historical record (Rig 10–11).

Antonio's words regarding the doves are from a sermon that he gave at Saint Martin's Abbey on November 3, 1226, as recorded by Stoddard (pp. 50–53).

Scripture verses are from Psalm 55:6 ("Who will give me wings . . ."); Jeremiah 48:28 ("Leave the cities . . ."); see Ephesians 2:20 ("This rock is Jesus . . ."); Genesis 28:11–15 ("Jacob slept on a stone . . ."); and Song of Solomon 2:10, 14 ("Arise, my love . . .").

17

Amélie

Manor House, Brive, France (1226)

mélie banged the wooden bowls in her mistress' pantry as loudly as she could. She was a woman now, but she didn't care if she acted like a child. She didn't care if the bowls scratched or if the banging noise disturbed her poor lord's headache. The household might as well know that she was angry. How could they send her out to the garden to pick vegetables in this violent rainstorm and then have her scurry all the way to that friary through the drenched fields? *What do they think I am? A fish?*

"What's going on in there?" bellowed a cook in the adjoining kitchen. "Get those leeks to the saint. He told the mistress that the brothers have nothing to eat."

The saint. All she ever heard about was the saint. Amélie tossed her head with such anger that her thick black braids whipped around and struck her in the face. *If he's such a saint, why doesn't he make his own vegetables appear?* Some saints miraculously fed multitudes with bread or rice, or so the ballad singers sang. But not this saint. This saint had to send her out into a storm to get his food. The miracle would be if she returned without catching a deathly chill.

Amélie slipped into her rain cloak and grabbed the biggest wooden bowl she could find and a long blade knife.

When she threw open the door, a wet blast of wind slapped against her. Pulling the door shut behind her, she pushed out into the storm.

The wind was whipping her master's pear saplings nearly to the ground and whistling like a demon through the well-ordered vines of his grape arbors. Heading directly into the gale, she hustled toward the vegetable garden. Leeks. She pulled their muddy, white bellies from the ground and threw them into the basket. Parsley. Dill. She plucked huge handfuls and tucked the feathery tops under the leeks so they'd not blow away. Carrots. Beets. Garlic. She sliced away their tops with the knife, then tumbled the muddy roots into the bowl. Cabbage. Its heavy outer leaves were bobbing in the wind. She sliced two heads and wedged them between the muddy beets and carrots. *So what if the friars have to wash the mud off the cabbages,* the maid thought. *Serves them right for asking for food in this weather.*

When the bowl was full, Amélie ran back to the kitchen to return the knife, then headed across her master's uncut hayfield with the bowl. She'd taken this route many times. Didn't her master love to tell of another of his fields, this one near the saint's convent? Her master had sown it with fine wheat for his mill. One moonlit night, a few friars who were coming out of the oratory in quiet meditation saw a host of marauders rampaging through the field, trampling and plucking the wheat. The friars ran to find their founder, Père Antonio. He was at prayer. *Of course,* the maid thought. *What else for a saint?*

"Don't be afraid," he had told the friars. "This is only a trick of the devil to distract you from your meditation. The field isn't harmed."

And the next day, it wasn't.

Thinking of the story made Amélie shudder. Demons, it seemed, must be in this very storm. *Lord, don't let me see one,* she pleaded.

At the end of the hayfield, she took a sharp right to a footpath that led through a forest. The path would eventually bring her to a narrow lane that led to the friary.

As she entered the forest, she thought of Antonio living like a hermit in a narrow cave in these very woods. People were certain that he had gone there in order to pray more and to more severely discipline his appetites. What did "disciplining his appetites" mean? Did he whip himself or roll in thorns or beat himself with rocks? What manner of distasteful things did he do? *One thing, for sure, is that he's not disciplining his stomach. No, he wants vegetables. Leeks. I hope they're strong enough to sear his throat,* she thought.

Folks said Père Antonio had hollowed out a fountain by his little grotto to receive water that gushed from a rock. He wouldn't need water today. If he put a pot outdoors, it would be filled quickly with water. If only he could do that for vegetables. Amélie imagined Antonio invoking vegetables and having leeks and parsley and carrots fall from the sky like rain. She grinned at her silly vision.

She lifted her skirt to hop over a fallen branch. That hadn't been down the last time she'd walked this path. That was last week. The wind must have brought down the bough. *God, don't let some falling tree limb hit me,* she prayed.

How many times had she pattered through these woods? If her mistress paid her extra for every trek she'd taken to the friary, she'd have been able to buy cloth for a new chemise by now.

All Amélie ever heard about, it seemed, was Père Antonio. Père Antonio needed this. Père Antonio needed that. Why hadn't he founded his little monastery of friars in Limousin instead of coming here to Brive? *Because Quintus de Falcici had built them a house here, you fool,* she chided herself. Oh, if only Seigneur de Falcici were not so pious!

Well then, why wasn't Père Antonio at his convent in Guienne on such a bad day? If he were, another maid would be out in this downpour instead of her. And why hadn't the mistress stayed home today in this storm? Why did she have to ride all the way out to the friary to attend Antonio's early morning Mass? Her mistress had returned home, soaked through her cape and proclaiming that the friars had no food.

Why couldn't the friars plant their own vegetable garden? *Bah, they have planted one,* Amélie thought. *Little good it does them when they give away all their produce to the poor.* She shook her head. Saints. They had no sense at all. They lived in another world.

She bounded out of the woods and onto the flooded lane. Three knolls and she would be at the friary.

Was it true that Père Antonio raised a dead child to life in Limoges? The mother had left the baby in the cradle, the rumors went, while she went to hear the friar preach. When she returned, the child was dead. Shrieking, she ran to the saint, who was detained speaking to those who had lingered behind after his homily. "Go, for God will show you His mercy," the priest told her. When the woman insisted that the priest accompany her, he told her again, "Go now. God will show you His mercy." When she hesitated, he sent her on her way with the same words. As she arrived home, she saw her son playing in the yard with some pebbles.

A second miracle had made its way through local gossip from Limoges to Brive. Another woman, this rumor said, had gone to hear the priest preach and, when she returned home, she found her son playing in a pot of boiling water, totally unharmed.

What's the matter with the mothers in Limoges? Do they care more about a supposed saint than about their own children? Amélie snorted to herself. When *she* married and bore children, she wouldn't leave them unattended even if Christ Himself came to Brive to preach.

Then this Père Antonio sometimes seemed almost like Christ Himself. Just three weeks ago, the mistress had returned from a shopping spree to Limoges. She had gone there to purchase new pottery for the kitchen. While there, she had heard a young novice friar preaching in the square. Of course, she sent a message to her cart driver to rein the horses so she could listen.

The preacher was a young, lightly bearded novice from Limousin, named Fra Pierre. He was preaching about the Holy Spirit when he related a curious incident. As a friar in the convent at Limoges, Pierre had been tempted to leave the ordine. One day, while he was thinking of this, Père Antonio happened to meet him on the grounds of the monastery. Without any questions, Père Antonio cupped in his hands the tall friar's cheeks. Then, tipping the youth's head toward his own, the saint had done what Christ had done to His apostles. He had breathed into the novice's mouth and said, "Receive the Holy Spirit." Smiling at Fra Pierre, the saint had released his grip.

The saint had better not breathe on me, the maid thought. *If he likes leeks as much as the mistress says he does, he probably smells like them.*

Fra Pierre, so the mistress said, was now fully convinced of his vocation as a friar. "And so," the mistress had concluded her story, "we must beg God to send His Holy Spirit upon each of us with the same power with which He conferred it on Fra Pierre. For he preached forcefully, almost as well as the saint."

Amélie groaned. To hear constantly about one saint in the area was bad enough. But two?

There, up ahead, was the friary. Quite breathless from her scurrying, Amélie skirted the main door and swung around to the kitchen. Antonio himself answered her knock, his tunic sleeves rolled back and his hands glistening wet.

"Pardon my casualness," he said. "I'm on kitchen duty and I am nearly done scrubbing the floor." Amélie noticed a pail of water and a brush to the right of the door.

Antonio grinned at the bowl of soaked vegetables. "And once I finish scrubbing, I'll have something to cook."

"Just give me back the bowl and I'll be on my way," Amélie said. *Let me go before you breathe on me, too.*

"I've made you some mint tea. Why don't you come in and warm yourself before you return home?"

Amélie felt exasperated. Couldn't the saint see anything? "Père, the storm is growing worse. I'll be soaked to the bone by the time I get home."

"Are you wet now?"

What a stupid question. Of course she . . . the maid shook her rain cloak. It was dripping with water. But her gown beneath it was dry, even at the hem, which had several times swept the underbrush in the woods, not to mention dragged through tall grass in the hayfield. Her toes felt dry and warm in her boots, too.

A bit confused, she replied, "Well, I guess I'm not wet. Not much."

Antonio pointed to a small table with a steaming wooden cup on it. "Have your tea." He carried the bowl of vegetables to a sideboard, where he dumped them into a tub of water.

"How do you think carrots would taste with"—he picked up the dill—"a touch of this?"

Amélie gulped the warm tea. "Very good, Père. Especially if you add a bit of leek and steam it all together."

"Fine. We shall have that tonight." The priest began rinsing the roots in the tub. "And the cabbage? I usually braise garlic in a bit of olive oil and then add the leaves."

"You might add a few carrots to it as well. It makes such a pretty dish."

"Good idea. You have picked us such an abundant supply of food. Please give your mistress our deepest thanks."

The cup was empty. "I've got to be going, Père."

Antonio rinsed the bowl and wiped it with the sleeve of his tunic. After handing it to the girl, he raised his hand over her in blessing. Alarmed, she turned her head aside, wrinkling up her nose in anticipation of a breath. But none came.

"In the name of the Father, and of the Son, and of the Holy Spirit," the priest said, making the sign of the cross over her head.

Amélie signed herself at his words.

"May the rain spare you on your return trip as well."

"Merci, Père."

She opened the kitchen door and felt the full force of the wind in her face. Drops as huge as acorns pelted her rain cloak. With the bowl firmly tucked under her arm, she raced the long route to her mistress' manor house. When she arrived, her gown and her feet and her thick black braids were still completely dry.

NOTES

Antonio's foundation of the monastery at Brive and his life in the narrow cave, with its hollowed-out fountain, are accurate. The miracles in this chapter are recorded in the following sources: Keller 6 (dead child raised to life and child who wasn't scalded); Rig 10 (devilish apparition in the wheatfield); Rig 8 (novice named Pierre who was tempted to leave the ordine); Rig 9 (unnamed maid who remained dry despite bringing vegetables to the friars during a rainstorm).

18

Minette

Brothel, Limoges, France (November 1226)

Plump Minette tugged her chemise down over her head and smoothed out its skirt as big, heavy Roland, sitting beside her, laced up his shirtsleeves. Now that he was dressing, having taken what he paid Minette good money to give, he would talk. He spoke before he undressed and then after he dressed again. During the heat of passion, he said nothing. Such was his habit. Other men had stranger habits, the strangest of all being Minette's father, who had used her ever since she was a child. "A beautiful Eve, my daughter, you be," he recited each time he came. "She made Adam to sin and you make me." Until she was nine years old, she endured his sick rhymes and sicker passion. Then she ran away to live in brothels. She was still a sinful Eve, she thought, making men sin.

Roland pushed Minette's long hair, the color of field mice, away from her face and kissed her. "Tomorrow I won't see you," he said. "Tomorrow is All Souls' Day and Celestine insists that I take her to hear the saint."

Minette pushed him away playfully. "Celestine again."

He tickled her chin. "Minette. She is my wife."

"So what saint is this? Every month there is a new saint in Limoges."

"You haven't heard of Père Antonio? He's custos of the Lesser Brothers. He stays in Limoges but travels about, preaching. No one you know speaks of him? I'm surprised."

Minette struggled with a memory. "I think Janine did mention him. She said he restored Claudine's hair after her husband had pulled it out."

Roland teasingly tugged on Minette's hair. "Is she the one who brought meats to the friars while her husband was away? And when he caught her, he beat her?"

Minette tossed her head. The pulling pinched. "Oui. Claudine. She's a good woman."

Roland let off pulling her locks and began to caress them. "Minette, there are no good women unless they be saints. Claudine was disobedient to her husband. She deserved to be beaten."

Minette shuddered, remembering the blows her own father had rained on her. "No one deserves to be beaten," she said bitterly. "The saint didn't think she deserved it. She sent for him, and he restored her hair and healed her bruises. That's what Janine said."

"The saint thinks more like a saint than a man. And now he has her husband thinking the same. I've heard that he accompanies Claudine to the Lesser Brothers to bring them meats."

"What's wrong with that?"

Roland shrugged. "Nothing, I suppose. He does penance while I have fun." He pressed Minette close, squeezing her.

"But no fun tomorrow. Tomorrow you have to hear the saint. Why doesn't Celestine obey you and stay home?"

Roland bellowed with laughter. He was so close to Minette that her body shook along with his. "She would obey me, but I would have to live with her nagging tongue and pouting face. It's better to hear the saint. And perhaps he'll speak out against the sins of the clergy like he did at the synod in Bourges. That, I would like to hear."

"A priest would never speak against the clergy."

"You've never heard Père Antonio. They say his sermon at the synod made the clergy blush. There were hundreds of them there, all prim and proper in their miters and copes. Père Antonio shouted out in his sermon, 'You there in the miter!' Then he told them all their sins."

"*All* their sins?" Minette giggled.

"Oui, my dove. And they say some came to him afterward and confessed. Archbishop Simon de Sully was one."

Minette laughed as she thought of the finely dressed clergy, parading about as if they were kings. How she would love to hear someone openly reproach one of these men!

"What did he confess, Roland?"

"Only his mistrust of the Lesser Brothers who follow Francesco and the Preaching Friars who follow Domingo. He said he would now welcome them into his diocese."

Minette groaned. "Is that all?"

"It was a lot to the saint. He follows Francesco, too."

Minette folded her arms and turned her shoulder to Roland. "So I won't see you tomorrow because you want to hear the saint. And then you will follow Francesco, too."

Roland guffawed. "If I follow Francesco, I can't have you." His thick hands pulled Minette back to himself.

When he finally left, Minette rolled over and dozed, thinking of the saint castigating the bishops. She'd like to have heard that herself.

The next day was busy. The men who came to her instead of going to hear the saint certainly couldn't tell her what he'd said. Nor could the other women in the brothel, all of whom chose to wait for customers. By the time Roland came the next evening, Minette was obsessed with knowing. Nevertheless, she forced herself to speak casually. If she seemed eager, Roland might tease her by telling her nothing.

"So how was the saint?" she asked while he sat on the side of her bed and removed his cap. Minette was sitting fully clothed beside him.

Roland dropped his cap to the floor. "The saint was good. He preached in the cemetery of Saint Paul."

Minette shrieked with glee. The cemetery. What better place for an All Souls' Day sermon!

"He preached on a line from the Psalms. Something about in the evening, weeping shall take place, but in the morning, gladness. He said there were three evenings and three mornings. The evenings were the fall of Adam and Eve, the death of Christ, and our own death."

Minette wrinkled her nose. "Not a sermon I would like."

Roland was peeling off his inner shirt, loosening the tight sleeves to slip over his thick wrists. "He said the three mornings were the birth of Christ, the resurrection of our Lord, and our own resurrection."

"That's more cheerful."

"I suppose," Roland said, dropping the shirt to the floor, "if one is going to the right place." He turned to Minette and put his hands on the shoulders of her gown. "But we can have better than heaven here tonight, can't we? And when we die, we shall both go to hell and then we can continue to enjoy each other."

When Roland slipped on his shirt again, Minette spoke first. She knew that she had better speak quickly or Roland would begin to talk. Then she wouldn't have an answer to the question that was troubling her.

"Do you really think I'm going to hell?"

Roland burst into laughter. "Where else, Minette? Purgatory? Purgatory is for people who are at least trying to be good. You don't even try."

Minette felt hurt. "But I'm not a bad person."

Roland cupped her face in his huge, hard-skinned hands. "Minette, all women, except the saints, are bad persons. Whom do men sin with, if not with women? Look at where you live. Look at what you do. I've come out of here many times with fewer coins in my pocket than I should have had after paying you."

Minette blushed. "Perhaps you lost them on the way."

He pinched her cheeks. "Perhaps you took them, my dove. But I don't care. I have learned to carry only a few coins when I come here. But you won't need any coins in hell."

Minette grabbed Roland's wrists and pulled his hands from her face. "You're not a priest. You don't know where I'm going."

He laughed again. "Then next time Canon Jacques comes to visit you, ask him." Roland teasingly attempted to wriggle out of her grasp.

"I'll visit the saint. I'll ask him."

"Him? Then you'll know. For you, Minette, and for me, God has no forgiveness."

The words stuck in Minette's mind like cart wheels in mud. When Roland left and other men came day after day and night after night, she couldn't chase the words from her mind.

"For you, Minette, God has no forgiveness."

Every time she sinned with one of her many visitors, the words dug deeper.

"For you, Minette, God has no forgiveness."

She could hardly rest. Why had she been so anxious to hear what the saint preached? She wished she'd never asked. Was hell a flaming inferno or an icy wasteland? Images of herself in one place or the other with the men who came to her darted into her imagination. She could feel the men beating her as her father had done, calling her not Minette but Eve. The pouch of pilfered coins hidden under her bed seemed to swell until they poked her back.

"For you, Minette, God has no forgiveness."

Was she going to hell? By the time she resolved to know, the saint had left Limoges to preach in Saint Junien.

After several days of inquiring of her clients about the saint, Roland told her, "Père Antonio is going to preach in the old Roman amphitheater tomorrow afternoon."

Oh, what relief! "Then don't come to me," Minette said, "because I'll be there to hear him."

Under gray, threatening skies, Minette made her way to the amphitheater. She pushed through the haggling crowd at the many market booths to the clearing in the center of the square where an immense crowd, possibly a thousand people, had gathered. Minette, feeling too unworthy to draw any closer to the saint, stood at the very back of the gathering. She could see that a wooden platform had been erected. Near her, two men were pointing to the platform.

"The devil made the one they built for him in Saint Junien collapse," one man said. "Père Antonio predicted it would happen. But no one was hurt, as he said no one would be." The man lifted his shirt and pointed to a hammer stuck in his belt. "I came prepared to help remake this one if it falls. That's what the men of Saint Junien had to do."

Minette looked curiously at the platform. The devil? All her life, she believed that the devil used her to harm men. Now the devil was after the saint?

When Père Antonio arrived at about noon, he mounted the pulpit and the restless crowd settled into silence.

"O Light of the world," the saint called out in a clear voice that betrayed just the slightest hint of accent. "You are the infinite God, Father of eternity, Giver of wisdom and knowledge, and ineffable Dispenser of every spiritual grace. You know all things before they are made. You have made darkness and light. Put forth Your hand and touch my mouth and make it a sharp sword to utter eloquently Your words."

Antonio's eyes were raised to heaven as he prayed. Minette bowed her head. Despite her distance from the platform, she heard clearly every word of the prayer.

"My dear friends," Antonio began, "thank you for coming. A church would have been more comfortable for you, but it would have taken you much longer to enlarge it to hold everyone than it took for you to build this platform for me."

Minette giggled as laughter rippled across the crowd.

"Do not be alarmed at the threatening sky. You will be dry if you remain here. And so, let us begin. 'I am the Way, the Truth, and the Life,' said our Lord in the Gospel of John. In the name of the Father, and of the Son, and of the Holy Spirit."

It had been so long ago that her mother had taught her, yet Minette remembered how to cross herself. She and the crowd did it in a smooth, sleek motion.

The priest's voice rose, gentle yet strong. "'I am the Way,' said Jesus, 'the Way' without error for those who search for it. Isaiah the prophet spoke of this way. 'A highway will be there, called the holy way. No one unclean may pass over it, or fools go astray on it.'"

The word "unclean" leaped out. Minette thought of all the men who came to her and she felt the filth of her many sins. "No one unclean may pass over it." That meant her.

"Christ's message consists in not giving importance to the things of this world. No, the wise appreciate and savor those of the next world, those that belong to God and to eternity."

Eternity. Where would Minette spend eternity? Roland said she was going to hell. Her father had said the same.

"The righteous do not walk across the cursed fields of worldly thoughts and they avoid the vineyards of carnal and wanton desires."

Minette felt weak and conspicuous. Surely everyone around her could see that she was a woman of wanton desires who satisfied those same desires in men.

"The righteous walk straight along the public and well-trodden road that is Christ Who said, 'I am the Way.' The way of Christ is public because it is open to everyone. It is well beaten because it has been followed by persecutors and has been stepped on and despised by almost all feet."

She had despised the Way. She had trodden on Christ.

"Only the righteous walk the way faithfully and humbly. They follow it faithfully until death and enter into the Promised Land. Thus, Christ is this Way.

"Christ is the 'Truth.' He is 'Truth' without falsehood for those who find Him. 'The truth is great and stronger than everything else. All the earth invokes the truth and the heavens bless it. There is no truth in wicked kings or wicked women or in all the offspring of iniquity. There is no truth in their wicked words. They will perish in their very sinfulness. But truth remains and grows strong into eternity. It lives and reigns forever.'"

So he had given her the answer that she sought. She was a wicked woman and, as the bastard child of a thief, the offspring of iniquity. She would perish in her sinfulness. Long ago, while yet a child beaten by her father, she had forgotten how to cry. She wished she could remember, for she wanted to weep now for the loss of her soul.

"Oui, even if the temptations of the flesh and impurity are strong, the truth of Christ is stronger and conquers all these sins.

"Christ is Life for those without life. 'Because I live, you will live also,' Jesus said."

Was she hearing clearly? Was there hope? Would Jesus save her from sin, bring her to life eternal?

A crackling split the air, and Minette shuddered in the lightning that arched across the amphitheater. A murmur of panic swept the crowd.

"Fear nothing," Antonio called out. "I have asked the One Who creates storms to protect us. The storm will pass by."

A few people raced toward the exits of the amphitheater. Most pulled cloaks over their heads but did not move. Minette drew up her hood and huddled, waiting for the rain.

"You who are going out through the gates of this amphitheater!" Antonio called out, "You will pass directly into the storm! Go instead through the gate that is Christ and He will protect you. For He said, 'I am the Gate. Whoever enters through Me will be safe. That one will go in and out and find pasture,' pasture in the eternal fields of heaven. For Christ's days are eternal and the days of His elect will also be eternal. 'I am the Life' means that Christ is our life in example, truth in promise, life in reward; a way that is straight, a truth that does not deceive, a life that never ends. He is the Gate to glory through Whom all must pass on their way to the Father."

How could Minette enter the gate of Christ? Surely there must be a gate-keeper, an angel, who would bar her entrance.

"There was a gate in Jerusalem called the 'eye of the needle.' It was so narrow that a camel could not pass through it, for a camel is a proud and haughty animal. It refused to stoop low enough to pass through the gate. This gate is the humble Christ. The proud and the greedy, those burdened with false pretensions and riches, cannot enter through this gate.

"Those who wish to enter must humble themselves by stooping. They must kneel in humility before Christ, the humblest of all, and admit their sins. Then they will enter through the gate and will be saved as long as they persevere."

Minette felt wetness on her face. Tears? Thunder crackled. The wind rose with a howl. The wet drops were rain. Minette pulled her cape more tightly around herself. She had been in storms before. She would leave only when the priest did. He continued his sermon, his voice rising above the wind. The crowd remained, waiting for a deluge that never came. That first smattering of drops was all the rain that fell in the amphitheater. By the time Antonio was completing his sermon, the thick black clouds were thinning out, revealing patches of limpid blue.

"Praise be to You, my Lord Christ, the 'Way, the Truth, and the Life,' the 'Gate' through which the humble sinner may enter the kingdom of God. Amen."

When Antonio's voice faded, the crowd surged toward him. Minette quickly lost sight of him as he was swallowed in the mob. Her mind was in turmoil. She must speak to him, but what would she say? As the crowd around her thinned, she was left standing alone. Unsure about what to do, she turned away from the crowd at the platform and, through muddy streets strewn with the storm's hailstones, skirted puddles and rivulets until she reached the brothel.

But when she opened the door to her room, she saw it with new eyes. Behind the hanging, rich brocades, she knew that the walls were gutted with rot and stained with rain. Her bed, nest for many men, repulsed her. Under her bed, pushed out of sight in the dust, a small pouch of pilfered coins testified to her greed.

She paced her room. What should she do now? Suddenly, living as she had been sickened her. But she knew nothing else. In an act of unthinking desperation, she pulled the pouch of coins from under her bed and, clutching it like a madwoman, ran out the door and into the sodden streets. If she hurried, she might get to the amphitheater before the saint left.

She need not have rushed. Many waited before her and she stood in her muddy shoes, leaning against the platform, for several hours.

She had time to study the saint's long, narrow face, his large, deep-set black eyes and the gracious smile that seemed a living part of his face. Obviously he was well bred. Whatever made her think that she could approach him?

She studied the crowd. Barons, nobles, peasants, serfs, women, men from every walk of life. Even two canons. Many wept. Several threw themselves on their knees before the priest. Others gave him purses or spilled laps full of coins at his feet. Some handed him their daggers and swords. Three other gray-robed brothers, who stood near him, silently gathered the booty into pouches while the priest spoke to the penitent people and sent each home with his blessing.

A few went away disgruntled. "All I asked him for was a thread from his tunic and he refused," one woman muttered.

"Why wouldn't he give it?" her waiting friend asked.

"He said the faithful take relics from saints, and he isn't a saint."

Minette had slid down to sit against the platform by the time the saint finally approached her. She jumped up from the platform steps.

"You've waited all this time," he said, "and now only you are left. Madame, what is your name?"

Madame? Never before had she been addressed with that title of respect. "Minette," she weakly replied.

"And what is troubling you, Minette?"

"Père, I . . ." Minette stumbled over the words. She bit her lip. Two bitter tears squeezed out of her eyes. The first real tears in over a decade.

Antonio noticed the moisture, she knew, but he turned from her to the three silent brothers behind him. "Leave now with what you have been given today. Discard the weapons and distribute the coins to the poor. Return to the convent when your pouches are empty." Raising his hand in blessing over the three men, he sent two away. The third walked out of earshot and sat on a hunk of stone facing the priest, waiting.

Antonio pointed to the platform steps. "Minette, let's sit down here."

She obeyed. She had never sat so close to any man who had not looked at her with lust. She recognized compassion in this man's face, a look she had seen occasionally on other faces, but on none directed to her. Minette turned her head away from his, her eyes smarting too much even to stare at her feet.

"My sister," Antonio whispered in a tremulous voice, "don't be afraid. I confess to you and will always confess it, that if the Lord had not been my helper, my soul would have fallen into every sin. Take courage. The Lord will console anyone who mourns for his own sin."

Minette nodded. How desperately she wanted consolation! She tried to speak. But the words wouldn't come. She tried again. The words stuck in her throat. Her sins were too horrible to be spoken to this holy man.

"Minette," Antonio said, "can you write?"

She nodded. "Oui. A little."

She heard the rustle of a robe and then blank parchment and a pen were pressed into her hands. Puzzled, she looked up through her tears and saw Antonio holding a vessel of ink.

"Write your sins," he said softly. He guided her hand to the wooden steps, placing the parchment onto it. Then he dipped the pen into the ink, releasing Minette's hand.

Shaking, she laboriously wrote. **I lie. I steal. I make men sin. I am going to hell.**

Weak with fear of his rebukes, she handed the pen and parchment to Antonio.

He glanced at the parchment, then spoke. "Minette, imagine that the platform behind us is Mount Calvary and you, like Mary Magdalene, are sitting here, exhausted with grief, at the foot of the cross. Can you see, Minette?"

She closed her eyes and imagined a huge wooden stake looming above her head, her back thrust up against it.

"Do you see Christ hanging naked on the cross of shame?"

Minette nodded. The gentle voice came again, "That is how Mary Magdalene saw Christ. Now look at the face of Jesus, swollen and bruised and covered with His tears. He suffered 'though He had done no wrong nor spoken any falsehood.' He 'prayed at all times for sinners' even on the cross when He asked His Father to forgive those who persecuted Him."

Minette's tears came faster. *Was He praying for me? Will He forgive me?*

"The Blood of Christ brings forgiveness and life to His persecutors. Can you see Him, Minette? Can you hear His prayerful cries?"

She could see, hear. *Oh, Lord, forgive me.*

"Now look again, Minette. Do you see the Mother of Christ weeping beside you at the feet of her Son?"

She could see her, a woman three decades older than herself, her face grimy with dust, streaked with tears, its beauty twisted with unbearable grief.

"Minette, you think that you are going to hell. But why despair of salvation when all here speaks of mercy and of love? Behold the two advocates who plead your cause before the tribunal of Divine Justice: a Mother and a Redeemer."

With a clearer vision than she had ever possessed, Minette could see the scene. The Son. The Mother. Herself.

Antonio's voice was like a salve. "See before us Mary who presents to her Son her heart transfixed with the sword of sorrow. See Jesus Who presents to His Father the wounds in His feet and hands and His heart pierced by the soldier's lance. Take courage. With such a mediator, with such an intercessor, Divine Mercy cannot reject you." He paused. "You say that you have stolen. Are you sorry for this?"

Minette fished up her sleeve for the purse and slid it into Antonio's lap.

"These are the stolen coins? And you wish me to give them to the poor?"

"Oui, Père." Her voice was barely more than a squeak.

"And you lie? So did Saint Peter. He repented and was forgiven."

"It's so difficult for me to tell the truth, Père."

"I know, Minette. But in Christ all things are possible."

"I'm sorry for those lies. I'll try harder to be truthful."

"Then the lies are forgiven."

"Père, I make men sin. The things I have done—to tell you would make me sick. I make men sin. I'm evil."

Antonio pointed to Minette's words on the parchment in his lap. "You don't make men sin. Men who sin with you sin of their own accord. Who told you that you were evil?"

She breathed deeply. "A man. Men."

"Were these men Christ? Or His true followers?" Minette started at the question. Antonio was smiling at her. "I thought not. Then why believe them?"

"But aren't women like me evil? Aren't I going to hell?"

"God created women. God doesn't create evil."

"But look at me. You know what I am."

"I know what you used to be. What you are now is between you and God."

"But, Père, I have sinned in ways that even God cannot forgive."

"Remember, Minette, that all sin that has gone before can be forgiven the one who wishes to make a new beginning. Is this what you wish? To make a new beginning?"

"Oh, Père, more than anything."

"Then leave the men who come to you and strive for purity. Our worst enemy can be our flesh. We must conquer lust and must keep it under control by wholesome penance, for it is a most dangerous foe."

Minette dared to look directly into the priest's dark eyes. She found no condemnation and no false pity there. Only acceptance and purity that is love.

Antonio's voice was soft. "Minette, in Christ's new covenant, even our thoughts come under judgment. How much more our actions! Sexual sin allows the unworthy to enter the heart and faith is lost. The life of the soul is faith, Minette. Fornication puts to death the soul that God formed in His likeness. Fornication robs the heart of faith and thus of life."

How could she gaze so intently at this pure man? He knew all about her. How ashamed she felt! She turned her head away from those eyes that were probing her soul.

Antonio's soothing voice continued: "We must prefer to die rather than sell our inheritance in heaven. We must prefer to suffer any hardship rather than surrender our eternal glory for carnal pleasure. If we do this, any sorrow that we feel at denying our own flesh will turn into joy. Do you understand, Minette?"

Without looking at the priest, Minette nodded.

Antonio put his hand under Minette's chin and turned it so that the two were again looking eye to eye. "Would you like to learn a prayer that I use very often myself whenever impure thoughts or temptations come?"

"Is there such a prayer? That works?"

Antonio smiled. "There is. Now sign yourself." Minette did so clumsily. "Now say, 'Behold the cross of the Lord.'"

"Behold the cross of the Lord." Her voice was trembling.

"Fly, you hostile powers!"

"Fly, you hostile powers!"

"The Lion of the tribe of Judah, the Root of David has conquered. Alleluia! Alleluia!"

Minette repeated the words softly. Antonio had her cross herself once more and repeat the prayer. Suddenly she grinned. She imagined shouting out this prayer the next time Roland came to her door. That would frighten him off!

"Minette, look at me." Antonio made the sign of the cross over her as he spoke. "In the name of the Father, and of the Son, and of the Holy Spirit. I absolve you of all sins of your past life. You're not evil, and you're not going to hell, Minette. Your sins are forgiven."

He handed her the parchment that still lay in his lap. The words she had written on it were gone.

"Père, the words," she stammered.

"You're not going to hell. Your sins are forgiven," Antonio repeated. "Your soul is as clean as that parchment."

Minette stared at the blank sheet. A sigh from deep within thrust up her throat and escaped like a frightened bird. With it went the vicious words of her father and of the other men. She wasn't evil. She was forgiven.

"I'm not evil, Père?"

"Anyone reborn of Christ is good, Minette." Antonio paused. "But still, I'm obligated to give you a penance."

"Even if it were to wear sackcloth the rest of my life, it wouldn't be harsh enough."

Antonio shook his head. "No, Minette. For your penance, I want you to pray daily the prayer I taught you. Pray it often, in every temptation. Think of Christ Who gave His life in exchange for yours. He will help you. Will you do this?"

"It's too little to ask. Oui, I will do that."

"In addition, you must leave behind your lifestyle and you must never return to it. Would you like me to send you someplace where you can find work and live a good Christian life?" When she nodded, he handed Minette the purse. "On our way, I want you to distribute these."

Through muddy streets trekked Antonio and the woman, accompanied by the brother who had waited silently in the amphitheater. Minette gave two coins to a blind beggar, a handful to a man on crutches, and the remainder, along with the empty purse, to a thin woman whose three children clung to her stained gown. How good to give the coins away!

Quite suddenly Antonio stopped at a small house and knocked. When a chubby young woman, broom in her hand, opened the door, the priest spoke.

"Minette, this is Madame Beaudoin. She is one of our benefactors. Madame, this is Minette." The woman smiled pleasantly at Minette, who squirmed at the unfamiliar goodwill. *She knows what I am,* Minette thought. *Yet she seems kind.*

"Would you kindly let Minette stay the night with you? Tomorrow I'll send two brothers from the friary for her."

"Certainly, Père," the woman said pleasantly.

The priest turned to Minette. "Minette, with your permission, the brothers shall accompany you to a monastery. There the nuns will love, shelter, and instruct you in weaving cloth. If you stay and do as they teach you, you will learn to make a living. You aren't to take the habit unless it's your will and the nuns test your vocation. I will ask them to keep you in their employ until you wish to move elsewhere. Are you willing to go to such a monastery?"

Minette's mind was swirling. A monastery? Her in a monastery? There she would be safe. There she would never again have to use her body sinfully.

"It will be difficult for you to change your life, Minette. But with Jesus, all things are possible."

Minette smiled. She thought of Christ gazing at her from the cross and of His Mother.

She thought of the saint's gentle words and of the blank parchment. She thought of learning to weave cloth in a monastery and of a new beginning.

With Jesus, all sin can be forgiven. With Jesus, all things are possible.

NOTES

The fictitious Minette represents the numerous prostitutes whom Antonio converted by his preaching (*Assidua* 18). No record exists of his personal counsel to these women. While his provision for Minette to live at a monastery was typical for the period, we don't know if he ever made such arrangements for repentant women.

Roland's attitude toward women—seeing them as vessels of sin—was common at the time.

The fictional Minette's writing of her sins parallels that of an unnamed penitent coming to Antonio with sins too horrible to speak of and being advised by Antonio to write them down and bring them back. When this weeping penitent presented the paper, the sinner and Antonio went over the sins and, when Antonio handed the paper back to the repentant sinner, it was clean (Purcell 170, Da Rieti 116).

Other incidents mentioned are also found in the historical record: the restoring of an unnamed woman benefactor's hair, which her abusive husband had pulled out (Da Rieti 56–57); the synod at Bourges (Rig 12); the collapsed pulpit (*Dialogus* 12); the storm that bypassed the crowd (Rig 13); and repentant people giving Antonio their weapons, money, and ill-gotten goods (*Assidua* 18).

Antonio's words are from Stoddard 53 (the prayer to preface his sermon each time he preached), SK 51–53 (his sermon), SK 46–50 (his meditation on the crucified Christ), and SerE 114, 145–46, 175 (his advice on sexual purity). His admission of his own temptations to sexual impurity and the use of prayer to combat them are from Rig 1, *Dialogus* 1, and Bierbaum 23. His belief that he would have fallen into every vice had not God helped him is from Bierbaum 22.

His well-known prayer "Behold the cross of the Lord" is used to drive away temptations to impurity. On May 21, 1892, Pope Leo XIII "granted an indulgence of 100 days which may be granted once a day by all who recite this blessing devoutly" (Bierbaum 23–24).

Scripture verses are from Psalm 30:5 ("In the evening . . ."); John 14:6 ("I am the way . . ."); Isaiah 35:8 ("A highway shall be there . . ."); 3 Esdras 4:35–40 ("The truth is great . . ."; during Antonio's time, 3 Esdras was part of Scripture; today it is considered apocryphal); John 14:19 ("Because I live . . ."); John 10:9 ("I am the gate . . ."); Isaiah 53:9 ("Though he had done . . ."); see Psalm 109:4 ("He prayed at all times for sinners . . ."); and see Matthew 19:26 ("With Jesus, all things are possible").

19

Agathe

Cottage, Marseilles, France (Late 1226)

Agathe had been kneading her bread dough for perhaps two minutes when she heard a soft rap at her cottage door. At least she thought she heard a rap. With the wind whipping a chill December rain across the countryside, she couldn't be sure if she had heard a knock at the door or the tapping of a tree branch against the roof. She shrugged and went on kneading. If she had visitors, they'd knock again. And they did.

Wiping her hands on her apron, Agathe waddled over to the door. She'd invite them in, of course. If they weren't heretics, that is. The Cathars, often called Albigensians in this region, were fleeing the French armies directed by King Louis IX, who was still a boy, and Blanche, his mother. The war, she had heard, was vicious. She herself had seen little of the fighting, but she had often watched armies of mounted knights and foot soldiers marching up and down the roads and, sometimes, scurrying bands of fleeing heretics.

Today the weather was horrid, but if these visitors were heretics, she would send them on their way with a curse. But what Cathar would be bold enough to knock at her door? The heretics had secret networks of their own supporters. Surely a heretic would go to a house known to be sympathetic.

Most likely, her visitors weren't heretics. Most likely they were pilgrims on their way to a shrine in Le Puy, Mont Saint-Michel, Vézelay, or any number of other spots in France. If they were true followers of Christ, she would offer them some bread if they were willing to wait for it to rise and bake. Didn't Christ say that those who welcomed strangers welcomed Him? Agathe fancied that someday she would open the door and, perhaps, the Savior Himself would be there.

Today there was no Savior. *But close enough,* she smiled to herself. There were two poor friars, drenched to the bone.

"Madame, we've come a long way," said the shorter one, who was just about her height. She recognized a certain tired heaviness in his voice that comes with a deep, deep grief. Her own voice had carried that thick tone for months after her husband had died.

Quickly she ushered them into her one-room cottage. She had very little, but what she did have was at their disposal.

She could tell at a glance that they were followers of the poor little man of Assisi, Francesco, who bore the name of her own country. So she knew what their grief was.

Holy Francesco, she had heard, had died in Assisi. These men were mourning their founder. Who wouldn't mourn for him? He was a legend. Tamer of wolves, preacher to birds, poet of prayer. And, rumor had it, bearer of the wounds of Christ. With Francesco had died a special love, gentleness, and humility that had been sung in song and told in story even here in France.

How Agathe wished she could ease the friars' grief! If only she had dry clothes to offer them, but she had nothing but her own thin, patched cloak and one extra chemise, hung on a peg by the fireplace. She couldn't ask them to remove their wet clothing to dry over the flames. She knew that these friars wore nothing beneath their tunics but their breeches.

With a start, she realized that she had rolled back the sleeves of her chemise to knead her bread. Never had any man except her deceased husband seen her bare arms. Embarrassed, she plucked at her sleeves to pull them down. What would she do? With them down, she couldn't knead the bread without dirtying her clothes. If she didn't finish kneading, she would have nothing to offer the two men.

The shorter friar touched her lightly on the hand. "Don't worry, Madame. I've kneaded bread myself." He raised his hand in silent blessing over her.

Agathe smiled and curtsied awkwardly. "Warm yourselves by the fire while I finish. The bread will rise soon and bake. You shall have that and wine."

"Merci," the friar said.

Agathe went back to her kneading. The friars sat silently before the fire, their tunics pulled out before them. Water dripping from their clothes formed muddy puddles on the floor.

"How far have you come?" she asked.

The taller friar turned toward the question. "From Brive," he answered.

How young he is! the woman thought. *Not yet twenty.* "Will you stay the night?"

The tall friar looked at the other for an answer. The shorter friar turned toward the woman and smiled. "Merci, Madame. With your good pleasure, we will stay until the rain stops. Then we must be on our way to Assisi."

Agathe grinned. At least until the rain stopped, she'd have company to relieve her loneliness and boredom.

Abruptly, the taller brother asked the shorter, "What do you think will happen at the general chapter? Do you think Fra Elia will again be chosen as minister? Who will take Fra Francesco's place?"

The shorter friar placed his hand on the youth's arm. "Fra Francesco created this brotherhood at God's command, and in God's hands it must remain. We must continue to pray that God's will be done. Fra Francesco is praying with us, you can be sure."

Agathe plopped the two loaves of bread onto a board and covered them with a scrap of linen. She placed the loaves on the floor near the hearth and glanced sideways at the friars. Thin, glistening lines of water squeezed from their eyes. She averted her head.

Something about the shorter one made her pause. She seemed to have seen him somewhere. Heard that voice.

"Do you think Fra Elia will have you preach in Spoleto?" the younger friar asked.

"I'll do whatever he tells me. With Francesco gone, we owe Fra Elia obedience."

Agathe gasped, then caught herself. This was Père Antonio! She had heard him preach four times, but each time she had been far back in the crowd. Her eyesight had grown so poor with age that she had never seen him clearly. But the voice. Oui, the voice was his.

Père Antonio held some sort of important position in Limousin, custos or something, she had heard. This Fra Elia, whoever he was, must have called all the important administrators of the friars back to Assisi to consult on what to do now that holy Francesco was dead.

Oh, dear, with such an important man in her house, what was she to do? He was so fatigued with travel and grief, and all she had to offer him was bread and wine! Her cheese was moldy in a leather pouch by her bed. She might nibble it herself, but she couldn't offer such a poor scrap to the friars.

She owned only simple, scratched wooden cups and plates on which to serve a meal. If only she had something fine to bring a bit of joy to these men! Her neighbor had a wine goblet. Père Antonio must drink from a goblet! Certainly, he was used to such niceties. Had he not called her "Madame" and been as polite as a noble?

Agathe pushed herself up from the hearth and reached for her hooded rain cloak. "I have only poor cups to drink from, Père. My neighbor has a fine glass goblet. I shall go and borrow it from her so you may drink from it."

Antonio looked dismayed. "Madame, don't trouble yourself. I've been living in a cave at Brive and drinking stream water with my hands. I need no fancy goblet."

"A cave? Père, please stop teasing. You shall have your goblet. Her cottage is just over the hill."

Antonio leaped to his feet. "It's a wretched day. Don't go. It's unnecessary."

"My cloak is old, but it doesn't leak," the woman said proudly.

"Then let me wear it and go for you," Antonio offered.

"Certainly not, Père. Stay here and I'll be back shortly. By then the bread will be ready to bake." The woman hurried out the door before the good priest could protest further.

The cloak did keep her dry, but her shoes were a muddy mess when Agathe returned to the cottage. No matter. She sloshed happily around in them while she slid the bread into the fire and then set the table, the delicate wineglass gracing it as if waiting for a bishop or for the Savior Himself. She invited her guests to sit down on the bench.

I have so little to offer, Agathe thought again. *The bread and wine will have to do.*

She'd get the wine while the bread finished baking. Already it smelled scrumptious.

"I'll be right back," she happily told the friars as she threw her rain cape over her head. Taking a pitcher, she bustled outdoors to draw wine from the single cask in her wine cellar. When she returned with a full pitcher, the younger friar met her at the door. His anguished face told her that something was desperately wrong.

He held his two hands out to her. In one lay the goblet, in the other its stem. Agathe nearly shrieked.

"I'm so sorry," the young man said in a high-pitched, trembling voice. "I was only looking at it and it slipped."

"My neighbor's glass," the woman moaned. "Her most precious thing. I can never replace it. Holy Mother of God, have mercy. What shall I tell her? Holy Mother of God, have mercy."

The boy looked helpless and about ready to cry. Why had she spoken so quickly? She should have stopped her mouth.

"Don't worry about it," she said almost too swiftly. "We're friends. She'll forgive me. I asked for it for Père Antonio. She'll forgive me."

A bit unsteady, Agathe walked to the table and placed the pitcher on it. Antonio was seated on the bench, his elbows propped on the table, his face in his hands. In the fire's glow, his tonsured head gleamed.

"Père, are you ill?" she asked.

As he shook his head, she suddenly remembered something.

"Dear Mother of God, I've forgotten to turn off the tap!"

She rushed outdoors to the cellar. The wine was running full tilt to the floor, dyeing the mud deep black. The woman turned the tap and leaned against the barrel, groaning. She began to tap the wine barrel from the bottom up. She had not yet reached the middle of the cask when she heard the thin echo of empty space. The barrel had been nearly full. Now it was nearly empty. The earth had drunk almost her full winter's supply of wine.

Agathe plodded back to the house. She would have to be cheerful for her guests. They were feeling enough sadness, and she was the only one here to comfort them. And one of the two the famous preacher! Oh, she almost wished he had gone to her neighbor's cottage rather than her own. First the wine glass. Now the wine. Was this how God rewarded those who served His servants?

Agathe trudged indoors and hung up her cape. She tried to smile so as not to worry the friars. She pulled the plump, nicely browned bread from the fire and set it on the hearth to cool. She would ask Père Antonio to give a blessing and then she would serve her guests. First, she went to her cupboard to bring out her second wooden cup.

As she turned toward the table, Antonio smiled weakly at her. "I'm glad that you decided to join us, Madame. Only I will be glad to use that wooden cup that you have taken out for yourself. I think you, as our gracious hostess, deserve to use the fine goblet."

He held out his hand to her. Astonished, she took the goblet from him. It was unbroken.

His voice, tired and thick, continued. "Now, so we may enjoy our meal together, may I ask you to check your wine cask again? I think, Madame, you will find it full. We'll wait for your return before praying together."

"Oui, Père," Agathe said. Without even bothering with her cape, she ran outdoors to the cellar and tapped on the wine keg. First the bottom. Then higher. Then the center. Then near the top. Each time, she heard the same dull thud that meant only one thing. Wine.

NOTES

When Antonio received news of Francesco's death in Assisi on October 3, 1226, he was acting as custos of the district of Limousin, France. As such, he was in a position of leadership over all friars in his province. At the time, he was living as a hermit in a cave at Brive (Purcell 146). Fra Elia, then minister general of the ordine, sent a circular letter to all the provincial ministers, calling them to a general chapter to be held in Assisi. Antonio and an unnamed companion set out to attend this meeting. On their way, either in late 1226 or early 1227, they would have walked the French roads with the king's armies and the heretics that were fleeing before them.

The two friars stayed with an unnamed peasant woman of Marseilles, where Antonio worked the miracles described in this chapter (Rig 7). The friars may have asked her for shelter, or she may have offered her home to them after seeing them in the street. History says nothing about the weather on the day of these miracles.

PART FOUR

Hope Is the Opposite of Looking Back

20.

Pope Gregorio IX

Lateran Palace, Rome, Italy (Late April 1227)

In the early dawn, Ugo woke slowly, remembering who he was. He had followed this process of self-examination nearly every morning for the past three-and-a-half weeks. To the world, he carried many titles. Cardinal Ugolino dei Conti di Segni. Grandnephew of the deceased Pope Innocenzo III. Previous Cardinal Bishop of Ostia and Velletri. Recently, chief counselor of the ailing Pope Onorio III. Once, long ago, Count of Anagni in the Patrimony of Saint Peter. Now, Pope Gregorio IX, Vicar of the holy Roman Church. But before God and himself, he was Ugo, pilgrim on a journey to eternal life. And to the doves cooing on the roofs and turrets of the papal residence, the Lateran Palace, he was merely another white-bearded Roman stirring awake.

As he lay beneath his blankets, watching the darkness begin to lighten, Ugo relived his election as if it were happening again. Onorio had died on March 18. After his burial the following day, the cardinals had assembled in the monastery of San Gregorio to celebrate the Mass of the Holy Spirit and then to elect the new pontiff. Ugo had been praying for guidance in making his choice, but, when all the votes were cast, he himself had been the choice.

"No!" he had screamed. He had seen firsthand how the papacy had devoured Onorio and Innocenzo. Was he to be consumed with worry and responsibility, carrying the Church until his death?

"I am not worthy!" he cried. "I am not capable."

As two cardinals holding the papal mantle approached him, the nearly eighty-year-old Ugo had bolted toward the locked door. Hands caught him. Anguish and horror erupted in his soul. Shrieking, he grabbed his cassock, his arms trembling with the strength that comes from unbearable pain.

"No!" His fingers clutched the red garment over his heart, pulling violently as if to wrench out of himself the overpowering fear and grief. As the cassock ripped across Ugo's chest, he felt the papal mantle forced over his shoulders.

DO NOT RESIST THE WILL OF HEAVEN, an interior voice seemed to say. Ugo's arms fell to his side, suddenly limp as he surrendered to the unavoidable will of God. Two days ago, on Easter Sunday, he had been crowned. The miter still felt heavy on his head. The papal throne on which he sat still seemed too large.

Lord, why have You given me this office? I am neither worthy nor capable, he prayed as he lay in bed. *Lord, Your Church seems to be crumbling. Many of Your clergy ignore the teachings of Christ. They are greedy, lustful, proud, dressed like peacocks when the poor are in rags. Even some of the cardinals fall into these sins. Thus, the people are without guidance and the faith is dying. What do You wish me to do?*

The early morning wore on until dawn, when Ugo sat on the papal throne, clothed in the robes of Pope Gregorio IX. All morning following Mass, he hosted audiences with this or that cleric. As noon approached, he anticipated another well-dressed official, but this time the large doors before him opened to reveal two barefoot Lesser Brothers dressed in tattered gray tunics.

What a welcome diversion! Ugo broke into a grin. Before becoming pope, he had been cardinal protector of the Lesser Brothers and he still loved them dearly. These two, however, were among the thousands he'd not yet met. Nevertheless, he had been expecting them. As minister general, Fra Elia had sent word that he was sending two brothers to him to clarify some matters before the May chapter gathering.

The canon who was acting as a page called out, "Fra Antonio and Fra Taddeo of the Lesser Brothers!"

Ugo had never heard of Fra Taddeo. But Fra Antonio. If this was the Fra Antonio he'd heard so much about, he would have to have him preach to the Curia and to the crowds of Rome.

The two brothers walked briskly up to Ugo and knelt before him, their heads bowed almost to the floor. Ugo traced the sign of the cross over their stooped shoulders. From the description he'd heard of Fra Antonio, he guessed that the short friar must be him.

"Rise, brothers."

Ugo first embraced the lanky, dark-eyed young man with the sparse black beard. "Fra Taddeo?" The youth broke into a bashful grin. Then Ugo turned to the lightly bearded shorter man. "Fra Antonio?"

"Sì, Lord Pope."

As he embraced Antonio heartily, his joy turned to perplexity. The Lesser Brothers were scrawny. Whenever he embraced one, he generally felt a bony rib cage beneath the tattered tunic. With Antonio, he felt plumpness.

Ugo released Antonio slowly. "Let me look at you." He studied Antonio, from the gentle face down to the slightly protruding stomach and the bare, somewhat puffy feet. Ugo had seen cardinals and bishops who were plump from eating rich food. Fat didn't look like this. This was swelling.

"Are you well, brother?"

"Sì, Lord Pope."

"Don't be too certain." Ugo had heard rumors that Antonio was severe in his fasting, much like Francesco. If that was true, the corpulence was from disease, not from gluttony. "Have you seen a doctor?"

"No, Lord Pope."

Ugo grunted. He had thought as much. He beckoned to the canon sitting near the door. "Find our physician and bring him here. I would like him to examine Fra Antonio." Bowing, the canon left.

Ugo turned to Antonio. "So you've come to me from France. I understand that you've been serving as custos of Limousin. How are the convents doing, both the established ones and those that you created? Did the brothers grasp the theology you taught? Will they be able to preach the Good News of Christ and combat heresy effectively?"

"They're good men, Lord Pope. They love Christ and serve Him. That alone will make their words effective."

Ugo nodded. "So it will. And how do the brothers in France feel about Francesco's Rule?"

Antonio shook his head. "Some think it's too strict. Others embrace it willingly."

Ugo nodded. "It's the same here. Fra Francesco's way of life is still dividing the friars. And Fra Elia sent you to speak to me about one of the disagreements. Possessions. Books. As if I can end the discussion."

"We're obedient to the Church, Lord Pope," Antonio said. "We'll abide by your decision."

"You meet in Assisi at Pentecost, sì? And I will be in Anagni. Rome is unbearable in the summer. Unhealthy. Never come here in the summer, brothers. You know, I have been to some of your chapters. How clearly I remember the first! I attended it as a cardinal."

Ugo led the two men to a large oaken table around which twelve chairs were arranged, six on each side, with one large, ornate chair at the head. In this chair, Ugo sat. He motioned for the brothers to sit as well, one to his left and one to his right.

"I remember riding along the plain around Assisi to that poor little Church of Santa Maria degli Angeli. And what do I see but endless huts no bigger than barrels, made of branches, with grasses, mud, and straw littering the floor of each. I could hardly believe it. *These men sleep like dogs,* I thought." Taddeo was grinning. "You've heard of this gathering, brother?"

"Sì, Lord Pope. The older brothers speak of it."

"I met many of those older brothers, as you call them. They were younger then, like a battalion of penitent knights! They thronged me. Cheered me. *This is Christ's army,* I thought. *If men can live like this before God, how will things go for those of us clergy who take our ease in comfort and luxury?*"

"The brothers who saw you will never forget," Taddeo said, "that you dismounted your steed, threw your cloak over the saddle, and took off your shoes."

Ugo nodded. "And we all walked to that poor little chapel to celebrate Mass. Fra Francesco preached the sermon. Because the chapel is so small, most of the brothers had to remain outside." Ugo leaned back in his chair. "Fra Francesco. You couldn't convince him of anything. You know, at another chapter gathering some brothers persuaded me to urge Francesco to follow an approved Rule. The brothers didn't have a written Rule then, just some words Lord Pope had orally approved. They asked me to convince Francesco of the wisdom of adopting an approved Rule, perhaps that of Saint Augustine or Saint Benedict or Saint Bernard. Did you hear what he did?"

The brothers shook their heads.

"He took me by the hand, led me up the steps to the speaker's platform, and addressed the chapter. 'My pope'—that's what he always called me—'My pope,' he said, 'wants us to take another Rule. Brothers! Brothers! God has called me by the way of simplicity and showed me the way of simplicity. I do not want you to mention to me any Rule, whether of Saint Augustine, or of Saint Bernard, or of Saint Benedict. And the Lord told me what He wanted. He wanted me to be a new fool in the world. God did not wish to lead us by any other way than this knowledge.' No one could convince him."

"Those founders allowed books," Antonio said. "Fra Francesco didn't want any books except breviaries. He wanted the brothers to remain unlearned."

"I spoke to him often and know his mind fully," Ugo commented. "I stood by him both as he composed the Rule and obtained its confirmation from the Apostolic See. I approved of him granting you permission, Fra Antonio, to teach sacred theology to the brothers because they requested it. You whom he called with great respect 'my Bishop.'"

Antonio smiled. "He admonished this unworthy so-called 'Bishop' that I could teach 'providing that, as is contained in the Rule, you "do not extinguish the Spirit of prayer and devotion" during study of this kind,'" Antonio quoted.

"I cannot imagine you, of all people, extinguishing 'the Spirit of prayer and devotion.' You have come to ask if this permission might be granted to others in the ordine. I understand Francesco's mind. What is unclear, I will be able to clarify. Fra Antonio, would you ask the Lord to guide us?"

Antonio bowed his head. "With humility and devotion, O Holy Spirit, we ask You to pour out Your grace upon us. Kindle over us the light of Your presence so that in Your radiance we can see almighty God in the splendor of Your saints. With Your help, You Who are one God in three, blessed throughout all ages. Amen."

Thus, Antonio and Ugo conversed while Taddeo occasionally offered an insight. Would Francesco have extended his permission to teach to all the learned brothers? How did the Rule reveal his thoughts about poverty, possessions, money, education? After much discussion, they concluded in the affirmative. For the ordine to grow and be a more effective witness, Francesco would have granted other learned brothers permission to teach provided that they did not "extinguish the Spirit of prayer and devotion." Antonio would present this interpretation to Fra Elia and the chapter.

With a conclusion reached, Ugo led a prayer of thanksgiving and then rose from the table to escort the two brothers to the door. "Fra Antonio, I ask of you three favors. Tomorrow, I wish you to preach to the cardinals in their assembly. The following day, you will preach from the steps of the Lateran to the crowd that has come here for the Easter indulgences." Ugo placed his right hand on Antonio's shoulder. "Brother, will you preach before you return to Fra Elia? Whom the Holy Spirit touches, He touches."

Antonio bowed. "With your blessing, Lord Pope."

Ugo again traced the sign of the cross first over Taddeo's head and then over Antonio's.

"And now my third request." He motioned to the canon sitting quietly by the door. He had returned while the men were in discussion.

"Give these brothers a meal," Ugo instructed, "and have the papal physician check Fra Antonio."

The canon bowed. "Sì, Lord Pope."

"Please usher in my next appointment."

The canon bowed again, brought in three well-dressed clerics, and then led out the two brothers. Ugo assumed his daily work for the Church. At the day's end, he fell exhausted into bed, thinking of Antonio's health.

When the brothers were ushered in the following afternoon, Ugo was quick to ask, "What was the physician's diagnosis?"

"He told me to eat more and drink more."

Ugo sighed. "I could've told you that myself. Are you doing it?"

"I've begun today." Antonio smiled. "Don't worry about me. I'm well."

"I pray so." Ugo rose. "Come, Fra Antonio. The cardinals are assembling."

Under the high, ornately carved ceiling of the papal court waited the cardinals in assembly. Ugo sat behind the pulpit, in which Antonio now prayed eloquently for God's inspiration. Ugo had a commanding view of the red-robed prelates, who were studying the barefoot friar in the patched tunic.

They're skeptical, Ugo knew. A smile played on his lips. *Soon they'll understand that Antonio deserves his reputation.*

Antonio's voice rang out as a herald. "'The word of the Lord was made known unto John, the son of Zachary, in the desert and he came into all the country about the Jordan. John came preaching the baptism of penance for the remission of sins, as it is written in the book of the prophet Isaiah, a voice of one crying in the desert.' In the name of the Father, and of the Son, and of the Holy Spirit."

As one giant crimson organism, every member of the assemblage crossed himself.

Antonio stepped away from the pulpit as he began to speak, his clear voice reaching easily to the farthest corners of the room. "The name Zachary means 'a remembrance of the Lord.' John, the son of Zachary, symbolizes a prelate or a preacher who ought to remember, to remember constantly, the memorial Passion of our Lord Christ."

He moved among the prelates, gazing at one after another as he spoke. "The Book of Exodus admonishes us, 'It shall be as a sign in your hand and as a memorial before your eyes.' Thus, Christ's Passion must be a memorial and a sign for us." He raised his long hands toward the prelates. "It must be a sign in our hands as we use these hands to touch others in the name of Christ and to consecrate bread and wine into His Body and Blood." Moving his arms outward and upward, he continued, "Likewise, the Passion of Christ must be ever before our eyes as we pray and as we see in others the figure and the creation of God."

Pausing, Antonio raised his eyes heavenward, then called out, "Are we true sons of Zachary? If a prelate or a preacher is a true 'son of Zachary,' the word of the Lord will be 'made known to him,' as it was made known to John. The word is a word of life and peace, of grace and truth. It will be a sweet word, offering hope and solace to a sinner 'as cold water to a thirsty soul, like good news from a far country.' So says the Book of Proverbs."

Antonio turned and looked directly at Ugo. "To the true son of Zachary, 'God will make known His word,' as it says in First Kings, 'like the whispering of a gentle breeze.' So softly comes the inspiration of the omnipotent God."

Antonio turned back to the cardinals. "The Book of Job says it well. 'It is a spirit in man, the breath of the Almighty, that gives him understanding.'"

Ugo's throat tightened with emotion. *Oh, God, You have spoken to me and I have fought the gentle breeze of Your word. Let me accept this office in which You have cast me. Let me embrace Your words and accept the will of heaven.*

"Fortunate indeed was John the Baptist to have the word of the Lord made known to him!" Antonio again raised his eyes and arms to heaven. "I beg you, Lord, 'since Your word is a lamp to my feet,' may Your word be revealed 'to Your servant, according to Your word in peace.'"

Antonio continued his sermon, admonishing the prelates to make haste in spreading Christ's message and to preach repentance and administer penance in love. They must be examples of Christ, he proclaimed, as they brought Christ's message to the world.

"What can I say about the enervated prelates of our times?" he called out. "Like young women about to be given in marriage, they clothe themselves in finery, dressing themselves in leather; their excesses evident in pretentious painted sedans, in the elaborate ornamentation of their horses and their spurs, stained red with the Blood of Christ."

Ugo studied the cardinals who stared at the beggar priest. He saw some faces turning a shade of crimson somewhat lighter than the color of the gowns the prelates wore. He saw some eyes turning away from Antonio's penetrating stare, which seemed to single out each cardinal in turn.

"Take a look at those to whom the bride of Christ is entrusted, the same Christ Who was wrapped in swaddling clothes and laid in a manger. These, in sharp contrast to Christ, wantonly loll in their ivory beds and bedeck themselves in leather. Elijah the prophet and John the Baptist girded their loins with skins. Let this be a sign for you, O prelates of the Church: 'You will find an infant wrapped in swaddling clothes and lying in a manger.' You who live from His patrimony, sign yourselves with the seal of the humility and abstinence of this Infant, with the seal of His priceless poverty. Mortify the skin of your body, which is destined for death. Then you will receive it glorified in the general resurrection."

Antonio spoke as he walked slowly back to the pulpit. "Descend to minister humbly to your downtrodden neighbor. Descend to assist and condescend to raise up your fallen brother. 'Men should regard us as servants of Christ and stewards of the mysteries of God,' Paul writes in the First Letter to the Corinthians. Isaiah says, 'You shall be called the priests of the Lord, ministers of God.'"

He stood now before Ugo, gazing at him again. "The ministers and stewards are prelates and preachers of the Church who attend to the word of God and who preach the baptism of penance for the remission of sins."

From the pulpit now, Antonio turned to face his audience. "Concerning these ministers, Isaiah says, 'How beautiful,' since they are free from the filth of sin. 'How beautiful are the feet of him that brings good tidings and that preaches peace!' The good tidings is the message of salvation offered through the peace that God Himself made between Himself and humanity. May we 'show forth good' and 'preach salvation' so that we may proclaim to every soul, 'Your God' and not sin 'shall reign' in you. Amen."

As Antonio stepped from the pulpit, he turned to Ugo and bowed. Ugo leaped up and embraced him, then turned Antonio to face the court again. "Behold, the ark of the testament!" Ugo called to the assembly. "Should the Bible be lost, Fra Antonio could write it from memory!"

A thunderous cheer rose from most of the cardinals and legates and swelled the hall. Ugo noticed immediately that those who were merely politely clapping were the very ones whom he had seen riding about the city in their painted sedans or on the backs of expensive steeds. Antonio's words had penetrated deeply. Ugo beamed at the red-cheeked priest.

"I speak God's word, Lord Pope," Antonio said softly, "not mine. God's. To Him belongs this praise."

The people will praise Him as well, when they hear your words tomorrow, Ugo thought.

⇝

On that warm and sunny April morning, the square outside the Basilica di San Giovanni in Laterano was jammed with pilgrims from every conceivable nation. As Ugo and Antonio walked together out of the basilica, a cheer rose from the crowd. Ugo raised his hands for silence, then introduced Antonio. Another cheer swelled. Ugo stepped back into the shadow of the basilica while Antonio walked forward to the edge of the top step and bowed his head.

After his opening prayer, Antonio called out the text that he had chosen. "Jesus said to Simon Peter, 'Simon, son of John, do you love Me more than these?' From the holy Gospel according to John. In the name of the Father, and of the Son, and of the Holy Spirit."

Ugo watched the sweeping motion of the cross pass over the crowd. These people, travelers from many lands both near and far, were his children who abided in the house of his Church. Could he be a good and holy Father to them? Would their Church stand?

Antonio's voice rang forth. "Jesus did not ask Peter the question only once, but a second and a third time. 'Simon, son of John, do you love Me more than these?'

"Three times the Lord heard Peter answer that he loved Him. 'Sì, Lord. You know that I love You.'"

Antonio paused. "Why, you may ask, did Jesus ask three times instead of only once? Because Peter had thrice denied his Lord." Antonio raised his left hand with three fingers held up to the crowd. To Ugo, the sun was visible just beneath his arm, its rays caught against the friar's dark habit, holding him in a glow. "Following Christ's arrest in the Garden, Peter had three times denied knowing Christ." The priest now held out his right hand with three fingers visible. "Now he three times proclaimed his love." As he spoke, he brought both hands together until the fingers of each touched the other. Sunlight gleamed around the two meeting arms, making Antonio's body into the shadow of a cross. "Peter's threefold admission of love parallels his triple denial. Peter thus shows that the tongue ought to be prompted no less by love than by fear."

Thus Antonio's sermon developed, contrasting Peter's denials, his repentance, and his admission of love. Ugo again found himself swept up in the message.

Suddenly, Antonio turned toward the Lateran and flung open his arms. "Behold the Church!" Then he turned to the crowd and extended his arms over them as if to embrace them all. "Behold the Church! The Church from the least of her members to the most noble of her hierarchy was commended to Peter by Christ with the words, 'Feed My lambs.' For we are the lambs of Christ. Christ cares for us. He, as the faithful shepherd, 'laid down His life for His sheep.' Having bought us at so high a price, He wished to commend us to Peter in His stead."

Antonio dropped his arms and turned directly toward Ugo. "Jesus commanded Peter, 'Feed My sheep.' Feed them with the words of your preaching. Feed them with the help of your devout prayers. Feed them with the example of a good life."

Antonio's direct address to him startled Ugo and broke his concentration on the brother's preaching. He noticed the sun again, considerably higher in the sky than when Antonio had begun preaching. How long had every face in the crowd maintained uninterrupted focus on the friar? Certainly, those who understood the Roman dialect that Antonio was speaking would follow his words. But many in the crowd were from Germany, England, Portugal, and other nations. How had he managed to hold their attention? Ugo couldn't spot one inattentive face.

Antonio turned again to the crowd. "Where does Christ feed His lambs? In the Church. Here in the Church the sinner is readmitted by means of faith and repentance. Here the repentant one can share in all the spiritual goods that abound in the Father's house."

Antonio flung his left arm backward to indicate Ugo. "Who is to lead the Church but Peter?" Drawing his arm forward and bringing his right arm up to meet it over his head, Antonio joined his two hands in a tight fist. "Jesus declared to Peter, 'You are "Rock" and on this rock I will build My Church and the jaws of death shall not prevail against it.'" Antonio opened his arms over the crowd. "Jesus did not say that Peter would be called a rock but that he is truly a rock." Now he drew his hands together, again forming a fist. "Peter was made a rock by Christ. He was made a sharer in the only foundation, which is Christ and on which the Church is built." Releasing his grip, he lifted his hands and face heavenward. "Indeed, Saint Paul writes in the First Letter to the Corinthians, 'No one can lay a foundation other than the one that had been laid, namely Jesus Christ.'"

Antonio turned and looked at Ugo for a brief moment, then again faced the crowd. "We need not, therefore, fear for the Church's stability. Even if the raging persecution of the devil and of human persons beats against it, even if heretical currents, like overflowing rivers, rip through the dike, even then we must not fear that devastation will come to our Church."

Again, he raised his arms and joined his hands above his head. "Our Church will always stand firm because it is built upon a rock."

Ugo bowed his head. *Lord, God, how wonderful You are! You have spoken to me through this man's words. Thank You for reminding me that Your Church will remain.*

"Jesus told Peter, 'I will entrust to you the keys of the kingdom of heaven.' Peter the rock was made head of the apostles and of the universal Church. He was entrusted with the power to bind and to loose. What is this power? It is the ability to distinguish the worthy from the unworthy and the power to admit the former and to exclude the latter from the kingdom of God."

Ugo, the Successor to Peter, felt a thrill of faith running through his blood. He knew what Antonio preached. He had heard it all his life. But now God was speaking it to his heart. The words had been directly addressed to less than two hundred men throughout history. Ugo was one.

Antonio turned toward Ugo and took his hand. Drawing Ugo forward, he raised Ugo's hand high. "Although the whole Church has power in its priests and bishops, although all the priests and bishops must feed the flock, God gave power and mission to Peter in a special manner. 'Peter, do you love Me more than these?' In his submission to God's will in leading all the faithful to eternal life, Peter has given his answer."

Still holding Ugo's hand heavenward, Antonio lifted his other hand to heaven and gazed skyward. "May we all pray for and obey Peter as he guides the flock of our Church. May the Holy Spirit grant him the words to feed the lambs of the fold. May the Son, the Good Shepherd, enable Peter also to 'lay down his life for the sheep.' May the Father increase in Peter the wisdom and holiness to direct the Church." His voice rose as his upheld arms trembled. "Oh, Lord, in unity of faith and communion with the Church, may we be absolved from sin and enter into heaven. Amen."

Antonio's grip tightened on Ugo's hand before he released it and dropped his arms. Ugo was left standing with his hand raised over the crowd.

A cheer rose from the listeners. The name Ugo heard was not Antonio's but his own. "Lord Pope, pray for us."

Antonio stepped back as Ugo moved forward and raised his other hand to quiet the crowd. Suddenly Ugo realized that everyone within listening distance of Antonio had understood every word that he had preached. How could that be?

DO NOT RESIST THE WILL OF HEAVEN, he again heard in his heart. I HAVE CHOSEN ANTONIO TO SPEAK MIGHTILY TO MY PEOPLE. I HAVE CHOSEN YOU TO LEAD MY FLOCK. LEAD THEM WELL IN MY NAME UNTIL I TAKE YOU HOME.

A profound peace penetrated Ugo's soul. Antonio's mission was to preach, and God would bless that preaching. Ugo's mission was to guide, and God would bless that guidance. Each man was where God had placed him. In that place lay each man's ultimate submission to God and ultimate salvation. In that place, each would be effective for Christ.

Bowing his head, his arms extended over his flock, Ugo called out to the silent crowd in a clear, deep voice. "May the Lord of all creation bless you. May His Holy Spirit guide you. May His Son save you and bring you to eternal life. I now bless you all in the name of the Father, and of the Son, and of the Holy Spirit. Amen."

NOTES

The election of Ugolino (also spelled Hugolin or Hugolino) and his reaction to it are accurate; he actually tore his garments and tried unsuccessfully to refuse the pontificate. He submitted because he felt that he should not resist the will of heaven.

Ugolino calling himself by the shortened Ugo is pure speculation.

Ugo's words about fully understanding Francesco's mind are from his bull *Quo elongati* (FA:ED I 571).

In the words used in this chapter, Francesco granted Antonio written permission to teach the brothers (FA:ED I 107).

Ugo's relationship to the Lesser Brothers and his attendance at chapter gatherings follow the histories (FA:ED II 104). Francesco's refusal to consider another Rule, proposed by Ugolino at the request of the brothers, is accurate (FA:ED II 132, III 124–25).

No one is certain when Antonio's body began to swell from edema (dropsy). The early histories mention his corpulence (*Assidua* 12, *Dialogus* 2). Whether or not Ugo spoke to Antonio about his health is unknown.

In some unstated year, "the minister of the order" sent Antonio "to the papal curia because of an urgent matter concerning the religious family" (*Assidua* 13). At this time, the pope asked him to preach to the Curia and called him "The Ark of the Testament" (*Assidua* 13, Rig 12, Ben 3, 2LJS 4, *Dialogus* 2, FA:ED III 631). He also asked him to preach to the crowds assembled "to gain the Easter indulgences," and the crowd miraculously understood him in their native tongues (Ben 5). History does not record Antonio's words on either of these occasions.

Antonio and other brothers were again sent to Rome for similar reasons after the May 1230 chapter meeting. By then, however, the Easter indulgences were concluded. The *Assidua* hints that Antonio went to Rome at least twice by placing his preaching to the cardinals after his visits to Rimini, which occurred in 1223 and again in 1227, but before the May 1230 chapter.

This book postulates that the "urgent matter" was whether Francesco would have permitted learned brothers to teach in addition to Antonio. Some brothers who had been university professors were teaching, but what about other learned brothers who were not professors? If they were deemed capable and theologically sound, would Francesco have permitted them to teach? A meeting, such as the one postulated in this chapter, must have preceded the permission, which was granted around this time.

Antonio would have gone to Rome with a traveling companion, unnamed in the histories.

Antonio's words are from Praise 52 (his prayer to the Holy Spirit) and SK 37–40, 111–15 (his sermon to the crowd). His sermon before the cardinals is from SK 161–65 and "You Will Find an Infant," published in *Messenger of Saint Anthony*.

Scripture verses are from Luke 3:2–4 ("The word of the Lord . . ."); Exodus 13:16 ("It shall be as a sign . . ."); Proverbs 25:25 ("As cold water . . ."); 1 Kings 19:12 ("Like the whispering . . ."); Job 32:8 ("It is a spirit . . ."); Psalm 119:105 ("Your word is a lamp . . ."); Luke 2:29 ("To your servant . . ."); Luke 2:12 ("You will find an infant . . ."); 1 Corinthians 4:1 ("Men should regard us . . ."); Isaiah 61:6 ("You shall be called . . ."); Isaiah 52:7

("How beautiful . . ."); see 1 Samuel 12:12 ("Your God shall reign . . ."); John 21:15 ("Simon, son of John . . ."); John 10:11 ("laid down his life . . ."); Matthew 16:18–19 ("You are 'Rock' . . ."); and 1 Corinthians 3:11 ("No one can lay . . .").

21

Madonna Delora

Castle Courtyard, Rimini, Italy (Fall 1227)

Youthful Madonna Delora made her way through the courtyard of Messer Tristano. Dogs yapped at her heels and chickens fluttered out of her way. This was the first time that she'd walked through Tristano's courtyard. Other times she'd ridden through on horseback, preceded by banners and followed by ladies-in-waiting. Her gown then had been of shimmering silk, its long, pointed sleeves rubbing the flanks of her steed, and her chestnut hair plaited in the center, wreathed with flowers. Those times, she had come as a noblewoman and a wife. Today, she returned as a black-robed, widowed perfecti.

The pain of her young husband's death came back to her swiftly and unexpectedly. Curses on these feudal wars that had claimed her spouse! Even as she walked, she pictured him in this courtyard as he had been three years ago, proudly astride his brown stallion while she followed behind. That same horse had carried home his broken and bloodied body. Madonna Delora sucked in a huge gulp of air. It chased her faintness and, she knew, brought color to her cheeks. She had promised herself that she wouldn't cry, that she would show, like all perfecti, that she knew that suffering in this world was the lot of humans.

Her husband's death had opened her to Catharist doctrine. Her wobbly faith had not sustained her in her loss. Nor had her priest been any consolation. He had been quick to take the funeral offering but made no move to comfort her.

She needed answers, so she sought one of the Good Men who had been preaching around Rimini. He had told her that her husband wouldn't enter eternal life since he didn't know the good God. Instead, his spirit would be reborn in another body. Only when he became a Cathar would he be guaranteed heaven.

Then he had asked, "And what of you?" Madonna Delora admitted that she knew very little of her Roman faith and nothing of Catharist doctrine. "Our canon told us to avoid listening to the Cathars, so we did," she had confessed.

The elder had counseled her, assuring her that her destiny was certain if she, too, became a Cathar. He used Scripture as he instructed her. Certainly he must be right. So she had fasted and studied for a year and taken the consolamentum. Then she had gone to live at a hospice where she prayed and fasted and instructed other women who visited there. Some of them were now on their way to becoming Good Christians.

Messer Tristano had invited Madonna Delora to his castle feasts several times since her husband's death. Today was the first time she had felt strong enough to come. A few Good Men were invited, too, Messer Tristano had told her. The rest, including the lord, were Catharist believers, not yet perfecti like herself.

"Madonna Delora!"

She turned to her right at the call and broke into a smile.

Messer Tristano bounded out of the stable area and hurried to the woman. She smiled at the muscular, red-and-black-silk-clad figure who immediately dropped to one knee before her and placed his hands on the ground. "Praise the Lord," he said, turning his head to one shoulder and bowing.

How strange it felt for a good friend to greet her in this typical Catharist fashion! Yet she was a Cathar now, she reminded herself. She turned her head to one shoulder and replied, "Praise the Lord. May God bring you to a good end."

The count rose to his feet. Madonna Delora wanted him to embrace her chastely as he used to do, but he refrained. She felt a rush of pain at the loss of this touch. No man was to touch a female perfecti.

"So good to see you," the count said with genuine enthusiasm. "But where is your traveling companion?"

"She grew ill with fever. I came alone."

"The roads are dangerous."

"God is with me."

"Sì. Of course. Let me lead you into the banquet hall, Madonna." Then the count turned toward the stable and shouted. "And feed well the steeds of my guests."

A hooded groom peeked out the door and called, "Sì, Messer."

Tristano grinned. "Tonight, Madonna, you shall have a surprise. Tonight, you shall see the advance of the Cathars in the Romagna."

"You tease me," she said as they ascended a curved staircase to the castle.

"Not at all. I have invited Fra Antonio to dine with us."

She tried to hide her dismay with a smile, but Messer Tristano had seen the brief pursing of her lips.

"I know. He's a threat."

A threat. What an inadequate word! Antonio had created a stir when he had come to Rimini years ago before traveling to other parts of the Roman Empire and to France. More than once, he had been at the papal residence. He was now provincial of the Romagna. As such, he had jurisdiction over all the Lesser Brothers in the region. At his word, they were under obedience to do and say as he dictated. And he could dictate that they stir up the people against the perfecti just like the followers of the preaching friar Domingo de Guzmán had done in France. If the French wars were duplicated in the Romagna, the Cathars would suffer pillage and murder at the crusaders' hands.

"You fear that Fra Antonio will urge the taking up of weapons against us," Messer Tristano said. He didn't wait for an answer. "We all fear it. It won't happen."

Tristano led the way into the banquet hall. Already many guests were present, a few of whom were robed all in black. Perfecti. She saw, too, that Antonio was standing near two of these Good Men. He was nodding as they spoke. A tingle of fear crept up Delora's spine and tightened her face. It was the same nameless but real fright that had knotted her stomach for the two days before her dead husband was brought home.

Tristano escorted her to a banquet table with other women, one of them perfecti and the remaining two dozen believers. He must have seen the startled look on her face as she noticed men seated across the room.

"I know it's odd," Tristano said, courteously pulling out Delora's chair for her, "but I wanted you and the other women also to hear the priest. So you will dine in here with us men."

Delora smiled demurely. "You have novel ideas, Messer."

She chatted with the women while the other guests took their seats. Then Tristano strode into the center of the huge hall between the two rows of tables. Directly across from Delora sat the gray-robed priest near the head of the table.

"Following our banquet, Padre Antonio will address us," Tristano called out. He nodded at the priest. "We all wish to hear your words, Padre," he grinned.

"Or perhaps you wish to see me eat another toad," Antonio returned the smile.

Uneasy laughter rippled through the banquet hall. Madonna Delora had heard the story about the toad. A Catharist baron had invited Antonio and several Cathars to dinner. They had intended to ridicule the priest by serving him a huge, plump toad, nicely roasted and lying on a bed of parsley.

As the plate had been placed before Fra Antonio, the other banqueters had burst into raucous laughter. No fastidious canon who graced his table with the choicest foods would dare to touch such a repulsive creature.

"We simply wish to see if you follow Scripture," the baron had said. "For Saint Paul wrote, 'If any unbeliever invite you and you be willing to go, eat anything that is set before you, asking no questions, for conscience's sake.'"

After blessing the hideous creature, Antonio had dug into it with as much relish as if he were eating a fine, baked hen. After the meal, he had explained his faith at length to the guests, some of whom were no longer Cathars when they returned home.

"No toads tonight, Padre," Tristano promised, taking his seat.

"It was quite good," Antonio said with a smile, "although most people would prefer trout."

Again, laughter burst from the feasters. After that, the mood of the gathering relaxed. Still, Madonna Delora felt that tingle of dread. Perhaps she was uneasy because Messer Tristano was being unusually kind to a priest whom he feared. He had seated the man at his right, where Madonna Delora could clearly see him urging the priest to eat heartily of this and that tastefully prepared dish.

As the banquet progressed, the women spoke quietly among themselves. The men were more spirited as they engaged in a verbal tournament with the priest. A baron would make a remark on a point of doctrine, backing it up with Scripture, and Antonio would counter with a point and Scripture quotation of his own. Terms like "Eucharist," "purgatory," and "angels" were being bandied about like balls.

Maidservants were setting small plates of cooked wheat seasoned with herbs, olive oil, and vegetables before each guest. Madonna Delora and the others would eat only after Messer Tristano took the first bite. Discreetly watching her host spoon a few grains into his mouth, Madonna Delora saw Antonio reach for his plate and then draw back his hand.

He spoke quietly. "So, my friends, you have invited me here to poison me." Swift denials rose throughout the room. "This does not please our good God Who, all here agree, condemns murder."

Madonna Delora stared in horror at Antonio's food. She could see absolutely nothing to distinguish it from anyone else's. And why should it look different? If someone wanted to poison the priest, the criminal would have chosen a substance that would be tasteless, invisible, and potent.

"Why do you want to kill me?"

"We don't wish to kill you," Messer Tristano said. "We only wish to test this text from the Bible. Is it not written of Christ's apostles, 'If they shall drink any deadly thing, it shall not hurt them'? Either you believe the words of the Gospel, or you don't. If you believe them, why hesitate to eat? Eat, then."

Antonio looked squarely at Tristano. "It is unnecessary that the truth of this text always be shown to everyone who tests it. God works this miracle only when it is necessary to His plan."

"You claim that God wills us to return to the Church. Is this not, in your opinion, God's plan?" one of the Good Men asked.

"We should never tempt God's infinite power with these trials, as you well know. Even your own faith doesn't depend on tests."

"True. God's truth is verified by divine revelation. We have never taught that this text should be taken as written. The deadly drink refers not to drinks or foods, which, being material, are products of the evil god. Rather, it refers to the drink of doctrines of false faiths, which Good Christians confront and confound."

"You are wrong," Antonio countered. "This passage must be taken literally. In the beginning of the Church, this and other miracles nourished the faith that, like a tender plant, needed roots to grow. Faith, now well planted and grown up, has no need of special miracles in order to flourish."

"You misunderstand," said Messer Tristano. "We mean that, if we see you eating this poisoned food without harm, then we will believe what you preach. We will join your Church because you will have proved that it holds the truth."

Antonio nodded and bowed his head, then raised his eyes to heaven. When his gaze returned to Messer Tristano, he said, "I will eat this food, not to tempt God, but purely to honor His Gospel. If I live, may you hold to your pledge. If I die, it will be due to my sin, not to the error of God's words or the powerlessness of our Creator."

Then, holding his right hand over the poisoned wheat, he made the sign of the cross. He picked up his spoon and dipped it into the food, then raised the spoonful to his mouth. Time seemed to halt. No one spoke. Even the dogs who roamed beneath the tables looking for scraps ceased to move.

The priest ate one bite and then another. He lifted the water glass to his lips, took a generous drink, and then finished the plate of herbed grain.

"You must tell your chef to poison your food more often, Messer Tristano. I have never tasted anything quite this good."

Madonna Delora stared at the priest. It was not so much that he had not been harmed but that he had eaten. She had never seen anyone with that much trust in God.

The guests returned to their meal. Discussion resumed at the men's table. Maids brought in more foods. The feast went on for another hour. At its end, Messer Tristano and several other believers had pledged to return to the Church. Madonna Delora was not one of them.

He may be a good and holy priest, she thought, *and certainly God is with him.* But she could not erase from her memory the coarse way in which she had been treated upon her husband's death. Antonio, she knew, would have treated her with kindness and understanding. *But he's a traveling brother,* she told herself. *He isn't the whole Church.* For now, she would remain with the charitable, compassionate Cathars. Miracles and theology would not make her follow the Church of Rome. Only love would do that.

NOTES

Madonna Delora and Messer Tristano are fictitious characters through whom two miracles regarding the saint are related. The Catharist dress, manner of greeting, foods, and lifestyle, as told in this chapter, are accurate.

The two feasts involving Antonio and the heretics are in the historical record. At the time, heresies other than Catharism existed. History doesn't record to which sect the heretics of the feasts belonged. The Cathars were the most numerous heretics and Rimini was one of their strongholds.

Da Rieti 80–81 states that the saint turned the toad (Keller 12 calls it a bat) into a capon, but this seems untypical for a Franciscan, since they frequently mortified the appetite by sprinkling ashes on their food. It seems more likely that Antonio would have eaten the toad with as much relish as if he were eating a hen.

Antonio's reaction to the poisoned meal is accurate (Rig 9). History doesn't record how many dishes were poisoned or what they were.

After both these feasts, many heretics returned to the Church. Most of Antonio's converts were believers. He had little success among perfecti, who had completed the consolamentum.

Scripture verses are 1 Corinthians 10:27 ("If any unbeliever . . .") and Mark 16:18 ("If they drink . . .").

22

Fabio

Highway, Padua, Italy (Lent 1228)

Fabio waited in the underbrush along with eleven other robbers, half on one side of the highway and half on the other. He had tucked his brown curls beneath his olive-green snood and tied a gray rag around his nose and mouth so that only his black eyes showed. His thick knees were tightly clamped to the belly of his chestnut steed and his big, pudgy hands securely grasped the reins. He had thought that he heard a tinkling of little bells. If he had, it meant that a wealthy band of Paduans would soon be along.

Padua was a treasure trove for Fabio and his band, a sensual place where wealth flowed like water. Rich silks, gaudy jewels, and luxuriant furs clothed those many citizens who lived in the extravagant palaces of the area. Money was in ample supply, and those who had too little found plenty of moneylenders from whom to borrow if they were willing to pay exorbitant interest.

Sì, he had heard the chimes. A gentle jingling filled the air. The bells, Fabio knew, were attached to the breast straps of mounted horses. His heart began to pound with excitement, anticipation, and dread. He hated these robberies, but how could he live without them?

Five years ago, when he was sixteen, Fabio had been a serf, working with his father, grandfather, and brothers for one of the barons of Padua. How he hated the sowing and hoeing and mowing! His eyes smarted from the work. His plump body sweated like an animal's. The chaff from the wheat and dust from the furrows caught in his knee and elbow joints and irritated him. How many times had he wished to be done with toil forever? Yet he had been born a serf and he would die a serf.

Then muscular, intelligent Drago, who was three years older than himself and the son of another serf, proposed a plan. They would run away and become thieves. At least they would be free from grinding labor and merciless sun. One night, according to plan, the two young men met and stole away from the estate. In the woods of Padua, they lived for a few days before meeting up with a band of eight other youthful thieves. Joining with them, Drago soon became the leader. Now the band had grown to twelve men and their corresponding stolen steeds. All the men now waited in the underbrush as the tinkling of the bells grew stronger.

As happened every time that the band gathered to ambush a group, Fabio fought an urge to wheel his horse around and streak off into the forest. He wished he could live alone, hermit-like, among the glades. He loved to wander among the thick, massive trees, the soft green feathers of ferns parting before his feet. More precious to him than the jewels he stole were the clear streams whose waters danced and sang over beds of smooth pebbles. The scent of autumn compost was, to him, headier than a woman's perfume, and the wild almonds and walnuts that he gathered in the woods tasted better to him than choice cakes. In the forest, life was free and he was at peace.

At camp, he felt differently. The coarse jokes of the other men often erupted into fights, frequently with drawn weapons. Wine, drunk too freely, intensified quarrels, and he had several times backed away from the protection of a night fire, preferring to take his chances with bears or wolves than to be part of escalating and dangerous arguments among beastly humans.

The robberies themselves were not to his liking either. Even now, as he prepared to commit another crime, Fabio regretted the fear in the eyes of those he robbed, as if he, no more dangerous than a kitten, would rape or murder or beat another human being. He was horrified at the thought that maybe he would actually do those things someday and turn into the beasts with whom he lived.

He hated the sickening reality that he could make a mistake and turn his back on a knife. He would feel it plunge into his side, and he would topple from his horse to die in the dust of the road.

Worse than all these thoughts was the one that lurked deep inside his soul. Continuously he harbored a persistent accusation that what he did was wrong, so wrong in the eyes of God that his thievery in this life would earn him damnation in the next. The thought of his final and eternal fate terrified him.

But how could he abandon the life that he led? He couldn't return to the fields to work. If he ever went back to being a serf, his spirit would shrivel like a fig in the sun.

The sound of the bells grew stronger. From it, Fabio could tell that this cortège had about half a dozen members. He tightened his grip on the reins and beat his wavering spirit into submission. Thievery was his life. It was do this or die.

As the richly blanketed horses came into view, Drago, followed by five other robbers, burst through the bushes on the opposite side of the road. Fabio spurred his horse as did the other robbers on his side of the road. Instantly the cortège was surrounded.

Immediately in his path rode a silver-haired matron in a maroon gown and blue cape. Sharply reining his horse in front of her dappled steed, Fabio pulled his thin-bladed knife from its hilt and wordlessly pointed to two gold rings on the woman's hand.

As the woman's horse jerked to a halt, she gaped at him. He looked into the woman's eyes, eyes that were as huge as a cornered rabbit's, and he longed to tell her that he wouldn't hurt her. But he said nothing. Instead, he again pointed to the rings.

With wildly trembling fingers, the woman tugged at the rings that, Fabio knew, were sticking to her sweaty fingers. Patiently he waited for her as he had waited for many other frightened women. Finally, the matron managed to twist off the jewelry. Fabio held out his steady palm and she dropped the rings into it.

Then, with the blade of his knife, he pointed to a big golden brooch that fastened the woman's cape. As he paced his steed up and down before her to block any escape, the woman fumbled with the clasp. Finally, the brooch came loose. Fabio thrust his dagger toward the woman, who, despite her violently shaking wrist, managed to slip the valuable piece over the tip of the blade. Flicking the blade upward so that the brooch dropped securely onto it, Fabio made a deep bow and then deftly dropped the brooch into his palm. As he tucked all the jewelry into a leather pouch attached to his waist, the other robbers pulled back from the cortège and Drago swept his arm toward the woods. In an instant, Fabio had wheeled his horse into the forest and was bolting back toward the thieves' campsite.

He reined his panting horse before the thieves' cave deep in the forest. Dismounting, he pulled the saddle from the horse's back and began to rub down his animal with a cloth that was hanging from a nearby pine.

Swiftly the glade filled with other robbers. Gray-robed Drago rode into the clearing last of all and slid from his golden horse. With a flourish, he pulled a frayed basket from a peg pounded into a maple and tossed the container to the ground.

One by one, the robbers pitched their loot into the basket. Fabio gladly dropped in the rings and brooch, whose luster mocked his own filth. He who had been born to spread dung in a field had robbed a baroness of her goods.

Shaggy-haired Drago picked up the basket and jingled its contents. "Well done, men. This will last us a while."

As the robbers rubbed the lather from their tired horses, they began their familiar banter.

"So, Drago, today you rob the rich. Tomorrow you go to hear the saint, eh?" one man called out as he massaged his horse's flank.

"They say he preaches like the prophet Elijah," another remarked.

"I will believe that when I hear it," exclaimed a third.

"Who isn't curious about him?" Drago said, heaving the saddle from his own mount.

"We'll all go to hear him preach."

Fabio rubbed white foam from the chestnut haunches of his winded horse and thought about hearing a saint preach tomorrow. Would God strike him dead before letting him sully the presence of a holy man?

→⫛

The following day, the robbers walked into Padua in clusters of two or three. Each had shaved and put on fresh, clean tunics and stockings. Each tried to appear confident and non-threatening. No one wanted to be noticed, so they left their stolen horses at the cave. Since the steeds belonged to the residents of Padua, they were likely to be recognized.

As the crowded main piazza of the city came into sight, the men dispersed themselves among the gathering people. Now they were merely individuals among many others. Fabio halted at the edge of the massive crowd a good distance from a small platform that had been erected in the piazza. Here, he could listen to the saint yet be able to sprint away quickly if recognized. He fished in his pouch for an almond, chosen from four huge baskets that the robbers had gathered in the forest the previous fall.

As he cracked the hard shell between his teeth, he studied the crowd. Judging by its immense size, Fra Antonio's reputation had preceded him.

"Sì, he preached in Treviso," observed a nearby butcher, his leather apron stained with blood.

The candlemaker whom he had addressed scratched his head. "I thought it was Venice."

Fabio thought he'd join in. "Maybe both places? What's he going to talk about?"

"Dunno," grunted the butcher. "Came here on Wednesday to preach the Lenten sermons."

"I thought he came on Tuesday," the candlemaker countered.

"Preaching every day, so I heard," the butcher nodded.

Every day? That would be a lot of preaching!

Fabio looked at that amazing man, a good distance away on the platform. His head, which had been lifted to heaven in prayer, now lowered. The priest gazed at the vast crowd from one end of it to the other and then called out in a resounding voice, "'Peter found at Lydda a man named Aeneas, a paralytic who had been bedridden for eight years. And Peter said to him, "Aeneas, may Jesus Christ heal you; arise and set your bed in order." Aeneas got up immediately.' The Book of Acts." Antonio bowed his head and crossed himself, "In the name of the Father, and of the Son, and of the Holy Spirit."

Fabio signed himself as well.

"Aeneas means poor and miserable. Aeneas is the sinner in mortal sin; he is poor in virtue and miserable because he is a slave of the devil. This sinner is a paralytic, for he lies in a bed of carnal concupiscence with all his members dissolute." Antonio lifted his left hand over the crowd. "And what will be the result of this paralysis?"

He paused while Fabio's mind, and probably every other listener's as well, fished for an answer to the question.

"Death! 'For the wages of sin is death,' Paul tells us in the Letter to the Romans. All of us shall die."

Antonio paused. His words penetrated the crowd, who waited as still as corpses. Fabio envisioned himself lying in a road, a dagger in his back.

"Genesis says, 'You are dust and unto dust you shall return.' How fragile we are! Psalm 90 tells us, 'Our years shall be considered like those of a spider.'"

Like those of a spider whose web often hung, dew-dropped, across the upper corner of the robbers' cave.

"What is more fragile than a spider's web? The flick of a hand can sweep it away at once. As easily broken is a person's life. A small injury or the slightest fever can destroy a life. When a miserable person considers how fragile he is, that person begins to think about eternity."

Goodness, the priest was right. Fabio would not always be young. Someday he would die. He might die of illness, or injury, or plague, or accident, or old age. He might be hanged as a thief or killed by someone he had attempted to rob. Someday he would die. That was certain.

"'The wages of sin is death.' Those who sin mortally have already established a place for themselves," Antonio paused again, "in hell."

Hell? Wasn't there a commandment that said, "Thou shalt not steal"? How much had he stolen in the past five years? Jewels? Coins? Gold? The peace of mind of his victims? Perhaps they awoke at night shrieking as they dreamed again of being ambushed on a highway.

"Sinners are bound by a yoke of eternal death. For the demons that beset a person and hold him captive impose a heavy yoke on his neck. They tug the sinner along with a rope, driving him like an ox or an ass and giving the wearied one no rest as they drive him from one sin to another."

Fabio had started out hating the fields. He had abandoned his father and run away. He had turned to thievery. He had laughed at coarse jokes and, although he had not yet assaulted a woman, he had not tried to stop Drago or some of the others from doing so. In only a matter of time, he would become like those with whom he lived. The yoke of sin was heavy on his neck. He would move from one sin to the next as surely as a rock kicked downhill would bounce along until hitting the bottom.

"Yet we are not beasts as oxen and asses are. We can command the demons that beset us to halt. Does the sinner do this? How crazy can one be, being worn out on a road and being unwilling to halt? Only when the sinner says, 'Enough. No more,' does he form a will to repent. And this will is not of the sinner's own creation. God beckons us wretches to a new life. By the inspiration of His grace and the preaching of the Church, the Lord calls the sinful soul to repentance."

Fabio lowered his head. If only he could repent. But repent meant to give up. How could he give up his way of life? He had no other talents. He couldn't return to the fields.

"Peter's vicar says to the sinner, 'Aeneas, poor and miserable, let Jesus Christ heal you. Arise through contrition and set your things in order through confession. You yourself, not another, must get yourself in order.'"

How? How could he possibly do this? The priest had no idea how difficult it was to change a way of life when no alternative existed.

"Surely when the sinner is truly sorry, God will forgive him. For the truly sorry person proposes to confess. When this happens, immediately the Lord absolves that person from the fault and from eternal death. Because of the sinner's remorse over his sin, his eternal death is changed into a purgatorial debt of punishment. The contrite person then goes to the priest and confesses."

Goes to the priest and confesses? Fabio shuddered. Tell a priest about years of stealing? How could he do such a thing? The very idea of baring his soul made his stomach flutter.

"As soon as the soul confesses, a wondrous thing occurs. The soul is forsaken by the devil and then lifted up to God. The devil cannot abide in a repentant soul. And the one whom the devil thus forsakes, Christ takes up." Antonio lifted his hands together as if lifting a child. "You see, God has greater care for the

salvation of human beings than the devil has for their perdition. Come, therefore. Admit your sin and the devil will abandon you into the arms of your
Father."

Could it be true? Could God truly want him, a sinner?

"'And immediately Aeneas arose.' He left his bed of carnality and with it the
paralysis of sin. He arose because Christ, in His forgiveness, healed him and
absolved him from every bond of wickedness."

How Fabio wished to arise as well, to walk again in freshness and goodness,
to know the power of grace!

"And, to show that forgiveness must be genuine, the priest imposes on the
repentant soul a temporal penance. This temporal penance replaces or lessens
the purgatorial punishment. If the temporal expiation is authentically completed, the person is ready to enter into glory. Thus God and the priest together
forgive and absolve."

What penance could he possibly be given for all his crimes? How many
lashes would it take to beat the sin out of him? How many hangings from the
gibbet to repay society for all he had unlawfully taken?

"And now the sinner, having confessed and been forgiven, having entered on
a path of penance, is not alone. For Jesus, Whose hand is strong, leads the soul
forward from virtue to virtue. Isaiah proclaims, 'I am the Lord your God, Who
take you by the hand and say to you, do not be afraid for I have helped you.' You
have all seen a loving mother holding the hand of her child trying to climb the
stairs behind her. She supports and encourages the little one to take the next step
and the next, never once abandoning the child who is just learning to walk."

Fabio imagined his mother teaching him to walk, leading him from one
step to the next. As he took those first faltering steps, he must have been a clumsy
child, one whose feet frequently tangled together. Yet his mother had helped
him, tugged him along, caught him when he fell, and kissed away his bruises.

"As a mother guides her child, even so, with an equally loving hand the Lord
takes the hand of the humble penitent to enable him to climb the steps to the
cross. The Lord supports and encourages the penitent as he moves ever higher,
never once abandoning the repentant soul. In fact, God helps that soul to reach
the level of the perfect wherein he may merit to behold the One so desirable to
see, the King in His splendor upon Whom the angels desire to look."

Was God as supportive as that? Would God lead him all the way to eternal life?

"So come, you who are paralyzed with sin and you whom the devil goads from one blunder to the next. Come, you who are weary of life and whose bed of carnality is full of all unpleasantness. Come to Christ in total trust, for the Son Himself says in Isaiah, 'I have made and I will bear; I will carry and I will save.' I have made you and I will bear you on My shoulders like an errant and weary sheep. I will carry you as a nurse carries a child in her arms. How can the Father reply to all this but to say, 'I will save you'?"

Would God be willing to save him, even him, a thief?

"'But,' you say, 'I have no faith that God will save me.' Jesus spoke in no uncertain terms about this. 'Ask and you shall receive,' He promised. 'Seek and you shall find. Knock and it shall be opened. For the one who asks, receives. The one who seeks, finds. The one who knocks shall be admitted.' Ask for faith. Before all else, 'seek God's kingdom and His righteousness.' Begin by asking for the things of heaven, where our treasure, which is our salvation, is and where our heart should be. For in the treasure of our salvation is perfect joy. 'Ask,' therefore, for forgiveness and for faith, 'and you will receive both, that your joy may be full. And that joy no one shall take from you.'"

Joy? What was joy? If only he could feel that, if ever he had.

"Be slaves of sin no more, 'for the wages of sin is death. But the free gift of God is eternal life in Christ Jesus our Lord.' The law of perfect freedom is the love of God, which is perfect in every way and makes us free of slavery. On the miry vastness of worldly pleasures, the works of sinners slip, so that they fall from sin into sin and finally tumble into hell. But the just man's steps do not falter because the law of love is in his heart. The one who continues in that law of love will be blessed in what he does. For love of God confers grace in this present life and happiness in future life. 'The gift of God is eternal life in Christ Jesus our Lord.' May He lead us to this Who is blessed forever, amen."

As Antonio finished speaking, the crowd broke into weeping. Fabio stood with his eyes fixed on the friar. He didn't know what to do with his life, but he had to lay it before that priest.

From the crowd walked men, most garbed in either black, gray, or white tunics, but some dressed much as a knight or noble. Each one found a stool, cart, or upturned barrel placed more or less equidistant from each other around the platform. The rest of the people backed away except those who approached the seated men and knelt, one per man, before one of them. *Those are the priests,* Fabio thought, *and the people confessing to them.*

He hung back, waiting for the crowds to disperse. Off to his right, he caught sight of one of his fellow thieves, who was kneeling, his face in his hands. Fabio went over to him and touched his shoulder.

"I, too, am going to confess," Fabio said. His friend, his eyes moist and red, nodded and rose.

The two men worked their way closer to Antonio, who was seated on the platform steps. From their left came three more of their group. Clustered around the priest were Drago and the others. The men looked at each other in wonder and embarrassment. The entire band was here.

Comments flew back and forth.

"He's shown us a better way."

"I'm done with thievery from now on."

"An honest life for me."

"Poverty is better than hell."

The men waited their turns. Hours passed as penitents filed up to Antonio, sat beside him on the platform steps, and often wept. Then it was their turn. Drago, being the leader, went first. Then another of his band. And another. The sun began to slip close to the horizon and Fabio realized that the day was nearly gone. Antonio had begun speaking in the morning, ended after noon, and had been hearing confessions ever since.

Finally it was Fabio's turn. He felt his pouch. He still had a few almonds left. As he sat beside the priest, he pulled out the nuts and held them out to the friar.

"You've not had anything to eat all day."

Antonio smiled. "I'm used to it." He picked up a nut and looked at it. "You're also a thief, aren't you?" The voice was mild.

Fabio hung his head. "Sì."

"And have you stolen these?"

"No. I picked them in the woods."

Antonio smiled. "Very well, then." He stuck the nut in his mouth and clamped down hard. The shell crackled open. Antonio picked the nut from his lips and held it in one hand and the shell in the other.

"You can learn a lesson from the almond, my brother. In the Book of Genesis, Jacob says, 'The Lord, the Almighty, appeared to me at Luz in the land of Canaan.' Luz means almond," Antonio said, holding the nut meat up to the sun. "The almond is a fitting symbol of penance, for, like penance, the almond has three parts to it."

Startled by the comparison, Fabio gawked at the nut suspended in the long, slender fingers of the friar who sat beside him.

"An almond has a bitter skin, a hard shell, and a sweet kernel. The almonds that you have brought today are missing the bitter, leathery hull. Why?"

"Well, when the nut is ripe, the hull splits open and the nut inside falls to the ground. I gathered these from the ground."

"Of course. In the bitter skin, we recognize the bitterness of penance, for penance is always bitter to begin. But you will note that you have already begun your penance by approaching the Lord. The bitter skin of admitting wrongdoing has split and fallen away, freeing you to find the joy of forgiveness."

Holding the nut meat in his fist, Antonio took Fabio's hand in his own and opened his palm. Then he dropped into it from his other hand the broken shell. "In the hard shell, we identify the strength of perseverance. Penance, if sincere, always requires perseverance. With perseverance, a sinner who is sorry can perform even the most difficult penance."

Then he held the nut meat to the light. "In the sweet kernel, we rejoice in the hope of forgiveness." He placed the kernel in Fabio's other palm, atop the small pile of uncracked nuts. "The Lord appears, then, in Luz in the land of Canaan. Canaan means change. My brother, you will have true peace if you change from sin to righteousness, for there, at the place of change, at the place of penance, the Lord appears." Antonio plucked another almond from Fabio's hand, cracked the shell with his teeth, and popped the kernel into his mouth.

"Now, if you are willing to change, confess your sins to God."

Fabio glanced at the broken shell in his one hand and the nut meat in the other. He thought of the bitter hull of penance, already split and freeing him to speak. He began his confession. He told Antonio everything that he could remember, including the times that he had lied to his father before he ran away. Antonio listened, nodding.

"Are you sorry for all these offenses? And do you resolve, with God's help, never to commit them again?"

Fabio's brain swirled. He wanted never to commit them again. But how could he? "Fra Antonio, I cannot resolve anything. I'm sick of robbery, but I can do nothing else. I cannot bear the thought of returning to the fields. I would feel trapped like . . . like . . ."

"Like a caged lark." Antonio patted Fabio's knee. "I, too, love the freedom of the forest. But a greater freedom lies with God. You must reject sin if you wish to be truly free."

Fabio's words caught in his throat. How badly he wanted to be truly free! But could he? What if Fra Antonio sent him back to the baron?

"You must repent and turn from sin. Trust God. He shall ask no more of you than you can bear." The priest's hand was warm on his knee, accepting, encouraging.

Within himself Fabio struggled. Could he truly repent?

"Repentance is an act of the will. Will it and God will give you the grace to carry it out."

He felt his opposition weakening. He glanced again at his hand that held the broken almond shell. Turning his palm upside down, he watched the shell slide to the ground. "I will it," he said in a thin voice.

Fra Antonio's voice leapt with a quiet joy. "Good. Then I absolve you from your sins." And he blessed the man. "Now I must give you a penance. Your sins were grave and deserve a grave recompense. You must make twelve trips to the tombs of the apostles in Rome. On foot. You must take nothing with you but the clothes on your back. Sleep wherever you find shelter." Fabio lifted his head and looked at the priest, whose eyes were twinkling. "Even in the woods. If you need food, you may glean the forests for it or you may work for it or beg. Make your pilgrimages, trusting in God's mercy. And, when you reach the tombs, remember me there in prayer. Will you do this?"

Twelve pilgrimages? To Rome? Walking and working along the way? That would take years. How many forests lay between Padua and Rome? How many glades of ferns, wildflowers, and nut trees? He would find these beauties during his journeys. His penance would make him free.

A grin broke across Fabio's face. "You are too good to me."

"No. God is good to you." Antonio touched Fabio's hand that held the almond lying amid a few uncracked nuts.

Curling Fabio's fingers around the nuts, he took the young man's fist in his own two hands and squeezed it gently. "You have made a good beginning. Now wait here until the others confess."

Just as the sun was flinging its night purple and pink across the heavens, the last robber finished with the priest. All twelve stood about clumsily as Antonio arose. Everyone else had gone home except one friar who, all this time, had sat far off to the side of the platform, well out of earshot. He had to be waiting for Antonio.

"I shall bless you all," Antonio said. The men knelt before him in a cluster of colorful tunics and caps.

"But before I bless you, I have one last word to say. You are twelve, the number of Christ's apostles, none of whom was perfect. So take heart. Christ transformed those twelve men and can transform you. You have expressed remorse for your sins and have each resolved to complete the penance which is yours. Now remember this. If you remain true to your God and follow Him faithfully, you will receive an eternal reward with those twelve who left all to follow our Lord. But if you turn back to sin, thus rejecting the One Who died to save you, you will come to a miserable end. Do you understand?"

Twelve voices called agreement.

Antonio extended his arms over the cluster of kneeling men. "Now bow your heads." He paused while the men bowed. "Dearest brothers, let us humbly entreat the mercy of Jesus Christ so that He might come and stand in our midst." Antonio's voice trembled with earnestness. "May He grant us peace, absolve us from our sins, and take away all doubt from our hearts. May He imprint faith in our minds so that, with the apostles and the faithful of the Church, we might merit eternal life." Antonio's voice began to rise in melody as if in song. "May He grant us this, Who is blessed, laudable, and glorious through all ages. Let every faithful soul say, 'Amen!'"

"Amen!" the robbers exclaimed together.

NOTES

In about the year 1292, an unnamed old man told a friar that he had known Sant'Antonio. One of twelve robbers who plundered travelers on the road to Padua, he, with the other disguised members of his band, had gone to hear the saint preach. Antonio's words so moved them all that they each went to confession to him in turn. He gave each a penance and exhorted them not to return to sin. If they persisted in their faith, they would gain eternal life. If they returned to a life of crime, their lives would end in torment. A few did return to the criminal life, the old man said, and their days ended horribly. But he and the rest had persisted in their reform, and those who had already died had gone peacefully.

Antonio had given to this man the penance of making twelve visits to the tombs of the apostles. In 1292, he was just completing his twelfth pilgrimage. With tears, he told the friar that he was now returning home to await his eternal reward, which Antonio had promised him (Rig 14). Rig 14 gives no personal background, name, or description of the robber, nor does it hint at the contents of Antonio's sermon.

Antonio's words for his sermon are compiled from SerE 62–63, 98, 99–100, 148, 179, 194, 196–97, 208, and SK 117–18. His comparison of the almond to penance is from SerE 87, while his final blessing to the robbers can be found in SerE 104.

Scripture verses are from Acts 9:33–34 ("Peter found at Lydda . . ."); Romans 6:23 ("The wages of sin . . ."); Genesis 3:19 ("You are dust . . ."); Psalm 90:9 ("Our years shall be . . ."); Isaiah 41:13 ("I am the Lord . . ."); Isaiah 46:4 ("I have made . . ."); Matthew 7:7–8 ("Ask and you shall . . ."); Matthew 6:33 ("Seek God's kingdom . . ."); John 16:24 ("That your joy . . ."); and Genesis 48:3 ("The Lord, the Almighty . . .").

23

Count Tiso da Camposampiero

Palazzo della Ragione, Padua, Italy (Fall 1229)

Count Tiso da Camposampiero pulled his blue silk cap over his shoulder-length graying hair and stomped down the long upper hall of Padua's Palazzo della Ragione. Years ago, when he was a young man, he'd sold to the city a house on this spot so that the comune could build a mercato and a justice and administration center. This immense building was here because of him, but that made no difference to the clerk he'd just dealt with.

"Messer Severo won't be in until after siesta."

He'd left his estate as the sun was rising to arrive here well before noon, complete his inquiries with the justice administration, and have a leisurely ride back to Camposampiero. Now he'd have to spur his dappled, smoke-colored steed into a slow gallop to arrive home before dark. Why didn't the justice administration have more clerks in its employ?

"Messer Severo won't be in until after siesta."

Tiso clomped down the stairs, his mood growing darker with each step. He supported his city. He lent its governing comune money and saw that the nobility were suitably protected by the statutes. He also loaned money to individuals at a reasonable interest and was patient in waiting to be repaid. Unlike other nobility, Tiso had only a few debtors in prison, and these three whom he'd come to ask about were irresponsible, lazy wretches who had incurred immense debts. Messer Severo would know if they had been able to acquire any of the money owed, but *"Messer Severo won't be in until after siesta."*

What was Tiso supposed to do until then? God knew that he had little time to waste waiting for Messer Severo to arrive. Tiso was embroiled in all the duties that go with being the head of one of the wealthiest and most powerful families of the region. Affairs of his family, estate, city, and territory consumed his days. Sometimes he felt like a rabbit who, in a futile attempt to sample the entire garden, skips from beets to cabbages to carrots without ever fully finishing off any particular plant. He had with him none of the paperwork he needed to get anything done.

In his impatience, he stumbled over the bottom step and almost tumbled into a cheese vendor's stall that was part of the immense covered mercato on the ground floor. Catching his balance, he noticed that the mercato was much less crowded than usual. Come to think of it, the streets also seemed emptier.

"Is something going on today?" he asked the cheese merchant.

"Padre Antonio is speaking right about now."

Tiso must have looked confused.

"Padre Antonio. He's been speaking here for weeks."

"Wasn't he here two summers ago?"

"Sì. When he founded the Lesser Brothers convent, Santa Maria. So many wanted to join that they needed a place to stay. Surely you've heard of Santa Maria?"

Tiso had heard something about it.

"Haven't you heard him speak?"

"No." Tiso didn't have time to hear preachers. The only one he had heard was Friar Preacher Albert, nephew of one of Tiso's friends. Albert, the son of a German count, had been studying at the University of Padua when Albert's uncle had asked Tiso if he'd like to accompany him to hear his nephew. How could Tiso refuse a friend? Albert had converted many, but Tiso was already a good man. He treated his servants fairly. He attended Sunday Mass, gave alms generously, and supported the Church. He confessed and received the Eucharist yearly as required. He had even given the Lesser Brothers a corner of his vast estate on which to build a hermitage, a quiet place for them to rest after their busy affairs in Padua.

"Padre Antonio is speaking today in the Church of Santa Sofia. Or outside it, if everyone can't fit in!" the cheese vendor laughed.

Santa Sofia? A good many people could stand in there. Was Padre Antonio growing so popular that a church the size of Santa Sofia couldn't hold his audience? Since Tiso had nothing better to do, he might as well go to hear the priest and see what all the fuss was about. Santa Sofia was only a short jaunt from the Palazzo della Ragione, and *"Messer Severo won't be in until after siesta."* Antonio's sermon would conclude long before that. Tiso had time to hear this priest.

When he rode toward Santa Sofia, he noticed that the crowd was standing in the piazza next to the church. He maneuvered his horse to the edge of the throng so that the stiff breeze would carry the priest's words in his direction even as it blew Tiso's straying hair away from his long, lean face.

Antonio was already preaching. When he was done, Tiso remembered the general tone of the address. Spiritual fulfillment. Only one phrase stood out, probably because Antonio repeated it several times.

". . . the penitent who sighs for his first conversion and perfection of behavior."

He kept thinking about this even as Messer Severo assured him that his debtors had found people to pay a portion of the debts owed. He thought about it as he spurred his steed the long distance back to Camposampiero, arriving there near dusk. And he shared it with his wife while they supped.

"You're already converted," she said lightly.

That's what he had thought. But maybe he wasn't.

Tiso increased his prayers.

His swineherd didn't ask questions when he requested a pig hide from a slaughtered boar. Nor did the kitchen maid ask him why he wanted her to scrub the hide clean. Beneath his handsome silks, the pig bristles made a suitable hair shirt.

When he asked his household's chaplain to offer Mass a few times a week, the priest was gladly surprised. Then Tiso surprised him even more by attending.

He found some excuse to ride all the way to Padua and listen to additional sermons that Antonio preached. Then Antonio told the crowds that he was preaching in other towns in Lombardy but would return to Padua for Lent. After that final homily, Tiso approached the priest and offered him a room at

Camposampiero, if he ever wanted to get away from the city. To Tiso's delight, Antonio accepted. "In the spring," he said.

So Antonio left. But Tiso's unease didn't. He could neither name nor suppress the growing agitation in his soul. He wasn't a great sinner. Why were Antonio's words so discomfiting? He struggled with these feelings that sometimes, for weeks on end, died down like wilting flowers. But then, just when Tiso convinced himself that he really was a good man who had given God so much, a flash of insight at Mass or during his prayers would flood him with a cloudburst of grace. The dying questions in his soul would revive and spring up, sturdier than ever.

Lent took forever to come.

On Ash Wednesday, Antonio would be preaching in Santa Sofia. The crowd spilled out into the piazza and street. When the time came, Tiso slowly moved forward to receive the ashes, hearing the words repeated over each penitent: "You are dust, and to dust you shall return."

He began to tremble with expectancy. Something whispered in his soul, "After this Lent, you will never be the same."

As Tiso knelt before Antonio, his head bowed to receive a cross of ashes on its crown, he felt the friar's sleeve brush his cheek. It thrilled him as would the touch of an angel's wing.

Thereafter, Tiso went to hear Antonio preach as often as his business allowed. The words that he heard were like a continual, gentle spring drizzle, watering the seeds of grace in his soul and coaxing new, green life from the barren landscape.

One drab day when he almost didn't make the trip to the city, Antonio's words stuck him like a dagger. "If the spirit does not put aside anxious care about temporal things, it never comes near to God. Those who are trapped in endless temporal concerns cause the burdens of sin and the weight of secular care to reach their souls. Temporal things are like a morning cloud. They are like nothing at all, but yet, like a cloud, they appear to be something. The morning cloud hinders our view of the sun, and the excess of temporal goods diverts the soul from thoughts of God."

Tiso, who daily was up early riding about the fields of his estate, had often seen the morning clouds that obscured the sun.

He returned the next day to hear, "The unfruitful soul is suffocated by an abundance of temporal goods. It is then buried and pressed down by the great weight of its own evil ways. The rich man who the evangelist Luke tells us was 'clothed in purple' was buried in the pains of the netherworld because during his earthly life he buried himself in pleasures. Solomon says in the Book of Proverbs, 'A man finds bread sweet when it is got by fraud, but later his mouth is full of grit.' The bread got by fraud is all worldly pomp and glory, which deceptively asserts that it is something whereas it is nothing. This world's glory, because it is sweet to man's taste, will fill his mouth with the grit of fiery ash in eternal punishment where he will be unable to swallow."

For days after, Tiso couldn't eat sweet raisin bread without remembering Antonio's words.

Midway through Lent, Christ Himself called to Tiso in Antonio's words. "The Lord said in the Gospel of Matthew, 'If you wish to be perfect, go and sell all that you have and give your proceeds to the poor. And come and follow Me.' To a person with charity and with a desire to share in the poverty of Christ, the Lord appears.

"For Christ says 'Follow Me.' You who have nothing, who have never possessed anything, follow Me. You who are weighed down with the troubles of life, follow Me. To follow Me, you must cast aside anything that will weigh you down or hold you back, for you will not be able to keep up with Me if you are burdened with extra weight. 'Whoever wishes to be My follower must deny himself,' renounce his own will, 'take up his cross' of denial and mortification 'each day' without ceasing, 'and follow in My steps.' That is what Christ meant when He said, 'Follow Me.'

"Since Christ alone knows the way, how reassuring are His words when He invites us to follow Him! When we follow Christ, we walk a very narrow path. It is the path of justice, poverty, and obedience, a path that Christ followed throughout His life. Although it is a narrow path of moral courage, one can walk along this path with great freedom. Although obedience and poverty appear to confine and restrict one's freedom, they actually liberate us from our chains and set us free. Whoever follows Jesus along the straight and narrow path will not be hampered by attachment to material things or by selfish dependence on his own will, both of which hinder and restrict spiritual progress.

"Follow Me and I will show you what 'eye has not seen, ear has not heard, nor heart of man conceived.' Follow Me and 'I will give you treasures out of darkness and riches that have been hidden away' and 'then you shall be radiant at what you see and your heart will throb and rejoice.' You will see 'God face to face, as He really is.' You will become radiant in body and soul; your heart will throb and overflow with wonder at the choirs of angels and the celestial kingdom of saints."

The sermon rooted Tiso to his corner of the crowded piazza. Through moist morning mist, he seemed to see himself older and ill, feebly lying on a couch surrounded by his possessions. Dying. What if Antonio's clear call to follow Christ was the very last invitation that the count would receive? How he longed for the joy and peace that radiated from that priest! But how could an old man dispense with his riches and follow the call that each day burned more intensely in his soul? He could no longer stand the relentless pain of a life grown burdensome and pointless. He was sick of the seemingly endless war with Ezzelino da Romano and now with his brother Alberico. What was the objective of all this hatred and killing? He needed to speak to Antonio, so he invited him to spend the night at his home within the city walls.

The night before that Tuesday on which Antonio was due to arrive, Tiso calmed his fluttering soul and slept nearly as soundly as the hound at the foot of his bed. But then, while the night was still and dark, he awakened as suddenly as if someone had poked him with a stick. Eyes wide open, he stared into the darkness as all his fears and questions rose in his soul like moths. They flew about his brain, alighting here and there, leaving him in agony. What did God want of him? What if it was too much to give? Should he change? How? What if he never reformed at all? Could he then live with himself in peace? If he did change, could he live with himself? Would Antonio ask him to renounce all his comforts? Could he?

Each question spawned another, and no answers came to swallow any of his wonderings. Finally, in desperation, he threw back his soft blankets and groped in the dark for his breeches that hung on the peg above his bed. He dressed quickly, as if pursued by demons, pulling on the silken garments that he had worn yesterday to a meeting with one of his notaries. He stumbled his way out of the room to the hallway and, taking one of the lamps with him, hurried through the hushed house and slipped outdoors.

As Tiso knew they would, his thoughts seemed to scatter a bit in the vastness of the sleeping city. In his many years of business deals and legal wranglings, he had learned that the problems that squeezed the life out of him in his bedroom always seemed smaller outdoors.

That Tuesday morning, the heavens were still black, but just beyond the outlines of the houses the subtlest shade of pink tinted the sky. Nothing stirred. Not a dog yelped. Not a rooster crowed. Not a maid scurried to market or tossed wastewater into the street. Using the lamp to guide him, Tiso walked through the dozing city.

Oh, God, he prayed, *I want Fra Antonio to come, but I'm afraid of what he'll demand. Help me, Lord. What do You want of me?*

Heavy dew clung in droplets to the flowers and vines that fronted the wooden and stone houses. Even the garbage piled up here and there twinkled with radiance.

In a flash of insight, Tiso recalled Antonio's message of the previous day.

"Dew is like the Paraclete, the Spirit of Truth, that comes gently into the sinner's heart and cools the desires of the flesh."

Could the turmoil within him be the stirrings of God's Spirit?

Lost in thought, he stood still in the street, the light of his lamp playing over a scattering of discarded root tips and wilted greens tossed beside the curb. The dew sparkled on them, making them look almost like gems, but underneath the luster they were still rotting refuse. He saw within himself the Spirit of God, drenching and transforming his indifference, neglect of God, and immersion in the world. Beneath the glitter, in the lamp of a soul being renewed, he now could sense the rot.

From the house that fronted the decaying pile came a startling shriek. Then another scream, a panting that ended in a cry and a low whimper. Then stillness. For a moment, he thought an irate husband was beating his wife. But then he heard the voice again, a woman's voice, sharp with sudden pain. Rapid, agonized breathing. A squeal of surprise. A prolonged moan. And then a man's voice, gruff. "Hold on. A few more pushes, and you'll have him."

Tiso smiled. In the room above his head, a child was being born.

What were Antonio's words in the last sermon that Tiso had heard? They were about birth. He tried to remember.

"Isaiah says, 'In Your presence, O Lord, we have conceived and have brought forth the spirit of salvation.'"

Sì. That was it.

"After it becomes pregnant with the Holy Spirit's grace, your soul feels distress because it is conscious of its sins. 'A woman, when she is in labor, has sorrow, because her hour has come.'"

Sì, his soul was straining to give birth, to bring the new man out of the old. There was only one way to do this, and it involved Antonio.

"The hour of birth is your hour of confession. Now your soul is sorrowful, expressing bitter groans, so that, shamed for your sin, your soul might acknowledge it, weep over it, and in tears receive grace. There you will be delivered."

From the room above Tiso's head erupted a horrifying shriek, a long moan, and then a peal of laughter. "Oh, Bambina! I wanted a daughter, doctor. We have all sons."

Tiso grinned as he imagined the woman holding to her breast her newborn.

"If the soul would endure the pain of labor, beyond a doubt it would rejoice at the birth. About this spiritual birth, the Lord says, 'There is joy in heaven over one sinner repenting.' For, as Isaiah says, 'The troubles of the past will be forgotten. Instead you will be glad and rejoice forever.'"

The woman in the room above him, the woman who had brought forth new life just beyond the dew-covered rot at Tiso's feet, rejoiced in her child. What her child would become she didn't know. Yet she trusted God enough to have brought the babe forth and to leave the future of the child up to the Lord Who created her. Tiso had been struggling over the birth of his own new man and worrying over what the new man might be. It was enough for him to bring the babe forth and to let God determine his future.

That evening, Tiso, who had worried about whether he could confront the priest with his sins, told him all of them in great peace. By the dying embers of a fire in an ornately carved marble fireplace, Antonio pronounced absolution and blessing. He administered penance—twofold restitution of any ill-gotten gains, release of those whom he had imprisoned for debt, and daily attendance at Mass for the remainder of his life. Tiso had invited him to spend more time at his house, both in Padua and at Camposampiero. Antonio accepted.

As Holy Week approached, the inspirations of the Holy Spirit increased. Tiso began to think more often about those known as penitents. Their numbers were increasing in Padua and all of Lombardy. In charity, holiness, and peace, these people gave God their lives, not in convents or monasteries, but in their own homes. Their Rule involved certain days of fasting and abstinence from meat, set prayers and times to pray, works of mercy, simplicity of dress in undyed cloth, and monthly meetings with other penitents. They relinquished their weapons. They desisted from taking oaths of loyalty to any human being. All the conflicts that Tiso had been in had not brought peace to this region. But if enough people became penitents, peace would happen.

The desire to surrender himself completely to God swelled in Tiso's heart. But could he do it? On the evening of the Monday after Easter, when Antonio was staying with Tiso at his city house, the priest suggested an evening stroll.

"Padre, do you think I could become a penitent?" There, Tiso had voiced it. "I'm old, much attached to the world, and feeble in resolve. I want to do this, but I wonder if I can."

"Ah, Count Tiso, you remind me of the women who went to the tomb of our Lord to anoint His body," Antonio mused. "To get there, they traveled through the streets of Jerusalem, but at a much faster pace than you and I are taking."

As Tiso and Antonio rounded a corner, a gentle gust ruffled past them. "The Holy Spirit drew them to the tomb," Antonio said, "and they so wanted to do our Lord this service of anointing Him. But on the way, 'they were saying to one another, "Who will roll back the stone for us?" for it was a large stone,' probably much larger than this." Antonio patted a thick pillar that supported a second-floor balcony. "When they got to the tomb, Messer, what did they find?"

"That the stone had already been rolled back."

"Sì. Now it would be difficult—in fact, I would say impossible—for you and me together to dislodge this pillar, even if it were not fastened above and below. Do you agree?"

"Perhaps even a team of oxen couldn't budge it."

Antonio nodded. "But a stone, probably larger than this, was already removed when the women reached the tomb. The Holy Spirit did that." Antonio touched Tiso's arm. "Messer, you have proposed to become a penitent. This idea hasn't come from you but from the Spirit of God. Yet you say, 'Who will roll back the stone for me? Can I stand the severity of the religious life? Can I tolerate the frequent fasts, the simple dress, the voluntary poverty, the required daily prayers?' Am I right?"

"Absolutely right."

"Don't be fearful, Messer Tiso. The stone has already been rolled back. Like the angel who removed the stone for the holy women, the Holy Spirit has already removed the stone for you. The Spirit says to you, 'I will strengthen your weakness, make severity easy, and sweeten every bitterness with the balm of My love. See, the stone is rolled back. Come and enter the tomb where you will see the place in which your Savior was resurrected.'"

Tiso looked at the pillar rising above his head. He looked at his own fearful heart. And he leapt into the arms of God. When Pentecost arrived, he was garbed not in his colorful silks but in the humble, undyed cloth of a penitent. He had never felt so finely dressed.

NOTES

Beginning in 1227, Antonio preached in Padua and the other towns in the March of Treviso. People crowded to hear him. So many men wanted to join the Lesser Brothers that Antonio founded the monastery of Santa Maria for them within the center of Padua. From Padua, Antonio moved to the surrounding towns and then south to Florence. By the end of 1229, he was back in Padua, living at Santa Maria.

The elderly Tiso (Tisone, Tiso VI) da Camposampiero (da Campo San Pietro or Camposanpiero), who died in 1234, sold a house to the comune of Padua that was demolished in order to build the Palazzo della Ragione. Messer Severo is a fictitious name for an individual who would have held his administrative position.

Tiso seems to have been married to his second wife at this time. He did invite Antonio to Camposampiero and to a second home he seems to have had in Padua.

Because of Antonio's sermons, Tiso experienced conversion and joined the Order of the Continent Brothers and Sisters. Such details as Tiso's age or the year of his conversion have not been recorded. However, in 1227 and 1228, he was involved in wars against Ezzelino da Romano and his brother Alberico. After 1228, no mention is made of Tiso's involvement in such conflicts. Since penitents would not bear arms, he must have entered the Continent Brothers no earlier than 1228.

The requirements of the Order of the Continent Brothers and Sisters, including their undyed clothes, are accurately described.

Antonio's sermons and words to Tiso are from SerE 77–78, 83, 149, 152, 157–58, 189–90, 205–06, 210–11 and SK 85–88. "The penitent who sighs . . ." is from SSF IV 72.

Scripture verses are from Genesis 3:19 ("You are dust . . ."); Luke 16:19 ("Clothed in purple . . ."); Proverbs 20:17 ("A man finds bread . . ."); Matthew 19:21 ("If you wish to be perfect . . ."); Mark 8:34 ("Whoever wishes to be . . ."); 1 Corinthians 2:9 ("What eye has not . . ."); Isaiah 45:3 ("Treasures out of darkness . . ."); Isaiah 60:5 ("Then you shall be . . ."); see Revelation 22:4 ("See God face to face . . ."); Isaiah 26:18 ("In your presence . . ."); John 16:21 ("A woman, when she . . ."); Luke 15:7–9 ("There is joy . . ."); Isaiah 65:17–18 ("The troubles of the past . . ."); and Mark 16:3 ("They were saying . . .").

24

Suor Elena Enselmini

Convent of Arcella Vecchia, Padua, Italy (Spring 1230)

Suor Elena Enselmini sat on a narrow stone bench in the convent garden, her bony back propped against the trunk of a tall oak that supported one end of the seat. The other end, she knew, was supported by a second oak. Today, her thin hands mended by feel the threadbare tunic in her lap. As her fingers felt out the holes and then stitched them shut, she rejoiced at the sun's warmth and the caress of a spring breeze.

All winter she had been chilled in the convent, along with the other Poor Ladies, while the bitter north wind rattled the walls. Daily she had hobbled through the corridors on legs so wracked with pain that she could barely keep erect. Then, the frosty convent walls or the warm arm of another sister had been her support.

Today spring was in the air. Elena had asked Suor Sancia to help her outdoors to sit in the welcome sunlight. She had brought her mending, for today her fingers, which had been stiff and clumsy all winter, were nimble. The sun and the spring breeze had wrought the change.

This was the season of new life in the fragrance of moist earth sprouting seeds and in mating birds calling. The season, too, of Christ's final weeks on earth, His Passion and death. From His bloody agony had sprung both resurrection and salvation. Elena felt joy stirring in her heart, a joy that, for weeks, she feared had left her. *Dear Jesus, Son of God, let Your sun renew my fervor,* she begged. *Let the wind of Your Spirit blow away my discontent.*

Ever since Elena could remember, she loved no human being as much as she loved Christ. She couldn't remember how old she was when she tired of playthings and playmates, of fresh gowns and trinkets for her hair. Christ, Whom she had heard about in church, didn't live this way. Christ was poor and Christ suffered. Surely He, Who was God, had chosen the best way. She would choose it, too.

Ten years ago, when she was barely a woman, Francesco of Assisi came to Padua to preach and to establish a monastery here outside the walls. The nobles of the Enselmini family, all good followers of Christ, went to hear him preach in one of the churches. Elena sat near her mother and gazed at the brother, who seemed to be Christ incarnate. Here was a humble man who had absolutely nothing but the Savior. Francesco's words and manner burned with zeal for God. Elena sensed that, if she stood close to him, she would feel warmth radiating from him as from a fire.

She remembered how he, his eyes raised to heaven, had concluded his sermon with a song, beautifully sung, of his own composing.

"Hail, Queen Wisdom!
May the Lord protect You,
with Your Sister, holy pure Simplicity!
Lady holy Poverty,
may the Lord protect You,
with Your Sister, holy Humility!
Lady holy Charity,
may the Lord protect You,
with Your Sister, holy Obedience.
Most holy Virtues,
may the Lord protect all of You,
from Whom you come and proceed.
There is surely no one in the whole world
who can possess any one of You
without dying first."

Desperately, Elena wanted to possess all the virtues, which obviously possessed the poet who sang about them. For the next few days, Elena had waited as impatiently for Francesco to complete his monastery as any other girl her age would wait for her betrothed to ready the home where he would bring his bride. When Arcella Vecchia was completed, she presented herself to Francesco and asked to be admitted. With his own hands, he had cut off the flowing black hair that she had come to despise and handed her a patched gray tunic. She had walked into an adjacent room where two Poor Ladies helped her remove her beads and jewels, her silks and chemise, her soft shoes and ribbons. She slipped into the tunic, kicked the heap of finery with her foot, and felt a deep peace. This was where she belonged.

Although the sisters of Arcella Vecchia sewed and embroidered for alms, the walls of their monastery shut them away from the world. Here, like the noble Madonna Chiara of Assisi, who founded the Poor Ladies, the sisters lived in utter poverty, frequent fasts, and scheduled prayer both day and night. The brothers, who lived in a small convent right next to the ladies' monastery, counseled the women and assisted them with alms. Among those had been one whose family in Padua was as respected as Elena's: Fra Luca Belludi, now traveling companion of Fra Antonio.

When Elena entered Arcella, she had never once looked back. Christ became her All. She gave Him her time, her prayers, her discipline, her love. He could take whatever He wished. And, six years after she entered Arcella, He did.

Pain and fever such as she had never known racked her body. She spoke to no one about it, but the sisters read the agony on her face and saw that she could take no nourishment but the Sacred Host. So they tended her and prayed. For months, the illness persisted, sometimes throwing her into convulsions and delirium.

Then she had recovered a bit, but not much. As the illness continued its hold on her, her legs grew weak and throbbed with pain. Her eyesight faded. Her voice grew faint. One day, she couldn't walk without support. Then her eyes no longer caught even the glimmer of a torch held in front of them. Her throat could no longer speak even the faintest whisper. Now she was painfully lame and completely blind and speechless. The illness continued to strike unexpectedly in fever and pain, then abate. Always it returned. Elena no longer cared about her sufferings. God had come to her.

Once, while at prayer, she had seen in a vision the glory of Francesco and his followers in paradise. And she was among them. How she rejoiced at it! Then a heavenly voice said, "Francesco was powerful on earth, but in heaven he is far more powerful." *Oh, Fra Francesco,* she had prayed, *speak to Jesus about my soul. Make it burn for Him.*

On another occasion, God had thrust her into the torment of purgatory. Ah, how the souls suffered in the fire that would purify them for their entry into eternity. Yet she saw how the prayers and good works of the faithful on earth were to these souls as cups and pitchers and buckets of water on the flames, slowly drowning the fire while giving life to the souls suffering in it. Ever after that vision, she increased her prayers for the souls suffering in that place, and she knew that some of them were in heaven because she prayed.

She was praying now as she mended in the sunlight. One of the nuns at Arcella had died a short time before. That nun was the focus of Elena's prayers.

But today, as she prayed, she remembered other days, winter days, when she had shivered in the convent and her prayers had come by sheer force of will without the spontaneity that she felt today. On those days, the flame in her soul seemed to die.

She had entered Arcella radiant with joy. Her joy had increased with the newness and simplicity and holiness of her poverty. Then her illness and her visions had come, plunging her more deeply into the sufferings and the ecstasies of Christ.

But these days, she sometimes felt as if she were in a stagnant spot such as that dead pool in a river above the rapids, far from either riverbank, where the waters simply lie. The pattern of convent life, the sameness of her maladies, the repetition of prayers were relaxing her, deadening her. Perhaps it was too much to expect that the joy she felt upon her entry into Arcella would persist. Suppose her love of Christ died. She couldn't bear the thought.

As Elena was thinking about these things, she heard three almost imperceptible pairs of footsteps approaching across the pebbled courtyard. Then, a touch of a finger on her left hand.

"Suor Elena." The voice was Suor Sancia's. "Fra Antonio is here to see you."

Fra Antonio! Her confessor. For the past several years, he had been preaching in Florence, Ferrara, and other cities and towns of the Romagna. Still he came regularly to visit her and some of the other nuns. Because of her illness, she had been permitted to communicate with him inside the enclosure. The other Poor Ladies had to confess to him through the convent grate, where they could hear his voice but see nothing.

Grinning, Elena thrust the needle into the cloth on her lap and raised her hands upward. Two other hands, warm and a bit pulpy-feeling, caught hers and clasped them tightly. "Pace e bene, sister!" She felt the bench slightly give way as Antonio sat down beside her.

Another pair of hands, these lean and strong, caught hers and grasped them briefly. "Fra Luca, sister. Pace e bene."

Elena smiled at Fra Luca as he released her hands. Then she heard the soft smacking of feet against the courtyard stones as someone walked off. Since Fra Antonio had come to see her, that would be Fra Luca leaving them alone to speak. Suor Sancia's familiar, almost inaudible footsteps also faded quickly. Although she could see neither Luca nor Sancia, she knew that both were watching some distance out of earshot. All a precaution for chastity.

Elena smiled. The nuns weren't to look upon the brothers without being granted a dispensation, which Suor Sancia, as the protector of virtue, had earned. Nevertheless, Elena imagined that several pairs of curious eyes were having a difficult time not peeking. The nuns would want to glimpse Fra Antonio, whom they, like the rest of Lombardy, regarded as a saint. But blind Elena had never seen him herself.

Elena was glad for all protectors of virtue as well as any sisters who were spying. She loved Antonio with a love that troubled her because it was so deep. She so wanted to merge her personality with his that she grew frightened. Such a love could turn from spiritual to physical. She doubted that he felt the same about her, for he had many spiritual children and preached constantly on purity in thought and action. She trusted Antonio. Yet, because she didn't fully trust herself, she was glad that her sisters in Christ, as well as Fra Luca, were watching.

In a familiar procedure, the somewhat puffy hands placed Elena's own hands into her lap. Then she felt a board placed on her knee. She caught the smooth plank and lifted her fingers to catch the edge of a parchment and then, with her other hand open, waited for the pen. Two fingers touched the wrist holding the parchment and Elena reached across that hand to feel for a narrow vessel of ink. There it was, held secure in Antonio's palm.

Then came the gentle voice. "Are you well, sister?"

She smiled and nodded, lifting her hand with the pen in the direction of the friar as a way to emphasize her answer.

"Have you anything you wish to tell me?"

Oh, how she wished she could speak! But God had taken her voice and she wouldn't ask for it back. Elena dipped the pen into the ink and began to write on the parchment. She tried to space her words so they'd not run together and become illegible. *I had another vision of heaven. Religious who live in community were more exalted than hermits. I asked our Lord why. Religious live under obedience as did He Who took our flesh and suffered and died on the cross, He said. Obedience makes their actions more meritorious.* She stopped writing.

"As Saint Gregory the Great says, 'Obedience incorporates in itself the rest of the virtues and preserves them all.'"

She again began to write. Antonio's hand touched hers and guided it down the parchment. She knew that she must have been writing over what she had previously penned.

This vision made me happy, but not like it once would have. I am growing dull. This frightens me.

Antonio's hand patted her own. "My sister, I know what you're thinking. Obedience is difficult. Affliction such as you suffer is burdensome. Prayer becomes routine."

Elena nodded vigorously. Antonio had read everything in her clumsy revelation.

"You ask, 'Why is my joy not what it used to be?'"

Elena held the parchment down with the pen in her hand. She placed her other hand on Antonio's wrist and squeezed. Again, she nodded. He must understand that he had spoken to her heart.

"When these thoughts come upon you, sister, think of this. The Father sent us His Son, the best and the perfect Gift, Who is co-eternal with the Father. Consider this needle you are using so skillfully." Antonio lifted Elena's hand off his wrist and laid the needle in its palm.

"The eye is the gentle mercy of Christ which He displayed at His first coming; the point is the penetrating justice by which He will pierce us in the judgment. With this kind of needle, Christ, our embroiderer, will make for the faithful soul a beautiful tunic, startling by the multiple colors of its virtues."

She felt the needle lifted from her hand, and then a gentle prick on her palm. The point startled her, but it didn't hurt.

"But justice pierces and pricks as these thoughts of yours do. Yet remain true to Christ. Let Him embroider on your soul as He sees fit. With each pain of soul, the eye of Christ's mercy is drawing a thread of virtue through you. Sister, do you remember colors?"

Elena nodded vigorously. How she remembered them! The flame of the sun. The brilliant blue of violets. The blinding white of snow.

"Try to picture the colors now."

She felt the thread being drawn across her palm as Antonio spoke.

"The purple of the Lord's Passion and your own suffering." The thread tickled her palm.

"The white of chastity."

The thread was again dragged across her palm. And so it went with each color.

"The blue of contemplation. The scarlet of love of God and of neighbor. And so on. Christ, the Gift of highest value, can stitch for you an everlasting tunic if you, despite these inner struggles, remain obedient to Him. And what a beautiful and colorful tunic it will be, woven of all the virtues!"

Antonio lightly laid the needle in Elena's palm.

She plucked the needle with her hand and rubbed it through her fingers. Oh, if only Christ would embroider for her such a tunic! Her Savior had favored her with visions, yet her internal deadness made her feel like Judas.

She felt for the tunic that she had been mending and threaded the needle into it. Then she fumbled for the pen. Antonio slipped the piece of parchment out from under her fingertips and replaced it with what Elena suspected must be a clean sheet. Then he guided her pen to the ink and she wrote again.

I feel like I betray my Lord.

"Then let us see how you are betraying. Christ wore a tunic that He Himself designed. It was a tunic of sackcloth, stretched on the cross for us, torn by nails and pierced with a lance."

Elena shuddered for, beneath the tunic that she was now wearing, unknown to anyone else, she wore a shirt of sackcloth. Did Antonio somehow know?

"Sackcloth is a sign of guilt, worn by a penitent, worn by a sinner, not by a Redeemer. Yet Christ wore this tunic, stitched of human flesh and suffering, when He assumed the burden and guilt of our sins.

"And the sackcloth of our sins, with which He had cloaked His divinity, led Him to death on the cross. Christ came to redeem us. For 'we were dead in sin' but Christ died so that we might live in God. Wasn't Christ, then, God's most perfect Gift?"

Elena nodded. Her hands began again to write. *I know this, yet I still feel as if I betray Him. I am so lax. He has given me so much.*

"My sister, as you sew and pray, think of the poor sackcloth of His earthly Body that Christ stitched for Himself, a garment that He restored to immortality by His wisdom and the power of His resurrection. Think, too, of the glorious tunic that Christ is making for you as you remain obedient to Him. Your garment, sister, is coming to resemble His, and your reward shall be with Him.

"And when you are tempted to give up, think of Whom you are exchanging and for what."

Antonio took the pen out of Elena's hand. He took her two hands and placed them both, palm up, on the parchment in her lap. Then, with his finger, he traced a cross on her right palm.

"'What will you give me,' Judas said, 'if I hand Jesus over to you?' What price can be set in exchange for the Son of God? What can they give you? Were they to give you Jerusalem . . ." Elena felt a pebble drop into her left hand. "Galilee . . ." Another pebble. "And Samaria . . ." Yet a third pebble. "Would these be a suitable price for the Son of God?"

Again, a finger traced a cross in her right palm. "Were they to give you heaven with all its angels . . ." A rain of pebbles in the left palm. "The earth with all its peoples, the seas, and all they contain . . ." A greater sprinkle of pebbles. "Would all these suffice in exchange for Jesus . . ." Again, the tracing of a cross. "'In Whom are hidden all treasures of wisdom and knowledge'?"

Antonio closed the fingers of both her hands. The one with the pebbles felt heavy and gritty, the one with the cross, light.

"Sister, God alone knows what is 'the way of the spirit.' The writer of Hebrews says, 'He is a discerner of the thoughts and intents of the heart. All things are bare and open to His eyes.' So He knows that, in these afflictions, you seek Him. And He has promised, 'The one who perseveres to the end will be saved.' As you remain obedient to Christ when fervor dies down, Christ is stitching your tunic of everlasting life with the gold thread of perseverance and the silver thread of obedience. And you will have a precious garment if you do not exchange the world . . ." he said, tapping the hand with the pebbles, ". . . for the Lord."

He patted the hand that had been traced with the cross.

"In time, the song of the bride in the Canticle will again be yours when she sings, 'Arise, north wind, and come, south wind, blow through my garden that its perfumes may flow.' The north wind, which freezes the waters of the soul, is the devil who, by his cold malice, removes the consolations of God. To the devil, you will say again, 'Arise and go away,' and to the south wind, the Holy Spirit, 'Come.'"

She felt a warm finger on her cheek, gently angling her face directly into the breeze, then a finger under her chin lifting her face full into the sunlight.

"Come, blow through my conscience so that the perfume of my tears may flow. You will experience again the hidden things of contemplation, the joy of the spirit, the sweet experience of inner delight, which are the secrets of the Holy Spirit, for He will dwell in you and by His indwelling blow through with the soft breath of His love."

Elena sat as still as a dove at rest, the cross in one hand, the world in the other, her face bathed with the breeze and the warmth. A fire seemed to burn in her hand with the cross. She felt herself transported into the Passion of Christ, reliving it as He lived it. Mockery of Herod. Treachery of Pilate. Whipping. Thorns pounded into scalp. Jeering of the mob. Wooden beam digging into soft shoulder blade. Bare toes grappling stones in a struggle to walk. Falling. Jerking upright. Being thrust onto hard wood. The sear of iron nails driven into flesh. Cross jolting upright. Indignity of nakedness. Sticky blood running down back, arms, belly, legs. Flies and gnats, buzzing, stinging, itching. Blinding sun. Burning thirst. Abandonment of God. Death. Then tomb. Resurrection. Life.

When her meditation had ended, her hands were still cramped closed in her lap. The breeze had turned cool and the sun's warmth had faded. With her fists, she felt in her lap for the tunic, but it was gone. Elena stretched and opened her cramped fingers. She threw the pebbles to the ground and clasped the imaginary cross to her heart. Then she groped at her feet and found the tunic that had fallen from her lap. As she went to pick it up, her finger caught the needle and its point pricked her. The sudden pain brought back to her Antonio's words about the needle of Christ's mercy and justice. She turned to thank him, feeling for his hand. But he was gone.

Holding the needle in one hand and pressing the tunic to her chest where she had earlier pressed the cross, she felt her way into the convent.

There is joy in joy, she realized. *And there can be joy in dryness. Where Christ is, all is joy. Compared to the perfect Gift of Christ, all the world is pebbles.*

NOTES

Biographies of Elena Enselmini say that Francesco of Assisi founded Arcella in 1220, but at least one biography of Antonio (Stoddard 69) states that Antonio founded it in 1227. Tradition states that Antonio was the confessor of Elena Enselmini, a nun at the convent of Arcella. Elena had a great devotion to the Passion of Christ, a fervor that Antonio fostered. No more about their relationship is mentioned, and some biographers question whether it existed.

Elena's background and illness, which most authorities agree struck her in 1226, are historically accurate. However, when she lost her sight and speech is unknown. Gamboso speculates that she was ill for about thirteen months when the illness deprived her of sight and speech. This would mean that she was most certainly in the condition that Antonio found her in this chapter.

However, Gamboso also says that Elena first became ill around the summer of 1230, that she lost her sight and speech just after Antonio's death, and that she died three months later. This information is based on an early biography that claims that her illness lasted sixteen months, whereas most other sources say sixteen years. Therefore, Elena may have been blind, mute, and lame for only the last three months of her life. On the other hand, she may have suffered from these maladies for most of the sixteen years of her illness. Some sources say she had these conditions while Antonio was her confessor. Others say she suffered from them "for many years."

Elena actually had the visions described (no dates given), but one or more of them may have taken place after Antonio's death.

Francesco himself received Elena into the religio of the Poor Ladies after he established the convent at Arcella. History doesn't record his sermon that so touched Elena. His poem in this chapter is a portion of "A Salutation to the Virtues" (FA:ED I 164).

Suor Sancia is a fictional character representing any nun who acted in her role.

Elena had a reputation for holiness from her youth. No history mentions that she felt an attraction to Antonio or that she suffered from spiritual dryness.

Elena died on November 4, 1242, at the age of thirty-four. Her body remained incorrupt for centuries. In 1695, she was declared Blessed by Pope Innocent XII.

Antonio's words are taken from SerE 86, 156, 166–67, 200–202 and SK 41–45.

Scripture verses are from Ephesians 2:1 ("We were dead . . ."); Matthew 26:15 ("What will you give me . . ."); Colossians 2:3 ("In whom are hidden . . ."); see Galatians 5:25 ("The way of the Spirit . . ."); Hebrews 4:12–13 ("He is a discerner . . ."); Matthew 24:13 ("The one who perseveres . . ."); and Song of Solomon 4:16 ("Arise, north wind . . .").

25

Messer Girolamo di Giovanni di Gualterio

Great Hall of the Messer Girolamo's Palazzo, Assisi, Italy (Mid-May 1230)

Messer Girolamo di Giovanni di Gualterio waited anxiously in the great hall of his palazzo. On this warm day, he'd had all the windows shuttered as if it were winter, not to keep out chill but to keep in the discussion that was about to happen in this room. That is, if Fra Elia came.

Where was he?

Girolamo had known Elia ever since they were youth together along with Francesco and Rufino and Nicola and Bongiovanni and so many others in Assisi. Francesco. Elia. Rufino. They'd given their lives to God as Lesser Brothers. Bongiovanni had followed God another way, by doctoring the ill, including Francesco when he was dying. Girolamo had never considered anything but knighthood and work to strengthen the comune. He never imagined that he'd be elected to the highest governing office in Assisi, but here he was, the podestà.

The big doors to the great hall swung inward. "Fra Elia, Messer," his servant announced.

The tall brother strode into the room, his gait not quite concealing a limp, his graying black beard hinting at aging and his sandals half slapping, half sliding against the tiled floor.

The two men embraced, first on one shoulder and then on the other. Girolamo pointed to a seat across the massive oaken table and Elia obediently sat, Girolamo sitting opposite.

"So, you're wondering why I asked you to come here," Girolamo said.

"Sì. But would it be better to wait for Fra Filippo and Messer Picardus?"

"They don't know about this meeting. It's not about the basilica."

Elia looked confused. Of course. The four men had met here frequently while executing the construction of the Basilica di San Francesco. With the ingenuity of Fra Elia's plans, the architectural expertise of Fra Filippo di Campello, and the accounting acumen of Messer Picardus Morico, the basilica was rising on the site of Assisi's former garbage dump. As podestà, Girolamo had hosted the meetings and made sure that the men had the supplies and manpower to keep building.

Girolamo removed his cap and placed it on the table. Then he ran the fingers of both his hands through his nearly white hair and, clasping them behind his cocked-back head, stared up at the ceiling. "I don't know how to say this, brother, other than to come right out with it. The planned burial of San Francesco is irresponsible. Imprudent. Inane. Shall I go on?"

Elia showed no surprise. "The burial is how Lord Pope planned it."

"I don't presume to tell Lord Pope how to run the Church, nor should he presume to tell me how to conduct the burial of a saint."

"He wants the burial to be reverent, joyful, faithful, in keeping with the spirit of San Francesco."

"Of course." Girolamo leaned toward Elia. "But was he there when Francesco was dying like we were? Was he there when a contingent of us knights escorted him all over Tuscany to Assisi so he could die at the Porziuncula as he requested?"

Girolamo had repeated these thoughts to himself so many times that they leaped out like goats released from a pen. "Was Lord Pope there when we knights accompanied his body to San Giorgio until it was interred? And why did we do that? Just because this holy man was a son of Assisi?" Girolamo slammed his hands on the table. "No! Because he's a saint, and now more miracles have taken place at his tomb than ever in his life. Does Lord Pope know what mobs this public burial will attract? Does he consider that Perugia may attempt to seize the body?"

Girolamo's seat was too confining for his agitated thoughts. He leaped up and began pacing the room. "Or, if not Perugia, the crazed mob itself. Lord Pope wants to protect the saint from desecration. Hosting a massive, public display to move the body from one place to another is an invitation to desecration." Girolamo ran his fingers through his hair again and groaned. "Who's going to get blamed if anything happens to the body? Lord Pope? Oh, no! Me. The podestà. I'm the one who should have ensured that nothing dire would happen. I'm the one who'll take the blame for Lord Pope's witless plan."

Elia stroked his thick beard. "You don't have to convince me," he said calmly. "I thought of this the first time I was told."

Girolamo threw his arms up in desperation. "Then why didn't you say something?"

Elia looked at him dumbly.

"Oh. I understand. You're a son of the Church. You're not supposed to talk against Lord Pope." Girolamo threw his hands into the air again. "So why did I call you? I should have called Filippo and Picardus."

"You called me," Elia said calmly, "because I can do something about it and they can't."

"Well, thank God somebody can do something." Girolamo wheeled around and looked Elia squarely in the face. "So what can you do?"

"Well, let's think this through," Elia said. He was so calm that Girolamo wondered if he'd already thought it through. "If we bury the body as planned by Lord Pope, you'll need to have many knights in attendance to keep order."

"Many knights?" Girolamo slapped the table again. "A battalion, you mean."

"Many knights," Elia continued, "and even then, there may not be enough. Trying to defend the body could cause bloodshed."

Girolamo moaned.

"People getting trampled."

"Or a knight drawing his weapon," Girolamo almost shrieked.

"It could get dangerous quickly."

"Do you have any suggestions?"

Elia didn't answer.

"Do you?"

No answer. *He knows,* Girolamo thought. *Something unthinkable.*

Abruptly he stopped pacing as a thought darted into his head. He lowered his voice. "We could bury the body early."

"Sì. That is the only safe solution."

The remainder of the night was spent in determining exactly how to do it. Thus, three days before the scheduled burial, Elia and Girolamo drove a straw-filled cart to San Giorgio's and knocked at the church doors, which had been locked for the afternoon siesta. The four knights guarding San Francesco's temporary tomb admitted them. Then, using two ladders that had been delivered the previous day, two of the knights removed the remains from the suspended stone sarcophagus while the remaining two laid them on a length of common cloth such as workmen use to bundle up tools. They gently wrapped the cloth around the shriveled corpse, then knelt and briefly prayed before carrying the priceless body to the cart, where they laid it on the straw with the ladders next to it. Girolamo nodded with approval. The knights reentered San Giorgio where, as if nothing had happened, they would take up their posts again as guards.

With Elia riding in the cart and Girolamo walking beside the oxen, the two men guided the cart to the Basilica di San Francesco. On their way, Girolamo acknowledged the scattered townspeople who were walking about at this hour. Some commented.

"Final work in the basilica before the big day?"

"No siesta for you two. Too much work to be done at the basilica."

"Indeed," Girolamo answered as he kept walking.

At the basilica, four workmen whom Elia could trust removed the ladders and took the bundled remains as nonchalantly as if they were carrying hammers and saws. They brought them into the basilica where, with Elia leading the way and Girolamo following, they carefully carried them to a simple wooden casket resting beside a deep excavation in the floor. The bundled remains were gingerly removed from the shroud and placed in the casket. The men knelt by the casket for a few moments. Then the lid was placed on it, ropes secured about it, and, with pulleys already in place, the casket was lowered into the tunnel prepared for it. Down, down it went until it came to rest on a floor.

A ladder was then lowered into the hole and the men descended. In one direction extended a tunnel. The workmen ignited two oil lamps. Elia took one and led the way, while Girolamo, taking the other, walked behind the casket, which the four workers carried into the short tunnel. There, they laid it on a ledge prepared for it. Elia removed the lid and repositioned the body. Nearby lay a squarish stone painted with a red stripe. Elia placed it under the head like a pillow.

"He always slept on a stone pillow, didn't he?" Girolamo asked reverently.

"Sì."

"But why the red stripe?"

"Do you remember the pillow he died on?"

Girolamo remembered well because it was so incongruous from how Francesco lived. A red silk pillow brought by a matron from Rome. "The red is reminiscent of his death pillow," Girolamo reasoned. Then, "We need to authenticate the body." Beneath the feet of the corpse, Girolamo placed his signatory ring, which authenticated the burial, and a handful of coins, which dated it. Beside them, Elia placed a circle of beads on a cord—some sort of prayer chaplet, Girolamo assumed. Elia added a small, odd-shaped hunk of metal.

"What?" Girolamo asked.

"It was on the shroud. Likely a fragment from the hooks that held the sarcophagus at San Giorgio."

If Elia were right, the fragment would also authenticate the remains.

The men knelt again, almost on top of each other in the cramped space. Then the lid was replaced on the coffin and the men made their way out of the tunnel and up the ladder. The workers drew up the pulleys and ropes.

"Immediately put the iron bars in place across the tunnel and then spaced to the top at intervals as instructed, with layers of rock in between," Elia told the workers. "Then rebuild this floor so that not even the keenest eye will know a hole has been cut here. No one but you are to be in this room until the translation of the relics three days hence. Remember your vows to secrecy. You are protecting the body of a saint."

Leaving the basilica, Elia and Girolamo guided the oxen to the basilica's convent, where a few young brothers scraped the straw out of the cart to replenish bedding. After returning the cart to the farmer who had loaned it to them, Girolamo and Elia walked back up the hill to the city, with Elia setting the gait.

"Where did you get the idea for that tunnel?" Girolamo asked. "You must have been building it for some time."

"This is how they bury kings in Egypt and Syria," Elia said.

Girolamo let out a low whistle of surprise. Elia had been provincial minister of Syria some years ago.

When they reached the city, they embraced wordlessly and parted ways, Elia to the basilica and Girolamo to his office. With the siesta ended, the city was busy again.

The next day, Girolamo took time to hear Fra Antonio preaching in the Piazza del Comune. The priest was in the city for San Francesco's burial and a chapter meeting of the brothers thereafter. Since he'd be leaving after the chapter, today was the only day he'd be preaching. Girolamo had heard him before. Who hadn't?

The piazza was packed with people who crowded into the merchants' stalls or gathered at windows and on balconies of surrounding buildings. Girolamo stayed on the edge, as he didn't know if he would have time to wait until the sermon ended.

In his loud, clear voice, Antonio was speaking about Anna weaning Samuel and taking with her to Shiloh an offering of calves, flour, and wine. He used the calves to represent three stages of penance and then began to discuss the flour. "Wheat is ground and broken down into flour, as you all know," he spoke. "What is then done with the flour? You women and kitchen maids know well how to mix it with water to bake bread. And for what use? 'To strengthen man's heart.' Thus, bread nourishes us. Sì?"

"Sì!" the audience called out.

"Sì! Our work is like grain. Have you ever thought of that? In the same way that wheat is ground into bread, so the grain of our work has to be ground and broken down in the examination of our conscience, that it may be purified like flour." Antonio paused. "Do we think of this? Do we examine our work? No? Then let us begin. How many bushels of flour did Anna bring as an offering?"

While he paused, Girolamo tried to remember. *Three. Three bushels.*

"Three!" Antonio called out as, with distinct movements, he indicated three directions. "This examination of our work must be threefold. Now think of the work you do. Do you farm? Do you sell? Do you beg? Do you govern? Do you serve? What is your work? Some of you perform many works. Think of one. Name it."

He paused.

My work as podestà, Girolamo thought.

"First, we must examine the nature of the act itself, its origin and purpose. Why are we doing this work? What purpose does this work serve? Who asked us to do this? What requires this of us? This is examining the nature of the act. If it is not a good work, we must abandon it for something better. If it is a good work, we have a second examination."

What could that possibly be? Girolamo had no idea.

"What evil have we already done?" Antonio gazed across the crowd, waiting.

Girolamo could think of many sins, impatience and lack of trust in God being two of the most prominent. But evil? Had he ever done evil?

"You ask if you have ever done evil? Let us think. Carnal desire. Lustful and unclean thoughts."

Oh, goodness!

"Worldly vanity."

His new cap. *Whew!*

"The work must be mixed with the water of tears of repentance for such evil. Thus, even though our work be tiresome or unrewarding, it can be offered with tears, as flour is mixed with water, to make 'the bread of tears.'"

Antonio gestured in a third direction. "Three bushels of flour. Three examinations. What is the third? No matter what our work, no matter if we have done evil previously, we can offer our work for the desire of eternal joy. All our work, which must be good work, is to make amends for past sins and to prepare us for future happiness. Return now to your work, with awareness of how the Lord wishes to use it to bring you to the refreshment of eternal glory. Amen."

The throng rushed forward to Antonio. Girolamo rushed to work. Today he would offer it to the Lord as reparation for his sins and as a sacrifice toward his own salvation.

The next few days, Girolamo's work was readying the final details for the great celebration on May 25. He heard nothing about the secret burial. The men sworn to secrecy were keeping their vows.

On May 25, Girolamo met Elia early at the Church of San Giorgio. The commissioned open-bed ox cart was in place at the doors, the two oxen draped in

purple silk. Resembling an animal's drinking trough, the covered stone sarcopha-
gus that had held Francesco's remains rested on the floor. The anticipated knock
came. The guards positioned at the tomb opened the doors to two cardinals of the
Church and the barefoot Fra Giovanni Parenti, minister general of the Lesser
Brothers. The cardinals introduced themselves. Well-dressed Cardinal Goffredo
Castiglioni. Stern-faced, black-bearded Cardinal Niccolò Conti di Segni.

"As Lord Pope's official representatives, we are to authenticate the body,"
Cardinal Castiglioni declared.

Girolamo looked at Elia. Neither of them had anticipated this.

Elia nodded to the knightly guards. They lifted the lid.

"It's empty!" Castiglioni gasped.

"Where is the body?" di Segni demanded.

"What did you do?" Fra Giovanni turned to Fra Elia, horrified.

"The crowds. We feared desecration. Theft." Girolamo was stammering.
How could he explain?

"Francesco's body is authenticated and buried already in the basilica," Elia
explained calmly. "It was necessary to avoid desecration and possible theft."

"Where?" Castiglioni barked.

"That will remain a secret."

"Lord Pope will hear about this," di Segni snapped.

"You will hear about this," Giovanni added, shaking his head.

"The crowds are immense." Castiglioni. "Thousands are waiting to see the
saint."

"We must proceed as planned," Elia replied, his face a blank slate. "No one
was promised access to the body, only to the sarcophagus."

"Sì," di Segni agreed reluctantly.

Cardinal Castiglioni glanced at Cardinal di Segni. "I have a small speech
prepared which I am to give before we begin."

"Give it. Just no mention of a body."

"The people will find out about this," Fra Giovanni fretted.

"But not today," Girolamo insisted firmly. "Today, there would be rioting."

"We must proceed as planned. San Francesco's body is safe. Now we must
keep the people safe," Elia said reasonably.

Lord Pope's representatives thought. And agreed.

Thus, as the sun approached its zenith, Cardinal Castiglioni exited San Giorgio. Standing in the oxcart, he first offered a prayer, asking San Francesco's intercession. Then he addressed the crowd, reminding them of the solemnity and honor of the occasion and conveying Lord Pope's blessings. Even with the cardinal's booming voice, Girolamo wondered how far his words would carry. Surely those at the rear of the assembled crowd could never have heard or even seen him.

When the cardinal completed his brief exhortation, the four knights who had guarded the sarcophagus and the four workmen who had sealed the tomb at the basilica hoisted the heavy trough out of the church and heaved it onto the oxcart. Fra Giovanni draped it with sumptuous purple banners and took his place along with the provincial ministers and custodes of the Lesser Brothers. They walked immediately in front of the cart, behind the two cardinals and other dignitaries at the head of the procession, which was led by the four mounted knights.

Elia climbed onto the cart beside the driver. Girolamo mounted his cream-colored steed and rode to the front of the procession while an armed guard of knights surrounded the cart on all four sides. When he reached the front, Girolamo turned his steed around and perused the procession. All was as planned. Additional knights spaced themselves alongside the attendees. Girolamo could not see the rear of the crowd that jammed the street, but he assumed that the four mounted knights he'd assigned to patrol the end of the procession were in place. All seemed in order. Girolamo raised his hand and a ripple of quiet beginning behind him quickly traveled through the mob. He brought his hand down slowly and spurred his steed into a solemn walk. The procession moved forward toward the Porta San Giorgio.

The air rang with shouts of joy and the music of countless pipes and tambourines. Behind the cart paraded innumerable brightly dressed archers, a cortège of mounted knights in full armor, and all the guilds of Assisi bearing a huge number of banners. Clogging the streets around all of these, as well as preceding the procession and surging along behind it, were nearly all the citizens of Assisi as well as visitors and endless rows of friars who had been sleeping in the streets and fields awaiting this glorious day. Everywhere people were dancing and leaping with happiness.

Girolamo felt like singing, too, but inside his breast nagged a persistent fear. *Lord, let the guards keep the revelers at bay.* But try as they might, the guards couldn't hold back the mob. Bodies pushed between the mounted soldiers; hands reached out reverently; fingers clawed at the fluttering purple banners; devotees stroked the sarcophagus.

"San Francesco, pray for me."

"San Francesco, bless me."

The procession was a stop-and-go march, the cart forced to pause periodically as the people in front of it blocked the streets or those to the sides pressed too close to allow easy movement. As the procession approached Paradise Hill, Girolamo saw the basilica before him rising in the sunlight like a giant altar. As the massive oak doors of the lower church came into view, the crowd to the right of the cart pushed against the guards. With a start, Girolamo saw that the guards were having difficulty holding them back. More pushing. Shoving. Shouting. A crowd of peasants, nobles, friars, and unfamiliar knights was hemming in the cart, surrounding it, reaching toward the sarcophagus. Hands were stretching toward the mounted knights, grappling with them, trying to tug them from their saddles.

Such commotion could spook the two oxen. "We need to get inside," he shouted to the captain of the knights leading the procession. He heard the blare of the horn calling forward knights who were lining the procession. Amid a swirl of noise, the knights forced open a path before the cart. Girolamo kept moving forward with the oxen. With knights like a wall on either side, the four leading knights entered the basilica. The dignitaries. The ministers and custodes of the ordine. The oxen. The cart with the sarcophagus. Girolamo heard the doors slam behind him and the captain of the knights ordering, "Hold them back!" above the angry shouts coming from the other side of the door.

The cart was at the tomb. "Quickly!" Girolamo ordered. Elia jumped off the cart. Eight sturdy knights slid the sarcophagus off the cart onto a low dais surrounded by posts with thick chains attached. Quickly, knights flung the chains across the sarcophagus, both lengthwise and widthwise, and locked them securely to the posts on the opposite side. With the sarcophagus chained down, a phalanx of armed knights took their posts all around the dais. Elia, Rufino, Leone, Egidio—all some of the first brothers who had known Francesco best—gathered the purple drapes and reverently replaced them on the sarcophagus. They knelt, heads bowed, hands touching the stone.

All was ready. "Let them in!" Girolamo ordered the knights holding back the crowd.

As the knights slowly retreated, the doors were shoved inward. Girolamo rode into the milling throng. "We will have order, or we will arrest the rioters," he shouted.

The pushing eased. Guards shoved the people into a semblance of order. Knights rode up and down among the crowd to maintain peace. The people began to file past the sarcophagus, touching it, pausing with bowed heads, kneeling, weeping.

"Messer Podestà." The voice was trembling and choked, as if with tears. Girolamo looked down into the tear-streaked face of a young friar. "Messer Podestà, I am Fra Giacomo of Iseo. I . . . I touched his coffin. Out there by the door. I . . . I just wanted to pray. And the hernia. I had a hernia since I was a boy. The hernia." The brother rubbed his hand over his belly. "It's gone, Messer."

Girolamo stared in wonder at the youth. San Francesco had worked another miracle. And its occurrence confused him. Antonio's words came to mind. *"First we must examine the nature of the act."* The act of touching the coffin. That was an act of veneration. No evil in it. And it would help to lead not only Fra Giacomo to glory but also anyone else who heard of the miracle.

But what of the act of secretly burying San Francesco? Was that evil or not? Had Girolamo done it to avoid blame if anything happened to the body or to protect the body itself? Or for both reasons? Was his action evil or good? Or both?

NOTES

Elia seems to have had some chronic pain in his feet. His description and that of Giovanni Parenti follow old engravings of these men.

According to Fortini (620–21), Girolamo was the podestà of Assisi at this time.

Historical accounts of what happened on the day of Francesco's burial are conflicting (Odoardi 75–84, Brooke 138–39). As evidenced by a papal letter condemning the actions of civic leaders in the matter, the body was buried in a fashion that was not in keeping with the pope's orders. The pope wrote that, "I had named the Minister General and some other devout and God-fearing members of the Minorite Order my delegates for the translation of the most glorious body of Blessed Francis.... But the men of Assisi incited by a spirit of furious madness failed to perceive that sacred things should be touched only by consecrated hands, and with uproar and insolence seized the body of the Saint and thus profaned the mystery of his translation damnably" (Gilliat-Smith, 119–20, translation of *Speravimus hactenus*, issued by Pope Gregory IX, June 16, 1230). What this means is debated.

Some accounts say that Francesco's body was buried three days earlier than scheduled. Others state that the burial was on the appointed day but that the body was whisked into the basilica and quickly buried in an unknown place. In the early 1800s, Pope Pius VII granted permission for an excavation to be made to find the tomb. The body was discovered with the items described in this chapter plus a piece of straw. The relics were removed to the tomb where they are visible today in the Basilica di San Francesco.

Franciscan scholar Jean-François Godet-Calogeras believes that Elia and Girolamo buried Francesco's body three days early because both would have been aware of the dangers of desecration or theft. This chapter speculates how that might have happened.

The description of the numbers of attendees and the joy at the procession is in the histories (FA:ED I 419–20). The histories state that cardinals (unnamed) were in attendance as the pope's representatives, and only they were given authority to touch the saint's body. Cardinals Goffredo Castiglioni and Niccolò Conti di Segni were members of the Curia at this time. Their description in this chapter is taken from old images of them.

Antonio must have been present for these festivities because he was provincial minister of the Romagna, a high office in the ordine, and all the provincial ministers who could attend did. In addition, his presence was required at, and he did attend, the chapter gathering held five days later. Since he was a popular preacher, it seems reasonable that he would have been asked to address the citizens of Assisi if he were in town.

The cure of Fra Giacomo of Iseo is in FA:ED II 673–74. Antonio's words on Anna's offering are from SSF II 33–35.

Scripture verses are from Psalm 104:15 (numbered at that time as Psalm 103:15; "To strengthen man's heart ...") and Psalm 80:5 ("The bread of tears ...").

26

Fra Giovanni Parenti

Monastery of the Lesser Brothers,
Basilica di San Francesco, Assisi, Italy (May 30, 1230)

I n a large meeting room in the monastery of the Lesser Brothers at the
Basilica di San Francesco, Fra Giovanni Parenti sat amid the provincial ministers and custodes. These men who held governance in the ordine were
responsible for making decisions that would direct the ordine for the next three
years. They'd prayed. Breakfasted. Reviewed business since the last chapter
meeting three years ago.

They'd also discussed the excitement and joy of the entombment and the
now public knowledge that Francesco's body was somewhere in the basilica but
not in the sarcophagus. The ministers and custodes were divided in their opinions as to the necessity and prudence of such an unanticipated move. Nothing
could be done about it, for those who knew where the body was were keeping
their silence. And no one could be certain of who exactly did know. All the
brothers could do was to pray for resolution and repentance. After they did,
they proceeded to the next order of business: the appointment of provincial
ministers.

"Before we begin the assignments, does anyone have something to share?"
Giovanni looked about the room. In the back, a hand waved. "Fra Antonio?"

Antonio stood. "Excuse me, but I request that I may be relieved of my position as provincial minister of the Romagna."

For the first time in these busy days, Giovanni looked closely at Fra Antonio. His belly was bloated, and his skin had lost that ruddy, healthy look that it had at the previous chapter gathering. Antonio was ill. It would be a charity to relieve him of that responsibility.

"Grazie, Fra Antonio, for all your service to the brotherhood. You have permission to retire from your office and go wherever you wish to preach and write."

"Grazie, brother."

"Anyone else?" No response. "Now, to assignments. Fra Agnello di Pisa couldn't be with us, but he will continue as provincial minister of England. Is that correct, Fra Richard?" Giovanni turned to the sage-looking old English priest.

"Correct," Richard confirmed.

"Buono. Fra Richard, Ireland is growing in vocations, isn't it?"

"Correct."

"Are you willing to serve as provincial minister of Ireland?"

Richard's gray eyebrows arched, but he mellowly replied, "As you wish, brother."

Just then the door to the meeting room was flung open, and a bevy of brothers burst in carrying on their shoulders Fra Elia Bonbarone, whom they let down next to Giovanni. Before Giovanni could react to this outlandish display, Fra Sebastiano shoved him aside. "Fra Elia will be our minister general."

Several provincials and custodes objected. A few pushed forward. The friars accompanying Elia held them back. Shouts flew back and forth.

"You have surrounded yourself with clerics. Fra Francesco wanted the ordine to be simple!"

"You allow us to possess breviaries. Fra Francesco never did!"

"Everyone, sit down!"

"Before he died, Fra Francesco blessed Fra Elia, not you."

"Fra Elia must be minister general. He's the one Francesco wanted."

"Let us have peace!"

"Fra Elia stepped down three years ago because he was building the basilica. It's time for him to resume governance."

"In God's name, brothers, let us have peace!"

"We brothers have all come to Assisi for Fra Francesco's burial. Fra Elia said we could attend this chapter meeting. You have no right to keep us out."

"You have barred us! Fra Francesco never would have."

"It's in the Rule! Only custodes and provincials may attend the chapter."

More shouts. More pushing.

Antonio had somehow moved to the front of the assembly. With his hands and face upraised, he began to recite, in a voice at once prayerful and commanding, a prayer composed by Fra Francesco. "Most High, glorious God, enlighten the darkness of my heart and give me true faith, certain hope, and perfect charity, sense, and knowledge, Lord, that I may carry out Your holy and true command."

Sebastiano pushed him aside. "You're not Fra Francesco. Didn't he change our Rule just so you could teach and use books? Didn't you allow the brothers to possess the church and convent at Bassano when Fra Francesco forbade us to hold property? You have no right to speak his words."

Antonio dropped to his knees, his head bowed, praying. Giovanni felt helpless as the chaos increased. Swiftly other provincials and custodes knelt. Some brothers who had carried Elia knelt as well.

Elia stood, silently watching. Was he behind this? What was happening with the brotherhood? Giovanni had given his life to the ordine. Yet he wanted nothing to do with a brotherhood that was going to trample the virtues of peace and humility. In anguished desperation, he tore off his habit and flung aside his breeches. Naked before them, he would leave behind this animosity. He would find a place of peace.

As he moved toward the door, the whole assembly seemed frozen. In the silence, five novices who had burst in with Elia spoke up, their voices trembling.

"We have been knights."

"We laid down our weapons to follow a way of peace."

"This will bring no good to our ordine."

"There can be no order with disorder."

"We are brothers here, not enemies."

The groups backed off. The riot fizzled. One of the men who had come with Elia handed Giovanni his breeches and robe. Giovanni reclothed himself. All this time, Elia had neither moved nor spoken.

Fra Richard shouted, "What do we do with these intruders?"

Fra Aymo answered back, "Assign them penance."

With face flushed, Giovanni turned to Elia. "I will assign some infractors to each provincial, who will give them a penance. Brothers, leave us now. Remain in your cells until summoned."

Nodding, Elia was the first to leave. The five novices who had been knights followed, then Sebastiano and the others.

Giovanni was suddenly aware that he was weeping. God had given him the gift of tears, but he tried to keep that gift hidden. Now, they were leaking from his eyes as thoughts of what was happening to the brotherhood flew like darts through his mind. He sat down, fearing he might collapse from emotion if he remained standing.

"Brothers, I'm sorry . . . about this. . . . I'm . . . shaken . . ." he stammered.

Aymo spoke up. "I think we're all shaken. Perhaps Fra Antonio has some words of encouragement."

"Fra Aymo, you're a gifted speaker. You will have words to boost our morale," Antonio remarked.

"You're more gifted than I am," Aymo said demurely. "The Lord will speak through you. With Fra Giovanni's approval."

Giovanni could hardly speak. "Fra Antonio, if you can."

Antonio bowed his head. "Brothers, please join me in prayer that the Spirit will give me the words He wishes you to hear."

The brothers bowed their heads. Silence. Peace.

"Brothers, I have a riddle." A murmur rippled through the brothers.

A riddle? Giovanni thought. *Are you going to make us laugh? Maybe a riddle is just what we need.*

"We're here at our Pentecost chapter. Pentecost is the culmination of Easter, and Easter the culmination of the Passion, and the Passion begins with Palm Sunday. We were speaking earlier about the translation of San Francesco's body and how frenzied everyone was. Let's imagine how much more excited were the inhabitants of Jerusalem to have the living Lord among them. Can you imagine the frenzy Jesus felt all about Him on that day?" He paused and looked from face to face. "Here's my riddle. During the translation of San Francesco's body, I saw two who were not excited at all. They were as calm as a lagoon."

Giovanni thought. He hadn't seen anyone who wasn't excited.

"I'm sure you all saw them," Antonio remarked.

More thinking.

"Fra Alberto. Did I see you wave? Do you have two in mind who were calm?"

"The oxen?"

The brothers laughed.

"Sì! The oxen."

Heartier laughter.

"Now I have another riddle. When Jesus rode into Jerusalem, who was calm?"

Voices shot out from all around the room. "The donkey!"

"Sì! The donkey. I understand that the oxen were borrowed from a farmer near the Porziuncula and the donkey who bore our Lord was borrowed from an inhabitant in Jerusalem. Here is another riddle. Are these beasts the servants of their owners?"

Calls of agreement smattered the room.

"You're partly right," Antonio laughed. "The owners work these beasts. They are his servants." He paused and looked from face to face. "But who cares for these animals? Who feeds and shelters them and tends to their needs?"

"The owners," the brothers replied, almost in unison.

"So who is the servant of whom?"

More laughter.

"Now listen. Didn't God become our servant for thirty-three years on this earth, even to dying for us to free us from slavery to the devil? Did you ever think that God became our servant so that we might become His?" He paused, and quiet descended. "It is easy to give ourselves completely to our Lord when we remember who we are. Consider the donkey who bore our Lord. He could have grown proud and vain, thinking all the joyous calls were for him. But none hailed him. They hailed our Lord on his back. The donkey was, after all, only a donkey. Let us realize that we are merely donkeys, humbly bearing Christ the King into the marketplace."

A murmur of assent ran through the room.

"The oxen were at the service of those who procured them for the translation of San Francesco. The donkey was at the service of Christ. Do you think these beasts thought, *I'm going to give a bit to this work but not my all?*"

The brothers shook their heads.

"You're right. Beasts give themselves fully to their tasks, holding nothing back. In the same way, we must give ourselves totally to God. God does not only want a part of us. If we reserve a part of us for ourselves, then we are ours and not His."

More nodding.

"We must give everything to God. Everything. All our works, all our actions. Everything. Whatever we do for the sake of our own glory, we totally lose. Brothers, I tell you that each time I have attributed the merit to me and not to our Lord, each time I have preached Antonio and not Christ and sought my things and not God's, I took nothing except perhaps some flatterer who sang my praises but on whom my words fell like pebbles against stone. How vital it is to submit one's whole will entirely to God! Only wholly in God do we become wholly who God intends us to be. Only then will we achieve heavenly glory! Brothers, let us pray."

He paused as the brothers bowed their heads.

"Christ Jesus, You conquered the pride of the evil one by the humility of Your Incarnation: grant also to us to shatter the chains of pride and arrogance by the humility of our hearts, so that we may be worthy of the gift of Your glory. With Your help Who are blessed from age to age. Amen."

The brothers cried aloud with one resounding voice, "Amen!"

NOTES

The description of the 1230 chapter meeting is accurate (13CC 154–55, Brooke 291–93). History doesn't record the name of the ringleader of the brothers who wanted Elia to be minister general, nor is history clear about Elia's acquiescence to this attempted coup. The oldest records don't reveal what Antonio said as he attempted to make peace, but they do say that his words were ineffective. The chapter quieted only when Giovanni Parenti disrobed and the five novices spoke as recorded in this chapter. Antonio was released from his duties as provincial at this meeting. There is no record that he addressed the gathering after the disturbance was quelled.

Francesco's prayer, "Most High, glorious God," is from FA:ED I 40. Antonio's words are from SK 9–13, SerE 191–92, and Praise 46.

27

Fra Elia Bonbarone

*Monastery of the Lesser Brothers,
Basilica di San Francesco, Assisi, Italy (Early June 1230)*

Fra Elia Bonbarone was sitting at his desk in his cell in the monastery of the Lesser Brothers. Before him lay an open ledger. His mind had been swirling with calculations. The provincial of Germany had sent this much money for the basilica, the provincial of Tuscany more. How much would Emperor Federico give if Elia asked him to donate again? What materials were needed to complete the basilica's upper level, and how costly were they?

A rapid, sharp knock at the door jolted him away from his work. When he opened the door, he was face-to-face with Fra Giovanni Parenti. Elia fell to his knees before the older man. "Forgive me, brother." He meant it. He should never have allowed Sebastiano and the others to haul him into that chapter meeting, demand admittance, and try to force his election as minister.

Giovanni placed his hands on Elia's head and spoke softly some words Elia couldn't quite hear. "I forgive you, brother."

Elia stood and invited Giovanni into his cell. "Let me remove these documents," he said as he began to clear off a bench.

"Leave them. I cannot stay. I came only to bring you news."

Elia paused in his cleanup.

"Lord Pope has summoned to Rome you, Messer Girolamo, the city council, and everyone else involved in the burial. He has threatened to excommunicate
everyone if he does not receive an explanation within fifteen days. He has put
the basilica under interdict, taken away all its privileges, and given its care to the
bishop. We may not occupy this monastery nor any place nearby. All is closed
until the resolution of your meeting with him. We must vacate here at once. Our
chapter meeting will resume at the Porziuncula. The brothers are building huts
for cells."

Huts for cells, like the earlier days, Elia thought. *Could this severity be true?*

"Don't trouble yourself about building a cell, Fra Elia. You won't return
here," Giovanni continued. "Until you can leave for Rome, you may sleep in the
chapel. Fra Sebastiano and the others who disrupted the chapter because of you
are being dispatched to various provinces. For your actions both with the burial
and the chapter, you are to do penance at the hermitage at Cortona until you are
sufficiently repentant. Such actions require reflection and reform."

Elia had expected punishment. "The decisions are just. I will do as you say."

"Grazie, brother. Pace e bene."

"Pace e bene." Elia closed the door behind Giovanni and sunk onto his
bench. He had no time to be amazed or dismayed. He only had time to act.

Quickly his mind reviewed what had to be done. He and Girolamo would
ease Lord Pope's mind. Once Lord Pope opened the basilica again, work must
continue in Elia's absence. The plans and documents strewn about this room
must go to Fra Filippo de Campello and Messer Picardus Morico. Elia would
have to sort out who received what.

Did the fifteen days begin from the time Lord Pope issued his request or
from the time Fra Giovanni received it? He suspected the former. He, Girolamo,
and the others had better begin the trek to Rome immediately. Perhaps they
could be ready to leave in two days' time.

He swiftly began to sort the ledgers, records, architectural plans, and documents. In a short time, he had two piles. He put the largest pile, the one for
Filippo, into his begging pouch. He tucked the smaller pile for Picardus into the
pocket sewn inside his tunic. Then he limped to the basilica, looking for Filippo.
He found him inside, directing the remaining workers to return home until
recalled.

"So you know," Elia said. He handed Filippo the documents from his pouch. "In my absence, continue the work on the monastery and the upper level. Here are the documents you'll need."

"You'll be gone no more than a few weeks," Filippo said.

"No. I'm banished to Cortona."

"For how long?"

Elia shrugged. "I don't know."

Filippo moaned. He took the documents and threw his arms around Elia. Then, with tears in his eyes, he bowed to Elia and strode toward the exit. There was no time to waste.

But for the remains of San Francesco and the presence of God, Elia was alone. In his mind's eye, he could see, as from a distance, the massive, half-completed rose-and-white stone basilica that he'd designed after the fortress sepulchers that he'd seen while provincial minister of Syria. His imagination saw work continuing, the upper level taking shape, the structure rising from the jagged rock promontory once called Hell Hill. Because of Elia's foresight, this outcropping that sloped steeply down to the river Tescio had a new name: Paradise Hill. For here was interred the body of the greatest saint of this age: Francesco of Assisi.

Elia walked through the basilica, caressing pillar, altar, and door, as if touching them would hold them in his memory until he returned. If he returned. He knelt before the sarcophagus and tried to pray, but no words came. He wished he could pray over the spot, so perfectly concealed, below which Francesco's body lay, but he was unwilling to take the slightest chance of revealing the burial location by being seen. Rising, he made his way to the exit, turning to whisper before he left, "Pace e bene, Francesco."

Elia limped to the monastery stable and asked to borrow the ass, stating that he would return it in two days. When he plodded up to the home of Picardus, he thanked God that the accountant was home. Elia gave him the ledgers and other documents he'd need. Tears. Hugging. Farewell.

"I was expecting you," Girolamo said when he arrived. The two made plans to gather the knights and workers who had assisted with the burial and those council members who had known about it. Girolamo, the council, and the knights owned steeds. Between all of them, they could loan enough horses for

Elia and each of the workers. Allowing for a slow enough pace so as not to exhaust the animals, the group should be able to reach Rome within the fifteen allotted days. They would leave at dawn the day after tomorrow.

The ride to the Porziuncula seemed both swift and endless. What disdain might he meet? What should be his response?

The plain around the Porziuncula was littered with newly built wattle and reed cells, just like in earlier times. Scattered between the trees stood tables around which the brothers sat, taking their evening meal. Some brothers hailed to him, but Elia wasn't hungry. How could he sit with his brothers when he felt disgraced? He rode instead to the Porziuncula and, dismounting, entered to pray.

No words came. He sat in silence before the Eucharistic Lord, letting the sorrow in his heart speak. He didn't know how long he sat. Perhaps he was dozing when he felt a light tap on his shoulder. Fra Antonio motioned to Elia to join him outdoors.

"I'm sorry to bother you at prayer, but may I speak with you before you leave? I think there is time before Vespers. I don't know when you're leaving." The voice was hesitant, gentle.

"The day after tomorrow," Elia said.

"I can speak to you tomorrow, then, if that's better."

"Tonight is fine, brother."

"Grazie." Antonio led the way to the now-empty tables and sat on a bench near one. Elia sat across from him.

"Brother, do you know that I cannot even build a sandcastle, while you build a basilica?"

Elia guffawed. As a boy, he had built marvelous sandcastles, complete with moats, bridges, and towers, all supported with inner gridwork of stone and branch.

Antonio whooped. "You're laughing at me!"

"So I am," Elia chuckled.

"The basilica is magnificent. Never have I seen such an edifice. It will some-day rise high because you sank the foundation deep into rock. So you can understand the truth of what Blessed Bernard says: 'The deeper you lay the foundation of humility, the higher the building is able to rise.'" Antonio smiled.

"Fra Elia, I need your help. Fra Giovanni is sending a delegation of seven to Rome to confer with Lord Pope about San Francesco's Testament. I'm to head the group. The brothers want to know what is and isn't binding. You were San Francesco's friend. You know better than any of us what he intended."

A lump rose in Elia's throat. How could Antonio, or anyone else for that matter, possibly know what Francesco and Elia had experienced together? There was one thing he could share. "Francesco always meant what he said. What he wrote in the Testament is what he meant. It needs no interpretation."

"That does seem clear. 'Rather, as the Lord has granted me simply and plainly to speak and write the Rule and these words, so simply and without gloss are you to understand them, and by holy deeds carry them out until the very end.'"

"You remember it well."

"Did Francesco consult anyone while composing it?"

"No. He said that the message was granted him by the Lord."

Antonio whistled softly. "Do you think Lord Pope will accept that?"

"I think he will want more than 'God told me to do it.'"

Antonio sighed. "Whatever Lord Pope decrees for the ordine, we must accept whether or not we agree. He's the head of the Church. He speaks in the name of Christ. Brother, will you pray for us, for the ordine, for me?"

"Fra Antonio, I'm better at work than at prayer. Since Francesco died, I haven't been able to pray well much of the time. But I will pray for you."

"Fra Elia, we have joined the ordine to follow Christ, not to follow Francesco."

The rebuke was soft but pointed. Why had Elia joined? Many times, he had tried to remember that time when his wife had died after their son was grown. Joining the brotherhood had been a call from God. Or so he thought. That was so long ago.

"Brother, do you mind if we get a drink?" Antonio asked.

"Not at all."

As the two walked toward the well, Antonio remarked, "Ah, how good it feels to have your thirst quenched, sì?"

"Sì."

"I think this may be why Christ called Himself the living water. If we drink of Him, we will never again thirst."

Elia let down the bucket, which sank into the water far below, and drew it up. He and Antonio each took a wooden cup from the small pile next to the well, and they drank deeply.

"Ah, brother, you see we sought this water. And we knew where to get it. Just so, we must seek the kingdom of God if we wish to quench our spiritual thirst. The kingdom of God is the highest good, the most important thing in our life. Do you agree?"

"Of course."

"Everything else must be sought in view of this kingdom; nothing should be asked beyond it. Whatever we ask must serve that end. Even banishment to Cortona." Antonio refilled his cup. "You will have much time to pray there. In this, I envy you."

"If I could pray." Elia drained his cup and placed it back into the jumbled heap.

Antonio drained his cup and placed it on the pile as well. "Do you mind if I share the Apostle Paul's instruction about prayer?"

Elia fished around in his mind, trying to remember such instruction. "I thought I might get a sermon from you," he said sheepishly after a long moment.

Antonio burst into a laugh as he led the way back to the tables. "Let's call it an instruction. Sì?"

Elia smiled. "You were born a teacher."

Antonio shrugged. "I was born what God made me. But Saint Paul is a much better teacher than I. In his Letter to Timothy, he shows how to pray. 'I desire, therefore, first of all, that supplications, prayers, intercessions, and thanksgivings be made.' Let's think about these. First was . . ."

"Supplications."

"What is that?"

"Asking for something."

Antonio nodded as he sat. "Supplication means a careful attention to God in one's spiritual exercises and in all other matters. But we must ask for things in the right order." Elia's face must have reflected the question. "You ask what that means. In supplication, anyone who prefers knowledge to saving grace gets only grief. We must, therefore, ask for grace first if we wish to obtain anything else. With God's grace, we will know how to act. You, brother, must go to see Lord

Pope. That's an action that must be undertaken. I'm sure that you're asking God to guide your words once you're in Lord Pope's presence."

That, Elia definitely needed to do. The news he'd received today had so shocked him that he'd never thought to pray. He'd not asked for grace before he acted on knowledge. "I'll ask God's guidance for that meeting," he said meekly.

"Buono. Do you remember Saint Paul's second instruction?"

Elia thought. "Prayers. But isn't that the same as supplications?"

"If it were, Saint Paul wouldn't have used two words. Supplication is asking for something. When we beg, we can ask a household for some scraps to eat. But do we have a relationship with that person from whom we beg?"

"Usually not."

"Supplications don't involve relationship. Prayers do. Prayer is the disposition of the man who holds to God. It is a certain familiarity and loving conversation with Him. It is the condition of the enlightened mind to enjoy it as long as it may."

"This is where I have difficulty, brother."

"You had a wife, didn't you? And you have a son?"

"Sì."

"Can you remember those days when you sat at home, your wife busy about her work, your son at play?"

"And me making mattresses." Elia had always been a worker.

Antonio chuckled. "And you making mattresses. Brother, did you love your family?"

Did he? Oh, mightily.

"You felt comfortable just being with them, loving them, enjoying them. If we love God, so shall we be with Him."

Elia was beginning to understand.

"Next was . . ."

"Intercessions. Isn't that the same . . . ?"

Antonio shook his head. "Intercession is the care to obtain temporal things that are necessary for this life. God approves the goodwill of those who ask, yet does what He Himself judges best, giving freely to whoever asks well. It is common to all, but more particularly to the children of the world, to desire tranquility and peace, health of body, fine weather, and other things useful and necessary for this life and for the pleasure of those who misuse them. Those who ask for them in faith should do so only from need, and even then they should always subject their own will to the will of God. In asking, one should pray with devotion and faith, yet not clinging obstinately to these things requested. We do not know, though our Father in heaven does, what is useful to us in our present circumstances."

"This is like begging for food, asking God to provide it, and returning to the brotherhood with nothing."

Antonio smiled. "You remember well the early days, it seems. The brothers weren't so well-liked then as now, I understand."

"Yet God provided for these intercessions as we asked for them in faith. He was blessing us."

"He still is blessing us," Antonio reminded. "And this is why we must offer God the climax of our prayers."

"Thanksgiving."

"Sì. Thanksgiving is the acknowledgment in mind and thought of God's grace and goodwill; and an unfailing and ceaseless reference of everything to God, though at times either outward expression or inner affection will be missing or at least sluggish."

How well Antonio expressed what Elia's attempt at thanksgiving would be like, facing what he now was facing!

"The charity that never fails is ceaseless prayer and thanksgiving, of which the Apostle says, 'Pray without ceasing' and 'Give thanks always.' Let's name them again, Fra Elia."

Together they recited. "Supplications. Prayers. Intercessions. Thanksgivings."

From the chapel rang the bell for Vespers. The men rose.

"Pray for me, Fra Elia. I will pray for you."

The two days ran swiftly by, swifter than the plodding journey to Rome that followed. And then the dreaded meeting with Lord Pope. Elia prayed fervently for God's grace and Spirit to direct that meeting, and he knew that the brothers were praying as well. In the end, Lord Pope understood, although he didn't approve, why Francesco was buried early. He lifted the ban on the basilica and rescinded his threat of excommunication. While the others returned to Assisi, Elia hitched rides on carts heading to Cortona. His hermitage was small and bare. In penance, neither bathing nor shaving nor changing his tunic, he prayed. This would be his life until the brotherhood chose to reinstate him to the ordine.

The months passed, days flowing into days. In autumn, as the leaves showed tints of red and yellow and the air grew cool with autumn, a letter arrived.

My dear Fra Elia, Pope Gregorio has spoken. San Francesco's Testament is not binding as he did not consult the ministers before writing it, and one minister may not bind another. We may have the use of houses to live in as well as furniture and books, as long as these are owned by another. Money may be accepted through an intermediary for future necessities.

Brother, you see that our ordine is changing. But San Francesco, who lived in utter poverty, possessed as well a poverty of spirit. With great effort and deep faith, it is possible to retain poverty of spirit amid any circumstances. No matter what we think of Lord Pope's decree, we must do as San Francesco always did and humbly submit to the decision of the Vicar of Christ.

I continue to pray for you daily. Please continue to pray for me.

Fra Antonio

Elia read the letter twice. If Francesco's Testament wasn't binding, then what was? The brothers whom Francesco had wanted to live in utter poverty were now going to become well-housed, secure monks just like in every other ordine. This wasn't what Francesco had wanted. This wasn't what Francesco had said Christ had revealed to him.

Even in his cell, Elia felt the autumn chill nipping his face through his thick beard. Now he felt a chill strike his heart. If only he had Antonio's faith and trust! If only he could give himself totally to the Lord! If he did, God might swallow him.

What did God want? Was it possible to know? Francesco had said that his Testament was from Christ. Yet Lord Pope, Christ's Vicar, had rejected it. Had Christ spoken to Francesco? Or had Francesco misunderstood? Or had Lord Pope? Had the Rule and Testament been good for their time but not good for this time?

Could anyone know the mind of God? And yet, long ago, when Elia joined Francesco, he thought he had known it. Maybe he had gotten away from that. Maybe, since Francesco's death, he'd been making supplication but putting himself, rather than God's grace, first. He was here to do penance. Was that penance once again to put himself last and to let God's will be done, whatever that was?

Antonio was praying for him. Now he prayed, "Francesco, pray for me."

NOTES

Pope Gregorio IX was so angry over the events around the translation of Francesco's body that he issued a bull that threatened to excommunicate the podestà and council of Assisi if they didn't explain their conduct. The bull forbade the Franciscans to live at the basilica or to hold general chapters there, and the tomb was placed under the care of the bishop of Assisi. Only when Elia and several others involved explained the reasoning for what had happened was the bull lifted before taking effect (Gilliat-Smith 109–11).

Antonio headed a delegation to Rome, which included Giovanni Parenti, to discuss Francesco's Testament and other rules of the Order. The result of that meeting was the bull *Quo elongati*, issued in September 1230, which stated that the Testament wasn't binding. We don't know Antonio's opinion of the decision, just that he accepted it.

History records no personal meeting of Elia and Antonio, nor any letter written by Antonio to Elia.

Elia was reconciled to the Order in 1232 when he was elected minister general. He then resumed his work on the basilica, which was completed in 1236. Later, Elia commissioned famous artists of the day to decorate the church with frescoes.

Elia served as minister general until 1239 and was then deposed amid much complaint and conflict. He was accused of cruelty to the brothers, disregard of others' opinions, unjust visitations of provinces, and indulgent living.

Against the orders of Alberto of Pisa, the minister general who replaced Elia, Elia continued to visit the houses of the Poor Ladies. When the pope insisted that he obey, Elia allied himself with Emperor Federico against the pope and was excommunicated along with the emperor in 1239. He remained excommunicated for years, while still wearing the habit of the Lesser Brothers, and was finally reconciled to the Church on his deathbed in 1253.

Antonio's words are from SSF I 368–69.

Scripture verses are from 1 Timothy 2:1 ("I desire, therefore . . ."); 1 Thessalonians 5:17 ("Pray without ceasing . . ."); and Ephesians 5:20 ("Give thanks . . .").

PART FIVE

His Grace Will Come Down to Us

28

Ezzelino da Romano

Castle Fortress, Verona, Italy (May 1231)

Astride his broad-chested, sturdy-legged brown steed, Ezzelino da Romano led his band of six knights within sight of his castle fortress. Behind him the mournful lowing of a cow almost overpowered the snorting of the lathered horses, who, Ezzelino knew, could now smell their stable. The animals wanted to be rubbed down and fed and were pulling against their bits in impatience.

Seeing his castle's massive stone walls made Ezzelino want to hurry, too. Now that he and his band had completed their patrol of Lombardy and had a bit of fun as well, Ezzelino was anxious to be out of his heavy chain mail. His servant Ariana, now nearly a woman, knew how to bathe his dark-skinned, hairy body and then massage the weariness out of his bulging muscles. She would ease the tangles from his luxuriant, sandy hair, and delicately shave his stubbled face.

Ezzelino had killed a peasant who had bumbled from his cottage, half-asleep and probably half-drunk. Why else would he threaten six knights and Ezzelino, the lord of this territory, with a scythe? The threat was a good excuse to slaughter the man. Ezzelino himself had taken care of the serf, riding up to him and thrusting him through with his sword. A woman, probably the man's wife, and two small boys emerged at the door of the cottage. The woman had shrieked. Ezzelino motioned to two of his soldiers. At once, they swooped down upon the cottage, killing the children and the woman. Then the men had dragged the four bodies into the cottage and set it afire.

Ezzelino had reined his horse to the pasture around back where he had spotted a tan cow, her udder plump with milk, and her youngster. Sliding off his horse, he had ambled over to the big-eyed, trusting calf. The wobbly-legged creature had let him approach and fondle its broad head while its mother watched. With a swift stroke, Ezzelino slit the little beast's throat and drained the blood while its curious mother looked on.

When the knights rounded the barn as they sought Ezzelino, he called, "Torch this too." With smoke rising from both cottage and barn, Ezzelino had flung the calf, its tongue dripping blood, over a knight's horse and then mounted his own. The cow, he knew, would follow her infant. And she did, all the way to his castle.

"Take the cow to the herd and the calf to the cook," Ezzelino barked at the knights following him. He slipped off his horse, handed the bridle to a groom, and strode straight to his room where Ariana, waiting for him, filled his tub with water warmed over the blazing hearth. Quickly, he undressed and climbed in, and Ariana proceeded to scrub him until his skin was as clean as a newly bathed infant. After she dried him, Ezzelino lay belly-side-down on the dais with a red silk pillow under his head, his right hand dangling down to stroke the droopy ears of a large black dog that snoozed beside him. On this warm May evening, he didn't mind waiting for Ariana to dispose of the bathwater and give his towel and garments to a maid to launder. The soft spring air across his body comforted him. He closed his eyes and sighed.

How good to be master of Lombardy! The boy who had once considered himself too short and squat to be a knight was now the terror of his region. He grinned at the thought. He, a terror? When he was a child, he had dreamed of being as powerful as his father and grandfather, both of whose names were the same as his. Now, in his late thirties, he had far surpassed his dreams, for he had retained the cities that his family had controlled and had brought others under his dominion.

Ezzelino's father disapproved of his son's lust for power. What did he know, he who had gone mad in the head in his old age? Ezzelino remembered well the day when his father, who in his youth would fight a man to the death in revenge, announced to his family that power was empty. Only weakness before God, he told Ezzelino and his other children, was strength enough to fulfill the soul. Ezzelino understood not a word. Struggling with bitterness and anger, he bid his father farewell as the man whom he had emulated left his family and his castle to become a poor, black-robed monk. The Church of San Donato near the bridge of Bassano was a constant reminder of his father's foolishness, for Ezzelino the monk had given that church to the followers of Francesco, the now-canonized Lesser Brother of Assisi.

Ezzelino would never go soft. He resumed the battles that his father had abandoned. One after the other, the towns of Lombardy fell to his men. With each victory, more barons and lords grew thin in his scattered dungeons. More peasants and clergy trembled at his approach. More tales of his army's bloodshed spread across the region, making the taking of successive towns easier. Nobles and religious were persuaded to align with him rather than risk imprisonment or death. He earned nicknames: "The Tiger," "The Ferocious," "The Devil." He loved them.

Grinning, Ezzelino scratched the dog's bony head. *Ah, you serve me,* he thought, *and I serve me. How right! All-powerful people serve themselves, even if they pretend to serve others.*

Ariana's soft touch to his back startled him. How soothing! With gentle skill, she began to knead the tension out of Ezzelino's well-scrubbed shoulders.

He thought of Federico II, head of the Roman Empire. The emperor, too, had women tend him, but he was far less honorable than Ezzelino. A fine example of self-interest he was, great in power and military prowess, who went about his dealings in despicable ways. The fair, reddish-haired emperor was a lecher and a hypocrite. He had two wives, both of them now dead, but whispers of his trysts with this or that maiden, even when married, filtered to Verona. Yet Federico pretended piety, attending Mass, carrying the papal banner, fawning on the pope.

Despite his cleverly worded promises, Federico never actually followed the pope's bidding if it conflicted with his own goals. Like Ezzelino, he regularly consulted astrologers rather than prayer. Their advice and his own insight guided Federico's schemes.

Emperor Federico had continually deceived Pope Onorio III, promising help with this or that crusade or papal project without following through. After Onorio's death four summers ago, crusaders thronged the ports of Apulia to set sail for the Holy Land. They found a lack of ships but an abundance of plague. Falling ill himself, Federico, who had promised to sail in August, postponed the crusade until spring. The new pope, Gregorio IX, didn't accept his excuse and promptly excommunicated him.

No matter. Eager to expand his empire, Federico sailed from Brindisi for the Holy Land three summers ago. Peacefully through treaties, he secured the Holy Land for himself and for Christianity, entering Jerusalem several months later. At the Savior's tomb, he placed the crown of Jerusalem on his own head. As the self-crowned, rather than papally crowned, king of Jerusalem, Federico considerably increased his popularity in the empire while making the pope look foolish. The excommunicated emperor continued to expand his territory and consolidate his power while pretending to be a pious man wronged by a corrupt papacy.

Unlike Federico, Ezzelino was too honorable to use deceit to gain power. He refused to pretend service to a legate of a Church in which he didn't believe. Nor did he pretend to embrace the beliefs of the Cathars, although he was in sympathy with their ideals. Ezzelino's loyalty lay with living mortals, not with a crucified God.

Ezzelino felt a soft tap to his shoulder, Ariana's signal to turn over. She had rubbed sweet perfume into every muscle of his perfectly clean body as she worked, then massaged her way across his arms, down his back and buttocks to his heavily muscled thighs and calves, ending with the soles of his feet. He rolled over so that she could complete the process. In this position, it was impossible to reach the sleeping dog. Lying on his back, Ezzelino studied the tightly fitted boards in the ceiling, each sturdy and in exactly the right position.

Those beams represented how he ran his life. With strength. Precision. Nothing out of place. Not a single decision that needed adjusting. Unlike other nobles who made and broke alliances for personal gain, Ezzelino's fidelity never shifted, for he made no alliances unless he meant to keep them. Loyalty was one of the strongest traits of the da Romano family. Two hundred years earlier, Ezzelino's ancestors had come to Lombardy from Germany in the suite of Emperor Conrad II. Ever since, the family had remained loyal to the emperor.

Ezzelino's father had ridden and dined with Emperor Federico's predecessor, Ottone IV. Ezzelino had secured Lombardy for Federico.

The victory hadn't been easy. Some cities were difficult to control. Ever loyal to the pope, Padua was one. Ezzelino's grandfather, Ezzelino I, known as "the Stammerer," had been a citizen of Padua and had built the exquisite palace of Santa Lucia. Ezzelino's father, Ezzelino II, had been friendly to the city. But as Ezzelino III consolidated his alliance with the excommunicated emperor, Padua increasingly allied with the pope.

Ariana was massaging Ezzelino's chest, the seat of the heart and the place of love. Ezzelino scorned both, preferring to act by wit. Indeed, he had a plan. For now, he would let Padua alone. Peace would relax the city's vigilance. Fra Antonio, whom Ezzelino had heard of, made the city his home. Good. Let him continue to exhort the citizens to lay down their arms. Soon the Paduans would forget how to fight. No matter how many years it took, when that time came, Ezzelino would launch a surprise and vicious assault and secure control. He had no doubt that he would succeed. No god could hold this "devil" at bay.

Ezzelino felt another tap to his shoulder. Ah, the massage was done and how good he felt! Standing, he allowed Ariana to help him don fresh, silken garments, white hose, and soft blue shoes. Before she bowed to leave, he slipped into her tender hands a few almond cakes and, as always, she dutifully smiled, "Grazie. You're a good master, Messer Ezzelino." He knew she was sincere. Ariana was safe here. In Ezzelino's castle, every female remained a virgin until her wedding night and loyal to her husband thereafter. If not, the unchaste parties were killed.

Ezzelino made his way to the dining area, grateful for his purity. Virginity was honorable, so Ezzelino insisted on chastity and practiced it himself. Even though he embraced no religion, he protected the Cathars and agreed with their emphasis on purity. If Ezzelino caught anyone, even his most capable knight, violating a woman, he would slaughter the assaulter on the spot. He followed this policy into battle and had personally cut down more than one knight whom he caught raping a captured woman. To take a woman's life, even to take it brutally, was typical in war, but to take her honor was criminal.

The dozen knights who headed his companies stood when he entered the great hall. He sat at the head of the table, then motioned for his men to sit as well and to pass the wine, which was part of the tithe Ezzelino demanded from the citizens of the March of Treviso. The men noisily poured the fruit of the vine into golden goblets and filled their bowls with veal soup, one of Ezzelino's favorite dishes. The chef had boiled in its mother's milk the tan calf whose throat Ezzelino had slit, then added some parsley, rapini, garlic, and a bit of salt.

Ezzelino was halfway through eating his second bowlful when a servant approached through the doorway to the entrance hall. He came up to Ezzelino and bowed low.

"Messer Ezzelino, a Lesser Brother requests entrance into the castle."

Ezzelino sopped a hunk of bread into his soup. "A Lesser Brother? You mean two."

"No, Messer. One."

Ezzelino turned to his knights. "Don't the brothers travel in pairs?"

They all agreed.

"Only one brother, Messer," the servant repeated.

Ezzelino popped the dripping bread into his mouth. Swift visions of clergy whom he'd personally disemboweled flashed through his mind. This one was either a fool or a saint to come to Ezzelino alone. What should he do to him?

"Show him in," Ezzelino said.

The ruddy, obese friar who walked into the banquet hall strode directly to Ezzelino. Breathing heavily, he bowed at the waist, then spoke. "I've come to request the release of Ricciardo, Count of San Bonifacio, and the other prisoners whom you're holding." The bold request was spoken gently but firmly.

Ricciardo? Ezzelino burst into loud laughter. "You come to me requesting the release of my brother-in-law? Since when do Lesser Brothers involve themselves in family matters?"

"Count Ricciardo and his men have been in your prison for four summers. This is a matter of justice, not a family dispute."

"It is justice only in the eyes of the nobles who ally themselves against our emperor. Which of them sent you here? That holy family of Camposampiero perhaps?" Ezzelino spat out the words. "Surely you have heard how courteously Count Gerardo di Camposampiero treated my father's second wife, Cecilia?" The brother stood blank-faced.

"So you haven't heard that he ravished her? This is how the nobility, so loyal to your holy Church, behave. Sì, I have another count in prison. I have robbed Ricciardo of his home, but not of his honor. Yet the noble Gerardo took that from Madonna Cecilia."

"Neither Count Ricciardo nor the other prisoners whom you are holding had anything to do with Gerardo," the brother said calmly. "They are not responsible for his vicious crime."

"I offered them freedom. If Ricciardo deeds to me his well-armed castle, they can all go free today."

"That is an unreasonable demand. In God's name, I beg you to free those men."

Ezzelino looked directly at the brother. "In God's name," he repeated with a snigger. "No."

"I have come to ask. You have refused to grant. 'Judgment is without mercy to one who has shown no mercy.' God will grant you mercy only if you extend it to others."

Ezzelino chuckled. "Mercy? Do you know who I am?"

"Who doesn't know the Devil of Lombardy?"

"Is that what you call me?"

"That is what you are called throughout this region."

"And what do you call me?"

"A rebellious child of God. A sinner on his way to hell. A man whom Christ died to save." The reprimand was given as courteously as a compliment.

Ezzelino dipped another hunk of bread into his soup and held it out to the brother. "Have some. You look like you enjoy a good meal."

The friar shook his head.

"Why not have a taste?"

"I want no food gained by bloodshed."

Ezzelino dropped the sop into his bowl. "Do you know that if I snap my fingers, any one of these knights will slay you in an instant?"

"I know it."

"Perhaps you would prefer torture."

"Whatever the Lord permits, I will accept."

Ezzelino gazed into the man's black eyes, looking for some unsteadiness that would denote fear. He found none. But he caught something else. The man looked to be about Ezzelino's age, yet not. The face was gaunt, the eyes hollow, with dark circles beneath them. He studied the man, his swollen bare feet and ankles, his long, fat fingers clutched together over a protruding belly. The friar was breathing too deeply. This was not healthy obesity. This was illness. Far advanced.

"How did you get here?" Ezzelino asked.

"I walked."

"From where?"

"From Padua."

Padua. His primary rival. He might have known. Ezzelino marveled. How had the friar come this far without collapsing? He motioned for the knight across the table from him to yield his chair. The knight rose. "Sit," Ezzelino commanded the friar. The man obeyed.

"I have heard that Fra Antonio stays at Padua."

"I am he."

Ezzelino crossed his arms on his chest and nodded. "So the saint comes to the devil."

Antonio smiled slightly. "I do not claim that either of those terms is correct."

Ezzelino liked this brother's directness. He decided to humor him. "What, other than releasing the prisoners, do you want me to do?"

"Turn away from sin to life."

Of course he would say that. But why didn't he raise his voice in condemnation? Ezzelino tipped backward in his chair, steadying himself on the table with his hands. "Why should I?"

"Because if you don't, you will die in your sins. Jesus said, 'you will die in your sins unless you believe that I am he,' meaning the Son of God. 'The wages of sin is death' forever. Look at me. We are about the same age, but you are in the prime of life, strong and secure, while I am nearing the end of my life. This dropsy from which I suffer causes an abnormal accumulation of water in the body. One of its symptoms is an unquenchable thirst. The more water I drink, the thirstier I become."

Antonio reached across the table to place his puffy hands on either side of Ezzelino's muscular ones. "You see how dropsy has misshapen me. Dropsy is fittingly compared to a person's addiction to power and greed." Antonio looked steadily into Ezzelino's eyes. "Power for power's sake and greed for worldly possessions inflict dropsy on the soul, misshaping it and producing in it a thirst which cannot be quenched. Am I not right, Messer Ezzelino?" The tone of the question was as mild as a caress.

Ezzelino stared at the man who had read his very soul.

"Greed and power are bottomless pits. They hold the soul imprisoned like an enemy in a besieged fortress." Antonio leaned toward Ezzelino. "Today I came to ask you to release prisoners who have given up hope of freedom. Suppose that you and not they were in prison. And suppose you heard that the man who would release you had finally come. Wouldn't you leap for joy? Most certainly you would." Antonio placed his hands on Ezzelino's. The friar's touch was gentle and warm, the voice earnest with concern. "Well, Messer Ezzelino, you are in prison. You are in the prison of sin and there is only One who will release you. The Lord Jesus has come to release you from the devil's power and from unending imprisonment in hell."

Ezzelino had heard enough. He would see just how peaceful this priest would remain.

Impetuously, he threw off Antonio's hands. Leaping to his feet, Ezzelino rounded the table and approached the man from the side. Antonio rose to face him. Ezzelino's hand flew to his waist, where it gripped the hilt of his sword. He scrutinized Antonio as a wolf stares down a cornered doe, waiting for some sign of fear before lunging to attack.

Antonio stood unflinching, his calm gaze locked on Ezzelino. Ezzelino couldn't bluff him.

Ezzelino let out a low whistle of defeat. The game had gone on long enough. Suddenly he ripped his belt from his waist and spun it around his neck like a noose. With exaggerated gestures, he bowed to the floor as he thrust the belt toward Antonio with a grand flourish. Then he raised his head to Antonio, black eyes fixing coldly on black eyes. "You want me to put my head in a noose, to bow to your God and to become His slave." Ezzelino paused and furrowed his brow. "Never. You are right. I am a prisoner of greed and power. And I love it. The only god I know is me."

Ezzelino whipped the belt from his neck and threw it to the floor. He jumped to his feet as his anger gave way to gratitude. By some act of grace, he hadn't killed this man. Had he murdered him, all of Lombardy would have risen against the one who had slaughtered their saint.

"Show him safely out," Ezzelino commanded the nearest knight. Then, impulsively, he grabbed one of the golden wine goblets and held it toward Antonio. "For you."

Antonio shook his head. "No, Messer Ezzelino." His voice approached a whispered sob. "The only thing gained by bloodshed that I want is your soul. Christ shed His Blood for that. I will pray for you."

As he watched Antonio follow the knight through the doorway, Ezzelino thought of his own father. *"Only in weakness before God is there strength,"* he had said. Today Ezzelino understood what his father had meant.

NOTES

Ezzelino (Eccelino) III da Romano was born in 1194, making him one year older than Antonio and the same age as Chiara of Assisi and Emperor Federico II. His reputation for cruelty against clergy and laypeople of both sexes and all ages was well known. The fictitious incidents with the serf and the massage from Ariana are perfectly reasonable considering Ezzelino's taste for brutality toward others and luxury toward himself.

Ezzelino considered chastity to be honorable and practiced it himself. His treatment of sexual offenders, as described in this chapter, is accurate.

Curtayne (81) and Wiegler describe Ezzelino physically. Wiegler gives his family history.

In May 1231 (one author puts the date at 1228), Antonio visited Ezzelino at his palace to negotiate for the release of the prisoners as described in this chapter (Purcell 244). No one knows if he took this visit upon himself or if he made it at Count Tiso's request. Antonio was unsuccessful. Seven months after his death, ambassadors from Venice and Wiffredo da Lucino, then podestà of Padua, succeeded in having these prisoners released (Purcell 245).

The earliest accounts of Antonio's meeting with Ezzelino simply state that he was unsuccessful. About thirty years later, embellished stories appeared. These state that Ezzelino was seated on his throne surrounded by murderous troops, that Antonio preached a fire-and-brimstone sermon to him, and that the tyrant undid his girdle, twisted it around his neck, and threw himself at Antonio's feet, confessing his sins and promising to amend his life. After Antonio left, Ezzelino told his servants that he saw lightning come from Antonio's eyes and was certain that, if he laid hands on him, the demons would take Ezzelino's soul immediately to hell. The legends then go on to state that a short time later, Ezzelino sent Antonio a costly gift, which he refused with the words that he wanted no gifts gained by bloodshed. The accounts say that, for a short time, Ezzelino tempered his cruelties but relapsed into them following Antonio's death.

In 1232, he and Federico formed an alliance and warred against Milan and other cities. Ezzelino later married Federico's fourteen-year-old daughter, further cementing their families. In 1256, when Padua revolted against Ezzelino, he entered the city and slaughtered twelve thousand of its inhabitants in one day. Wounded in battle in 1259, he died unrepentant, having rebuffed the efforts of friars who urged him to confess.

All his life, Emperor Federico II, whose physical description in this chapter is accurate, fought against the papacy by deceit and false promises. In time, he actually engaged papal armies in combat for key cities. Twice he was excommunicated. Federico's success greatly diminished the power of the papacy. He died unexpectedly in 1250.

Antonio was suffering severely from dropsy when he met Ezzelino (Purcell 244). Antonio's words are from SK 137–40 (dropsy and its spiritual counterpart) and SK 170–75 (the imprisoned soul set free).

Scripture verses are from James 2:13 ("Judgment is without mercy . . ."); John 8:24 ("You will die . . ."); and Romans 6:23 ("The wages of sin . . .").

29

Count Tiso da Camposampiero

Convent of Santa Maria, Padua, Italy (May 1231)

O utside the convent of Santa Maria in Padua, the aging Count Tiso da Camposampiero was tastefully dressed in gray and white, resembling the colors of the speckled horse he'd just dismounted. By coincidence, the hues accented his ruddy complexion and silvery, shoulder-length hair, making him look nearly as handsome now as he had thirty summers ago. He had come today to invite Antonio to spend some time at his country estate.

Tiso's knock at the convent door was swift and sharp. The young brother who answered disappeared inside when Tiso asked for the priest, so Tiso sat on one of the log seats next to the convent to wait. Long moments later, a short, swollen friar appeared, his deep-set eyes looking darker against his yellowed skin. Antonio. Tiso had never seen him so ill.

Tiso stood and bowed. "You need a rest, Padre. May I invite you to spend some time at Camposampiero? There you can work on your sermons in peace. These sermons are on the saints, I heard. Isn't there a cardinal who commissioned them?"

"Sì," Antonio smiled. "Our ordine's cardinal protector, Cardinal Rinaldo dei Conti di Segni, commissioned them."

Antonio averted his gaze from Tiso and looked beyond him. "Madonna, may I help you?"

Tiso turned. He'd not heard anyone approach.

The woman standing a little distance behind him was youthful and well-dressed in reds and golds, likely a member of the minor nobility. Accompanying her was a drab older matron, likely a servant. "Padre," the younger woman shyly asked, "we're going on pilgrimage to Rome. Would you bless us?"

Antonio raised his hand in blessing. "In the name of the Father, and of the Son, and of the Holy Spirit."

"Grazie," the women said and, bowing, left.

Tiso resumed the conversation. "The cardinal would be glad to have you be able to work in peace, I would think."

For Antonio, Tiso knew, had had little peace during these past months. This Lent he had preached daily for forty days. Tiso had attended some of these sermons, held in piazzas and fields to accommodate the crowds. After Antonio finished preaching, the mob would throng forward. But for a group of burly Lesser Brothers who surrounded the priest, he might have been crushed in the frenzy to touch a saint or to snip a piece of his habit as a relic. The brothers would force the audience into a sort of order so that only one or two people at a time had access to their saint. The lines for confession to Antonio and other priests seemed endless.

Antonio had continued to preach, not always daily, until Pentecost. Then, as the grain was ripening, he had dismissed his hearers to begin the harvest. Yet many still came to him daily for any number of spiritual favors.

"Ah, peace. Solitude. Where would be best? Thank you for your invitation to Camposampiero. I will consider that. Before I go anywhere, I must complete my business concerning the debtors."

"I imagine that the prisons are empty of debtors because of you."

"Not yet. But perhaps soon!"

Hardly two months ago, Padua had enacted a statute that Tiso had inscribed in his memory so as to understand it in dealing with those who owed him money. It stated that "no one, henceforth, should be held in prison for money debts, past, present, or future, if he forfeited his goods. And this applies to both debtors and their bondsmen. . . . This statute has been enacted at the instance of the venerable brother and blessed Anthony, confessor of the Order of Friars Minor."

Since the statute took effect, scores of debtors, clad only in shirt and hose, had each sat three times on the blaming stone in the Piazza delle Erbe. Before the required hundred witnesses, each had proclaimed, "I give up my goods," invoking the statute that bore Antonio's name. Any property belonging to the debtor would be sold to repay the debt, but the humiliation on the blaming stone replaced the mandatory imprisonment for those whose debts exceeded what the sale could bring. Each duly humiliated debtor had to then leave Padua forever unless his creditors allowed him to return.

Tiso smiled at the priest. "I am certain my debtors would have used your statute had I not already forgiven their debts and released them. I am most grateful to you for your sermons."

Antonio's forceful sermons against usury, pride, and avarice were converting moneylenders, some of whom, unlike Tiso, charged exorbitant interest with no care about its effect on the borrower or his family. The entire region had heard of Antonio's sermon at a usurer's funeral in Florence. He had spoken on the text, "Where your treasure is, there will your heart be." So moved were his listeners that they visited the dead man's treasure trove and discovered a human heart, still warm, among the coins.

The clatter of cantering hooves caught Tiso's attention. A servant on a magnificent charger. How incongruent! Without reining the steed, the youth tossed a fat leather bag toward the two men and rode off. The bag had landed near Tiso's feet, so he picked it up and handed it to Antonio.

"Another usurer?"

"Most likely," Antonio said. "Not all of them come for confession. Some send their servants, like this one, to bring their offerings. That, they feel, absolves them." He fingered the lumpy bag. "Feels like coins in here. And daggers. Coins to the poor. Daggers to the river."

"The River Bacchiglione must be getting clogged with weapons," Tiso smiled. "I've seen men laying their swords at your feet."

Antonio grinned.

"I've heard talk of usurers making two- and threefold restitution to those whom they have cheated. And of sinners and heretics living together in repentance in a house you suggested they purchase." The men were recognizable, for their penance extended to their garb: a long, rough, ash-colored tunic with a cord about the waist.

"Praise God for the graces which He is giving to these men!" Antonio's voice was exultant. "But, Messer, I should take this offering to the guardian. And I will ask if he would permit me to go to Camposampiero." With that, Antonio, carrying the sack, shuffled inside. Tiso took a seat on a log bench.

Suddenly he smelled the unmistakable odor of a tanner. Sure enough, one was approaching. As he walked, the tanner pressed his hands against his dark hair that was sticking out in all directions and attempted to smooth it. Then he rubbed his hands over his grimy apron. "Is Padre Antonio in?" he asked Tiso.

"Sì." Antonio had reappeared in the doorway.

"Padre, I need to confess."

"Wonderful." Antonio was beaming. "Just a moment." He turned to Tiso. "The guardian gave approval if Camposampiero seems best to me."

Tiso's heart leaped with joy.

"Before you leave, may I ask a favor of you, Messer?"

What might this be? Perhaps to intercede with Ezzelino? As if Tiso had any positive influence over that man even though he no longer warred against him. At the not-so-subtle hinting of Tiso and other nobles of Padua, Antonio had undertaken a failed mission to have the tyrant release his prisoners. What could Tiso do against the "Devil of Lombardy"?

You can pray for him, the thought came.

"Would you pray for me, Messer?"

Pray for Antonio? "Sì." Tiso was already praying for him.

Add Ezzelino's name to Antonio's in your prayers.

Tiso nodded. He would have to do that. Only prayer could convert that man.

"Grazie, Messer." Antonio clasped Tiso's hands, then nodded to the tanner, who followed him into Santa Maria. Tiso knew where they were going. He, too, had confessed in the front parlor.

"Excuse me, Messer." The deep, manly voice hailed him from up the street. "Do you know if Padre Antonio is here?"

The young man was holding the hand of a small boy, and beside him a young woman was carrying a bundled infant. Their dress was simple but clean. Likely farmers from the countryside.

"He's here, Messer, but he's hearing a person's confession."

The couple looked at one another. "We'll wait," the man said.

The two of them sat on the log seats by the door. The child busied himself with twigs and stones at the couple's feet. Tiso turned his palfrey and started home.

His heart sang as he rode. He had seen the man whom he, like many others, considered a saint. Maybe he would host Antonio at his estate, but, whether or not he came, Antonio knew he was welcome.

A few days later, while Tiso was riding about his fields, checking on the harvest, he decided to visit the Lesser Brothers who, at Tiso's invitation, had constructed a hermitage at Camposampiero.

An unfamiliar brother was walking across a cleared area near the cells. Tiso rode up to him. "Pace e bene, brother. Do you know if Fra Antonio might be coming here?"

"He's already here," the brother said. "With Fra Luca. They walked in that direction." He pointed to the forest.

"Grazie, Fra . . ."

"Ruggerio."

Tiso nodded and directed his horse into the woods. He hadn't gone far when he found Antonio and Luca gazing up at the most magnificent tree on his estate, a giant walnut from whose three massive trunks spread six great branches lifting upward like a crown. The brothers turned at the sound of his approach.

"Count Tiso!" Antonio called out. "I hope our coming is of no disturbance to you. A benefactor offered to cart us out here, and we accepted. If your kind invitation to remain here to work on the sermons still applies, here we will stay."

Tiso's heart leaped. "Of course it applies. Welcome!" Dismounting, Tiso clasped Antonio's hands and kissed him, first on one cheek and then on the other.

"Fra Ruggerio and Fra Luca have come also at my guardian's request."

"Welcome!"

Antonio turned to the walnut tree. "Messer, see how this tree lifts his branches in praise as if saying, 'Glory to you, Mighty Lord!' Might I be able to have a wattle cell built up there, like a nest, with two additional ones below mine, one for Fra Ruggerio and one for Fra Luca?"

"I will begin at once." Tiso bowed.

"Fra Luca, find Fra Ruggerio and bring him here," Antonio requested. "You both can help Messer Tiso."

Luca sprinted off as Antonio smiled at Tiso. "I will be able to weave reeds but not much else with this poor body."

"I have two serfs who can do four times what we can do together. I'll find them."

Within a short time, Tiso, two muscular serfs, and three brothers were at work. They worked all afternoon. When evening arrived, the huge walnut tree sported three wattle cells complete with sturdy wooden floors, wattle doors, window shutters, and ladders. Tiso walked around the finished cells, their floors level and smooth, their little windows open to the breezes and the birds.

"We should see if they're waterproof," Tiso said to the brothers.

"We'll find out if they're waterproof," Antonio laughed, "because we'll be in them from now on."

NOTES

With his own hands, and at Antonio's request, Tiso built the saint a wattle cell in a "nut tree," either a walnut, chestnut, or oak. Most biographies favor walnut (*Assidua* 20–21, Ben 8, Rig 16, 2LJS 6–7). The biographies say nothing about any helpers, but it seems that Tiso would have needed help to finish this quickly, as Antonio simply showed up at Camposampiero and requested the tree huts.

The details regarding the effect of Antonio's sermons, his founding of convents, his advice to purchase a home for communal living for repentant sinners, and his inspiration of the debtors' code are accurate. The translation of the debtors' code and the use of the "blaming stone" are in Purcell (228–29).

The story quickly spread of Antonio's funeral sermon for a Florentine usurer whose heart was found among his coins (Da Rieti 94–95, Keller 16).

The Scripture verse is Luke 12:34 ("Where your treasure . . .").

30

Fra Luca Belludi

Road Outside the City, Padua, Italy (May 30, 1231)

Through the smattering of trees lining this narrow road out of Padua, Fra Luca Belludi gazed at the slope of the grassy hill that rose on his right. Halfway up the hill, a cluster of sheep grazed in a lush, flower-dotted meadow. The slope was not especially steep for someone in good health. But for Antonio?

"I want to see Padua one last time," he had told Luca. But should he climb this hill to view it? Just after Lauds, as dawn was breaking, the two brothers had left Santa Maria to begin their half day's journey to Camposampiero. Already, as the sun was climbing to its zenith, Antonio's deep, labored breaths strained his lungs. They still had a way to go.

Luca looked at his companion's haggard face, its skin dry and pale as parchment. "Are you sure you want to climb, brother?"

"I'll rest under this tree," Antonio said, easing himself down. With the tree propping up his back, he sat with his legs splayed out before him. "If I rest, I'll be able to make it."

Luca slipped from his own shoulder the wool pouch that held Antonio's sermon manuscripts and breviary as well as his *Moral Concordances* and *Commentary on the Psalms*, books Antonio had written for his own use. Today was the first day that Luca had ever carried these precious burdens. Previously,

Antonio had always insisted on carrying them himself, flung over his left shoulder, as the two men trod from place to place to preach. It was not that Antonio didn't trust Luca to carry them; it was simply that he felt responsible for bearing his own burdens. But today Antonio's swollen legs could barely carry his body.

"I'll carry the writings," Luca had told Antonio that morning. "It's difficult enough for you to walk without having to carry around more weight."

Antonio had conceded to the favor.

Luca placed the precious sermons next to him on the grass, then pulled his long legs up to his chin and tucked his habit around them. After wrapping his gangly arms around his legs, he rested his bony chin on his knees as he used to do when he was a boy.

Out of the corner of his eye, he glanced at Antonio. From beneath the priest's habit thrust bloated feet that joined legs as thick as logs beneath a tattered gray drape. Antonio's hands were clasped over his distended abdomen and his head was listing toward his bony right shoulder. Eyelids the color of a rain-battered sea drew closed. A charcoal blush encircled his eye sockets.

Antonio was snoring.

Luca felt a sense of relief. If Antonio slept, his heaving breathing might ease and he could possibly make the climb.

When the minister general had first assigned Luca to accompany the priest, Antonio had already been ill. The dropsy that had been swelling his abdomen now so inflated the man that, despite his continual fasting, his belly was as stretched as a glutton's and his ability to hurry was gone.

Luca reached over and gently tugged the hood of Antonio's tunic from behind the man's back. Pulling the hood over Antonio's brown neck, he carefully tucked its point over the tonsured head, pressing the fabric around Antonio's ears. Then, in a swift motion, he pulled up his own hood. Now the gnats would annoy neither man. Luca closed his eyes to rest.

Born near the dawning of the century, Luca had left behind the opulence of the Belludi family, who lived just outside Padua, to join the followers of Francesco. Ten summers ago, San Francesco himself had clothed him. Now he accompanied another man whom he likewise highly esteemed.

As Antonio fulfilled his duties as provincial, Luca had traveled with him through the towns of the Romagna: Milan, Vercelli, Varese, Brescia, Breno,

Lake Garda, and Mantua. On the roads, they had seen the common parade of clergy, religious, nobility, knights, and farmers, but also exquisite and strange animals brought from Asia and Africa by the emperor. Elephants. Lions. Apes. Antonio noted these exotic beasts and sometimes used them to illustrate his sermons. If he but mentioned a leopard, wild cow, or rhinoceros, his curious audience was immediately attentive.

On their journeys, Antonio had pushed both men to their limits and sometimes beyond them. The priest had preached, prayed, established convents, welcomed novices, forgiven sins, shared alms, healed the ill, and raised the dead. In him, Luca had seen the intimate union of both the divine and the human.

In one town, a woman had approached the two friars. In her arms lay a pale, limp child whose legs were curled tightly to his chest as if in a death agony. The pallid, twisted body filled Luca with grief.

"Can you heal him, brother?" Luca begged.

"I will bless him," Antonio offered.

Making the sign of the cross over the child and his mother, Antonio sent the two away. The following morning, the woman approached the platform on which Antonio was preparing to preach. With quick, short steps, the child trundled along beside her.

"Padre!" the woman called out.

Antonio had raised his hand to silence her. Again making the sign of the cross over the two, he sent them off into the crowd with the words, "Give glory to God for His mercy."

Another time, a young man named Leonardo had come to Antonio for confession. As he did with all repentant sinners, Antonio had listened patiently, given counsel and absolution, and sent the youth home. Not long afterward, word came to Antonio that Leonardo had cut off his foot. Antonio's face grew wan. "Precious Jesus, no!" he had whispered.

He and Luca had hurried to the young man's house, where they found his mother weeping and the young man bleeding profusely from his stump.

Cradling Leonardo's face in his hands, Antonio had asked in a voice full of agony, "Leonardo, why did you do this?"

"Padre," the trembling boy cried, "when I told you that I had kicked my mother, you said that the foot of him who does such a thing deserves to be cut off."

With bowed head, Antonio had moaned in a voice so full of anguish that it startled even Luca, "Oh, Leonardo, my sincere penitent. Where is the foot?"

Leonardo pointed to a basket. Antonio lifted by its big toe the blue, bloody foot. With his eyes raised to heaven, he had knelt at Leonardo's side while pressing the foot to the stump. Then he closed his eyes and shuddered.

"Madonna, quick, a rag," he had said.

The boy's sobbing mother grabbed a cloth from a peg on the wall and handed it to Antonio. "Tear it in strips, Luca," he had ordered.

Using a kitchen knife to help him, Luca had made some ragged bandages with which Antonio wrapped the foot and stump. When Antonio's bloody fingers slowly uncurled from the heel, the foot remained attached.

"Stay in bed, Leonardo. May God have mercy on you." Antonio blessed the young man, then took his hands in his own. "Leonardo, the body is God's temple. Never, never mutilate it. How I repent for having said what I did! Please forgive me." Antonio bowed his head to the boy's hands. "Please forgive me."

The boy arched his eyebrows and glanced from Luca to his mother and back again to Luca. Timidly he slid one hand out from underneath Antonio's face and, with a quick, light movement, touched the priest's shoulder. Then he drew back his hand and held it to his chest as if unsure what to do with it.

His voice came in hesitant syllables. "That's all right, Padre. I guess you didn't mean for me to really cut it off."

Antonio raised his head, his closed eyes fluttering open, a deep sigh escaping from his chest. "Let's pray, Leonardo." For long moments, the four in the house prayed together. Then Antonio rose to leave. "Don't remove that bandage for many weeks. I will continue to pray for your healing."

Many weeks later, when Leonardo undid the bandage, the foot remained attached. He had shown Antonio and Luca the huge, jagged scar that indicated where the foot had been cut off.

On another occasion, Luca and Antonio had been part of a crowd gathered to hear one of the preaching friars, who quoted the speech of Saint Paul to Dionysius and the other citizens of Athens.

"The God who made the world and everything in it, being Lord of heaven and earth, does not live in shrines made by man, nor is he served by human hands, as though he needed anything, since he himself gives to all men life and breath and everything. And he made from one every nation of men to live on all the face of the earth, having determined allotted periods and the boundaries of their habitation, that they should seek God, in the hope that they might feel after him and find him. Yet he is not far from each one of us, for

'In him we live and move and have our being';

as even some of your poets have said,

'For we are indeed his offspring.'"

As Antonio listened to these words, a great smile spread across his lips and his entire face seemed radiant with joy. He sank to his left knee, his right knee bent, his clasped hands resting on his right thigh, his face lifted to the sky. For the remainder of the sermon, he remained in this position, unmoving even when the preacher stopped speaking and the crowd dispersed. Luca held the curious back. "He's in ecstasy," Luca told them. Luca waited, standing guard, until Antonio lowered his gaze and stood.

"What did you see, brother?" Luca had asked.

Antonio had raised his hand to his lips and shaken his head. Luca didn't ask again. Nor did he question subsequent ecstasies, which were now becoming more frequent. Truly, sometimes Antonio seemed already to be living in heaven. But other times, like today when Antonio's labored snoring indicated the progression of his disease, the man seemed very much rooted on earth.

Antonio had pressed a rigorous schedule, finally coming to Padua, where he had worked diligently on his sermon notes. He was still working on them; that's why Luca was carrying them to Camposampiero.

Luca had read parts of them. "I have tried, insofar as divine grace imparted it to me and my poor little supply of knowledge responded, to establish a concordance," Antonio had written in the introduction. "While quite aware of my own insufficiency for accomplishing such a great and difficult labor, yet I let my fear and awe of the task be overcome by the prayers and the charity of the brothers who urged me on." Luca had smiled when he read that. He had been one of the encouraging brothers.

Later Antonio had added, "And so, dear brothers, I the least of all of you, your brother and servant, have somehow composed this work on the Gospels around the year, for your comfort, for the edification of the faithful, and for the remission of my sins. I humbly pray and beseech you, that when you read this work you will remember me, your brother, before God the Son of God, who offered Himself to God the Father on the wood of the Cross."

Luca swallowed a lump that rose suddenly in his throat. Would only Antonio's writings soon be all that was left of him? Oh, Luca would read them and pray for the man who was napping at his side.

Antonio had worked on those sermon notes until Lent and then had preached daily throughout the forty days. When Luca had tried to dissuade him from this brutal schedule, Antonio had been inflexible. "No, I must preach," he said. "The harvest is great, and I must work while there is still time. For me, night is coming, but while it is still day, I will labor in the vineyard of my Lord."

Every day Antonio had preached, not in the churches as planned, for they were too small to hold the crowds who came, but in the meadows. At night, the streets of Padua were alight with torches and lanterns. Citizens of all ranks and backgrounds made their way to the place where Antonio was to preach. Every morning, the grass was crowded with listeners who had camped overnight to hear their saint. Sometimes the crowds swelled to thirty thousand, with all voices—including those of vendors who had come to sell their wares—falling silent when Antonio began to speak.

Luca and several other brothers who accompanied Antonio would line the people up for confession while Antonio, who daily ate nothing until sunset, became so absorbed in hearing confessions that even rain showers didn't slacken his zeal. So many came to confess to him and to the other priests of Padua that clergy from neighboring towns were called in to help. Padua was entering God's kingdom in a wave.

Like clouds of mosquitoes, the crowds sucked from Antonio his ebbing strength and went away strong, faith-filled, and encouraged. At the day's end, Antonio pushed his body to the little monastery of Santa Maria in the heart of the city where sleep, interrupted by prayer, never quite replaced the energy he had lost.

Sometimes disturbances other than prayer interrupted that precious rest. One night around the beginning of Lent, Luca awoke to what he thought was an anguished choke. Throwing his tunic over his body, he had rushed out of his tiny cell into the adjoining one. Antonio was sitting bolt upright on his pallet, staring at the wall.

Luca stood helplessly in the doorway. In weak candlelight, he could see by the radiance of the friar's face that he was experiencing another ecstasy. In a moment, Antonio closed his eyes and sighed deeply.

Luca took one step into the room and knelt by the friar. Swiftly he took the blanket that lay across Antonio's loins and wiped beads of sweat from the man's bony chest and neck.

Antonio reached up and took Luca's hands in his own. His voice was gentle but shaky. "You are the father coming in to console his child who is troubled by terrors of the night."

"Did you have a dream, brother?"

"It seemed to me as if the devil tried to choke me. I could scarcely breathe."

Luca felt horror rising in himself. "Brother, no."

Antonio smiled. He patted Luca's hand. "I'm all right. I begged the Blessed Mother to help me, and I sang her hymn, 'O Glorious Lady.' When I made the sign of the cross on my forehead, I was freed from the demon's power."

"Did you see him?"

Antonio shook his head. "No. I thought I would when I awoke. But, instead, my room was lit with a heavenly brilliance. I saw our Lady."

Luca feared for Antonio's safety. "Perhaps Satan will return. I'll stay with you tonight."

Antonio smiled. "No. I have nothing to fear from the devil. In the light of God's love that flooded my cell, the angel of darkness couldn't possibly remain. You return to bed now. I'll be fine."

Lent continued and ended, and Easter came and went. If Antonio had confronted the devil again, he didn't mention it. The only confrontation that came close occurred when he, earlier this month, had visited Ezzelino da Romano. Refusing to take Luca along on the dangerous mission, Antonio had pleaded on behalf of Count Tiso's relatives, whom the tyrant had imprisoned. Luca had prayed fervently for their release and for Antonio's safe return, but God had answered only one of his prayers.

After Lent, and up until now, Antonio had continued to preach on Sundays and on many weekdays. Daily he wrote, consoled, forgave, visited the sick and the poor. Then, as the grain ripened in the fields, Antonio ceased preaching during the week. "Your duty, my people, is to the grain," he called out in his final daily sermon. "As you glean it, remember that Christ came to you as a humble grain of wheat. Crushed and broken for your sins, He feeds you with the Bread of His life and thus gives to you life eternal."

Today before dawn the two friars had left Santa Maria to go to Camposampiero. There, Antonio could rest and work on his sermon notes in peace. And he desperately wanted to finish them. They were intended for itinerant preachers and clergy who had difficulty composing their own sermons. These men would gain inspiration, knowledge, and guidance from his words and be able then to pen their own homilies. When he finished these intensive writings, which were filled with Scripture, examples from nature, and analogies, he wanted to write a book for all Christians to read. He wanted God's Spirit to bathe with light the people who would read his words.

At Camposampiero, Antonio had the chance to finish his sermon notes and begin his next work without too many interruptions from his devotees. Only those Paduans who needed to see him personally would make the long trek out to Messer Tiso's estate, especially during the stifling heat of summer. Of course, Antonio would continue to receive all visitors graciously as he always did. Devotees in Padua who simply wanted to see and speak to the man whom they venerated as a saint would have to content themselves with the other brothers at Santa Maria.

Luca was nearly asleep. Suddenly a flutter of wings swept his face. Startled awake, he caught a turtledove winging upward. At the same moment, Antonio's eyes fluttered open. The priest laughed. "For a moment, I thought I was again singing the responsory in Santa Maria's Church."

Luca grinned. On the feast of the Purification of Mary, Antonio had been singing in his sweet voice, "They offered 'a sacrifice according to what is said in the law of the Lord, "a pair of turtledoves, or two young pigeons."'" Suddenly two turtledoves had flown over the pulpit. Antonio's song had risen with joy. In his sermon he asked in astonished glee, "Have you ever wondered which gift the Holy Family offered? I had just been wondering myself. 'My Lady, was it two turtledoves or two young pigeons?'" Antonio's hand had swept upward to where the two turtledoves were perched in the rafters. "Today the Blessed Mother has revealed the gift to us."

Today the turtledove winged into the sky and disappeared.

"I'm no agile turtledove, brother. I'm an old mare that dozes in the harness," Antonio said. "But she's ready to press on, if you are."

Luca pushed to his feet and stretched his sleep away. He shook the cramps out of his legs. "I was napping, too." He held out his hand to Antonio, who, with a struggle, pulled himself to his feet. Luca picked up the pouch of Antonio's writings and hoisted it over his shoulder.

The two men climbed the hill, brushing through soft grass and trampling pink and purple blossoms whose fragrance wafted upward in fragile waves. Sheep bleated and parted as the men passed through. The two climbed silently. At times, Antonio paused to catch his breath while Luca waited. Other times, when they came to a particularly steep incline or to a heap of rocks, Luca helped pull and push up the friar's thick, clumsy body.

"I'm a bother," Antonio said.

"No. You're my brother," Luca replied. And they both laughed.

At the crest of the hill, Antonio paused. Far beyond them to the north rose the Tyrolean Mountains, their snow-capped peaks jutting into the pale sky. Nuzzling up to them like suckling lambs lay the hills of Vicenza. Closer to the east wound the serpentine mountains of Este thrusting through a vast green plain of grass and trees. Before them in the valley lay Padua, a city resting between the hills as naturally as a child sleeps between its mother's breasts. In the sunlight, marble palaces glittered. Domes and bell towers thrust gloriously toward the heavens. Dotted with moving workers and beasts, a vast array of brown and green fields and vineyards surrounded Padua's red roofs, gray stone walls, and open market spaces. From this height, even the hovels of the poor looked quaint and inviting.

Luca felt a warm hand on his own. "Look at Padua," Antonio said. "Is there a more beautiful location in all the world? Its beauty is a testament to God."

Antonio threw his arms open wide as if to embrace the entire scene. "Blessed are you, O Padua, for the beauty of your site!" His voice, firm and powerful and full, rang across the hills. "Blessed are you for the harvest of your fields! Blessed are you in your people who follow the Lord." Then, lifting his hands heavenward, he cried out, "Blessed also shall you be for the honor with which heaven is about to crown you!"

For long moments, he remained with his hands stretched heavenward, his eyes fixed on the skies, his whole body straining toward heaven as if it could fly there just by willing it. Luca bowed his head and clasped his hands. Wetness trickled down his cheeks, but were they tears of joy or sorrow? Or both? *Oh, Lord, is he telling me that he will die? Does he know how people will flock here if he does?*

Until the sun began to cast long shadows over Padua, the two men remained, Antonio reaching upward, Luca kneeling with bowed head. With the rise of an early evening breeze, the intensity of the Spirit blew aside and the friars gazed again at Padua, which now appeared gray and drab in the dusk.

Antonio was the first to speak. "Goodbye, beloved city," he said in a trembling whisper. "I shall not preach in you again."

Through the twilight, the two friars made their way down the hill to Camposampiero. By the time they arrived, dusk had deepened to dark.

NOTES

Luca Belludi, who was twenty when he entered the Lesser Brothers, was born between 1200 and 1210. He was assigned as Antonio's traveling companion. Luca became a provincial minister of the Franciscan Order and was mainly responsible for erecting the basilica that enshrines Antonio's remains. Active in preaching and good works, Luca, who was always known as Luca di Sant'Antonio, died in 1285 and was interred in Antonio's original tomb. In 1927, the Church declared him blessed.

Antonio bid farewell to Padua sometime around May 30, 1231.

Incidents from this chapter are:

Antonio's preaching, sermon-writing, and response in Padua are recorded in *Assidua* 15–19; Rig 10, 14; *Dialogus* 2–3; Ben 3; and 2LJS 5–6. His blessing of Padua is also found in the histories (2LJS 6, Rig 16, *Assidua* 19). His struggle with the devil is in Rig 10, 2LJS 5, *Assidua* 16, and *Dialogus* 2. Luca's request to heal a boy with crippled limbs is detailed in Ben 5–6, and the healing of Leonardo's foot, which some accounts say was instantaneous, is in Ben 7.

Antonio's ecstasy at hearing the sermon on Saint Paul's words to the Athenians is recorded in the histories, but the account does not tell what the ecstasy was like or what words caused it. His encounter with the turtledoves is also in the historical record.

Antonio desired to write a book for all Christians to read. While still working on his sermons, he died (SSF I), thus never fulfilling this ambition.

The words at the beginning of his sermon notes are taken from SerE 64; the words at the end of his sermon notes are from SSF III 387.

Scripture verses are from Acts 17:24–28 ("The God who made . . ."); see Luke 10:2 ("The harvest is great . . ."); see John 9:4 ("Night is coming . . ."); see Matthew 20:1–16 ("Labor in the vineyard . . ."); and Luke 2:24 ("They offered a sacrifice . . .").

31

Fra Ruggerio

Convent of the Lesser Brothers, Camposampiero, Italy (June 13, 1231)

On his wooden platform in the boughs of a great walnut tree, a huge, round-cheeked brother squirmed in his slumber. Although it was nearly dawn, Fra Ruggerio was not quite asleep. These nights, he never seemed to be quite asleep. Not that he minded squeezing his lumbering body onto this tiny platform, nor did he bother about sleeping with his oversized hands and feet thrust against the willow-woven walls of his cell. Discomfort was not keeping him awake. Antonio was.

Antonio, who slept on a larger, gabled platform above him, breathed laboriously all night long and occasionally snored. Fra Luca, who also lived in the tree, in a little hut built slightly above Ruggerio's and to the right of the trunk, mumbled in his sleep. Those noises, however, didn't disturb Ruggerio, who had learned to sleep well in the company of brothers who snorted and coughed the whole night through. What bothered him was Antonio's illness and the fact that, at any time, it might claim his life.

When the men had first begun to live in the tree together, Luca told Antonio, "If you need help during the night, you must call for us."

Antonio had shrugged and looked from Luca to Ruggerio. "You brothers will need your rest for whatever you might find in the morning. I'll be all right."

Would Antonio cry out if he encountered a crisis? Ruggerio sickened at the thought of finding the priest's stiffening body in the morning, and he cringed at the possibility of tending him in his final death throes during the night. When dark descended and the men lay down to sleep, Ruggerio couldn't relax. All night he listened for a scream, a choke, a gurgle, or total silence that would mean that death had entered the covered cell above his own.

Every night as he listened, the memories of Nonno's death returned. When Ruggerio was just a boy, he and his grandfather had been weeding the family carrot patch when pain's demon-talons had plunged into Nonno's chest. Nonno had buckled, grabbing his breast, his brown eyes filled with fear and agony. As he had crumpled over the feathery green shoots, he had clawed at Ruggerio and hissed, "Get your papà."

Terrified, Ruggerio had run to the meadow where Papà was plowing under the stubble left from the wheat harvest. "Nonno fell down and screamed in the garden," Ruggerio had shouted. He had seen Papà's eyes widen with fright, seen the panic as he threw down the reins and thrust the plow deeply into the ground to anchor it. Leaving the oxen standing stupidly in the furrows, he had outraced his son home. By the time pudgy Ruggerio arrived, breathless with running and fear, Nonno was lying indoors on his bed, squeezing his son's hand and screaming in anguish.

For ten minutes the man whom Ruggerio loved even more than he loved his own papà shrieked and trembled. Then, convulsing terribly, his entire body went limp. As Nonno's eyes rolled backward in his head, the town canon had rushed breathlessly into the cottage. Over the still body he recited the prayers and performed the anointing that would escort Nonno's soul into heaven.

The incident left one impression on Ruggerio. Death was horrible. He never, ever again wanted to see anyone die. And up to this point, he never had. Even though he had knelt beside dying brothers and recited the penitential psalms for them, he had not seen anyone die. In what must have looked like piety to others, he had kept his eyes tightly closed, his body unmoving, his mind focusing on the words of the prayers. He would pray this way until someone else announced the death, and then, taking a deep breath and averting his eyes from the corpse, he would rise and file out of the body's presence, his gaze on the floor.

Ruggerio hated his childish, secret aversion. Even though he believed with all his heart in God's saving mercy, even though he had joined the Lesser Brothers to die to the world, even though he knew that he must think of his current life as nothing but a preparation for death and what came after, even despite all his faith, he still feared seeing anyone die. Whom could he speak with about this unchristian terror? Who would understand?

Ruggerio had sometimes thought of speaking to Fra Antonio about his trepidation, for Fra Antonio was gentle and good. But Antonio was ill, weakened even more by the continuous stream of visitors who kept coming to Santa Maria seeking his counsel. Ruggerio thought too highly of the man to bother him with a fear that should have no hold on a follower of Christ. And, deep inside, he dreaded being alone with a man whose swollen body was obviously nurturing death. Suppose Antonio should be stricken in Ruggerio's presence? So he preferred to smile at the priest, greet him, listen to him teach, and then leave him alone.

Now all had changed. Two-and-a-half weeks ago, the guardian of the brothers at Santa Maria had summoned Ruggerio.

"We all realize that Antonio isn't well," the guardian had begun. "Now he does not even have the strength to greet his many visitors. Count Tiso has invited him to Camposampiero, and Provincial Fra Alberto has given him permission to go."

Ruggerio nodded. He had been to Camposampiero himself a few times. It was a restful spot indeed.

"Someone must be with Antonio at all times. That will be Fra Luca," the guardian continued. "But you are to tend him as well."

The assignment came like a punch to Ruggerio's groin.

"Should he require pen or parchment or a drink of water, you are to get it. He may send you back here or to Arcella on business. He may need help walking. As he grows weaker, he may be unable to rise from bed. You're strong and can assist him in his bodily needs. You'll go to Camposampiero two days in advance of Luca and Antonio to make sure that all is ready for their arrival. With Luca, you'll remain at Camposampiero to tend Antonio until the end, if necessary."

As the full import of the assignment sank into Ruggerio's brain like a stone into muck, nausea overwhelmed him and he nearly gagged. The guardian seemed not to notice. On jellied legs, he left the guardian's cell and, just outside the door, he retched. The guardian had assigned him to watch Antonio die.

For days, Ruggerio secretly hoped for the unspeakable—that the priest would die at Santa Maria or on his way to Camposampiero. But he didn't. Two weeks ago, after dark, Antonio and Luca had arrived at Count Tiso's estate.

It was obvious that Antonio was failing. While he loved to sit in the tree house that Count Tiso had built for him, he had great difficulty climbing into it. Ruggerio knew that the priest tried his best, but it took both him and Luca, one tugging Antonio's hands and the other guiding his grotesquely swollen feet, to get him up the ladder. Antonio would remain in the house all day except for the times of Office and the two small daily meals, which he ate with the other brothers in the small, rustic refectory.

Frequently Antonio called out notes or comments to Luca, who wrote them down in his own leafy cell. Ruggerio was the errand boy. He supplied quill pens and parchment and, on breezy days, stones to hold down the pages. On warm days, he passed cups of water through the clouds of leaves that hid the brothers from sight.

To those visitors who came from Padua seeking the priest, Ruggerio, towering over most of them, spoke with authority. "Fra Antonio isn't well. And he's very busy. Cardinal Messer Bishop of Ostia has requested that he compose notes about the saints for their feast days. If you must see him, you may speak to him from down here or, if you wish, you may climb up to him." That explanation discouraged most people from bothering Antonio.

Ruggerio had listened to a dozen sermons preached from the leafy heights to eager ears below. Once a crowd of careless listeners had trampled underfoot one of Count Tiso's wheat fields in their eagerness to cross the estate and surprise Antonio in his tree. When Antonio heard about the destruction, he asked Ruggerio and Luca to join him in prayer. The following day, Ruggerio had to skirt the field on his way to Count Tiso's manor house to request some additional parchment for Antonio. The wheat stood erect in the field.

Frequently, individual pilgrims came to see Antonio. Ruggerio had helped several climb the tree, including a few well-endowed noblewomen who unsuccessfully attempted to hold their billowing skirts around their ankles while making the ascent. Ruggerio was patient. He knew that these people came seeking God's forgiveness and guidance reflected in Antonio's words.

Whether Antonio was alone or with a visitor, Ruggerio always subconsciously listened for those deep, labored breaths. He had become used to them and often entertained a fantasy. Perhaps Antonio was not as ill as everyone thought. Perhaps in the summer air, he would recover and move back to Santa Maria. But at night Ruggerio's hopes dwindled. Even above the distant howling of wolves, he could hear Antonio gasping above him.

This Friday, as a tint of light began to whiten the darkness, Ruggerio stirred awake. He heard a rustling above him and to his right. Rising, he brushed the straw from his tunic and pushed it into a pile in one corner of his cell. This evening he would fluff it out again across the floor to create a bed. As he pushed aside the supple branch that he had come to regard as his door, he saw Luca ascending the ladder to Antonio's cell. Ruggerio climbed up after him.

After helping Antonio down the ladder, the three men proceeded a short distance through the forest to the tiny chapel that Count Tiso had built for them. There, before a wooden altar and a tiny tabernacle illuminated by a single candle, the three brothers joined a half-dozen others as they stood to chant the Morning Office.

After the Office, Luca and Ruggerio helped Antonio climb back up to his leafy oratory, then took their places on their own platforms. Although the day was already warm, Antonio was busy. His continual, muted dictation to Luca, the rustle of parchment, and the faint scratch of a reed pen above him lulled Ruggerio into a kind of torpor.

The sky brightened. Morning birdsongs swelled. Tiny black ants that perpetually climbed up and down this tree scurried along the bark. Hours passed with Ruggerio at prayer and Luca taking notes that Antonio called out to him. When the sun was high in the heavens, a bell rang from the convent. Ruggerio and Luca climbed the ladder to help Antonio descend for the first meal of the day.

As usual, several brothers were missing from this noon meal because they had gone into Padua or other neighboring towns to preach, work, or beg. The two left at Camposampiero, one of whom was the guardian, were standing at the table in the refectory. When Antonio took his place, with Luca and Ruggerio on either side of him, the brothers bowed their heads while the guardian recited the blessing. Then the brothers sat as the guardian broke the bread that Count Tiso's servants had brought and passed the loaf around the table. As Antonio attempted to pick up his portion, his hand trembled and fell. His heavy body sagged as his thick fingers clutched at the table. Had Ruggerio and Luca not caught him, he might have toppled to the floor.

The guardian of the convent leaped to his feet. "Is he in ecstasy?" he demanded.

Antonio shook his head.

"Brother, perhaps you should lie down," Luca suggested.

Antonio nodded, then attempted to stand. As he did so, his legs collapsed beneath him. Luca and Ruggerio caught his arms. The other brothers grabbed at the body. In a cluster of gray and tan tunics, Antonio was half carried, half escorted to the nearest straw hut. Once inside, he seemed to lose all strength as his body bent headlong on the mattress of vine branches. With great difficulty, the brothers turned him so that he was lying on his back. The hut was barely large enough for him. Ruggerio's back pressed against one wall, Luca's against the other. The other two brothers stood helplessly at the door.

"Fra Luca, don't leave my sermon notes in the tree," Antonio said weakly.

As Luca left, Antonio turned to Ruggerio. His dark eyes held Ruggerio in a gentle grasp. "Fra Ruggerio, I'm dying."

The whispered words screamed in Ruggerio's brain. He stared at those eyes, looking especially huge and deep-set in the gaunt face, and saw again Nonno's eyes roll backward in their sockets. As a huge wave of terror swept over him, he began to tremble uncontrollably.

Antonio's left hand slowly, slowly lifted until his fingers touched Ruggerio's wrist. "Don't be afraid, brother. Now comes the end of night which is life darkened by sin. Dawn is breaking for me. There is no need for any more struggle." The smile on his face was faint. "Life's misery is at an end and glory is beginning." Antonio's hand felt heavy on Ruggerio's wrist, heavy and warm and calm. Warmth and peace flowed from the touch.

"Brother, I'm going home."

Ruggerio nodded, pushing away the fear that dizzied him.

Antonio continued to speak. "Brother, can you do a little job for me? These hermits have been kind to us. But they have come to Count Tiso's to live in peaceful solitude. For these past two weeks, they have patiently endured visitors coming to see me."

Ruggerio nodded.

"I don't wish to put these brothers to the expense and trouble of my funeral. If I die here, they and Count Tiso will have to suffer endless lines of pilgrims to this lovely estate."

"The whole world calls you a saint, brother," Ruggerio managed to choke out.

Antonio nodded weakly. "A great burden to everyone concerned. If you approve, we'll go home to Santa Maria at once. Oh, that I might die and be buried there! There at the church dedicated to the Mother of God! Will you get a cart ready, brother?"

As Luca entered the hut with Antonio's manuscripts, a surge of relief came over Ruggerio. He would leave quickly. Perhaps Antonio would die in his absence. Carefully, he picked up Antonio's warm, puffy hand and placed it on his chest. "I'll get a cart," he said in a voice that rasped.

Ruggerio flew through the woods to Count Tiso's stable. His mind raced. *Lord, let him die before I return.*

In a quavering voice, Ruggerio told a stable hand, "Fra Antonio needs a cart to go to Santa Maria."

The gray-bearded man shook his head. "Count Tiso is out with the best cart. Got a second one left."

Ruggerio nodded assent as the stable hand settled a pair of oxen into a double yoke. Together he and Ruggerio threw huge armloads of hay into the cart and then the servant hitched the beasts to it. Ruggerio climbed into the seat and took the reins and a light whip in his hands. He called to the oxen, and they lumbered forward.

As he approached the convent, the guardian ran up. "You'll have to take him. He refuses to stay here."

Ruggerio's heart pumped wildly. Antonio was still alive.

Luca and Ruggerio and the two other brothers carried the bloated body out of the hut and placed it on the cart's bed of hay. Then, with Ruggerio driving and

Luca sitting in the back holding Antonio's hand, the cart jerked away from Camposampiero.

If only Ruggerio could make the ride smoother! He was striking every rut and rock in the road. Any moment he might hear an anguished moan or a shriek of pain. None came. The cart slowly jolted along. Whenever it traveled on a smooth length of road, which was not often, Ruggerio could hear Antonio's gasping over the creaking of the wood. He was still alive.

The sun was dipping lower. In the distance Ruggerio could see the peaceful suburb of Capo di Ponte. But who was this coming toward them? Another brother?

As the tan habit drew closer, Ruggerio recognized Fra Ignoto, the chaplain at Arcella.

Ignoto waved. "How is Fra Antonio? I'm on my way to visit him."

Ruggerio shook his head and waved to the back of the cart. Ignoto gave a little cry as Ruggerio reined the oxen to a halt.

"He wants to go to Santa Maria." The voice was Luca's.

Ruggerio felt a tug at his sleeve. Ignoto. "He won't make it to Santa Maria," he whispered in Ruggerio's ear. Then in a louder voice, Ignoto added, "Fra Antonio, if you go to Santa Maria, so many people will be coming and going that the brothers will be unable to keep them out of your cell. No one there will have a moment's peace. Why don't you come to Arcella? It's very close, and you can stay in my cell."

"Buono," Antonio said in a faint voice. "But I beg you, please give me your command of obedience. When I die, if it is in any way possible, bring my body for burial to the Church of Santa Maria, the house of the Mother of God."

"I promise, brother," Ignoto said. Then he hopped onto the seat beside Ruggerio, who directed the cart toward the abbey.

At Arcella, at the chaplain's door, Ignoto helped the two others lead Antonio into a small room and laid him on a straw mattress. They had no sooner gotten indoors than the other brothers at Arcella began to gather. Soon the thin, sweet songs of the nuns filtered through the walls. They were singing the psalms for the dying, praying that the gates of heaven would open for their beloved confessor, Antonio.

Ruggerio went outdoors to see about the oxen, but one of the brothers was already removing the yoke. Another was rubbing down their sweaty ribs with the skirt of his tunic.

"Go inside, brother. He may need you," the rubbing friar said.

That was the last thing that Ruggerio wanted to do.

As he entered the room, he saw at once that Antonio could scarcely breathe. His chest was heaving in great waves and his brown face was smeared with sweat. His eyes were wide, his mouth gaping.

"Ruggerio, quick!" Luca shouted. "Hold up his head."

Ruggerio felt as if he would vomit. His breaths rolled over each other in swift, shallow waves.

"His head, brother. He needs to sit."

Ruggerio shoved his hands behind the priest's head and neck. With Luca's hands behind his back, the two lifted Antonio to a sitting position. Ignoto pulled a chair next to the bed. Together, the three men lifted Antonio into it. Kneeling at his side, Ruggerio continued to hold Antonio's head erect, for he hadn't the strength to hold it up himself. As the three brothers tended to Antonio, the other brothers from Arcella crowded into the small room and knelt along the walls, their heads bowed.

Antonio's breathing continued to burst out in gasps. His wide-open eyes focused on a spot near the door and his body shuddered like a leaf in a November breeze.

"The water is rising in his chest," Ignoto said. "He's choking."

"Perhaps a demon has appeared to torment him," Luca offered.

He's afraid to die, Ruggerio thought.

Ruggerio stared at the spot near the door as the moist neck beneath his hand trembled. Ruggerio saw nothing.

Suddenly Antonio sighed deeply, and the trembling ceased. His eyes closed and he sank back in the chair, the tension gone from his body as surely as it leaves a goat that has jumped a chasm and left the pursuing wolf on the other side.

"Fra Ignoto, I must make my confession." The voice came in a husky whisper.

Ruggerio and Luca exchanged glances. Antonio seemed to read their thoughts. "It matters not if you hear my sins. You shall hear them all anyway at the final judgment."

In an attempt to drown out Antonio's whispered words, Ruggerio shut his eyes tightly and prayed the Our Father over and over in rapid succession. Nevertheless, he could not help overhearing. "Illicit thoughts. Distraction in prayer. Desire for comfort. Pride in my preaching. Attraction to popularity. Failure to trust fully in the mercy of God." Then, with a shaky voice, "Doubt over my salvation." Finally his voice was silent.

But deliver us from evil. Amen, Ruggerio prayed, concluding the prayer. He opened his eyes.

"I absolve you of all your sins," Ignoto was saying, "including those confessed and those forgotten." Then he took Antonio's right hand in his own and traced the sign of the cross over him. "And I bless you in the name of the Father, and of the Son, and of the Holy Spirit. Amen."

"Amen," said Antonio with a sigh. Then a great smile spread across his face and in a faint but clear voice, Antonio began to sing.

"O Glorious Lady,
Raised above the stars,
He who created you with foresight
You fed with milk from your holy breast."

Antonio's voice grew stronger, louder. His head pressed against Ruggerio's hands as he lifted his gaze heavenward.

"What sad Eve took away
You give back through your beloved Son.
So that we poor wretches might ascend the skies,
You become the window of heaven."

Was this how someone ought to die? Ruggerio felt fear begin to crack inside him as Luca, Ignoto, and the other brothers joined in singing the third verse.

"You are the door of the High King.
You are the gleaming gate of light.
O redeemed nations,
Acclaim life given you through the Virgin."

The clear, strong voices, the meaning of the familiar words sung during the Morning Office, sank into Ruggerio's soul as water into bread. Antonio had faced the terror of death and banished it. As Antonio sang his way into eternity, God's eternal light bathed Ruggerio's own soul with a similar peace. In a deep, strong voice, he sang the final verse with the others.

"Glory to you, O Lord,
Who were born of the Virgin,
With the Father and Holy Spirit
Unto endless ages."

As their voices faded, Antonio raised his head even more. His eyes focused on the upper corner of the room and widened with wonder and joy. A gasp of surprise squeezed from his lips as his smile grew in radiance.

"What do you see, brother?" Ruggerio asked.

"I see my Savior."

Ruggerio stared at the corner. *My Jesus, what am I to do in Your presence? Thank You for coming to him. For coming to me. My Jesus, I am a sinner. I don't deserve to be here in Your holy presence.*

"Fra Antonio," Ignoto interrupted Ruggerio's prayer. "I have brought the sacred oil to anoint you."

Antonio's gaze left the corner and turned to Ignoto.

"Brother, there is no need for you to do me this service," he said gently. "I have this unction within me. Nevertheless, it is good and gives me happiness." He stretched out the palms of his hands for the anointing while, through the walls, the songs of the nuns continued to drift.

The priest anointed Antonio's eyes, ears, nose, mouth, hands, sides, and feet, praying that God would forgive any sin committed through each body member in turn while Antonio prayed with him.

As the priest put away his holy oils, the kneeling brothers began to recite the seven penitential psalms. With his hands clasped, Antonio joined his tremulous voice to theirs.

With his hands supporting the head of a dying man, Ruggerio began to recite Psalm 6. He watched Antonio's face as he prayed, searching for any sign of breathing difficulty, adjusting the angle of the head to help him breathe better.

"Be gracious to me, O LORD, for I am languishing."

As he prayed, Ruggerio realized that he was supporting a saint. Yet he who had forgiven the sins of so many prayed with passion the words of Psalm 32. "I said,

'I will confess my transgressions to the LORD';
then thou didst forgive the guilt of my sin."

Antonio's voice deepened in fervor with Psalm 38.

"But for thee, O LORD, do I wait;
it is thou, O LORD my God, who wilt answer."

Ruggerio felt a shiver run through the friar. Was it a thrill of anticipation, delight, awe?

Antonio's neck trembled. The friars were praying their way through Psalm 51.

"The sacrifice acceptable to God is a broken spirit;
a broken and contrite heart, O God, thou wilt not despise."

By Psalm 102, tears were welling in Ruggerio's eyes. He and the man whose head he supported were close in age. Why was the Lord taking the one who knew so much, who loved so deeply, who forgave so readily, and leaving the other, a clumsy ox?

"He has broken my strength in midcourse;
he has shortened my days.
'O my God,' I say, 'take me not hence
in the midst of my days,
thou whose years endure
throughout all generations!'"

The tears were dripping swiftly from Ruggerio's cheeks, tickling him and dampening the chest of his tunic. He couldn't wipe them away without dropping his grip on Antonio. The words of Psalm 130 penetrated his sorrow.

"I wait for the LORD, my soul waits,
and in his word I hope;

my soul waits for the LORD

more than watchmen for the morning."

Then the final psalm. Ruggerio's voice was no more than a whisper while Antonio's quivered with emotions:

"In thee I put my trust.

Teach me the way I should go,

for to thee I lift up my soul . . .

for I am thy servant."

As Psalm 143 ended, Antonio sank back into Ruggerio's arms. The brothers remained on their knees, their quiet prayers rippling throughout the room, droning over the higher-pitched lull of the nuns' voices. Keeping his eyes on Antonio's face, Ruggerio prayed over and over the psalms, the Lord's Prayer, his own anguished pleas and his glorious praises. Antonio lay quietly, his eyes closed. The priest's breaths came deeply, measuredly, gradually growing farther apart until, after a short time, they came no more. The head felt heavy in Ruggerio's hands, like a melon fully ripe and sweet.

Ignoto, who had remained kneeling by Antonio's side, was the first to speak. "He has gone home. Amen. Alleluia."

"Amen. Alleluia," the brothers echoed.

Ruggerio and Luca eased the heavy body down. Through his tears, Ruggerio could see that already the color was draining from the skin. The brown tint was fading and, at its disappearance, Antonio's skin was whitening.

"He looks like a child," one of the brothers remarked.

"This is no child," Ignoto said abruptly. "This is a saint, and when Padua finds out that he's died here, they will swarm this place."

"What should we do?" another brother asked.

"We mustn't let anyone know that he's dead. Not yet. Perhaps if we take the body secretly to Santa Maria, the brothers there will know what to do."

Ruggerio nodded. He would go to prepare the cart.

A knocking sounded at the chaplain's door. Ruggerio, who was on his way out, brushed the tears out of his eyes and opened the door. A little girl stood there.

The child cocked her head curiously. "Are you sad?" she asked.

Ruggerio tried unsuccessfully to ease the huskiness out of his voice. "What do you want?"

"I want to see Padre Antonio."

NOTES

Along with Luca Belludi, Fra Ruggerio tended Antonio during the last weeks of his life. Ruggerio may have been a brother at Santa Maria or Arcella when he was assigned to attend Antonio, or he may have already been at Camposampiero when Antonio arrived. He may have been Antonio's helper even earlier than this chapter suggests. At least one biographer describes him as being a large, strong man about the same age as Antonio. Whether he feared death is nowhere recorded.

The account of Antonio's last day follows the historical record. Coming down from his tree, he collapsed during the noon meal and was put to bed. He asked Fra Ruggerio to take him to Santa Maria to die, but the cart was met en route by Fra Ignoto (also called Fra Vinoto), who may or may not have been chaplain at Arcella. Ignoto told the brothers to go to Arcella because Antonio would never survive the journey into Padua.

At Arcella, Antonio was placed in a chair, with Fra Ruggerio supporting his head, for the water was rising in his chest. After experiencing anxiety, Antonio regained his calm, made his confession (the records do not tell us what sins he confessed), then sang (or chanted) the ancient Latin hymn "O Glorious Lady" in a clear, strong voice. His vision of the Savior and his words regarding his last anointing are accurate. Following this, he recited the seven penitential psalms with the brothers, then maintained a peaceful quiet for half an hour before dying. The brothers immediately decided to keep his death a secret to avoid crowds at the convent (*Assidua* 22–27, 55–56; 2LJS 7; Rig 16–17; *Dialogus* 3–4; Ben 6).

Antonio's words to Fra Ruggerio about death are from SerE (p. 214).

Scripture verses are from Psalm 6:2 ("Be gracious . . ."); Psalm 32:5 ("I said, 'I will . . .'"); Psalm 38:15 ("But for thee . . ."); Psalm 51:17 ("The sacrifice acceptable . . ."); Psalm 102:23–24 ("He has broken . . ."); Psalm 130:5–6 ("I wait for the Lord . . ."); and Psalm 143:8, 12 ("In thee . . .").

32

Paduana

Paduana's House, Padua, Italy (June 13, 1231)

P aduana sat at the table and rubbed her bare feet up and down a table leg as she nibbled the bread Mamma had given her for breakfast. Mamma and Papà were eating, too, but Mamma was wearing her usual cream-colored tunic while Papà was dressed up in his deep-brown tunic and matching stockings that he wore only when he was traveling somewhere important. He had combed his drooping mustache and pointed beard, and Paduana could smell his costly and rarely used perfume. But before Paduana could ask where he was going, Papà, whose big mouth was stuffed with bread, mumbled, "I wonder how Padre Antonio is."

Paduana swallowed the bread she was chewing. "Is he all right?"

"Bambina, you know that he's very sick." Papà tickled her chin. "That's why he left Santa Maria."

Paduana thought of Nonna, who had been very sick before her death. She looked at her gentle, round-faced father. "Will he die, Papà?"

"We all die sometime, Bambina."

"But not Padre Antonio. He's too good to die."

"Even Jesus died, Paduana," Mamma interrupted. She poured Paduana a cup of goat's milk. "I baked Padre Antonio some fig cakes. He likes those. Maybe they'll make him feel a little better. Today Papà has to take Count Tiso ten bolts of cloth. He'll take Padre Antonio the cakes."

"Can I go, too, Papà?" Paduana was so excited that she almost tipped her cup. "In the cart? Please? Please?"

"If you promise not to eat the cakes on the way, Bambina," Papà said.

"Papà!" Paduana protested.

"Promise," said Mamma.

Paduana twisted her smile into a grimace. "I promise."

"I baked a few extra for you," Mamma said with a smile.

So Paduana drank her goat's milk and then wandered outside to pass the time until Papà was ready to leave. Spying some wooden stubs at the edge of the family's garden made Paduana think of playing "Mercato." Three days ago, she had gathered stray lentils from the lentil patch for her dolls to buy and sell. But she was tired of "Mercato." What could she play today?

Today she was going to see Padre Antonio. Maybe she would play "Being Cured." She hadn't played that for a long time. But Papà had told her the story so many times that she remembered it well.

Paduana gathered the stubs of wood and found a shady spot under a big tree. She was glad that Mamma had twisted her frizzy hair into two braids because they kept the curls out of her face. Digging her bare toes into the dust, she snatched the stubbiest, fattest stick she could find.

"This is Padre Antonio," she said, balancing it upright in the gray dust. "And this is Papà." Papà's stick was longer and a bit knotty. "And this is Mamma." Mamma's stick was smooth and slender, just like Mamma. "And this is me." Paduana chose the tiniest stick to represent herself. She still had a fistful of sticks left. She pushed them to one side. "And these are everybody else."

She put herself and Papà and Mamma into the pile of "everybody else." She put Padre Antonio a little distance from the pile. "Now believe in God and do what is right," she said in a deep voice. "Or else you'll go to hell." That was Padre Antonio preaching to the citizens of Padua. "Amen."

"Hurrah! Hurrah!" she called out. That was the citizens cheering for Padre Antonio.

Now she made Papà's stick carry her stick up to Padre Antonio. Mamma's stick went along, too.

"Padre Antonio," Papà said. "This is my little daughter, Paduana. When she was four summers old, a disease struck her and she could no longer walk. She crawls like a lizard. Many times she has shaking fits. Often she falls to the ground and rolls about senselessly. She's a good girl. Will you bless her?"

Paduana liked the next part best. She made Padre Antonio nod. "Of course I will bless her," she said in a deep voice. "In the name of the Father, and of the Son, and of the Holy Spirit."

Papà made a deep bow. "Grazie, Padre."

Paduana made Papà and Mamma walk home, taking turns carrying her. She decided that home, today, would be the broken piece of crockery that Papà kept by the door. He used the pottery shard to scrape mud off his boots before coming indoors. She leaned the crockery against the house, then searched in the dust for a pebble to represent a chair. Here was a smooth one that would do just fine.

Now Paduana walked the little family home. Papà stood Paduana on her feet and placed her hands on the chair.

Humming to herself, Paduana made her stick teeter and totter as it remained erect.

"Look!" Papà called to Mamma. "Paduana is standing."

Paduana hummed a lullaby as she put the sticks to bed, then whistled like a morning birdsong. Again Papà placed Paduana next to the chair. Again she stood. Bed again. Birdsong. Today, Paduana pushed the chair around the house.

"Look!" Papà called. "Paduana is walking."

Bed. Birdsong. As the days and nights sped by, Paduana was walking about the house unaided. Then she was running. And then the little family was walking all together to see Padre Antonio to tell him what his blessing had done.

Paduana had vague memories of being unable to walk and then of struggling with standing and a chair. Now she walked and ran just like all the other children. All because Padre Antonio had blessed her.

"Paduana!" Papà called from the tiny stable. "The mule is hitched, and the cart is ready. Get in!"

Paduana leaped up, leaving her sticks in the dust.

On the bumpy way, Paduana kept thinking about visiting Padre Antonio in his tree hut that Count Tiso had built for him. Once before, she'd visited the priest there. He allowed her to climb up and sit next to him. Up there, she knew how birds felt. She wanted to jump off and try to fly, but Padre Antonio had caught her and told her "No!"

However, when Papà delivered the cloth to Count Tiso and then drove to the monastery, Padre Antonio wasn't there. "He left earlier this afternoon for Santa Maria," a brother said. Santa Maria! That wasn't even far from home.

Paduana stopped thinking about tree houses and started to think about Padre Antonio. He could still tell her a story even if it wasn't in a tree house.

Papà drove up to the familiar convent. He and Paduana got out of the cart. He allowed Paduana to hold the basket with the fig cakes while he rapped at the door. A wrinkle-faced brother opened the door. His hair was so white that Paduana thought that he might have been alive when Jesus was.

"We've come to see Padre Antonio," Papà said. "My wife baked these cakes for him."

"Padre Antonio isn't here. He went to Camposampiero over two weeks ago."

"The brothers there said he returned here today."

"Did you pass him on the road?"

"No."

"He's not here. Maybe he went to Arcella first."

Papà groaned. The brother closed the door gently. "Bambina," Papà said, leaning down toward Paduana. "The mule is tired. I must get him home and rub him down and feed him. We will take the fig cakes to Padre Antonio tomorrow."

Paduana's lip trembled. She wanted to see Padre Antonio today. He would bless her and tell her a story and share a fig cake with her.

"Papà, I can walk to Arcella. I went there before all by myself with some bread for the nuns. I went often. Let me go today, Papà. Please."

Papà smiled. "All right, Paduana. But be sure to start back early enough so that you get into the city before the gates close."

Paduana grinned. "I promise, Papà!"

So he gave her the basket of fig cakes and off she went. She tried to imagine what it was like to be a nun—not that she had ever seen one, for the nuns remained within the convent. But sometimes she heard them singing the psalms, their voices joyful with prayer and praise. However, today when she drew near, the songs were different. The nuns seemed to be sobbing the words.

Are they sad? Paduana wondered.

Paduana knew that Padre Antonio wouldn't be at the convent. He'd be at the brothers' monastery off to the side. Usually she saw a brother or two in the garden. But not today. Where was everybody? Praying?

She walked around to the chaplain's tiny house. Under a nearby tree, two oxen grazed peacefully next to a cart of straw. She would have liked to pet them, but Papà had warned her never to do so. Too many people had been gored. So Paduana just looked at the cream-colored creatures as she knocked at the monastery door.

A huge, wide-shouldered brother who looked a lot like Paduana's red-faced Uncle Rocco answered her knock. The brother's eyes looked puffy. People had puffy eyes when they cried. Mamma's eyes had been puffy when Nonna had died. And the nuns were singing sad songs today.

"Are you sad?" she asked.

"What do you want?" the brother asked. Paduana smarted at his gruff tone.

"I want to see Padre Antonio. Mamma baked him these cakes." Paduana held up the basket.

The brother took the basket. "Tell your Mamma, 'Grazie.'"

"But I want to see him," Paduana insisted.

"You can't see him," the brother said, about to close the door.

"He likes to see me. Isn't he here?"

"He's here."

"Then let me see him. I want to see him. He tells me stories."

The brother bit his lip and closed his eyes. Hard.

"Why are you making a face at me?"

The brother took a deep breath and spoke slowly, accentuating each word. "Fra Antonio can't see you."

"But why not? He always sees me."

The brother gulped a big gulp of air. "Bambina, please go home." He began to close the door again.

Suddenly a realization struck Paduana with as much force as if someone had smacked her cheek. When Nonna had died, no one let Paduana see her. Her father had closed the door to Nonna's room to keep Paduana out. Nonna had been very sick when she died. Papà had said that Padre Antonio was very sick. Mamma said that everyone died sometime, even Jesus.

"He's dead," Paduana shrieked. "You won't let me see him because he's dead."

"Shhh! Bambina, be quiet."

"Padre Antonio is dead!" Paduana screamed. She thought she would burst with pain. Dead like Nonna, who never came to life again to sing to her. Dead like her dog, who never got up after being kicked by a horse. Dead meant still, and dead meant gone. "Padre Antonio is dead!"

"Bambina, please. Don't tell anyone."

She had to tell. She would explode if she didn't tell. Leaving her basket in the sad brother's hands, Paduana ran sobbing from the monastery, stumbling in ruts that she couldn't see through her tears. As she raced through the streets of Padua, children that she had seen at the mercato and at church looked up at her from their play. "Padre Antonio is dead!" she cried. "The holy priest is dead."

Soon the streets of Padua were overrun with children, shouting to one another and to everyone else, "The holy father is dead! Sant'Antonio is dead!"

NOTES

History records that Pietro, a citizen of Padua (his occupation isn't given), took his four-year-old daughter, Paduana, to Antonio to bless. The child was unable to walk and had epileptic-like fits. Following Antonio's blessing, Pietro took the little girl home and stood her by a chair. Over a period of time, she learned to walk by pushing the chair about the room. The cure was attributed to Antonio and was the only miracle that he worked during his lifetime that was included in the list of forty-seven miracles approved by the Roman Curia and read at his canonization (*Assidua* 55–56).

Whether Antonio liked fig cakes and whether Paduana's mother prepared them for the priest isn't known. Nor is it anywhere recorded that Paduana visited him at any time.

The brothers' attempt to keep Antonio's death a secret was thwarted by the children of Padua. History doesn't explain how the children learned of his death and mentions no role that Paduana may have played in relaying the news. However, almost as soon as Antonio died, the children began running through the streets shouting, "The holy father is dead! Sant'Antonio is dead!" (*Assidua* 26, 2LJS 7, Rig 16–17)

33

Abbot Thomas de Gaule

Monastery of Sant'Andrea, Vercelli, Italy (June 13, 1231)

Abbot Thomas de Gaule sat at his desk in his small cell, his forehead pressed against his fingertips. As he massaged his temples in a vain effort to stimulate his brain, his black tonsure flecked with a great deal of gray bobbed up and down like a narrow halo. Try as he might, he couldn't concentrate on the manuscript that lay before him. He was in the midst of writing a treatise on heaven, but his words had stopped flowing.

A few weeks ago, Thomas had developed a sore throat which, despite his best doctoring with herbs and olive oil, had only grown more severe. When he swallowed, he felt as if he were forcing down a chestnut burr. How unfair that one small part of his body should make all the rest of him miserable! His painful throat had robbed him of sleep, and lack of sleep always hindered his logic and creativity. Today he might as well have been just an average, middle-aged canon instead of, as many theologians declared, the greatest living doctor of theology in all the world. Being a doctor of theology meant nothing to Thomas today. Today he wished he had seen a medical doctor.

Thomas leaned back in his chair and closed his eyes. The thoughts just weren't coming. Instead of thinking about heaven, he began thinking of Fra Antonio. Pain didn't seem to impede Antonio. Thomas knew that Antonio was

ill in Padua, but he was under obedience to write his notes for preaching ser-
mons and he was doing it there. He was writing in a tree, nonetheless! Maybe if
Thomas climbed a tree, the breezes would clear his brain and he'd write better.
He shook his head. No, the way he was feeling today, he'd probably topple out.

If only he had a quick mind like Fra Antonio. When Antonio had begun his
preaching mission, Francesco had sent him to Vercelli to lodge with the Lesser
Brothers in their convent near the Church of San Matteo. Antonio was to
preach in Vercelli and Milan and to confer with Abbot Thomas to make certain
that his theology was sound.

Thomas moaned. Sound? Antonio's theology was so sound, deep, and broad
that he had enlightened Thomas. The two men had sat up well past sunset several nights, discussing this and that matter before Antonio would depart for the
night. After hearing a few of his sermons and spending hours in discussion with
him, Thomas had insisted that Antonio teach some of the abbot's theology
classes here at the monastery.

At the same time, Thomas had spoken fervently and frequently with
Antonio about one of his deepest convictions: namely, that the Church
should be stressing individual confession to a priest as Pope Innocenzo III had
declared in 1213. Unfortunately, not everyone followed the pope's directive
to confess yearly. Many misunderstood it and still believed that the rigor and
embarrassment of public confession was the only type of repentance acceptable to God. Many of the faithful waited to confess until they were approaching
death. Others felt that true contrition could be effective without the absolution of a priest. Nothing fed these attitudes more than one alarming fact: the
Church had a shortage of ordained clergy who were themselves morally pure.
No wonder conversion progressed slowly, if at all! The faithful should be
urged to confess and return to God at once, Thomas argued. Every priest
should promote this return and, if in sin, should himself repent. Antonio had
agreed wholeheartedly.

Thomas realized that he had been in the presence of one of the greatest
minds and hearts ever found in the Church. He thought of God-centered men
he would have loved to have met—the apostles, the Church Fathers, the martyrs. Marveling that he had enjoyed extended fellowship with one such person,
he had sent Antonio back to Francesco with the words: "Many men have

penetrated the mysteries of the Holy Trinity, as I have found had been done by Antonio during the course of the familiar relations which I had with him. Knowing little of profane science, he yet so quickly acquired a knowledge of mystic theology, that within he was on fire with heavenly ardor, and to men he seemed lit up with divine knowledge."

Thomas had seen Antonio periodically over the years when he had passed through Vercelli or preached there. When Antonio had come through Vercelli in 1229 on his way to build a convent in Varese, Thomas had noticed the friar's unhealthy corpulence and apparent weakness. Antonio had said nothing about his condition, and the two men had discussed spiritual matters as they had done several times before.

Thomas had heard that Antonio had blessed a well in Varese whose waters had healing powers. Thomas hadn't tried the water, but today he felt tempted. Still, the waters had not healed Antonio. Thomas, and all of Lombardy, knew that Antonio was very ill in Padua. Yet Antonio was still writing his sermon notes. Antonio could write of heaven even if he felt that his throat were aflame with the fires of hell.

Heaven. Heaven. Thomas rubbed his temples. *Lord, can't You give me a little insight the way You give it to Fra Antonio?*

Tap. Tap. Someone was knocking at Thomas' door.

"Come in." The hoarse words scratched Thomas' throat.

The door opened. Fra Antonio.

Before Thomas could force out a greeting of joy, Antonio spoke. "See, Father Abbot, I have left the ass near the gates of Padua and am hastening to my homeland."

Antonio was stocky but not swollen, his carriage straight, just as he had been on his first visit to Thomas.

"You're well again!" Thomas managed to choke out.

Antonio smiled as he bent over the desk. "And you aren't," he said, gently touching Thomas' throat.

"Can you stay a bit before returning to Lisbon?"

Antonio straightened and shook his head as he turned toward the door. "No, Father Abbot. I'm going home."

With that, he walked out the door, leaving it ajar.

Thomas leaped up from his desk. The manuscript could wait while he walked Antonio to the monastery gates.

The hallway was empty except for a canon with a breviary in his hand. How could Antonio have walked the corridor's length so swiftly?

"Which way did Fra Antonio go?" Thomas asked.

"I didn't see him," the canon replied.

Thomas decided to go in the direction of the courtyard that led to the street. Here a group of canons sat on a bench.

"Did Fra Antonio come through here?"

"No."

Thomas was puzzled. He began to methodically search the monastery, asking everyone he met, canon and servant alike, if Antonio had passed that way. No one had seen the priest.

Finally, Thomas went to the monastery gates. He asked the canon who was acting as porter. "Did you let Fra Antonio in to visit me?"

"I let no one in to visit anyone," the porter said.

Thomas heaved a great breath of disbelief. He gazed down the road. Of course, Antonio was not walking it. Thomas looked upward. Heaven?

Suddenly he knew. Antonio had left the ass, the friars' word for their body, in Padua.

He was going home to heaven.

A lump of wonder, joy, and grief pushed up in Thomas' throat. As he swallowed hard to keep from bursting into tears, he was astonished that the fire in his throat was gone.

NOTES

The visits of Antonio, when he was still alive, to Abbot Thomas, a brilliant theologian and great advocate of yearly confession, are accurate. History doesn't record Thomas' physical appearance. Thomas' words to Francesco about Antonio may never have been addressed to Francesco, but Thomas did write the accolade in one of his commentaries.

On June 13, 1231, Antonio appeared to Thomas as recorded in this chapter, speaking the words recorded here and healing Thomas' sore throat. When Thomas couldn't find Antonio anywhere or locate anyone besides himself who had seen him, Thomas returned to his cell and carefully wrote down the date, time, and details of Antonio's appearance. He didn't record what sort of work he was doing in his cell at the time of Antonio's appearance. A few weeks later, news of Antonio's death reached Vercelli. Thomas took out his notes and read them, realizing then that Antonio had appeared to him shortly after his death in Padua (Ben 8–9).

Works Consulted

Early Biographies of Saint Anthony

Dialogus Sanctorum Fratrum Minorum. ca. 1246. Personal translation by Paul Spilsbury.

Julian of Speyer. *The Second "Life" of St Antony Together with Extracts from the Office of St Antony Composed by the Same Brother.* 1233–34. Personal translation by Paul Spilsbury.

Peckham, John. *The Life of St. Antony, Commonly Called the "Benignitas."* ca. 1280. Personal translation by Paul Spilsbury.

Przewozny, Bernard, trans. *Life of St. Anthony: Assidua.* Padua: Edizioni Messaggero, 1984.

Rigauld, Jean. *The Life of Saint Antony of Padua (Rigaldina).* ca. 1280. Personal translation by Paul Spilsbury.

Early Documents on the Franciscan Order

Armstrong, Regis J., J. A. Wayne Hellmann, and William J. Short, eds. *Francis of Assisi: Early Documents.* Hyde Park, NY: New City Press (The Franciscan Institute of St. Bonaventure University, St. Bonaventure, NY). 3 vols (1999–2001).

Later Biographies and Other Writings about Saint Anthony

Beahn, John E. *A Rich Young Man: St. Anthony of Padua*. Milwaukee: The Bruce Publishing Company, 1953.

Bierbaum, Athanasius. *Saint Anthony of Padua: Life Sketches and Prayers*. Translated by Kilian J. Hennrich. Detroit: Third Order Bureau, 1931.

Butler, Alban. "St. Anthony of Padua." In *Butler's Lives of the Saints: Complete Edition*. Edited by Herbert Thurston and Donald Attwater, Westminster, MD: Christian Classics, Inc., 1956.

Curtayne, Alice. *St. Anthony of Padua*. Chicago: Franciscan Herald Press, 1931.

Da Rieti (de Pandolfi), Ubaldus. *Life of St. Anthony of Padua*. Boston: Angel Guardian Press, 1895. Reprinted by Andesite Press, 2017.

Gamboso, Vergilio. *Per Conoscere S. Antonio: La Vita-il Pensiero*. Padua: Edizioni Messaggero, 1990.

———. *St. Anthony of Padua: His Life and Teaching*. Translated by H. Partridge. Padua: Messaggero di S. Antonio–Editrice, 1991.

Gilliat-Smith, Ernest. *Saint Anthony of Padua According to His Contemporaries*. New York: E. P. Dutton & Co., 1926.

Hardick, Lothar. *Anthony of Padua: Proclaimer of the Gospel*. Translated by Zachary Hayes and Jason M. Miskuly. Edited by Cassian A. Miles and Janet E. Gianopoulos. Paterson, NJ: St. Anthony's Guild, 1993.

Huber, Raphael M. *St. Anthony of Padua: Doctor of the Church Universal*. Milwaukee: The Bruce Publishing Company, 1948.

Keller, Joseph. *Miracles of Saint Anthony of Padua*. 1899. Revised and edited by Darrell Wright. Monee, IL: CreateSpace, 2022.

LePitre, Albert. *St. Anthony of Padua (1195–1231)*. London: Burns, Oates & Washbourne Ltd., 1924.

Marin, Vito Terribile Wiel. "Sulle Possibili Cause Della Morte di S. Antonio di Padova." In *Ricognizione del Corpo di S. Antonio di Padova: Studi Storici e medico-antropologici*, Virgilio Meneghelli and Antonino Poppi, 193–98. Padua: Edizioni Messaggero, 1981.

Meneghelli, Virgilio. "La Revisione dei Resti Mortali di S. Antonio di Padova." In *Ricognizione del Corpo di S. Antonio di Padova: Studi Storici e medico-antropologici*, Virgilio Meneghelli and Antonino Poppi, 153–56. Padua: Edizioni Messaggero, 1981.

Purcell, Mary. *Saint Anthony and His Times.* Garden City, NY: Hanover House (Division of Doubleday and Company), 1959.

Stoddard, Charles Warren. *Saint Anthony: The Wonder Worker of Padua.* Notre Dame, IN: The Ave Maria, 1896. Reprinted Rockford, IL: TAN Books and Publishers, Inc., 1971.

Writings of Saint Anthony

Anthony of Padua. "God's Love for His Children." Translated by Claude Jarmak. *Messenger of Saint Anthony*, May 1986, 4–5.

———. "Knowledge, Virtue, and Faith." Translated by Claude Jarmak. *Messenger of Saint Anthony*, February 1990, 4–5.

———. *Praise to You Lord: Prayers of St. Anthony.* Edited by Livio Poloniato. Prov. Padua: F.M.C. Editrice Grafiche Messaggero di S. Antonio, 1986.

———. "The Preacher Warrior Against Sin." Translated by Claude Jarmak. *Messenger of Saint Anthony*, September 1989, 4–5.

———. *Seek First His Kingdom.* Edited by Livio Poloniato. Translated by Claude Jarmak, Leonard Frasson, and Bernard Przewosny-Porter. Padua: Grafiche Messaggero S. Antonio, Padua, Conventual Franciscan Friars, 1988.

———. *Sermons for Sundays and Festivals.* 3 vols. Translated by Paul Spilsbury. Padua: Messaggero di Sant'Antonio Editrice, 2007–10.

———. *Sermons for the Easter Cycle.* Edited by George Marcil. St. Bonaventure, NY: The Franciscan Institute, 1994.

———. "To See, To Speak, To Hear." Translated by Claude Jarmak. *Messenger of Saint Anthony*, July–August 1988, 4–5.

———. "Washing the Feet." Translated by Claude Jarmak. *Messenger of Saint Anthony*, March 1989, 4–5.

_____. "You Will Find an Infant." Translated by Claude Jarmak. *Messenger of Saint Anthony*, December 1990, 4–5.

Additional References

Abulafia, David. *Frederick II: A Medieval Emperor.* London: Allen Lane, The Penguin Press, 1988.

Arnald of Sarrant. *Chronicle of the Twenty-Four Generals of the Order of Friars Minor.* Translated by Noel Muscat. Malta: Tau Franciscan Communications, 2010.

Augustine Fellowship, Sex and Love Addicts Anonymous. *Sex and Love Addicts Anonymous.* Boston: The Augustine Fellowship, Sex and Love Addicts Anonymous, Fellowship Wide Services, Inc., 1986.

Barraclough, Geoffrey. *The Medieval Papacy.* Norwich, England: Harcourt, Brace & World, Inc., 1968.

Barton, Lucy. *Historic Costume for the Stage.* Boston: Walter H. Baker Company, 1935.

Blanchard, Gerald T. "Sexually Abusive Clergymen: A Conceptual Framework for Intervention and Recovery." *Pastoral Psychology* 39, no. 4 (March 1991): 237–45.

Bonaventure. *Major Life of St. Francis.* Translated by Benen Fahy. In *St. Francis of Assisi: Writings and Early Biographies*, edited by Marion A. Habig, 613–787. Chicago: Franciscan Herald Press, 1973.

Brooke, Rosalind B. *Early Franciscan Government: Elias to Bonaventure.* Cambridge, England: Cambridge University Press, 1959.

Brown, Harold O. J. *Heresies: The Image of Christ in the Mirror of Heresy and Orthodoxy from the Apostles to the Present.* Garden City, NY: Doubleday & Company, 1984.

Carnes, Patrick. *Out of the Shadows: Understanding Sexual Addiction.* Minneapolis: CompCare Publications, 1983.

Cianchetta, Romeo. *Assisi: Art and History in the Centuries.* Narni, Italy: Plurigraf, 1985.

Coulton, G.C. *Life in the Middle Ages.* 4 vols. Cambridge, England: Cambridge University Press, 1967.

———. *The Medieval Scene: An Informal Introduction to the Middle Ages.* London: Cambridge at the University Press, 1931.

Cristiani, Leon. *Heresies and Heretics.* Translated from the French by Roderick Bright. New York: Hawthorn Books, 1959.

Cummings, Juniper M. *The Christological Content of the 'Sermons' of St. Anthony.* Padua: Il Messaggero di S. Antonio Basilica del Santo, 1953.

Curran, Charles. *Absolutes in Moral Theology.* Washington, DC: Corpus Instrumentorum, Inc., 1968.

DeClary, Leon. *Lives of the Saints and Blessed of the Three Orders of St. Francis,* 36–38. N.p.: Taunton Franciscan Convent, 1886–87.

Englebert, Omer. *St. Francis of Assisi: A Biography.* Translated by Eve Marie Cooper. Ann Arbor, MI: Servant Books, 1979.

Francis of Assisi. *The Prayers of St. Francis.* Translated by Ignatius Brady. Ann Arbor, MI: Servant Books, 1987.

Gregory IX. *"Speravimus Hactenus."* June 16, 1230. Unpublished translation by Claude Jarmak. Granby, MA: n.d.

Habig, Marion Alphonse. *The Franciscan Book of Saints,* 122–123, 912–913, rev. ed. Chicago: Franciscan Herald Press, 1979.

———, ed. *St. Francis of Assisi: Writings and Early Biographies—English Omnibus of the Sources for the Life of St. Francis.* Chicago: Franciscan Herald Press, 1973.

Hastings, Margaret. *Medieval European Society 1000–1450.* 1st. ed. New York: Random House, 1971.

Holmes, Urban Tigner. *Daily Living in the Twelfth Century Based on the Observations of Alexander Neckam in London and Paris.* Madison, WI: The University of Wisconsin Press, 1953.

Isely, Paul J., and Peter Isely. "The Sexual Abuse of Male Children by Church Personnel: Intervention and Prevention." *Pastoral Psychology* 39, no. 2 (November 1990): 85–99.

Jordan of Giano, Thomas of Eccleston, and Salimbene degli Angeli. *Thirteenth Century Chronicles.* Translated by Placid Hermann. Chicago: Franciscan Herald Press, 1961.

Jorgensen, Johannes. *St. Francis of Assisi.* Translated by T. O'Conor Sloane. Garden City, NY: Image Books, 1939.

Kantorowicz, Ernst. *Frederick the Second—1194–1250.* New York: Frederick Ungar Publishing Company, 1957.

Kunz, Jeffrey R. M. *The American Medical Association Family Medical Guide.* New York: Random House, 1982.

Laaser, Mark R. "Sexual Addiction and Clergy." *Pastoral Psychology* 39, no. 4 (March 1991): 213–35.

"A Lutheran Pastor." *Pastoral Psychology* 39, no. 4 (March 1991): 259–63.

Maitland, S. R. *Facts and Documents Illustrative of the History, Doctrine, and Rites of the Ancient Albigenses and Waldenses.* London: C. J. G. and F. Rivington, 1832.

Mandonnet, Pierre. *St. Dominic and His Work.* Translated by Mary Benedicta Larkin. St. Louis, MO: B. Herder Book Company, 1945.

Mann, Horace K. *The Lives of the Popes in the Middle Ages*, vol. 13. London: Kegan Paul, Trench, Trubner & Co., Ltd., 1925.

Moorman, John. *A History of the Franciscan Order from Its Origins to the Year 1517.* Oxford, England: Clarendon Press, 1968.

Mundy, John Hine, and Peter Riesenberg. *The Medieval Town.* Princeton: Van Nostrand, 1958.

Odoardi, Giovanni. "St. Francis and his Basilica, Brother Elias, Gregory IX and the Transfer of 1230." Translated by Edward Hagman, OFM Cap. *Greyfriars Review Supplement* 13 (1999): 65–89. Originally published as "S. Francesco e la sua basilica, Frate Elia e Gregorio IX nella translazione del 1230" in *Miscellanea Francescana* 82 (1982): 116–37.

"One Priest's Reflections on Recovery." *Pastoral Psychology* 39, no. 4 (March 1991): 269–73.

Powicke, Frederick Maurice. *The Christian Life in the Middle Ages and Other Essays*. Oxford, England: The Clarendon Press, 1968.

Russell, Jeffrey Burton. *Dissent and Reform in the Early Middle Ages*. Berkeley and Los Angeles: University of California Press, 1965.

————, ed. *Religious Dissent in the Middle Ages*. New York: John Wiley & Sons, Inc., 1971.

Stanford-Rue, Susan M. *Will I Cry Tomorrow?: Healing Post-Abortion Trauma*. Old Tappan, NJ: Fleming H. Revell Company, 1986.

Strayer, Joseph Reese. *Western Europe in the Middle Ages: A Short History*. 3rd ed. Glenview, IL: Scott, Foresman, 1982.

Stuard, Susan Mosher. *Women in Medieval Society*. Philadelphia: University of Pennsylvania Press, 1976.

Timmermans, Felix. *The Perfect Joy of St. Francis*. New York: Farrar, Straus, and Young, 1952.

Wakefield, Walter L. *Heresy, Crusade and Inquisition in Southern France 1100–1250*. Berkeley: University of California Press, 1974.

Walsh, James Joseph. *The Thirteenth, Greatest of Centuries*. "Best Books" edition. New York: Catholic Summer School Press, 1907.

Walsh, Michael. *An Illustrated History of the Popes: Saint Peter to John Paul II*. New York: St. Martin's Press, 1980.

Wiegler, Paul. *The Infidel Emperor and His Struggles against the Pope: A Chronicle of the Thirteenth Century*. London: George Routledge & Sons, Ltd, 1930.

Also by Madeline Pecora Nugent

Continue your journey through early Franciscan history with Madeline Nugent's accounts of the lives of Saint Francis and Saint Clare.

FRANCESCO
A Story of Saint Francis of Assisi

0-8198-2754-1

544 pages

CHIARA
A Story of Saint Clare of Assisi

0-8198-1686-8

384 pages